A Season of Angels

A Season of Angels

A Cape Light Novel

THOMAS KINKADE

& KATHERINE SPENCER

BERKLEY BOOKS, NEW YORK
A Parachute Press Book

THE BERKLEY PUBLISHING GROUP
Published by the Penguin Group
Penguin Group (USA) Inc.
375 Hudson Street, New York, New York 10014, USA

Penguin Group (Canada), 90 Eglinton Avenue East, Suite 700, Toronto, Ontario M4P 2Y3, Canada (a division of Pearson Penguin Canada Inc.) • Penguin Books Ltd., 80 Strand, London WC2R 0RL, England • Penguin Group Ireland, 25 St. Stephen's Green, Dublin 2, Ireland (a division of Penguin Books Ltd.) • Penguin Group (Australia), 707 Collins Street, Melbourne, Victoria 3008, Australia (a division of Pearson Australia Group Pty. Ltd.) • Penguin Books India Pvt. Ltd., 11 Community Centre, Panchsheel Park, New Delhi—110 017, India • Penguin Group (NZ), 67 Apollo Drive, Rosedale, Auckland 0632, New Zealand (a division of Pearson New Zealand Ltd.) • Penguin Books (South Africa) (Pty.) Ltd., Rosebank Office Park, 181 Jan Smuts Avenue, Parktown North 2193, South Africa • Penguin China, B7 Jaiming Center, 27 East Third Ring Road North, Chaoyang District, Beijing 100020, China

Penguin Books Ltd., Registered Offices: 80 Strand, London WC2R 0RL, England

This book is an original publication of The Berkley Publishing Group.

This is a work of fiction. Names, characters, places, and incidents either are the product of the authors' imaginations or are used fictitiously, and any resemblance to actual persons, living or dead, business establishments, events, or locales is entirely coincidental. The publisher does not have any control over and does not assume any responsibility for author or third-party websites or their content.

FIRST EDITION: November 2012

Library of Congress Cataloging-in-Publication Data

Kinkade, Thomas, 1958–2012.
A season of angels / Thomas Kinkade & Katherine Spencer. — 1st ed.
p.   cm
ISBN 978-0-425-25277-2
1. Cape Light (Imaginary place)—Fiction.   2. Grandmothers—Fiction.   3. Brothers and sisters—Fiction.   4. Families—Fiction.   5. Christmas stories.   I. Spencer, Katherine, (date)   II. Title.
PS3561.I534S43   2012
813'.54—dc23   2012026357

PRINTED IN THE UNITED STATES OF AMERICA

10 9 8 7 6 5 4 3 2 1

CHAPTER ONE

＊

*T*HE DRIVE TO CAPE LIGHT FROM VERMONT HAD BEEN challenging. Adele Morgan rarely drove on the interstate these days. Her travels were confined to the back roads near her home and then, only in good weather and daylight. She had left for Massachusetts right after breakfast and crept along the right lane of the highways for hours, enduring the honking horns and sour expressions as other cars and trucks flew by her little green Subaru.

She was not the driver she used to be, that was for sure. She had been wise to take a few breaks to rest and check the map. It was hard to remember the last time she had made this trip on her own. Too long ago, she knew that much.

These days, as she neared the impressive age of ninety, memories seemed to float just below the surface of her awareness, elusive and slippery, like golden fish darting about in a dark pool.

You had to keep a sense of humor and plug along; that's what the years had taught her. To take life one day at a time. One hour at a time, if necessary. To fret far less about the small stuff and have more patience with herself and everyone else.

These days she was happy just to open her eyes in the morning and put her two feet on the ground. To know God had blessed her with another day in this beautiful old world.

Adele knew this well. She knew it in her heart. It was a large part of the reason she had come all this way, sneaking into town without a word of warning to her family—her oldest son, Joe, and his grown children, with children of their own now.

She drove through the village of Cape Light without turning off to see any of them. She remembered the way to Angel Island without checking the map at all, though it was nice to spot a few signs along the way, confirming that she was on the right track.

After all this time, it was still the same. One road on to the island and one road off. How much simpler could it be? Luckily, the tide was low and the old land bridge was open for crossing. It was all just as she recalled, and the stark beauty of the place still took her breath away.

A brisk wind off the water battered her little car, the salt air reminding her how much she missed living near the sea. Vermont was a lovely place but there was no ocean, a definite drawback in her book. Moving from Cape Light to Vermont had been her husband George's doing. They never would have left this place, but George had been transferred by his company and didn't want to lose all his seniority and retirement benefits. Their two sons were grown and on their own, so off they went, planning to return once he retired.

But as the saying goes, "Man plans, God laughs." That was another thing she had learned. A few years later, well before retirement age, George was downsized and out of a job. Adele had wanted to return to Cape Light then, but George decided they should take their nest egg and the severance package from his firm, and buy a little business. Something they could run part time as they got older.

George found a variety store for sale in Highland, the town where they lived, and that was that. She had loved him dearly, but he'd been a strong-willed man who always got his way. So up in Vermont they stayed, leaving behind their closest friends and family and never returning to live here again.

Adele drove across the bridge slowly as the memories came rushing back. She forced herself to focus on the road, the wide blue sky above and the dark blue waves that washed up on either side of the rocky shoulder. The wind pushed at her car, and she gripped the wheel hard to stay on course.

Just like life, she thought. *You have to hold on tight to stay aimed at your destination.* Her decision to come back here this weekend had been impulsive. But she did feel focused and determined in her mission, driven by a sense of urgency that only someone at her stage of life could truly understand.

Once she crossed the bridge, she headed north up the main road, one of two that crossed the island. The stunning panoramic view on her right, of the sea and sandy hillside that led down to the beach, was distracting. On her left, she saw open fields, wooded spaces, and the occasional house or farm.

Just a few miles down, the grand Queen Anne came into view. "Just where I left it," Adele said aloud. She pulled into the gravel drive and parked near the front porch. A hand-painted sign read, ANGEL INN—ALL ARE WELCOME. She remembered that, too. The inn looked very much the way she remembered, back in the day when Elizabeth and Clive Dunne ran it. Adele heard the place had been falling apart and was even closed for a time. That was when Elizabeth was ill and finally passed on. But the news that Elizabeth's niece, Liza Martin, had taken it over was heartening, and now Adele could see that the place was thriving once again.

In fact, the inn had never looked better, she thought as she got out of the car and slowly got the kinks out of her arms and legs. The grand old house was painted a rich cream color with sea-green trim. The porch was decorated with autumn's bounty, with cornstalks framing the entryway, pumpkins in various sizes stacked near the door, and the hardiest, last blooms of the season—purple and white kale plants. Bunches of mums in the fall colors of harvest gold, burnt orange, and deep burgundy lined the window boxes and stairway. Adele expected the decorations would be even more lavish once Christmas rolled around.

It's the perfect headquarters for my campaign, she thought. *The perfect place to plan my strategy.*

"Adele? You're early. We didn't expect you until three."

Claire North was coming down the porch steps to meet her. When Adele was living in the village, she and Claire had attended the same church together, the old stone church on the green. She had not seen much of Claire since her move to Vermont, but amazingly, Claire did not look any different at all.

"Dear Claire. How are you?" The two women greeted each other with a hug. "Must be something in the water down here. You don't look a day older."

Claire leaned back and laughed. "I could say the same about you, Addie. You look wonderful."

"Oh, go on. I'm old now. But I feel pretty good and I've still got my marbles . . . most of them," Adele added with a grin.

"That's plenty to be thankful for," Claire replied with a smile. She opened the hatch and grabbed Adele's suitcase and tote bags, carrying them easily. "I'll take your things," she explained as she led the way inside. "I'll get you settled right away. We've fixed you a lovely room with a water view. It's very quiet here right now. There's only one other guest checking in today."

"Fine with me. I like the quiet."

Adele had expected as much. In fact, she had been counting on it. The first weekend in December was too late for the leaf-peepers and apple-pickers who roamed New England in herds during the fall. And it was too early for Christmas visitors.

"How long will you be staying? Liza didn't say."

They had reached the first landing, and Adele followed Claire down the hall. Adele was relieved to be on the first floor. One flight these days was plenty. Just enough to keep her fit without making her breathe too heavily.

"Oh, I'm not really sure. Maybe a week, maybe more." Adele shrugged. "I'm just going to play it by ear," she said honestly. "I hope that's not a problem."

"Not at all. We have very few guests this time of year. But Liza has done a wonderful job renovating the place and we're very busy in the summer and fall. We fill up some weeks."

Claire sounded pleased and proud. Adele smiled. It was good to see her old friend. Claire had such a warm, calming manner that it made Adele instantly glad she had come here. *It was the right decision,* she told herself.

Claire stopped and put down the bags. "Here we are. Number five, one of my favorite rooms."

Claire opened the door and allowed Adele to walk in first. Adele went straight to the wide double windows that framed a view of the sea and sky. The upholstered window seat looked inviting, but she just stood and stared out.

"What a sight to wake up to. I may just stay up here and look out the window all day."

"You're not the first to say that." Claire arranged the suitcase on a stand and put the tote bags on the floor, near a small standing wardrobe. "Lunch is almost ready, but Liza is out running some errands. She should be back soon. I can knock in an hour or so if you'd like to take a rest. That was a long drive."

For someone your age, Adele knew she had almost added. It was true, spoken or unspoken.

"I am tired, but I'm ready anytime for some of your cooking, Claire. Why do you think I came all this way?"

Adele had been a good cook in her day. Claire's cooking, however, was in a league of its own. Claire was known all over the county for her unique versions of classic New England dishes.

"Thanks for the compliment. But I'm sure you have some better reason to come all this way than a bowl of chowder, no matter who cooked it."

Claire was still so intuitive. *She hadn't lost that special gift*, Adele thought. "Well . . . I did come for a pressing reason," Adele admitted. "But your chowder was high on the list, too."

The two old friends laughed. Adele was relieved, but not surprised, when Claire did not press her for any more explanation. They both knew Adele would tell her the whole story in due time. When she was ready.

Once Claire left the room, closing the door softly behind her, Adele walked back to the window seat and gazed out at the sea, watching the waves wash in and out of the shoreline and rocky coast.

Everything in due time, she reminded herself. She had taken the first step and would soon be ready for the next. There was something in the Bible about that, wasn't there? "To everything there is a season, and a time to every purpose under heaven . . . A time to break down, and a time to build up . . ."

Well, here I am, God, ready to build things up again, to mend them once and for all. I hope this is the right season to take up that task. I don't know that I have any time left to put the job off longer. You got me this far. Please help me with the rest.

"OH, DAD, THANKS FOR COMING. YOU DIDN'T HAVE TO BOTHER."

"You called me, honey. So here I am. Who could help you out of this jam better than your old man, huh?"

Molly Willoughby just shook her head and smiled. Nobody but her dad, Joe Morgan, was the answer to that question.

She would have hugged her father, but she was elbow-deep in a box of melted mini-meatballs. She was all alone in the back of her shop, Willoughby Fine Foods, trying to pull together the appetizers for a cocktail party in town that was due to start in a few hours. She was shorthanded on staff today, and to top it all off, one of the freezers had died during the night and all of the food for the party was ruined.

"What a mess, Moll. What a waste." Joe Morgan shook his head and quickly exchanged his jacket for a white cook's apron and a pair of food-handling gloves.

"Tell me about it. It's not just the meatballs. It's the mini ravioli, the shrimp, and the spinach puffs. The extra freezer went south on me overnight. No warning."

"Might be something simple to fix. I'll take a look later. I can run to the restaurant supply place in Beverly for you." Joe looked at his watch. "What time did you have to start the setup?"

"There isn't enough time, Dad. We have to find something around here . . . I just don't know what."

Molly knew she was stressed and not thinking clearly. She had been running this business for eight years and was a seasoned pro by now. Willoughby Fine Foods was always in demand. But the holidays were the craziest time of the year and, as usual, today she had totally overbooked.

Which wouldn't normally be a problem. Her partner, Betty Bowman, was so capable and organized she could run three parties at the same time. But Betty had called at six this morning, her voice tight with pain. Betty's back had gone out, and there was no way she could run any parties today. Meanwhile, a winter flu had also sidelined two of their most experienced workers, and Molly was down to a skeleton crew.

No wonder she had called her father in a panic. But, as usual, he was always willing to lend a hand and share his ample knowledge. Joe

Morgan had worked in commercial kitchens—in hotels, schools, and restaurants—all his life. He had not only passed on his culinary talents, but he had been her coach, mentor, and cheerleader—sometimes her only cheerleader—when she finally took the leap and started her own business.

Her father had always wanted to run his own business, Molly knew. But with six children to support, that was a risk he could never afford. Now he watched from the sidelines as she carried out his dream, one he was happy to help prod along, with his own spatula and whisk whenever necessary.

"How many pieces do you need, Molly?" Joe asked, staring into the big pantry.

"At least two hundred. I could put out bowls of nuts to fill in but—"

"Nix the nuts. This is no problem, baby. I have a few ideas. Go grab me an armful of those nice baguettes you have out front and slice them up real thin. We'll do some crostini with these tomatoes and some herb dip with the parsley, scallions, and that tub of cream cheese . . ."

Molly could practically hear the wheels turning as he gazed into the big refrigerator. Her father did some of his best cooking under pressure, in a total culinary crisis.

"Good thinking. Keep going." Molly grabbed a pad and pencil to jot down notes. This food had to be prepped at high speed, and they would have to work separately to get done on time. Once they got a game plan, Molly was going to pull one of her workers, who were staffing the front of the shop, to help out.

Her father took some big cans and containers off the open shelves of the pantry and came up with even more inspirations.

"Artichoke hearts. Perfect." He held up the five-pound can as if it were a prize. "Your grandmother used to make a really nice starter with artichokes and Gruyère. I think I spotted some Swiss. That will work fine."

Molly made a note. She remembered that dish, all baked and bubbling with melted cheese, and very tasty. But she was surprised to hear her father suggest it. Her father didn't talk about his mother much. Or her cooking.

Still, Molly remembered. Grandma Addie used to make all kinds of delicious things when the family traveled up to Vermont during the week between Christmas and New Year's. It was an annual reunion, just about the only time of the year when both sides of the Morgan clan, Joe's family and his brother Kevin's, visited.

The family didn't get together like that anymore, not since her grandfather George had died seven years ago. Now her father rarely mentioned his mother, Adele. He dutifully called her once a week, asking about her health and other needs. But there was always tension, even in these brief conversations. He rarely visited, unless there was an emergency. Grandma Addie was closer to her younger son, Kevin, and his family now.

Joe was a good man with a warm heart. He could never turn his back completely on his aging, widowed mother. But Molly knew that he had no interest in healing the rift that had begun with his father's death. And this was no time to remind him of it. She knew he wouldn't talk about it anyway. Over the years, the Cape Light side of the Morgan clan had established new traditions, and hardly anyone mentioned those Vermont gatherings anymore. Though sometimes on a snowy afternoon during the holiday season, Molly did feel wistful for a cup of hot cocoa and those good times in Grandma Addie's kitchen.

Molly shook off the memories and glanced over at her father, who was busy at work. He had opened the huge cans of artichoke hearts and dumped them quickly in big metal bowls.

"You could be on one of those TV cooking contests, Dad," Molly said as they got to work. "I bet you'd win the grand prize."

Her father just laughed. "I'd rather help you out of a jam any day, honey. That's all the glory I need. Now go get those baguettes and do what I told you. We'll turn out a pile of the tastiest appetizers you ever served in no time."

* * *

THE INNKEEPER HAD TOLD JONATHAN THAT THEY SERVED THREE meals a day. A good bargain, he thought, even if the place didn't turn out to be half as nice as it looked on the Internet.

He had left Boston late and then hit traffic on the highway, all the early-bird shoppers clogging up the lanes leading in and out of the malls. It had taken twice the time he had expected to reach Cape Light. The map said the village was only a few miles from the island. But who knew if he would find any place to eat over there. By all accounts, Angel Island was a fairly deserted spot, and it was nearly three p.m. His best bet was to stop here for a bite, or settle for afternoon tea and cookies at the inn. He had a feeling it was that sort of place.

He cruised down Main Street, looking for a likely spot. A neon sign for the Clam Box caught his eye. He slowed his car and parked in front. The old-fashioned diner was just the sort of place he had hoped to find. He hoped the prices were old-fashioned, too. Living on a graduate student's budget was a challenge, especially compared to the way he'd been raised—a bit sheltered and spoiled. Not the way most people lived, that was for sure.

The monthly allowance from his father was not lavish, but it still bothered Jonathan to accept even that small support. He knew it was given halfheartedly, for one thing, and he also felt he was old enough to be making his own way. He couldn't wait to finish his degree and start earning a decent salary. Though that was another flaming hoop to jump through. Faculty positions were hard to get these days, even with a PhD from Tufts University.

That's why the project he had come here to research was so important. The topic was new territory in his field, which was something like saying he had found a secret gold mine. If he could get a paper out of it and get published in a respectable journal, it would give him a huge advantage over other post grads. And maybe then his father would accept that he had made the right decision by quitting law school.

There were a lot of "ifs" in his life, weren't there? Jonathan smiled to himself and pulled open the door of the diner. Maybe that's why he loved history so much, where there were only facts left to sort through.

The diner was just as old-fashioned looking inside and practically empty. Though it was not as quiet as he expected. A uniformed policeman sat at the end of an otherwise empty counter, talking—arguing almost—with a man on the opposite side. Judging from his white apron, Jonathan guessed he was the cook. The two were engaged in an animated discussion as the cook refilled catsup bottles from a giant plastic container. He suddenly paused at his task and looked up.

"Sit anywhere you want. Waitress will be with you shortly." Then he turned and shouted into the kitchen, "Tess? Where the heck are you? You've got a customer out here waiting."

Jonathan chose a table near the window, happy to put some space between himself and the obstreperous cook. He noticed a blackboard listing specials and scanned the offerings. A waitress walked out from the kitchen and headed for his table, grabbing a glass and a water pitcher on the way.

"Sorry to keep you waiting. Would you like some water?" She leaned over and quickly filled his glass before he could reply.

"Thanks, and I wasn't waiting long." Jonathan smiled briefly, trying to put her at ease.

She stood back, holding the pitcher with two hands. She was chewing a big wad of gum and looked rushed and nervous.

"Here's a menu." She pulled one out of her apron pocket and handed it to him. "The specials are up on the board. I think we're out of the chili . . ." She paused and glanced over her shoulder. "No great loss. Same for the hot roast beef hero," she added in a quieter voice.

He laughed and looked up at her. She had bright blue eyes and reddish-brown hair pulled back in a long ponytail. Curly wisps framed a pretty face. Her large hoop earrings and lace tights were a little bold for his taste, but they looked good on her.

"Thanks for the warning. Red meat isn't my thing anyway."

"Me, either. It's bad for your health, not to mention the planet. I'm trying to reduce my carbon footprint."

Jonathan looked back up at her, intrigued by this turn in their conversation. Before he could reply, the grouchy cook called out, "Tess, I need you. Pronto."

"Be right there, Charlie." She turned back to Jonathan. "Do you know what you'd like? I can come back in a minute if you're not ready. If I don't get fired in the meantime, I mean."

Her wry humor made him smile again. "A bowl of clam chowder and the tossed salad," he said quickly. "And some coffee, please."

"Wise choice. I'll be back with the coffee."

Jonathan nodded and watched her walk back to the counter. She had long legs and an easy, swinging stride. She was just tall enough, he thought, and slim. Her frumpy waitress shoes and gray uniform did little to detract from her good looks, though the outfit would have been a deal breaker on most other girls.

Jonathan turned away and looked out the window. She was not exactly his style, but very attractive. Not that he would ask for her number or anything like that. He was here to work. Period. He didn't need any distractions. And he was taking a break from dating. His last charge into that battlefield had left his heart and ego battered. His ex-girlfriend, another student in his program, had dumped him for an assistant art history professor. He was better off without any female entanglements right now.

He reached into his briefcase, searching for something to read. A slim hand-bound manuscript caught his eye and he pulled it out. A white label on the brown paper cover bore the title: *Folklore Origins of the Massachusetts Bay Colonies—Original research by Martin Pilsner.* Dr. Pilsner was

Jonathan's advisor and had written the paper years ago when he was at Jonathan's stage in his academic career, still working on his doctorate.

It was generous of his professor to share this manuscript with him. Jonathan had been touched by the gesture. Martin was the professor who truly encouraged his work and reminded him what important work historians were called to do. Jonathan knew he would have never stuck with history if it had not been for Dr. Pilsner. He was grateful to his mentor and wanted to make him proud. *I will, too,* Jonathan promised. *So . . . no girls for now,* he reminded himself as he saw the waitress approach with his order.

"Here you are. Chowder. Salad. Coffee." The waitress announced each item as she set the dishes down before him. She pulled a handful of oyster crackers in cellophane packets from her pocket and put them next to the soup bowl. "Milk and sugar are on the table. If you need anything else, just let me know."

"Thanks." Jonathan nodded, trying not to look at her. He took a taste of the chowder instead. "This is sort of . . . thick," he said honestly. He didn't really like chowder when it was full of flour and potatoes. He liked a thinner broth and more clams.

"Gluey, I think, is the culinary term. But I know what you mean. I guess you've never been here before?"

"This is my first time in town."

"Are you just driving through or visiting awhile?" she asked.

"Driving through." He quickly took another spoonful of soup. That wasn't exactly true. He *was* driving through the town but planned to stay only a few miles away, on Angel Island, which technically was still part of the village. But he didn't elaborate.

"Would you like a newspaper while you're eating?" She glanced at the counter, where he saw a pile of papers. "We have the *Cape Light Messenger* and today's *Boston Globe* . . . Oh, and this week's *You Swap It.*"

The last choice made him laugh again. "Very tempting. But I'm all set, thanks." He glanced at the study that sat on the table next to his food and she did, too. He could tell she was reading the title upside down.

He wondered what she thought. Pretty dull stuff, he guessed would be her conclusion. He couldn't imagine her reading a historical analysis of colonial traditions during her work break. Fashion magazines, maybe, or the latest bestselling novel.

She looked up and seemed about to say something. Then her boss bellowed at her again. "Tess? Done chatting over there? I need you to stack these glasses and get the tables ready for the dinner rush."

"Okay, Charlie. I'll be right there." She rolled her eyes and spared Jonathan a quick grin, then headed back to the counter.

Jonathan watched her again for a moment. He wondered what she had been about to say. Some comment on his choice of reading material—or a question about it? What did it matter? She seemed nice enough, but he doubted they had much to talk about beyond the dos and don'ts on the menu here.

As he ate his meal he tried to read the introduction to Dr. Pilsner's study, but was too conscious of the waitress standing a short distance away, stacking the clean glasses. She hummed a song while she worked. She had a nice voice and a temperament to match to be so cheerful working here, he thought.

He sat back and sipped his water, staring out the window at Main Street. It was a pretty little town, classic New England. He knew that the village had been settled in the mid-1600s, and the villagers had played their part in the American Revolution. He was looking forward to exploring the area and checking out some of the older homes and buildings.

The street was busy with lots of people walking about. The main thoroughfare led down to a large harbor, park, and village green. Most of the shop windows were decorated for Christmas, and the parking meters were covered in red and white stripes, like candy canes. Free-parking candy canes, he'd noticed when he'd left his car. Green wreaths with red bows hung from the old-fashioned lampposts, and out on the village green, he saw the town Christmas tree covered with lights and topped by a big star.

A stone church at the opposite side of the green looked as if it had been built in the nineteenth century. It might not go back to the time of the original settlers, but it seemed like it would be worth a visit.

"Would you like anything else? More water?"

She was back. He hadn't heard her coming. He turned quickly, still holding his glass, and she misunderstood the gesture and started to pour.

"No, I didn't mean—" He jerked his hand away then realized it was a dumb move. She was suddenly pouring the water into midair.

"Oh no . . . I'm so sorry!" She stepped away from him, righting the pitcher, but not quickly enough.

Jonathan jumped up and stared at the table, speechless as water streamed down the table edge, on to his pants and shoes. "Oh, blast . . ." He quickly scooped up the manuscript, but it was too late. The pages were soaked through. He held up the soggy pile, suddenly shocked and angry.

"Your papers! Here, let me help you . . ." She reached over with a dry towel she had found somewhere.

"That's all right. Please don't touch this." He snatched the manuscript out of her reach. His words were mild enough, but his angry tone made her flush.

"But I could help you dry it off. You should blot that between some towels right away." Her voice was quiet and shaky. He could tell he had hurt her feelings and felt sorry, but he was too upset to apologize.

"It won't dry that way," he said, embarrassed and annoyed. He exhaled a long breath. The pages on the bottom were wet, the ink already running. "It's just that I need to read this, and I need to read it while I'm here. For my research—" He stopped himself, feeling it was futile to try to explain.

"Yes, I understand. Where do you think you are, Mars?" she answered without looking at him. She was using the towels to quickly wipe the table and seat. He could only look on and wave the paper in the air a bit as drops of water dripped down.

He could tell from her expression that she was mad—and insulted. Before Jonathan could say anything else, her boss ran over with a mop and began cleaning the floor.

"What's going on here?" the man named Charlie grumbled. "Looks like Niagara Falls. What did you do, Tess? Give this guy a bath?"

Charlie grinned at Jonathan. Trying for a man-to-man thing at the cost of belittling the waitress, Jonathan thought.

"It was my fault. Totally," Jonathan said.

"No, it was my fault," Tess insisted. "No charge for your meal. It's on the house," she added.

"On the house?" Charlie stopped mopping and glared at her. "I'm the only one allowed to say that."

"Don't worry, Charlie, I'll cover it," she snapped back.

She had a lot of character, that was for sure. Jonathan felt bad now about his reaction and getting her into trouble with her boss.

"It was just an accident. Nobody's fault," he said quickly. The whole situation was so uncomfortable. He had to get out of here. He had already grabbed his bag and leather jacket from the other chair, which luckily was clear of the spill. He tucked them under one arm, the soggy manuscript in his hand. Then he reached into a pocket with his free hand and pulled out some bills. "This should cover it." He set the money on the table. "Keep the change, miss." There would be enough left over for a good tip.

She glanced at the money. "Wait . . . take this back. You don't have to do that." She tried to get the bills off the table, but the surface was still wet and they stuck as if glued.

"Let it be," Charlie said, waving his hand. "If he wants to pay, let him."

Jonathan headed quickly for the door. Once out on the street, he took a few deep, calming breaths. Well, that was hardly his usual lunch hour. He didn't mean to look back through the window, but he couldn't help it.

She was still wiping the table, her boss still hovering and giving her a hard time. He suddenly wondered how long she had been working there. She didn't look as if she was going to last much longer.

I might not even see her if I go back. You don't need to go back to see her, he reminded himself. *You don't need to go back to the Clam Box ever again, in your entire life. Are we clear on that?*

He nodded to himself as he got back into his car. The smart thing would be to forget this entire episode, except for the soggy research paper. He found his gym bag on the floor and took out a clean towel that was stashed with his workout clothes. He folded it twice and pressed the wet manuscript between the fabric. She had been right. The towel did help dry it. Perhaps he could get some extra towels at the inn when he got there. Maybe it wasn't a complete disaster.

He started his car and headed out of the village, following the signs to Angel Island. He soon came to the land bridge that connected the island to the mainland and slowed his car a bit to take in the full view.

He couldn't see the legendary cliffs from the bridge, but he had seen photos and could picture them clearly. The cliffs that were shaped like an angel's wings. Were they a sign that the island was blessed in some mysterious way? Or simply the erosion pattern caused by the wind and sea? Jonathan tended to believe the latter, more logical explanation. But he had come to investigate the former, the folklore, which he had heard was widely believed around here. He had come to research the legend and make a name for himself by digging up the truth.

He drove across the bridge, followed the road onto the island, and headed for the inn, which he knew from the map was only a few miles more. The landscape was beautiful, he had to admit, wild and unspoiled. But that was another distraction that he couldn't indulge in.

You're here to deal with the facts, my friend. And absolutely nothing—and no one—else.

CHAPTER TWO

When Adele reached the old stone church on the green, she knew that the Sunday morning service had already begun. She parked her car and made her way to the side door, then slipped into the sanctuary and found a seat in one of the rear pews.

She wasn't too late. The choir was singing the opening hymn. She saw the minister, Reverend Ben Lewis, standing at the front of the sanctuary, singing along from his hymnal. It was nice to see Reverend Ben still here after all these years. She had heard he had a heart attack last winter and was going to retire but at the very last minute decided to come back. It was a wise decision, she thought. He wasn't that old. Not when you consider that some people, herself included, live far longer than anyone expected.

The church had not changed much either. It still held the same cool, damp smell—all the stones and the sea air caused that, she guessed—mixed with the scent of the wood polish used on the pews.

Adele picked up a hymnal and found the right page. But her eyes eagerly searched the rows up front for her family. She did not see her son Joe or his wife, Marie, which was somewhat of a relief, she realized. She didn't see her granddaughter Molly and her family, either. But Molly had a catering business and was probably busy with holiday parties today.

She did see her grandson, Sam, still handsome as ever with broad shoulders and dark looks that stood out in any crowd. He was in his mid-forties now, she knew, though these days she didn't keep track of the ages of her grandchildren the way she had when they were younger.

Jessica, Sam's wife, sat beside him along with their two sons, Darrell and Tyler, and the little one, Lily, up on Sam's lap. Adele tried to recall her great-grandchildren's ages. Darrell had to be at least seventeen now, and Tyler, seven and a half. Lily Rose was just shy of three. Adele felt her heart race with longing as she looked at them. She had not seen them since the summer, when they had dropped by on their way home from a camping trip. Darrell had grown even taller since then; he was nearly the same height as Sam now. And Tyler looked very different. He had chopped off the long, curly bangs he'd had since kindergarten and now wore his hair short.

Only little Lily seemed mostly the same. Held in the crook of her father's arm, she looked out over his shoulder and stared straight at her great-grandmother. Adele gazed back. For a moment she thought the little girl recognized her. Then the child turned away, and Adele realized that Lily didn't know her well enough to recognize her. Adele hadn't seen the child more than half a dozen times, and it hurt to realize that.

She looked forward to surprising them when the service was over. She wondered what they would say. Adele had always felt that of all Joe's children, Sam was the most understanding and sympathetic to her side of things. She hoped that coming out of church, he and Jessica would be in a charitable frame of mind.

Aside from her family and Reverend Ben, Adele felt fairly anonymous among the unfamiliar faces. She did notice a few old-timers like herself, still marching on like good Christian soldiers—Lillian Warwick, sitting front and center, as was her due. Or, as she believed was her due. Lillian's younger daughter, Jessica, was married to Sam, so that practically made Lillian a relative. Though one would never know it by the way Lillian acted whenever they met. Lillian sat beside Dr. Ezra Elliot, as she usually did. But the news that Lillian had married her old friend had been surprising. Then again, not that surprising once Adele thought about it. It was a sweet story, despite Lillian's sour temperament. Adele wondered if marriage had improved her disposition.

Sophie Potter, who owned the Potter Orchard, was still in the choir, bless her heart. And she still had a strong, clear voice. She had always been a kind, generous person without a harsh word for anyone. Adele knew that she had lost her husband, Gus, a while back and joined the ranks of widowhood. But Sophie still looked healthy and active.

The only other churchgoers Adele recognized were Grace Hegman and her father, Digger. The old fisherman had always looked old—even when he was young—and Adele was unable to remember his age, though she knew he had to be even further on in years than she was. And that was saying something.

It was funny how a church was like a family. It seemed like only yesterday that she and George were among the young couples here, sitting beside small children who squirmed in their seats. Now, even her own grandchildren were making way for the next generation. Time seemed to pass faster and faster as you grew old. She wasn't sure why, but it did make life feel very precious and even urgent.

Reverend Ben had started his sermon, and his words finally caught her attention. "It's easy to be negative and fearful, to be full of worry," he was saying. "Some people might even think such an attitude shows that you're realistic and well-informed. Why, a few minutes of watching the news will do it easily, with scenes of war and crime, and reports on the economy. Or maybe you don't even have to look to the news for reasons to worry. Maybe plenty of good reasons are close to home—illness, a troubled relationship, financial pressures—"

A family torn apart by an old grievance, Adele filled in silently.

"I think we can all agree that no one needs to look very far for worries. That's easy. The greater challenge in this life is to cast aside worry and fear. And to trust in God's plan for our lives. To trust that God is working to help us, even when we can't see it. God doesn't want us to worry. In fact, throughout the Bible, we find verse after verse telling us to 'fear not,' 'have courage,' and 'trust in the Lord.' You see, fear robs us of our faith and makes it practically impossible to see how God has blessed our lives in so many ways, every day. It makes it impossible for us to feel gratitude and peace. It makes it impossible to trust in God's love for us."

Reverend Ben paused, looking out at the congregation. "Am I immune to this pitfall? Not in the least. Just like all of you, I often feel paralyzed with fear, facing some problem that seems overwhelming. Or thinking about my loved ones and worrying for their safety or success or simply, their well-being. But at those moments we have to stop, and, like a small child being woken up from a bad dream, we have to seek comfort in God's presence and trust that He is always right there with us, through the darkest hours. That He is right there, no matter what we are facing or undertaking. He is there, with His power, protection, and provision. As we have just heard in the reading from Isaiah 41, verses 10–13: 'So do not fear, for I am with you; do not be dismayed, for I am your God; I will strengthen you and help you . . .'"

Adele did not know the Bible very well, except for the most famous passages. This one struck a note deep in her heart. She took out a pen and a scrap of paper and jotted down the citation. She would be needing the encouragement in the days to come.

She was afraid. Just like Reverend Ben had said. Full of fear, truth be told, to confront her family with this mission of hers. But it had to be done. She had woken up one morning, right after Thanksgiving, thinking about her family and the past, and she knew it had to be done. It was a "now or never" sort of moment. But after all these years of estrangement, she was afraid to confront them all. Especially her son Joe. He barely spoke to her as it was. He might cut her off completely. Then where would she be?

She knew that the Bible said it was right to take on the role of peacemaker: "Blessed are the peacemakers." She recalled the exact verse, Matthew 5:9. But the Bible never said it was easy. She could start with Sam, right here and now. But sooner or later, she would have to face Joe.

Up in Vermont, she had felt so sure that she was ready to do this, to open all these old wounds again. But as Reverend Ben invited them all to sing the final hymn, Adele felt her courage and conviction fading. She bowed her head in silent prayer. *Dear God, please give me strength to bring my family back together again . . .*

When she lifted her head, Reverend Ben was giving his silent blessing. She saw everyone rise and begin to collect their things. She saw Sam and his family begin moving out of their row.

No one had noticed her yet. With her heart pounding, Adele bowed her head and made her way out the side door, before anyone could notice.

OUTSIDE THE CHURCH, ADELE FELT HERSELF MOVING IN A STREAM OF people making their way to cars or walking across the green to the village. She guessed that quite a few were going to the Clam Box for a bite to eat. The place was always crowded on Sundays, even well into the afternoon. She and George used to take the kids there, back when Charlie's father owned it. It was their favorite spot in town. Joe would order a clam roll and fries and banana pancakes with a side of bacon, no matter the time of day. His knowledge of food had branched out quite a bit since then, she reflected.

Adele slowly made her way beyond the churchgoers and followed a path across the village green. It was a crisp day but there was little wind, and the water in the harbor was calm and dark, reflecting the sunlight and patterns of clouds. The big Christmas tree stood in the center of the green, strung with lights. She remembered the annual tree lighting, which was always held the Sunday night after Thanksgiving. How she and George had loved that. Singing carols and drinking hot cocoa. Taking the boys to see Santa ride into town on a fire truck. What would she give to go back to those days and live them all over again? A lot, she thought. Though it was useless to even imagine such a thing.

She walked along and came to the street that faced the park and town dock. She hadn't even realized where she was going when suddenly she saw a burgundy and gold awning over a sign on a storefront that read, WILLOUGHBY FINE FOODS & CATERING.

It was her granddaughter Molly's shop. Adele had seen it only once before, the last time she visited, when she drove down for the christening of Molly's youngest daughter, Betty. Molly was doing so well for herself now. She was always a smart girl and a hard worker. But she had made some mistakes, like marrying the wrong guy right out of high school. Molly had gone through hard times after that marriage ended, but she never lost her spirit or hope. Adele was so proud of her.

Wouldn't she be surprised to see her grandma Addie in her shop today? She would be surprised for sure . . . but happy? Molly and she were not that close, not the way they used to be. Partly because Molly was so busy juggling her business and caring for her family. But also because Molly and Sam had both pulled away from her. Ever since the rift with Joe, things had been awkward with his children. But Adele always suspected that Molly regretted having to take sides at all and missed the way the family used to be, familiar and close. As she opened the door to the shop, she hoped that was true.

Inside Willoughby Fine Foods, a rich buttery smell filled the air, making Adele instantly hungry. There were two large displays of food, a bakery area and one with dishes for taking out. A crowd of customers waited in front of each. Adele could only catch a glimpse of the selections and it all looked delicious, beautifully displayed and very gourmet.

She glanced behind both counters but didn't see her granddaughter. A door to a work area was open, and Adele could tell that there were people working back there, but all she could make out was a flurry of white and green aprons.

Maybe this was a bad time. Molly was probably working hard, off catering a party.

"Can I help you, miss?" Adele looked up to find a pretty teenager behind the counter smiling at her.

"I'm here to see Molly. Is she here today?" Adele heard her voice come out in a shaky, old lady croak. Oh, she hated when that happened.

"She's back in the kitchen. I'll get her for you."

Adele started to smile then suddenly heard the unmistakable sound of Joe's voice coming through the open door. Was he back there, too? Adele took a breath. She wasn't ready for that. Not yet.

"Don't worry, dear. That's all right. I'll come back another time. When it's less hectic in here."

The girl stared at her with a confused expression. "Would you like to leave your name or phone number?"

"Not necessary. I'll catch up with her," Adele said. She quickly left the shop and headed back across the green. She felt suddenly exhausted. Her hands were practically shaking, and her legs felt weak.

All the anticipation . . . and then the letdown, she realized.

She sat heavily on a bench and looked out at the water. *What now, God? It seems visiting Molly today wasn't meant to be.* She had hoped to take one little step toward Joe, to approach Molly or Sam first and get them to understand. But she wasn't ready to face Joe, head-on, with no warning.

Maybe God wants me to think about this a little more, she told herself. *Maybe I should just go back to Vermont. If I left now, I could make it back in time to sit in front of the TV and wait for my weekly phone calls with the family. None of them would ever even know I was here.*

Adele sighed and closed her eyes a moment. *Fear not. That's what the scripture says. All things are possible with God. Even winning over my stubborn, angry son.*

She would go back to the inn and have lunch. After all, Claire was cooking crab cakes. Not worth missing out on that, Adele decided. *Maybe I'm just shaky because I need a bite. Low blood sugar. Not because I panicked at the mere sound of my son Joe's voice.*

JONATHAN WAS WORKING IN HIS ROOM WHEN CLAIRE KNOCKED ON his door and announced that lunch was about to be served. When he walked into the dining room the only other guest staying at the inn was already seated, the old woman named Adele Morgan. They had met at breakfast but had not talked much.

The long dining room table was set with embroidered cloth linen napkins and silver flatware, with a centerpiece of fresh flowers in a low silver bowl. Even in this remote spot, the innkeeper, Liza Martin, was attentive to all the fine details. The inn was not only as comfortable as he had hoped but quietly elegant.

Dinner the night before and this morning's breakfast had proved that the food was just as high caliber as the table settings. The smells from the kitchen were enticing, though he could not guess the menu.

"Sit anywhere you like," Liza told him. She walked around the table, filling water glasses from a large glass pitcher.

He chose a set across from Adele, not wanting to be rude, though he would have preferred to eat by himself with a book or some of his research material. *You can make polite conversation for a half hour or so. It won't kill you,* he reminded himself.

Still, he was wary of encouraging an old woman, who would doubtlessly go on about her children and grandchildren and her family Christmas plans.

Jonathan had not been raised with a lot of family around. In fact, his life had been just the opposite. After his mother died when he was seven, his father remained at a distance from all their relatives. Jonathan saw his maternal grandparents and a few cousins once or twice a year at best, and he rarely saw anyone on his father's side at all. That's why the holidays didn't have much meaning for him, even though most people seemed obsessed by them at this time of year.

As they ate the first course, a light but creamy lobster bisque, Adele talked mainly to Claire about the church service she had attended that morning and all the people there that they knew in common. Jonathan enjoyed his soup and the fresh, fluffy squares of corn bread. But when the second course came out, a platter of delicious crab cakes, plump and golden and almost as big as his fist, the attention of the three women suddenly turned to him.

"Have you seen any of the island yet, Jonathan?" Liza asked him.

"Not much. I meant to take a walk or a drive around this morning, but I got distracted with my work."

"What is it that you do?" Adele asked.

"I'm a grad student at Tufts. I'm studying American history, the colonial period." Jonathan paused, not sure how much he should say.

But he had already told Liza a little, and she filled in the blanks for the others. "Jonathan is researching the legend of the island. He's writing a paper about it." She turned and smiled at him.

"Yes, I'm researching the historical facts surrounding the story," he politely clarified.

"How interesting. Have any other historians done that before?" Adele asked.

"There are many people who have worked from secondary sources and revised or recycled different versions of the story. I'm looking for firsthand accounts. Original documents, letters, diaries, accounts in the records of town meetings."

Liza had left the room and now returned with a fresh basket of rolls and corn bread. "That is interesting. So you're looking for the testimony of actual witnesses to the epidemic and what happened after that?"

"Exactly. The epidemic in the village of Cape Light is well documented, as well as the sick who were brought here to be quarantined. But the events afterward are well . . . historically cloudy, you might say."

He suspected that some at the table believed the legend, and he didn't want to insult anyone. So he stopped himself just short of admitting that he highly doubted the story. According to legend, after the sick were quarantined and more or less abandoned on the island, angelic beings arrived and nursed them through the winter.

"The story *is* improbable," Adele spoke up, her voice surprisingly strong and clear, though her hand shook a little when she picked up her water glass. "But when you reach my age, you realize that miracles can and do happen. Sometimes there is just no rational explanation."

Jonathan nodded, not wanting to seem rude. "I've just begun my research, so I don't know if that's so," he said honestly. "I do know that once the facts about an event are gathered and considered, one can usually arrive at a likely, or plausible, explanation."

Claire North had not said anything so far, he noticed, though he had a feeling, just from her expression, that she was among those who believed in the legend. But she did not seem the type to debate with him. Something about Claire sent a message that she was very certain of her beliefs and didn't need to prove anything, least of all to a student like him.

"So how did you come to get interested in this tale, Jonathan?" Claire asked as he reached for the platter of crab cakes to take a second helping. "Did you come across it in a history book? Or did someone tell you the story?"

"My mother told me the story, when I was a little boy. There were relatives on her side of the family who were among the early settlers of Cape Light."

"So you know the legend well," Claire said.

"Well, I heard it a number of times." *Before my mother died,* he added silently. "But as a historian, I appreciate and even collect different versions of a story. Especially one that has such little documentation and has mainly survived through oral history." He paused and glanced over at her. "You seem to know the story. Would you be willing to tell me your version? I'd be interested to hear it."

Claire looked surprised, then nodded. "All right. I'll tell the version I know."

"Would it be all right if I recorded this?" he asked. "It's more accurate than taking notes. I think I have my recorder right here." He reached into the breast pocket of his shirt and took out a small digital recorder, then set it on the table.

"I don't mind at all. Go right ahead." Once she saw he was ready, Claire began. "The version I've heard goes like this . . . The first colonists settled in the village of Cape Light in the mid-1600s. I believe they migrated up from settlements around Cape Cod. Things were going all right, and they were getting some help from the local Native American people, the Wampanoag. But about six months after they arrived, a sickness broke out. I don't know if it had a name or if doctors can now identify the illness. There were many types of contagious diseases back then that we don't see anymore, thank the Lord. But this was a deadly fever, and highly contagious. None of the usual cures, herbs, or bleeding could cure it. Most who caught the fever did not survive. There were very few doctors back then, of course, and much of the medical knowledge was pure superstition. Though there were some good herbal treatments for illness. But many times a cure was more likely to make a patient sicker than help them—"

"Like poor George Washington," Adele interrupted. "It was thought that he died of a simple throat infection. Today we know that his physicians actually killed him by taking so much blood, over nine pints, I read somewhere. The poor man was bled to death."

"Yes, that is true." Jonathan knew that for a fact. "This illness sounds something like Yellow Fever," he said to Claire. "It was prevalent in those times."

"It was something like Yellow Fever," Claire said with a nod. "But the colonists believed that even when a person survived the worst bouts of this fever, they could pass the infection on for weeks after, due to the boils that broke out on the body and took as long as three or four weeks to clear. So the village leaders decided the sick ones had to be quarantined and chose to send them out here, to the island. The outbreak began in the fall, and they reasoned the rest of the villagers would not survive the winter otherwise. Nearly a third of the colony had already been lost in only a few weeks' time. So the sick were taken from their homes and carried to this island and given shelter in crude huts. They were left with some supplies and firewood. There wasn't much to give, and most people believed they would soon die anyway."

"No matter how many times I hear this story, the quarantine always strikes me as harsh and cruel," Liza said.

"It was harsh," Claire agreed. "But those were hard times to live through. I believe a boat from Cape Light was sent out once a week or so with food and wood and not much more than that. Family members were not permitted to come, lest they carry back the infection. Few were brave or merciful enough to help the sick after they were left. A harsh winter came with many storms and high snow," Claire continued. "No one went out to the island for several weeks. Christmas came and went. There was no great celebrating back then as there is today. But it was still recognized as a holiday," she added. "The patients should have been home by then, but no one could get to the island. Most believed all the sick had died. Finally, a boat was sent to search for survivors. The rescue party braced themselves for a grim sight. But the truth was even more shocking than what they had imagined. The quarantined had not only survived but were completely healthy, living in sturdier shelters with ample provisions, clean water, and firewood to spare."

Claire paused and glanced at her listeners. Though they had all heard the story before, the conclusion still drew an amazed reaction, Jonathan noticed. He suddenly realized that he had also fallen under the spell of Claire's storytelling.

He sat up straight and cleared his throat . . . and his head. "And what was their explanation for their recovery . . . I mean, according to your version of the story?" he asked.

"The quarantined claimed that a group of able, gentle people had visited the island and nursed them through the winter. But no one could say exactly where these mysterious visitors came from. Once they returned to the mainland, many of the survivors searched for them. Some spent years traveling around to other colonies, inquiring with the ship captains who traveled back and forth from England. But it's said that the settlers never found anyone who had gone to the island that winter. Many believed that they were saved by the angels, who were disguised in human form," Claire added. "Some believe that the angels' powers can still be felt on the island and will be forever. The believers even point to the interesting shape of the island's cliffs that jut out like an angel's wings. The place came to be known as Angel Island. The name just stuck," Claire added.

Before Jonathan could respond, Adele spoke up. "That's pretty much the version I know, too. Though the way I heard it, this place was already called Angel Island because of the cliffs. When the illness struck and the town leaders had to decide where to bring the sick, they chose the island because many believed it was a sacred, protected place. And it turned out that was true," Adele concluded.

Jonathan's eyes widened at her matter-of-fact tone, but he didn't want to interrupt. Still he had to wonder: How could she possibly know that was true? People did use the word lightly.

"How about you, Liza?" Adele asked their hostess. "Is this the same story you always heard?"

"More or less. Aunt Elizabeth loved to tell the tale, especially on a beach walk to the cliffs. It was always a little different each time," Liza recalled with a smile.

"What sort of variations were there?" Jonathan turned the recorder in her direction, curious to hear her reply.

"Oh . . . let's see." Liza's blue gaze wandered as she tried to remember. "I think in my aunt's version, the villagers didn't expect to find anyone on the island still alive, just as Claire said. But the survivors surprised them by coming across the water on a raft or some sort of roughly made boat, and then they walked into the village, astounding everyone. My aunt would say that as they walked down Main Street, all activity stopped and everyone came out of the shops and houses to see them. But no one dared to say a word until the minister arrived and begged for their forgiveness on bended knees. They gave it, of course. And then he led everyone in a prayer of thanksgiving for their care and survival."

"My goodness, that ending to the story gives me goose bumps all over again." Adele hugged her thick cardigan sweater closer.

Jonathan also felt a few goose bumps at that ending to the story. But he didn't want to admit it. "In your aunt's story, did the survivors also say they had been nursed by mysterious strangers?"

"Oh yes." Liza nodded. "My aunt told us the helpers were angels in human form who had come on Christmas Day. And they also made the boat," she added with a smile.

Before he could say more, Claire caught his attention again.

"So, what do you think, Jonathan? Are these versions similar to the one you grew up hearing?"

"There are some interesting differences. I never heard the detail about the angelic beings arriving on Christmas before. Though that does make sense, in the context of the narrative," he quickly added. "And the variant with the boat is very interesting, too. It's a small detail, but sometimes those are the biggest clues."

"What sort of clue do you think that is?" Adele asked eagerly.

"Well, a roughly hewn boat or raft could suggest contact with the Native American people who were living in the area at the time. Perhaps they came to the island and helped the quarantined group. Though I would have to study some firsthand descriptions of the boat to support that theory."

"How interesting . . . I never thought of that," Adele said.

"So you don't believe the story about the angels visiting," Claire said. It wasn't a question, he noticed, more of an observation. She didn't seem offended as he had expected, but merely curious. However, he felt put on the spot and tried to frame a diplomatic answer.

"Let's put it this way: I believe any part of the story I can verify with factual evidence. How many people were sent to the island, and how long they were there, for instance. There could be village records to document that . . . and other details of the event, too. I believe that something happened on the island during those winter months that has never been fully explained, and that's what I'm trying to discover."

"But you must have some feeling about it," Claire persisted.

Now Jonathan didn't know what to say. He didn't want to insult Claire. He didn't want to hurt anyone's feelings here. They had all been so helpful to him and were so nice. But finally, he had to answer.

"I have to be honest . . . I don't believe it's possible. But when I'm researching, I put my personal opinions aside and keep an objective, open mind. Think of me as an archaeologist, digging things up—hard, tangible bits of evidence that I try to fit together. Then I see what I've got. I'll have some guesses as it takes shape. But I can never assume I know for sure until all of it, or mostly all of it, is there."

"I see. Well, it is a fantastic, improbable story. There can be no argument about that." Claire smiled, putting him at ease again. "But you know what Albert Einstein said: 'There are only two ways to live your life. One is as though nothing is a miracle. The other is as though everything is a miracle.'"

Jonathan had to smile. She had him there.

Liza turned to him. "I'd heard that quote but didn't really get it until I moved out here. When you look at the natural world—the ocean, the flowers, the trees—it's all so amazing, so miraculous. Anything seems possible."

Jonathan nodded and slipped the recorder back in his pocket. "Nature is fascinating and inspiring . . . and very mysterious. No doubt about that. I just can't quite make the leap to angelic beings nursing people on a deserted island." He gave a helpless shrug. "Sorry."

The three women smiled and exchanged looks. He felt as if they were sharing some secret message about him. He didn't mind. He had enjoyed the discussion and had collected some good information for his study.

"How long will you be working around here?" Claire asked.

"Hard to say. It depends on what sort of documents I find. I've only just started."

"Yes, that's true." Claire nodded and smiled.

What was true? That he had hardly scratched the surface and in time would change his mind? With all due respect to everyone at the table, Jonathan sincerely doubted that.

"Would you like some dessert and coffee?" Liza stood at the sideboard, collecting dessert dishes and flatware.

"Thanks but I'm really full." Jonathan meant it, too. But when a slice of lemon meringue pie—with mile-high sugary peaks, perfectly golden on top—was set in front of him, it looked too good to resist.

Afterward, he pushed back from the table, feeling pleasantly full. "That meal was awesome. At this rate, I'll gain fifty pounds before I go back to Boston."

"Nonsense." Claire waved her hand as she cleared the dishes. "I bet you survive on soup and crackers at school—and maybe some pizza and Chinese food."

"I'm not that bad." Jonathan laughed. He was, in fact, worse. She had forgotten the old standby, cold cereal.

"A good meal will never hurt you. But you need to get outside today and get some fresh air, or you won't have any appetite for dinner."

He nodded agreeably. He usually bristled from too much advice, but Claire's motherly prescription made him feel cared for.

"Just what I was thinking. I'd love to see the cliffs. Is it too far to walk?"

"The cliffs are on the other side of the island. It's a nice hike in the summer but it might get dark by the time you head back, this time of year." Liza glanced at her watch. "If you walk one way, I can come pick you up there. Or you can take a bike. We have a few in the barn. Just pick one you like and be sure to take a helmet and a map."

"Good idea. I haven't been riding in years. I'll definitely come back with an appetite." He glanced at Claire, and she smiled back approvingly.

A SHORT TIME LATER, JONATHAN WAS ON HIS WAY, PEDALING PAST THE goat farm that bordered the inn's property. The grass-covered meadows were golden brown but very pretty, Jonathan thought. There was a rambling old farmhouse, not far from the road, and a big red barn behind it. He had already noticed the goats from his window, frolicking in the big field. They were still out, grazing at the back of the meadow, which created a peaceful scene.

He pedaled on, down a long, sloping hill and a tight curve that made him remember the sense of freedom and the feeling that he was practically flying—feelings he had loved as a boy.

The road swung into a small town center and suddenly was all bumps. He noticed there were Belgian blocks on the roadbed. He bumped along through a small village square. A general store with a long, wide porch looked interesting, but he didn't need anything. Liza had even sent him with a water bottle and energy bar.

Across the way, he saw a small cottage encircled by a rickety picket fence. It looked like an elf from a fairy tale might live there. No wonder people around here indulged in these magical beliefs. Closer inspection revealed it was a shop or café. Or maybe both. He slowed down to read the sign: WINKLER TEAROOM & LENDING LIBRARY—BOOKS ARE OUR BEST FRIENDS. He was almost curious enough to go in, but the windows were dark. He decided to come back some other time, if he remembered.

On and on he pedaled, following the road past more cottages and gracious old houses, some in good condition and others quite run-down. Then past vast empty spaces filled with woods or meadows or acres of tall marsh grass, or a stretch of open coastline that would suddenly appear, running parallel to the road.

The island really was a beautiful place, natural and untamed even now, and he could well understand how the landscape here might have helped inspire the story about angels.

He was starting to feel tired and wondered if the cliffs were much farther along. But as he came around a bend, the legendary cliffs—jagged, golden sandstone, at least ten stories high—came into view.

It was nearly four. As Liza had predicted, the sun was already low in the winter sky, coloring the horizon with a rosy hue that reflected on the dark blue waves. The road inclined sharply uphill, and he battled to make it through the final stretch. He stopped for a break a short distance from his goal and stood on the sandy shoulder, holding up the bike. The outline of the cliffs stood out in stark contrast to the backdrop of dark blue sky. The cliffs did indeed look like wings, crescent-shaped and cupped, a point flaring out at the bottom like a long feather.

Quite unusual, he had to admit. He could understand how the early settlers came up with the angel explanation. They fell back on their spiritual beliefs to explain most anything out of the ordinary, and this landscape lent itself perfectly to those sorts of fantasies.

Pure fantasy, Jonathan reminded himself as he pulled out a slim digital camera and snapped a few photos. He left the bike on the roadside, then followed a rambling path to the beach, where he treaded through a few more yards of sand to finally examine this local wonder, up close and personal. He stood in the shadows of the towering rock wall and stared straight up while strong gusts off the water beat at his back. It didn't take a geologist to see that the odd formation had obviously been shaped by the salt winds and hard rain on this side of the island. Yet he hadn't heard one person propose that idea. So far, anyway.

Claire North was a sweet old woman, but . . . Well, what was it to him? She had a right to believe whatever she pleased. He hadn't come here to pull people kicking and screaming into the twenty-first century. He had come to investigate and get a good paper out of his findings.

He took more photos from different angles. The wing shape was best seen from a distance, but close-ups were important, too.

Standing at the base of the cliffs, he turned to look out at the water. The tide was coming in high. Wild waves rolled toward him, crashing on the shoreline and along a natural jetty that extended from the cliffs into the sea. He felt the cold spray on his face and squinted into the sun, which had dipped even closer now to the horizon.

It was getting late and he had to head back. He was walking back to his bike when he found he couldn't resist. He turned toward the cliffs again for one last look. The sandstone peaks were bathed in a glorious golden light, looking strangely softened. Supple enough to spread and take flight. An eerie feeling swept over him as he stared at them. Then he blinked and shook his head.

Get real, Jonathan. Claire North is a good storyteller. But you're a historian. An objective reporter. Don't let a charming old lady and a pretty sunset mess up your head. You haven't even gotten started yet.

CHAPTER THREE

~~~

ON MONDAY MORNING, ADELE WOKE UP FILLED WITH DETER-
mination. She called Molly's shop first thing before she was
even dressed or had gone down for breakfast. She had taken a business
card the day before and noticed that the shop opened at seven a.m.

"I'm sorry, Molly won't be in until the afternoon," a pleasant voice
informed her. "Would you like to leave a message?"

"Um . . . no . . . thank you. I'll try back later," she spoke quickly,
and hung up.

She sat on the edge of the bed and took a deep breath. She had been
all stirred up and now felt the wind leave her sails. It was hard to believe
she had been here since Saturday and hadn't faced anyone in her family
yet. How long could she stay without being discovered? Was this God's
way of telling her that she had made a mistake and ought to go back to
Vermont? Adele was starting to wonder.

She took a shower and dressed. It was still early, not even seven-
thirty. She went down to breakfast and ate in the kitchen with Claire.

"You're quiet this morning. Are you feeling all right?" Claire looked across the table at her with concern as they finished their coffee.

Adele was tempted to confide her troubles, but something held her back. "I'm all right. I don't like to talk much when I first get up," she said, which was true.

"I feel the same."

Adele just smiled, tempted to add that Claire wasn't exactly a chatterbox the rest of the day, either.

Claire began clearing the table, but paused to offer Adele a copy of the local paper, the *Cape Light Messenger*. "Why don't you sit on the porch and get some air? I don't think you'll be cold. It's a very fair day, considering it's December."

Adele was used to Vermont's harsh winter, so it almost felt like spring down here this morning. "I think I'll take a walk out on the beach," she decided. "It will do me good."

Maybe it will help me get my thoughts together and decide whether I should stay here. Is this the desperate crisis I'd thought—or just a fool's errand?

Claire was standing at the sink and glanced at her. "I wish I could come with you. Sometimes I think the beach is even more beautiful in winter, though that wooden staircase can be treacherous. There's a path that winds down to the shoreline, on a gentle slope. The opening is in the brush across from the goat farm. I think you'll be better off taking that route," she advised. It was a polite way of saying she would be less likely to break a hip or otherwise injure herself on this little adventure.

"I remember the way. Good idea."

Adele put on her down jacket and took a scarf and gloves just in case the wind kicked up near the water. She set off down the road and soon found the right path. It should be marked "For Seniors" or "Slow-Moving Vehicles," she joked to herself. It would take a bit longer to reach the shoreline this way than with the stairs, but she would get there in one piece.

She heard that sea air was a tonic and actually lifted your mood with positive molecules. She wasn't sure if that was true, but a walk on the beach always made her feel better. Maybe because you were so close to nature and standing by the sea and sky, you realized the enormity of the universe and your own insignificance. And the relative insignificance of your problems, she thought.

She took her time on the sandy path that wound through the dunes and soon reached the beach. Then she ambled over the sand until she reached the flat, smooth shoreline.

The sky was very blue with high, puffy white clouds, and the waves rolled gently to the shore, smooth and calm. If it had been July or August, it would have been a perfect day for swimming. She used to love to run into the water and dive under the waves. Even the rough breakers hadn't scared her when she was young and strong. That was one thing her husband, George, had loved about her. She wasn't afraid of taking on the ocean, diving in without a care.

Why am I such a scared rabbit now? George would not be proud of me so far on this trip, she thought. *Is he looking down at me right now, shaking his head?*

I'm doing my best, George, she silently countered. *We decided together and thought we were doing the right thing. But you can see now, it turned out wrong. And I'm left to sort out this big mess.*

"Adele Morgan? Is that you?"

Adele looked up. She'd been watching her steps, careful not to lose her balance and had not noticed the man who now stood just a few feet in front of her. She recognized him instantly, even in his baseball cap, red down vest, and high green wading boots. Even though he was carrying a fishing rod and a tackle box.

"Yes, Reverend, it's me." She smiled at him shyly.

"How good to see you. You're looking very well." He set his gear down and took her hand and held it for a moment between both of his.

"I thought I saw you yesterday at the service, sitting toward the back. Then I thought I had to be imagining it. You suddenly disappeared."

"You did see me there. I enjoyed your sermon as always," she said honestly.

"Thank you." He seemed embarrassed by her praise and peered down at her from behind his gold-rimmed glasses. He still had the same round cheeks and cheerful smile, the same thick beard, though it was now mostly gray. He was still a modest man, too, she thought.

She quickly filled the silence with some small talk, asking about his family and how his fly-casting was coming along. There were good reports on both fronts.

"What brings you out to the beach today? Are you staying on the island?" He finally asked the question she had been avoiding.

"Yes, up at the inn. Liza Martin's done a wonderful job renovating."

"Yes, she has." His curious stare remained. She could tell he was wondering why she wasn't staying with any of her family in the village. "Sam and Jessica didn't mention that you were visiting. I guess that's why I wondered if I'd even see you."

Reverend Ben was indirect at times, Adele recalled, but somehow always hit his mark.

"My family doesn't know I'm here, Reverend. I guess you could say I've snuck into town and I'm lying low," she tried to joke, but didn't quite manage it. "It's a long story," she added.

He shrugged. "I don't have anywhere to go. The fish aren't biting this morning, either," he added, stabbing his pole into the sand.

Adele hesitated. She had been worrying herself sick about this problem for years, but she had never really told anyone about it before. It was too hard to discuss, too painful. But maybe she did need to talk about it, and she couldn't think of anyone better to tell than Reverend Ben.

"The reason I've come is a little complicated," she finally began. "There's an issue in our family, an unsettled argument, one you probably don't even know about. It started when my husband, George, died seven years ago. My son Joe was very angry at the terms of my husband's will, which"—she hesitated, because even saying it aloud sounded so unfair—"which favored my son Kevin."

"I didn't know that. Seven years? That is a long time."

Adele felt a bit embarrassed by her admissions of these family matters, but she also felt relieved, finally bringing it out in the open.

"It's always pained me deeply, Reverend, but it seemed that there was nothing I could do. So I've lived with it. Like my bad knee or the aching in my old bones." She paused and glanced at him. He was listening intently with a thoughtful expression. "I don't know why, but suddenly I just couldn't live with it any longer. Maybe it's just Christmas coming. At my age, you know each holiday might be your last. I just felt this urgent need to make my family patch things up. So I've come down here to try to do that . . . I'm just not sure how."

Reverend Ben's blue eyes shone with sympathy. "I admire you for simply trying, Adele. It's a hard job but an important one."

"That's what I think," she said. "I just don't even know where to begin."

They were both silent for a moment, then he said, "Would you like to tell me a little more about it?"

Adele nodded. "You remember that we ran a variety store up in Highland?"

"Yes, I do, now that you mention it. But that wasn't the reason you and George left Cape Light, was it?"

Reverend Ben had a good memory, she thought.

"No, that wasn't why. George was transferred by his company and he didn't want to lose his retirement benefits and have to find a new job in middle age. I guess we were in our late fifties. We thought we were old . . . little did we know," she added with a smile. "So we moved up there, then it turned out that he was laid off anyway, about two years later. I wanted to come back to Cape Light, but he heard of an opportunity to buy a good business in town, the Five Star Variety store. George had always wanted to own his own business, so we used our savings and took a chance. It turned out to be a good decision. George had a knack for running the store, and it did very well."

"Was he still running the store when he got sick?"

"Yes, he was, with the help of a manager. He didn't put in the same long hours, of course. But he wouldn't let it go. He had promised the business to our son Joe. You know Joe, Reverend. He's worked in restaurants all his life, but he's always wanted to go off on his own. He could never afford to take the chance, though, not with the responsibilities of such a large family."

"So George changed his mind and left the store to Kevin? Is that right?"

This was the hard part to explain. "Kevin had a lot of problems at that time. His first wife had just left him, he had lost his job . . . and was trying very hard to get sober. He was an alcoholic back then. The drinking started in college and it got worse." She glanced at Reverend Ben. "He was floundering, Reverend. He was also minding the business for us while I took care of George."

Reverend Ben didn't interrupt.

"It was a very hard decision. But Kevin had lost so many jobs due to his drinking. George and I thought he needed the help much more than Joe did. George wanted to know that Kevin would be able to make a decent living after he was gone. I'm sorry now for the way things turned out, but it seemed the right thing to do at the time. We both saw Kevin as the weaker one, the one needing more help. He was always that way—going to three different colleges before he could finish his degree, going out and getting jobs and then losing them just as fast. I think we were good, loving parents, but Kevin had certain weaknesses in his character. He couldn't beat drinking, though he tried many times. We thought the business would give him hope and a new start. A reason to get up every morning. A good reason not to drink. That's what we both thought and hoped would happen. We *had to* do something."

Adele let out a heavy sigh. "Joe was always the strong one, very independent, never asking or even willing to accept our help. He had always been so close and protective of Kevin when they were growing up, we felt sure he would understand. My husband had planned to explain it all to Joe before he died. But he never got the chance. So I was left to break that news."

"And Joe didn't understand."

"No, he didn't understand at all. He felt very angry and betrayed. Betrayed by all of us . . . but mainly by Kevin. Joe didn't see the alcoholism as an illness. He thought Kevin had played on our sympathies. He thought Kevin should have been a man about his setbacks, not come crawling home to us for help or turning to the bottle to drown his problems. Joe told Kevin that the right thing to do would be to refuse the store and give it to him, as George had always promised."

"Joe has always been so responsible," Reverend Ben said. "I suppose that was to be expected. How did Kevin react to that? Was he willing to make any compromise at all?"

"Oh, he tried to apologize and even offered to pay Joe half of what the business might be worth, over time. But Joe wasn't talking to him by that point. He felt Kevin had manipulated George when he was sick. And just as bad, Joe felt he had been cut out of the will—and all for nothing. In a way, he was right. The store only lasted about two years more with Kevin managing things. He started drinking again and lost it all." Adele winced at the painful memories. "At that point, even I lost my patience and sympathy for him."

"That must have been a very difficult time for all of you. How is Kevin doing now? Did he ever manage to right himself?"

"Yes, he did," she said. "Losing the business was probably his rock bottom. He finally faced himself and made a commitment to get sober. He had reached out for help countless times before. But this time, for some reason, the program worked. Kevin's been sober now for almost five years. He married again and has a good job in telecommunications. He's doing very well, too. I spent Thanksgiving with his family, and he's been offered a big promotion."

"That's terrific. I'm glad to hear it," Reverend Ben said sincerely.

"It's a great relief to me. I would hate to leave this world knowing Kevin was still struggling with his illness. But he will be moving far away, to New Zealand. That's where his firm is moving him, right after the New Year," she added. "So you see, Reverend, there are many good reasons why I want my sons to make peace now. While I'm still alive, for one thing, and before Kevin moves halfway around the world and out of reach."

"Yes, I see. There is real urgency." Reverend Ben's expression was somber.

"I know we weren't fair to Joe, but I can't help thinking this was the way it was meant to be. It was only when Kevin hit rock bottom, when he lost the precious gift his father gave him, that he was able to finally face himself, take hold of his life, and truly change. Maybe he wouldn't have been able to pull himself together otherwise. Maybe that was God's way of doing it, the price we all had to pay so that Kevin could live a productive life again. Wasn't it a small price, all things considered?" she asked. "Wouldn't a parent pay any price to save their child's life? Shouldn't his brother feel the same way?"

"But Joe doesn't see it that way?" Reverend Ben guessed, his tone gentle.

Adele shook her head. "I doubt if he will even hear me out. The truth is, I'm afraid to bring the matter up to him, Reverend. Our relationship isn't what it used to be," she added sadly. "He hardly speaks to me anymore. Just a call once a week or so. Or he comes if I have an emergency. He leaves the rest to Kevin. Joe just does his duty by me now. I don't know how I'll ever get through to him," she admitted.

Reverend Ben was silent for a long moment, his gaze going to the endless waves sweeping in to the shore. Finally, he said, "I wish I knew what to tell you, Adele. There are no shortcuts to forgiveness of such a painful episode. It sounds to me as if this breach is about more than who got the store. It seems you're saying that you and your husband treated your younger son differently, gave him more attention and support. Because that's what he needed from you. While Joe was different, independent, and undemanding. This final gesture of your husband's, to take care of Kevin, even though it meant breaking his promise to Joe . . . Well, I guess that was the last straw for Joe. It would be hard for anyone to let go of that," he said honestly.

"Yes, you're right." She suddenly felt tears welling up in her eyes. Confessing her biggest, most regrettable mistake—even to a minister— was terribly upsetting.

"It won't be easy," Reverend Ben predicted, "but don't give up hope. You're doing the right thing. I believe that, come what may, your family must finally see that."

She dabbed her eyes with a tissue and nodded. "I believe that, too. But so far . . . I keep feeling as if God is telling me to go back home and leave it be. My dream was to bring them all together again, to have one big Christmas like the old days. Now I'm not sure I can do it. Maybe it's too much to ask."

"Nothing is too much to ask, Adele. Though I can't guarantee that God will get things done just the way you imagine it. I think you'll have to chip away at this mountain of resentment a little bit at a time. It might not even be solved by the New Year. But you should take comfort in knowing that you tried."

Adele drew in a long, shaky breath and nodded. It might take a long time to smooth these troubled waters. But she hoped to take comfort in succeeding, not just trying.

Reverend Ben rested his hand on her shoulder a moment. "Don't lose heart, Adele. Don't let yourself get discouraged. Keep asking for God's help. Just remember that even if He often moves in ways that are unfathomable to us, His love is always with us. And if there's anything I can do to help you, please let me know."

"You've already helped a lot just by hearing me out."

"I was happy to. In fact, I think I was down here on the beach, not catching any fish this morning for just that reason," he added with a smile. "I'll be praying for you and your family."

"Thank you, Reverend. It will take a lot of prayers," she added. "I'll let you know how it's going."

A few moments later they said good-bye, and Adele headed back up the beach, feeling much better than she had when she left the inn.

I'm no longer ready to pack up and sneak out of town, she thought with a smile. *How lucky to have run into Reverend Ben down here. Telling him my tale of woe really helped me get back on track. It wasn't luck,* she realized. *There was God's hand in that meeting. It was a sign, for sure. I have to march on back to town to see Molly or Sam, or both of them. Work my way to Joe. Chip away at the problem, like Reverend Ben said to do. I know in my heart I just have to. Even if I can't solve it, I won't rest easy until I've tried.*

JONATHAN SET OFF FOR THE CAPE LIGHT HISTORICAL SOCIETY RIGHT after breakfast but had a little trouble finding the place. He could see from his map that it was located outside of town on a long, curving route with few houses and many stretches of woods and meadows covered with marsh grass. The houses he did spot along the way were all old and unique, some Victorian and even colonial-era architecture. Claire had told him that the historical society building was past the Potter Orchard and Sawyer's Tree Farm, but even those two landmarks did not help much.

Finally, he backtracked and noticed a small sign that hung on high wrought-iron gates set in a long, stone wall. LILAC HILL—THE WARWICK ESTATE, he read, and below that in even smaller lettering, HOUSING THE OFFICES OF THE CAPE LIGHT HISTORICAL SOCIETY.

He'd read a little about village history, and as he drove through the gates and down a long drive bordered by trees, he realized he was passing the famous row of lilac trees that gave a spectacular show every spring. The first mistress of the house had planted the trees and named the estate in their honor.

He remembered that Lilac Hill had been owned by the Warwicks, the most prominent family in the area during the nineteenth century. They had made their fortune in the late 1800s with canneries and built the massive stone mansion just after World War I, copying one of the great houses in Europe. Jonathan had read that not only had the stones been brought over by boat, but with them came a team of masons, who lived on the grounds for several years while the mansion and outbuildings were constructed.

The estate covered more than three thousand acres and the house held about forty rooms, he recalled, with several wings to the building and too many chimneys to count. He parked the car and walked up a gravel path to the front entrance, feeling a little unsettled by the stares of stone gargoyles, which were perched at various points on the edge of the roof.

Enormous mansions and huge estates of this type were nearly impossible to keep up these days. This one had become impossible to keep for its last owner. Oliver Warwick, the last heir to live here, went bankrupt. His widow, Lillian, sold the estate and many of the furnishings in the mansion to the village to cover their debts. But she required that the property be maintained as a historical landmark and never sold for development. She must have been a strong woman with foresight. The mansion certainly was a landmark and well worth preserving, he thought as the looming stone building came into view.

A stone portico covered the entrance. Jonathan walked beneath it and climbed the steps to the large wooden front door. Just as he was about to enter, the door swung open. An older woman with a gaunt face, silver hair, and an expensive-looking wool coat with a fur collar swept by. She was followed by a man about her own age, who wore round spectacles and a bow tie.

The woman spared Jonathan a quick glance as he held the door for her, but she didn't thank him. It was as if he were paid to do that job, or as if she simply expected such service from the world at large.

"I don't know why they keep electing me to the board if they over-rule all my motions and barely listen to a word I say," she complained to the man. "They just want someone with the name Warwick on the let-terhead. I'm an endangered species . . . and I've been totally exploited."

"They do listen to you, Lillian. They just don't always agree with you. And your last name is now Elliot. Need I remind you?"

They walked the short distance to a shiny black sedan parked by the entrance. He held the door open for her on the passenger's side, and she made a grumbling sound as she got in. "Very funny. You ought to do stand-up comedy on a TV show."

"I'm glad you're amused, dear. That's why you married me, to keep you smiling." The husband had come around to the driver's side now.

Jonathan could see that the man was chuckling, having gotten the last word in with his wife. Jonathan stood there a moment and watched the car drive off. Was that really Lillian Warwick, the woman he had read about? She seemed about the right age and had the right attitude. The old man, Elliot, must have been her second husband. He certainly had an amazing disposition. Jonathan did not see himself marrying for a long time, but when he did, he would never choose anyone like Lillian Warwick or Elliot or whatever she called herself.

Love chooses for you. You don't have much say, someone had once told him. Jonathan recalled the words though he didn't really believe that.

He entered the building and found himself in a large foyer with a black-and-white tile floor. It looked like marble, but he couldn't be sure. There was a long circular staircase and a lot of carved woodwork and antique furniture.

He finally noticed a desk, like the kind you see in a library, and spotted two people working there. An older woman was already helping someone, showing them a self-guided tour map to the mansion and grounds. A younger woman stood with her back to him, answering the phone. He cleared his throat noisily and waited. She finally finished her call and turned to face him.

She just stared and he stared back.

It was the waitress from the diner. Tess. She even wore a nameplate again. She was hardly recognizable otherwise. Large black-rimmed glasses framed her blue eyes. Her hair was loose, pulled off her face by a wide black band. She wore a tailored shirt, pearl earrings, and a slim black skirt. She was exceptionally pretty.

"Oh, it's you." She frowned at him. "Did your research paper ever dry out?"

He had to think a minute; he was so shocked meeting up with her again. Then he realized that she was asking about the paper by his professor. He quickly nodded. "It's fine. A few pages are a little blurry."

"Good to know."

He couldn't quite tell if she was being sarcastic or not, but he felt a hot flush of embarrassment. "I'm sorry . . . I overreacted at the diner. I borrowed that paper from my advisor. It's a copy, but it was something he entrusted me with and—"

Now she looked genuinely concerned. "Did it really dry all right?"

"It's fine. You were right about pressing it between towels. That seemed to do the trick."

She nodded, looking relieved. "So, what brings you to Lilac Hall? Want to tour the local sites?"

"In a way, I guess I do. I'm researching the legend of Angel Island. I'm looking for primary sources from that time period, firsthand accounts about the epidemic. Any records the villagers might have kept, like personal journals, letters . . . that sort of thing."

"You've come to the right place. We do have some records from the early settlement. Why are you researching the legend? Are you a writer?"

"I'm a historian . . . Well, I plan to be. I'm working on my doctorate at Tufts."

She nodded again. He couldn't tell if she was impressed. But he did realize he wanted her to be.

"It's a fascinating story and there are many versions," he continued. "But, to my knowledge, it's never been investigated and documented in depth."

"No, I don't think it has," she agreed. "So you want to document it—create some authorized, scholarly version?"

"I guess you could say that."

She frowned, clearly not buying his answer. "Are you trying to disprove the legend? To debunk it?"

Was she sensitive about the story, too? She seemed so sharp and intellectual and not the type to believe in angels. He definitely didn't want to insult her. They were just recovering from the water-spilling incident.

He chose his words carefully. "I'm trying to piece together all the facts I can find about the event and hopefully come up with an explanation for what really happened, supported by hard evidence. I don't think that's ever been done. I've just begun the research, so I don't know what my conclusion will be. Does that matter in regard to using the library here?"

"No," she said, her tone softer. "You can see the documents, no matter what. I was just curious." She turned and chose a key ring from a row of hooks over the back counter. "You'll need to give me some identification and sign the visitors' book. And you'll have to leave your coat and things in a locker. You're allowed to bring a pad and pencils and a laptop, if you have one. Then I'll take you to the room where we keep the collection from that period. Documents from that period are kept in a storage vault. But you can view copies and transcriptions and some items on microfilm."

"Very good. Thank you." He wasn't sure why, but he felt a sudden and immense wave of relief. As if this attractive, sassy girl held his fate in her hands.

Tess handed him a form, and he handed over his driver's license and school ID. She watched him as he filled out the form, hastily printing his answers, which she read upside down.

Butler, Jonathan. PhD candidate at Tufts University. Local residence: The Inn on Angel Island. Permanent address: Phillips Street in Boston.

She brought his ID cards to the copy machine and set them on the plate to make a copy. She couldn't believe it. The guy from the diner! The last person in the world she ever wanted to see again. Hadn't that first time been embarrassing enough? Why did she have to be the one at the visitors' desk when he walked in? She wished she could pass him off to someone, but they were short on staff this week, and it was impossible.

Funny how he didn't seem quite as arrogant today. Though he did live on Phillips Street in Boston, which she was pretty sure was a Beacon Hill address. Then again, maybe he wasn't so bad. Maybe she had caught him in a bad mood at the Clam Box? He had stuck up for her with Charlie after all was said—and splashed. Tess felt bad that she hadn't thanked him. It seemed too awkward now.

When Tess returned from copying the ID cards, Jonathan was still filling in the form. He was pretty cute. She noticed how his thick brown hair hung in his eyes a bit as he leaned over the counter. His square jaw and dark eyes gave him a serious air as he squinted at the form. But when he smiled at her before, she had seen deep dimples and noticed how he could be friendly—even charming—when he wanted to.

He was also clever. The legend about the island was a little known but fascinating tide pool, which no true scholar had ever investigated. The epidemic was an event she had thought about digging into herself.

He finished filling out the form, and she handed back his IDs and then stapled his form to the sheet from the copy machine.

"Is that it?" he asked warily. "I don't need any personal references? Or emergency contact numbers?" He was teasing her, of course.

Tess wanted to smile but managed to keep a straight face. "I have to take a small DNA sample . . . but it won't hurt much," she promised.

He laughed, showing those dimples again.

"Let's stash your stuff in a locker. Then we can go upstairs and I'll get you started."

Jonathan looked cheered by that news. He grabbed his book bag and stood at attention. "After you," he said politely, letting her pass.

He quickly deposited his things in a locker, then Tess led the way, feeling a bit self-conscious as he walked beside her up the winding staircase and down the long, dim hallway on the second floor. He didn't offer any conversation, and her mind drew a sudden blank, though she usually had a lot to say to other visitors she helped with research. Something about him made her nervous.

Just chill, Tess, and don't go near him with any liquids. You'll be fine, she coached herself.

Tess stopped at one of the doors about halfway down the hall and unlocked the door, then led Jonathan into a large, elegantly furnished room with tall bookcases that held rare, old volumes. There were also many antique cabinets, whose shelves held cardboard folios filled with copies and transcriptions of the documents and cassettes of microfilm. Jonathan could hardly wait to get his hands on them.

He slowly looked around. "Wow, this is a beautiful room. Was it always a library?"

"Yes, this room was the original library when the mansion was built. Though some of the cabinets and furnishings have been changed since."

The ceilings of the room, like those throughout the mansion, were twenty feet high. Walls that were not covered with bookcases were covered by beautiful wood paneling and elegant moldings. There were two wooden library tables in the room, set up with low glass reading lamps and machines to view the microfilm.

The room was cool and dry, kept at a certain temperature and low humidity to preserve the paper. Wooden shutters kept out the sunlight, which was also damaging to the documents. Still, the scent of old books was unmistakable. Perfume to his soul.

Tess opened a glass cabinet with a key and carefully removed two maroon binders then brought them to his table. The white labels on the outside of the cases read: CAPE LIGHT 1633–1650 AND ANGEL ISLAND 1633–1650. "These are the earliest documents we have," she explained. "As you probably know, the village was founded in 1633. The settlers arrived in June of that year and the epidemic and quarantine occurred about six months later, during their first winter. This binder contains copies of the village records. They had appointed a governor back in England, John Ames, and there are a few pages of his journals here as well. We have other material that would be relevant," she added. "I can show you more when you're done with this. The curator, Mrs. Fisk, doesn't like us to take out too much at once."

He quickly opened his laptop, eager to get to work. "This is a great start, thank you." He realized that he was almost as curious about her as he was about the old artifacts. "So do you work here as an intern?" She was too young to be librarian with a full degree, he guessed. She was younger than he was, a few years anyway.

"I'm just a docent. I'm a senior at Boston University. In the history department, in case you were wondering." Her tone had that challenging edge again. But he was starting to like it.

"I was wondering," he admitted. "But I should have guessed that next. You seem to be in your element when you talk about village history. I bet you know everything about it."

"Enough," she admitted. She stared at him a minute. Did he want her to stay and help him? She would have liked that. His research topic was exactly the sort of thing that interested her, and being stuck down at the visitors' desk was unbelievably boring.

He had put on a pair of reading glasses and was squinting at the documents as he removed them from the binder, handling them with reverence and care. Even though they were just copies. He seemed the type who preferred to work alone, and she didn't want to seem pushy. If he needed help, he would ask, she decided.

"I'll be downstairs if you have any questions. When you're done, just return the documents to the cases. I'll re-shelve everything later."

"I'll do that. Thanks for your help, Tess." He didn't even realize he'd used her name—until he saw her surprised expression.

"No problem . . . Jonathan."

She turned and left the room, and he pretended to be focused on the documents. But couldn't help but sneak a look at her as she walked away.

Her voice seemed to echo in the emptiness after she disappeared. He liked the way she had said his name and wondered when he would see her again. Probably not until he left, he realized. Then he caught himself. *You can't sit here thinking about a pretty girl all day. You have a lot to do and better get started.*

Despite the distraction of meeting up with Tess again, Jonathan soon found himself totally engrossed in the carefully written records kept by the area's first settlers. There was a ship's bill of lading; some sort of dry goods inventory; three land grants; an agreement to purchase a horse, a cart, and five chickens; and records from a few of the town's early meetings.

The handwriting, written with a quill pen and sepia-toned ink, was difficult—almost impossible—to read. After several hundred years, the lettering had faded and the pages had practically deteriorated. Many were torn, with pieces missing and some were only fragments. Luckily, researchers before him had painstakingly studied and translated each mark, and the copies of the original documents were accompanied by a neatly typed and easy-to-read version on the opposite page.

Still, he read very slowly, carefully considering the information as he made notes on his laptop. He never tired of reading about this time period: The great hope and optimism of the early colonists, who left the thriving cities of Europe behind for a strange, wild land. How they willingly began to build a new civilization where there was absolutely nothing familiar. What optimism, what energy, what courage . . . and faith. He could never imagine doing such a thing. Maybe that was why this period of history and the people who lived then were endlessly fascinating to him.

Jonathan sat studying the documents for several hours. He only noticed the time had passed when the grumbling in his stomach became too loud to ignore. He decided to pack up and return to the inn. He had plenty of information to work on back there and would return again tomorrow to read more of the village records.

He was shutting down his laptop when Tess walked into the room.

"Oh . . . you're still here. Did you find anything to help your research?"

"Yes, I found plenty. I guess I'll be back tomorrow. Are you open the same hours?"

"Yes, ten to four. There's a card at the front desk. You ought to take it." She had come over to the table and looked over the binders before she put them in a stack. She looked very pretty standing there. Today she did look like the kind of girl he might ask out. It was funny how she seemed so different. Or maybe he had rushed to judge her too quickly at the diner. He had made a lot of dumb assumptions.

"It's a fascinating period of history," Tess said. "Is this the area that you're specializing in?"

Her question broke into his rambling thoughts. He nodded quickly. "Yes, it is."

She carried the binders to the bookcase and began to re-shelve them. "It's mine, too."

"Really? Then working here must be a big plus. You can do research any time."

"Almost. If I'm clever about it," she added.

He had a feeling she was clever about most things. That part probably wasn't any problem.

"So, what did you find out so far? I'm not sure I've ever read those early town meeting records."

"Oh, you should if you ever have the time. I love the way the colonists were so careful about recording their experiences. Almost as if they knew that hundreds of years later, someone like me would be sitting all alone in a room, studying every word."

"They had to report back to England," Tess reminded him. "And I think they did have a sense of their own place in history. Of the enormous adventure they had taken on, coming here and building a whole New World from a wilderness—"

"Exactly," he said excitedly. "I was just thinking the very same thing. I'm not sure I would ever have the guts to do something like that. Would you?"

Tess considered the question a moment, slipping one last binder into place. She turned to him. "Yes, I think I would. But that's easy to say now . . . and please don't tell me that NASA is enlisting volunteers to colonize outer space. I'm definitely not interested."

He laughed at the analogy. "Well, that's fine with me. Because I could really use your help again here. After all these town meeting records, I would love to find some more personal accounts. Letters maybe . . . or a journal?"

He was looking at her with those large dark eyes, as if she were the only person in the building who could help him . . . maybe the only person in the entire world. It was a thought that made Tess smile.

"I think I can help you with that."

"Will you be here tomorrow?" He picked up his laptop and notepad.

"Yes, I'll be here." Tess nodded, feeling a tiny ping of excitement when she met his gaze.

"Good. I'll see you then, Tess. Good night." Then he smiled at her and left the reading room.

Tess closed the bookcase and locked it. Then she looked around the room to make sure it was in perfect order. Mrs. Fisk checked every room, every night, and would be up soon.

Well, that was an interesting afternoon, Tess reflected as she straightened the chair Jonathan had used and shut off the reading light. Much more interesting than most. And he was much more attractive than he had seemed at the diner. He probably wasn't in town for very long, but it would be fun to see him tomorrow and help with his research. She already had a few ideas about sources. She was glad now that he had run into her here. It turned out that Jonathan Butler was not the last person in the world she ever wanted to see again. Not by a long shot.

CHAPTER FOUR

IT WAS LATER THAT SAME MONDAY THAT ADELE GATHERED
her courage and returned to Willoughby Fine Foods. The shop
was emptier this time, the lunch rush long over. She had a clear view of
the counters with their appetizing displays. Best of all, she saw a familiar
figure coming through the back door that led to the kitchen.

"Excuse me, miss, can you help me?" Adele bit back a smile at the
shocked expression on her granddaughter's face. But she was so glad to
see Molly, with her bright blue eyes and dark, curly hair, the famous
Morgan coloring.

Molly was carrying a tray of miniature fruit tarts and nearly dropped
it when her eyes met Adele's. "Grandma . . . what are you doing here?"
She set the tray down on the glass counter and brushed her hands on
her apron.

Adele walked closer, though they were still separated by a glass case
full of pastries.

"I decided to come down and visit since no one ever comes up to see me anymore. Well, rarely," she added, forcing a light tone. It wouldn't help her case at all to sound cranky and complaining. Light tone or not, she saw Molly's cheeks flush. She always had such beautiful fair skin and did still, even in her early forties.

"Oh, you know how it is, Grandma. We're all so busy." Molly avoided Adele's glance, skillfully sliding the tray of pastries into the case.

At least she had the good grace to make a polite excuse, Adele thought. The real reason was not so easy to admit.

"Did you just get into town?" Molly asked, standing up again. "You didn't drive all the way down here by yourself, did you?"

"I came down on Saturday, and I didn't drive very fast but yes, I did drive down here by myself," Adele said, feeling a touch of pride in her feat. "I'm staying on Angel Island, at the inn," she went on. "It's very pretty. Liza Martin's done a wonderful job with the renovation."

"Yes, she has." Molly seemed to be recovering from her shock. "I'd offer for you to stay with us, but I'm so insanely busy right now. You'd be pretty much alone all day . . . But if you want to leave the inn for any reason, we have plenty of room."

Adele appreciated Molly trying to make an effort, but suspected that the hospitality was offered more because it was the right thing to do than because Molly really wanted her there. Her granddaughter sided with her father in the argument, and their once-warm relationship had been strained ever since. It was sad how the anger and resentment between Joe and Kevin had spread through the family, like a drop of black ink falling into a pitcher of milk.

"Thank you for inviting me," Adele said quickly. "But once you find out why I came, you might not want me staying over."

Molly stared at her a minute, then brushed a loose strand of hair back from her face. She stepped out from behind the counter to give Adele a quick hug. "It must be important," she said ruefully, "if you drove all the way down here. Why don't you come around the back to the workroom, where we can talk?"

"That's a good idea. Lead the way," Adele said, and followed Molly into the back of the shop.

Molly closed the door and offered Adele a seat near a long metal worktable. "Can I get you something, Grandma? Some lunch? Some pastry? A cup of coffee?"

Adele smiled. That was Molly. Hard feelings could be swallowed back a lot easier with some tasty food, couldn't they? "No, dear, I'm fine. I know you're very busy but just sit with me a moment. I need to talk to you."

Molly took the seat across from Adele at the table. "What's up, Grandma? You're not sick, are you?"

She thinks I've come down here to tell everyone I'm battling some fatal illness, Adele realized with a start. *Not that I'm wishing ill on myself, but that sort of news might actually win me some sympathy*, she thought wryly. But she couldn't lie. It wouldn't be right.

"No, I'm not sick, thank the good Lord. But I'm not getting any younger, either. I came down to ask your father to forgive me and make peace with his brother," she said. "After all these years, Molly, I can't stand the idea that they're still angry at each other—and your father is still so angry with me. I know I'm not blameless and neither is your uncle Kevin. But it is long past time that those two talked things out and forgave each other. And it's time that your father forgave me. Oh, he still calls once a week to see if I'm alive, but there's not much more to our relationship than that." Molly seemed about to speak but Adele rushed on. "I want to see this family together again, like in the old days. Just one more time before I die? Remember when you all would come see me after Christmas?"

Molly sighed. "Of course I remember, Grandma, and I miss those gatherings too. But . . . I also remember how bad Dad felt when Grandpa died and he didn't get the store. After all those years of waiting and expecting? He and Mom even drove up there a few times to look at property." Molly shook her head. "I don't think he'll ever forgive you or Uncle Kevin for that. I'm not sure I would, either," she added in her blunt way.

Adele was not surprised at her reaction, but it still hurt to hear that hard note in her granddaughter's voice. She struggled not to interrupt. Molly needed to have her say, no matter how much it hurt to listen.

"I can't help taking Daddy's side of it," Molly explained. "Grandpa always promised Dad that business. And Dad was working such long, difficult hours to support all of us and he was never around to help Mom. Taking over the store was the chance he always wanted—and counted on. Uncle Kevin didn't have to take the store. He could have just refused to take it. I'm sure he knew in his heart that it wasn't fair. It wasn't the right thing to do. Or he could have even shared it with Dad. Dad would have kept it going. Uncle Kevin couldn't even run it. We all know what happened. All Grandpa's hard work and all the money he invested, down the drain two years later . . ."

"Yes, we all know what happened," Adele agreed. "But people can change, Molly. They can learn from their mistakes and improve themselves. You know that's true."

Molly caught her meaning. Adele could tell by the expression on her face. Not so long ago, Molly had been a single mother, living in a tiny apartment above a store with two young daughters whom she supported with odd jobs—cleaning houses and driving a school bus. But she hoped, dreamed, and worked for much more and eventually achieved it—her own business, a second marriage, a beautiful new home and a new life. Molly, of all people, should not sit in judgment of her uncle Kevin. Not if she was fair-minded about the question.

"Yes, your uncle lost the store. He lost everything he had and even disappeared for a while. But maybe that was all necessary. He finally hit bottom and saved his own life. He's been sober for almost five years and has a good job and a happy marriage."

"Yes, I know he's cleaned up his act. Good for him." Molly shrugged and looked down at a clipboard on the table that bulged with papers and yellow sticky notes. For her many jobs and orders, Adele guessed. Molly was a busy woman, and Adele knew she did not have much time left to plead her case.

"Your uncle is getting a big promotion. His company is sending him to New Zealand, right after the first of the year. Who knows when he'll be back?" Molly looked up at her again. Adele felt she had her attention. "I'm getting old. I may never live to see my sons reconcile. Do I have to wait until they meet again at my funeral?"

"Grandma, come on. Don't say things like that." Adele thought she'd gotten to her, just a little. But she also seemed even more irritated by the conversation. "Did Uncle Kevin send you here to talk to us? Was this his idea or something, because he's moving away?"

Adele sat up straight and looked her in the eye. "It was not his idea, none of it. Kevin doesn't even know I'm here. I know your father won't listen to me. He won't even talk to me about this. But he might talk to you. Will you help me, Molly? Will you help me bring the family back together again?"

Her granddaughter sat back, looking shocked by the question. Before she could answer, one of the counter workers opened the door and looked in. "Mrs. Breslin is here, Molly. She needs to talk to you about her party. Something about the vegetable pâté?"

"Oh, sure. Be right there. I'll just be a minute."

Saved by the vegetable pâté, Adele thought. *And I was just getting somewhere.*

The door closed again and Molly turned back to Adele. "I'm sorry, Grandma. I have to get back to work. And the truth is, I get mad just thinking about all this again. What you and Grandpa and Uncle Kevin did to my dad—you pulled the rug right out from under him, as if his feelings didn't matter at all. It wasn't just the store, or even what it was worth. You all just brushed him aside. I don't know . . . but I do know I'm not the right person to help you. I have a lot of sympathy for my father and just about none for Uncle Kevin."

Or you, Adele almost heard her add.

Thankfully, Molly did not go that far. But she had gone far enough. Her position was clear. She was not going to help Adele plead her case. Adele rose to her feet and picked up her handbag.

"I'm sorry if I was too blunt, Grandma. That's just the way I feel."

"You don't have to apologize," Adele replied. "We all have to be honest if we want to get to the bottom of this thing."

This murky, black pit of grievances and hard feelings. Was there a bottom to it? Adele hoped so. She hoped she could find it before she drowned trying. Adele saw a back door that led to a parking lot and decided not to walk through the store again. "I'll just go out this way. It looks easier."

"Yes, it is." Molly walked her to the door. "Are you going back up to the inn now?"

Adele shrugged. "It's such a nice afternoon. I'll take a walk in town first." *Lick my wounds and regroup,* she added silently. "Good-bye, dear. Thanks for taking the time to talk to me. It's been too long since I've seen you," she added honestly.

She leaned over and gave Molly a quick kiss on her cheek. Molly didn't respond, but that didn't matter to Adele. She knew Molly was upset. That was just her way. Talk bold and blunt, and then get moody for a while, wondering if she had done the right thing.

Molly held the door as Adele stepped outside. "What about Dad? Should I tell him that you're in town?"

Adele hadn't thought about that. "I'd rather you didn't. I'm not ready to talk to him," she said. "I'll get in touch with him when I'm ready."

Molly didn't look pleased by that answer, but she had to get back to work. Adele watched as she waved good-bye and shut the back door.

Adele stood out in the parking lot, not sure of which way to go or what to do next. The weather had been mild again today, but it was at least half past four. The daylight was fading, and the air was growing much chillier. She felt a chill deep down in her heart. She had hoped to find an ally here and now felt very much alone in her battle.

She took a deep breath and slowly walked over to Main Street, then headed up toward the post office and the Bramble, Grace Hegman's antiques store. From his wife Jessica's chatty Christmas letters, Adele knew that her grandson Sam still had his workshop in the barn behind the store. Half the barn was his shop and the other half was a storage area for the antiques shop. He was doing very well in his business, by all accounts, and might be there working right now.

She wondered if Sam was going to react the same way Molly had. Would he, too, refuse to help her? She really couldn't blame him if he stuck up for his father. She just hoped that Sam could also see her side of the story.

Adele soon came to the Bramble, a Victorian house that now had a shop on the bottom floor and a large apartment on the second and third floors. The shop was decorated very nicely for Christmas with a big wreath on the door and a pine garland around the porch. Nothing too lavish and everything looked very nineteenth century.

Adele spotted Grace Hegman inside arranging some pieces of china in the window, which was decorated for Christmas, too. Adele felt a twinge of guilt, knowing she ought to stop and say hello to Grace and Digger, but she couldn't afford to waste her powder. She only had so much energy these days and right now, she needed every drop for her family.

She marched down the gravel drive toward the barn and was happy to hear the roar of power tools on Sam's side. She knocked on the door and waited, then guessed he couldn't hear her. She opened it slowly and walked in. Sam had on goggles and big gloves and was running a power sander over a long tabletop, sending up clouds of fine white dust. She felt a little cough coming on and covered her mouth with her hand.

"Grandma Addie, is that you?" Sam put down the machine and stared at her. It was suddenly silent. Except for her coughing.

"Yes . . . here I am. Surprise," she coughed out.

"Come and sit down. I'll get you a glass of water."

Adele did not feel weak in any way, but she let herself be led to a chair with Sam's firm touch on her shoulder. She sat down and gratefully accepted the glass of cold water. "That tastes good. Nothing like a simple glass of water when your throat is dry."

Sam pulled off his goggles and face mask. "Do you feel all right?"

"I'm fine, dear, just fine." She smiled up at him. He was in his mid-forties now with a touch of silver in his thick dark hair, but she still saw him as a sweet, energetic little boy, always eager to help her. She hoped he felt the same way now.

"Was I supposed to know that you were coming to visit?" He gave her a wry grin. "It's really not a great idea to surprise a guy working with power tools."

"I realize that now. It wasn't very smart of me. But it is good to see you, Sam."

"You, too, Grandma. When did you get here?"

"On Saturday, actually—" The phone in Sam's shirt pocket rang. Adele paused while he checked the number.

"It's not important," he told her. "I'll call back." He stopped the ringing and put the phone back in his pocket. "So you were saying, you came down on Saturday?"

"Yes, I drove myself down and went straight to the Inn at Angel Island." She paused again, wondering how to broach the subject this time. "You see, I have a problem, Sam. I was hoping you could help me."

He looked at her with concern. "What sort of problem, Grandma? I'll help you if I can."

That was Sam. So openhanded and openhearted, bless him.

Adele felt encouraged. "I've come to make peace in the family, Sam. To bring your father and his brother back together and to ask your father to forgive both of us." She watched Sam's expression change from open and eager to serious and doubtful. "Now before you say anything, just hear me out, please?"

"I'm listening, Grandma. Go on."

Adele took a deep breath and told her grandson how she and George had felt desperate to help Kevin all those years ago, but how it was time that the rift in the family was healed. She told him how Kevin had changed and how he and his family were now moving to New Zealand.

Sam sat down on a nearby stool and crossed his arms over his chest. "Is that why you decided this was suddenly so important? Because Uncle Kevin is moving?"

"Not exactly. I guess it was part of the reason. No one likes to talk about it, but I might be going on a long journey myself pretty soon." She hoped she didn't sound maudlin, but facts were facts. "I'd rather see my children reconcile face-to-face than watch from some cloud up in heaven."

Sam laughed, his blue eyes twinkling. "Don't worry, I'll bet you'll make sure they give you a cloud with a good view, Grandma. And I know you're trying to do the right thing," he added in a more serious tone. "It's good to hear that Uncle Kevin has straightened out his life. I'm happy for him, honestly. But I don't know about Dad. He just has a block about that entire chapter in his life. It meant more to him than just losing that business."

"I know, dear, I know. But we have to start someplace, don't we? We have to get them talking to work through this."

Sam gave her a look. He could see she had assumed he would help her, and that wasn't necessarily the case.

"I think I can understand why Grandpa thought Uncle Kevin should get the business," he said at last. "And if I were in Dad's place, I guess, after all this time, I would try to forgive my brother. I'd at least hear him out. But I'm not sure I can really help you with all this. I can't force Dad to get together with Uncle Kevin. I'm not sure what you expect me to do."

"I know we can't force your father to forgive Kevin," Adele agreed. "All I'm asking for here is a first step. I want him to at least hear me out."

"Have you tried to talk to him about this?" Sam asked.

"A few times over the years, though perhaps not as often as I should," she admitted. "He would hang up the phone or walk right out of my house and get in the car." She looked up at her grandson, meeting his blue eyes. "I'm afraid I've been a bit of a coward, Sam. I never wanted to risk angering Joe so much that he shut me out completely." She lifted her shoulders in a helpless shrug. "We're barely speaking as it is."

"I know," Sam said quietly. "Dad's like Molly and me and every other Morgan—strong-willed and stubborn. We don't change our minds easily when we think we're right. Let's see . . . how can I get him to listen?" Sam rose and looked around the shop. He picked up an elastic cord that he used to secure ladders in the back of his truck, and arched one eyebrow. "I could tie him to a chair . . . or fasten a weight on his leg." He picked up a metal vise. "He won't get very far with this baby strapped to his ankle."

Adele had to laugh. It was the first time she had laughed in days, she realized. "I hope it doesn't come to that. But keep the equipment handy."

"When do you want to see Dad? I could bring you over there tonight, I guess."

"Soon. But not tonight. That's too soon. I just saw your sister Molly," Adele added. "She doesn't want to help me."

Sam didn't look surprised. "She's close to Dad. I'm sure she would feel like she was betraying him or something."

"What about you? Do you feel that way, too?" Adele wondered if she should even be asking that question, giving her only ally a way out, but she had to know.

Sam thought about it for a moment then shook his head. "I love Dad as much as anyone. But that doesn't mean he never makes mistakes. Holding a grudge against his brother—and you—all this time is a mistake. It's hurt the family and robbed him of his own peace of mind."

Adele knew that was true. "Thank you, dear, for saying that. It helps me. But let me think a little about when I should go see your father. I'll have to call you."

"All right, Grandma. Here are all my phone numbers, in case you don't have them handy down here." He handed her a card with the numbers at his shop, his cell phone number, and his home, scrawled on the back. Adele took it and put it in her purse.

"Can I at least tell Jess and the kids that you're here?"

"Of course you can. I can't wait to see them." She had seen them from a distance at the service on Sunday but didn't bother to tell Sam that. They had looked so different to her, she reflected.

She hardly saw Sam's children or any of her great-grandchildren on this side of the family. It pained her to be a stranger to them, especially the very young ones, who barely remembered her between their infrequent visits.

Sam brushed off some dust from the table he had been sanding. "I would take you back home for dinner tonight," he said, "but I have to be at church for a deacons meeting in a little while. There's a lot to do with Christmas coming."

"That's all right. I've had a big day. And you have work to do. I'm just going back to the inn for dinner. The food is very good," she added.

"So I've heard, but Jessica is a good cook, too. I'll check with Jess about a good night to have you over and call you."

Adele was cheered by the invitation. "Anytime would be fine with me." She stood next to him and smiled. "Thank you, dear, for agreeing to help me."

Sam looked down at her with a quizzical expression. "I'll do what I can, Grandma. But I have to be honest, I don't think you'll get very far with Dad. He can really dig his heels in when he wants to."

"Yes, I know. I raised him. He's just like his father, that's the funny thing. But you said it yourself, I'm trying to do the right thing. So we have to go forward with faith, Sam. You of all people should remember that."

He nodded and smiled. "That is true, Grandma. I'll try to remember."

The moment Adele closed the door to the shop, she heard the sander start up again. It was too late to stop in the Bramble. The sign on the door said CLOSED, COME AGAIN. She was too tired anyway for more conversation. She headed back down Main Street toward the harbor where her car was parked. Her meeting with Molly had been deflating, but at least she had Sam on her side. Partly, anyway.

Thank you, God, she said, sending up a silent prayer. *We're batting one for two today. That's not too bad.*

MOLLY WAS JUST WRITING OUT THE COOKING ORDERS FOR THE NIGHT crew and getting ready to go home when her cell phone rang. She recognized Sam's number and quickly picked up the call.

"Did you get my message?" she asked without bothering to say hello.

"Grandma Addie is in town," he said simply. "I didn't have to pick up your message. She came to see me, too."

"I figured that was her next move. So, what did you tell her? You're not siding with her against Dad, are you?"

Molly heard her brother sigh. Not a good sign. *If he is going to get all thoughtful and patient about this, it is going to make me nuts,* she thought.

"It's not that simple, Moll. It's not about taking sides, for or against. If you start thinking about it that way, we're never going to get anywhere."

"Call it whatever you want, Sam, but it is simple. Real simple. Grandpa and Grandma broke Daddy's heart when they didn't give him the store after all those years of promising it to him. Remember how he used to talk about it at the dinner table? When we get the store *this*, and when we get the store *that*, and when we move up to Vermont—"

"I remember, Molly. I was there, too."

"Well, you don't sound as if you were. If you start taking Grandma's side in this now, it's as if he's being betrayed all over again. Now, by his own son." Molly knew she was raising her voice, but she couldn't help it. She just got like this sometimes.

Sam was so quiet, she wondered if he had hung up.

"Yes, it was wrong," he said at last. "The way they all handled it was very wrong. Grandpa should have figured out some other way of trying to help Uncle Kevin, to make sure he had some security. But all this anger and bitterness is wrong, too, Molly. Grandma Addie is nearly ninety now. And even if she weren't, I don't think it's right for Dad to stay so angry at his own brother and mother. I think Grandma is right; it's time to sort this out and make peace. Before it's too late. Dad might regret it if he never even tries. I love him, too. But he's not perfect."

Molly felt her blood pound in her head. "Oh, he's not perfect? Well, he's perfect enough for me. I'm sticking by Daddy. He's done nothing wrong here. How about blaming the victim, ever hear of that? If Uncle Kevin wants to make amends so badly, he should come on his own. And he should have done it a long time ago," she added, "not send poor old Grandma."

"Oh, Molly, calm down. Kevin didn't send her. It's all her idea."

"That's what she says. I'm not sure I believe her . . . and don't 'oh, Molly' me, okay?"

"Okay. Look, I've got to go. We're not going to figure this out, shouting at each other over the phone. She's here and she wants Dad to hear her out. I think we can agree on that much, can't we?"

Molly didn't know what to say to that. "Yes, she's here. But honestly, I wish she would go back to Vermont and not stir everything up. And right before the holidays. Do we really need all this drama right now? Isn't life insane enough? I know mine is. I have about five hundred parties to do between now and January second and the girls are coming home soon and Laurie and the twins are coming for Christmas—"

"I know, Molly. Everyone's holidays are out of control. But maybe Christmas is the right time to face these things. Peace on Earth, good-will toward men . . . Isn't that what the season is really all about?"

Molly sighed. Trust her brother to fire back with Christmas carol lyrics instead of plain old insults. Sam just didn't fight fair.

"You got me there, pal. But that still doesn't persuade me to help Grandma."

"Fine. Everyone is entitled to their own opinion. Have a good night," he said finally.

"Yeah, you, too."

Molly hung up, still fuming. When had she been this mad at her brother? She couldn't even remember. But she couldn't help it. And she was even more annoyed at her dear old grandma.

What's right is right, she reminded herself. *Dredging up all these old family problems and painful memories right before the holidays was just not right.*

CHAPTER FIVE

WHEN ADELE GOT UP THE NEXT MORNING, SHE WONDERED IF she would hear from Sam soon. She was looking forward to visiting his family. She wanted to bring little Lily a present—a stuffed animal or maybe the pink princess hat and glove set she had seen in town. She wondered if she should bring the boys something, too. They were getting so big, she didn't know what they liked anymore. She would have to ask Sam.

But when would he call? Would he have any ideas on how to approach Joe? That was the main thing. It was hard to sit and wait, but she realized she had done all she could for now. The last thing she wanted was for Sam to feel pestered or nagged. He had been so good to agree to help, which Adele appreciated even more after Molly's refusal.

Adele followed the scent of pancakes to the kitchen, where she found Claire spooning batter onto a sizzling skillet. A stack of pancakes, fragrant and steaming, were already piled high on a platter on the counter near the stove, with a pot cover keeping them warm.

"Those look and smell simply delicious," Adele said. "Sure beats my daily bowl of high-fiber cereal."

"Everyone needs a change from their routine now and again," Claire said with a smile. "Even a health routine."

Adele agreed, especially when the change was so appetizing. "I can't remember the last time I had pancakes," she told Claire. "Doesn't seem worth the bother for one person." *And almost nobody comes to visit and stay over anymore,* she added silently.

Claire set the platter on the table then poured Adele a mug of coffee. Dishes and place settings were already laid out. Claire took the seat she had the day before. "Help yourself. No need to wait."

Needing no further encouragement, Adele slipped two thin, golden pancakes off the plate and onto her dish, then added butter and syrup and a shake of cinnamon. She was just about to dig in when a knock sounded on the back door. Adele and Claire turned at the same time. Claire wiped her hand on a towel and walked over to answer it. "Who could that be at this hour?"

Adele felt her fork fall from her hand and heard it clatter on her dish. She knew who it was. She saw his face through the window on the door, looking cross and impatient. It was Joe. Either Molly or Sam had broken their word. And she had a good guess it had not been Sam.

"Oh, hello, Joe. How are you this morning?" Claire opened the door and let him in. If she thought there was something odd about Joe Morgan showing up at seven in the morning, without Adele ever mentioning him, she didn't show it.

"Can't complain, Claire. How are you?" Joe said the words mechanically. Adele was sure he could complain, given the opportunity, about her being here for one thing. She felt his gaze fixed on her and slowly turned to him.

"Hello, Joe . . . You've surprised me."

He took a few steps closer to her. "No, Mom. You've surprised me. Molly says you've been here since Saturday. Hiding out."

Molly. She knew it. "Not exactly hiding. But I did get here on Saturday. I saw Molly yesterday. And Sam," she added.

"And you asked them not to tell me that you're here. Why is that? Are you sick? Did you have a health scare?"

Well, at least he had some feelings for her, she reflected. He did seem concerned.

"At my age, closing your eyes and falling asleep every night can be a health scare, Joe."

He shook his head, looking annoyed. "You know what I mean, Mom. So, you're not here because there's something wrong? That's all I'm asking."

She was tempted to jump right into that opening. But he seemed so put out just to find her here that she wasn't sure this was the right time to begin that difficult conversation. Besides, she wasn't sure what he already knew. "Didn't Molly tell you?"

"She wouldn't say. She barely told me you were here. She sort of slipped last night on the phone and then wouldn't tell me anything more. Sam was no help, either. He practically denied seeing you."

"It's not their fault. I asked them not to say anything."

She wished now that one of her grandchildren had told Joe her reason for coming. It would have taken some of the pressure off now.

"So, are you sick or not? Is that the secret they were keeping?"

"I'm totally fit and have no other pressing situations that might usually concern you—like a broken boiler or a leaky roof, if that's what you mean."

Before he could reply, Claire interrupted. "Would you like some coffee, Joe? And some pancakes? I made plenty."

"Coffee would be nice. Thanks." He took a seat at the table across from Adele, and Claire brought him a mug of coffee. He fixed it with milk and two sugars, the same way he had liked it as a teenager.

An awkward silence fell between them. Joe's expression was brooding as he stirred his coffee. Not a good sign, Adele thought. Before she could think of anything neutral to say, Jonathan Butler, the history student, came to the kitchen door. "Pancakes . . . those smell good."

Claire stepped forward from the stove, practically blocking his entry. She handed him a mug of coffee. "Good morning, Jonathan," she greeted him cheerfully. "Why don't you have a seat in the dining room? I'll be in with your breakfast in a moment."

Adele was thankful for her sensitivity. Claire quickly set the platter of pancakes and other breakfast items on a tray and headed for the door to the dining room. "You two sit and visit. I'll be back in a while," she said over her shoulder.

"So, how is Marie?" Adele asked once they were alone. She had loved Marie from the moment Joe brought her home all those years ago, and now she missed her daughter-in-law. "Does she know I'm here?"

"Of course she does. Marie knows everything. Usually before I do." He smiled for a moment then sipped his coffee. "She wanted to come and say hello, but she had to get to work."

"Still at the insurance office?"

"That's right, still there. And I'm still in the kitchen at the Spoon Harbor Inn."

Joe made light of his job, but he was actually the executive chef at a large, upscale restaurant that also hosted weddings and big events. It was a high-level job for his field, and he had worked hard to get there. He was earning a good salary now, better perhaps than what he might have made in the store, and he was working in the field he loved. Adele was proud of him.

"And you're still in Highland, Vermont," he concluded. "Or you should be. So what's up, Mom?" he added, his voice stern. "You still haven't told me."

Adele sat back from the table. Her pancakes, cold and uneaten on her dish, no longer looked very appetizing. In fact, the mere sight was making her a little queasy. She focused instead on her son's familiar face. His square jaw had softened with age. His dark hair, gone thin on top, was now all gray. He still had remarkable, sparkling blue eyes and thick dark brows and lashes. He still had a wide smile with deep dimples . . . when he cared to smile.

He was not smiling now. He looked very serious, his chin thrust out as he waited for her reply. She wished Sam were here. This was not how she had planned or pictured starting this discussion with Joe. But there seemed little choice now but to lift her banner and march on.

"The reason I've come, Joe, is that, after all these years, I think it's time that we all sat down and talked about your father's will and how much—"

"Stop right there." Joe held up his hand like a traffic cop. "Just stop."

"Joe, please . . . please hear me out." From the scowl on his face she was sure he wasn't listening to a word, but she plowed on. "I've lived a good life. I've been greatly blessed. But I can't rest easy while you and your brother continue this estrangement. I'm nearly ninety years old. What if I die? I can't leave this world without at least trying to bring you two together."

For a moment, Joe looked as if he might answer her. Then he stood up from the table. "If that's why you've come, then you've wasted your time. The damage is done. It's ancient history. There's nothing you or my brother can say to change that. That ship has sailed, Mom. So don't start stirring all that up." He stopped himself and she could almost see him biting back his next thought. Then he said, "I've got to go. I just wanted to find out if you were all right."

Adele swallowed back a lump in her throat. How could she be "all right" when he was still so angry at her? Didn't he understand that? She felt her eyes stinging, but she didn't want to cry in front of him. That wouldn't help at all.

"My health is fine. No worries there, thank God," she said firmly.

"All right then . . . I don't know how long you're staying. Marie wants to have you over to the house, but I'm working a lot of nights this week and next. We'll give you a call, okay?"

Adele nodded. "Give me a call whenever you get around to it. I'll be here."

Joe left the way he'd come, through the kitchen door, practically slamming it on the way out. Adele reached for her coffee but her hand was shaking so badly, she couldn't get it to her lips. She put it down and took a few deep breaths.

Oh, this was getting complicated. More than she had ever expected. Sam was with her. Molly was against her. Joe had snuck up and fired a warning shot. Why did it have to be so hard? She wasn't an ambassador at the United Nations. She was just an old woman, trying to make amends for her mistakes.

Stop it, stop it right now, Adele Morgan, she chided herself. *You'll never get anywhere feeling sorry for yourself. Your son just barks and you start whimpering? You brought him into this world. You wiped his bottom and fed him at your breast. He wouldn't exist without you. Buck up and get a grip. No one ever said this was going to be easy. I have to call Sam,* she realized. *If he plans on talking to his father on my behalf, he ought to know Joe and I have already had words.*

Adele was about to leave the table to find her cell phone when Liza Martin walked into the kitchen and poured herself a cup of coffee. "Morning, Adele. Did you sleep well?"

"Very well, thank you."

Liza walked over to the table and noticed Adele's untouched plate.

"Would you like something else besides pancakes? I can make you some eggs or oatmeal. We have fruit and yogurt, too."

"The pancakes are fine. I was just . . . interrupted," she explained.

"They look cold. I'll get you a hot stack." Without waiting for a reply, Liza swept the dish away and walked over to the stove to make a fresh batch.

Adele was about to stop her. Then she just thanked Liza for her trouble. She did want those pancakes and wasn't going to let Joe ruin her nice breakfast, too. Besides, she needed her strength and energy more than ever. Nothing short of a miracle would patch up this mess, she could see that now. And it looked like she was the one who had to make that miracle happen.

JONATHAN HEADED BACK TO LILAC HALL ON TUESDAY, FEELING EAGER and excited. He was ready to dig back into all that research material. The day before he had barely gotten into the records from the town meetings, and he knew they might be a gold mine of information.

But he also knew his anticipation had as much to do with seeing Tess again. He walked into the large, echoing entry hall and headed for the reception desk. There was only one person there to help visitors, the older woman he had seen at the desk with Tess yesterday.

Maybe Tess was in the office behind the desk, or upstairs helping another visitor. He wanted to ask, but decided not to. *She said she was working today. If she's here, I'll find her.*

After he left his things in a locker, the woman led him back up to the same reading room he had worked in the day before and took out the binders he needed. She did it the same way Tess had, but it wasn't quite the same, he thought.

He settled down in the same seat but couldn't concentrate. He felt suddenly deflated, like a balloon with all its air leaked out. He glanced at his watch. Maybe she was coming in later. *I'll go down and look for her in a little while, when I need to take a break,* he decided. He didn't want to seem too obvious. Besides, he did have important work to do and she was a distraction. *An attractive, charming distraction,* he corrected himself as he flipped open his laptop.

He forced himself to focus on the documents and found the place where he had left off the day before. Entries about the mysterious illness started to appear in the town records in the fall of 1633, about six months after the settlers had arrived. The first cases were noted in September.

". . . Elijah Haywood and William Stanton taken sick with fever. The men had been clamming on the marshes for two days prior," Jonathan read in an entry dated September sixth. "Ruth, wife of William, stricken as well. The affliction commences with profuse sweating, violent chills, high fever, and vomiting. Boils and rashes strike on the third day. Apothecary Simon has dosed the sick with boiled elm bark and ginger root. They are also bled."

Excited by the entry, Jonathan quickly looked ahead. But the next place he found mention of the fever was over a month later. The number of victims had grown to thirty, with many more unnamed also sick with the disease. The settlers had never seen anything like it back in England and called it Marsh Fever, owing to the first victims. It was unclear whether the marshland was truly the source of the illness, though it was possible that mosquitoes or some other airborne insect was carrying the disease, he thought.

The germ was highly contagious and could sweep through an entire family in a few days. He knew that this was partly owing to the lack of knowledge about how diseases spread and poor hygiene in the 1600s. But it sounded like a sickness that would be dreadful in any era.

There were so many illnesses of that time that simply did not exist in this modern day. The descriptions were hard to evaluate completely. As

Jonathan had told the women at the inn, Marsh Fever sounded similar to Yellow Fever, except for the boils and the fact that the illness lasted longer. Also, the settlers believed it was still contagious for several weeks, even if one survived the first phase of fevers.

Doctors in that era used leeches and drew cups of blood from patients, believing that they were draining the illness from the body. Apothecaries and even the Wampanoag people offered herbs and tree bark to lessen the fever and other symptoms. Jonathan suspected that some of that probably did help, though nothing could cure it.

He looked further and found scraps of notes from a town meeting held in early November. The death toll was mounting. The list of the recently deceased filled an entire page. ". . . Benjamin Walker, Daniel Walker, Joshua Thurgood, Jane Thurgood, Olivia Thurgood, Lillian Thurgood, Thomas Smith, Rebecca Smith, Charity Smith . . ."

Jonathan knew, of course, that epidemics killed large numbers of people, but somehow seeing the individual names—a great number of them seeming to be family members—made this one so much more real than others he had studied. The town was under siege. "So many innocent lives lost," wrote the governor, John Ames. "We dig graves night and day, praying for God's mercy that He might lift this pestilence." Jonathan paused, feeling deeply saddened by the words. He could practically hear the governor's despairing voice echoing in the reading room.

Tess paused at the doorway for a moment, her gaze fixed on Jonathan as he worked. He was concentrating so deeply, she didn't want to startle him. She liked the way he looked, frowning over the pages laid out on the table and tapping some quick notes on his keyboard.

She wondered if he had looked around the building for her, or wondered where she was. She had looked for him—and found him. But now it seemed as if she should come back later. He might not like being disturbed, she thought as she slowly turned away.

"Tess! Wait . . ."

She had barely taken two steps down the hall when she heard him call out to her. As she turned to go back to the room, they nearly collided in the doorway. Jonathan had to catch her shoulders for an instant so they wouldn't crash. His touch was gentle but firm, and any doubts that he was eager to see her were quickly dispelled by his brilliant smile.

"Hey . . . there you are. I was just about to come down and look for you."

"Mrs. Fisk asked me to do some filing in the office this morning. I just noticed your name in the visitors' book."

Whoops, she had given herself away. Now he knew for sure that she had been looking for him, too. She quickly changed the subject, hoping he hadn't noticed. "So, how's it going? Did you find any good information today?"

"I did. Great stuff. The village records document the first appearance of the disease and its spread. Reading these firsthand accounts is different from the secondary sources I've seen. It's very, very sad. The husband and wives, and so many children . . ." His voice trailed off. Tess understood. These struggles happened so long ago, but it was still very moving to read the firsthand accounts.

"Did you read the entry written by Governor Ames, where he asks God for mercy?"

Jonathan nodded. She could see it had affected him. Maybe that was why he looked so serious before. "I just read that one. . . . Did he catch the fever, too?"

"Yes, he did. He died very quickly. Within three days."

Jonathan ran a hand through his hair. "That's too bad. I was hoping he survived it. But I haven't found anything about survivors. I haven't even found any mention of the quarantine yet."

"I'm not sure you'll find any. The records are so incomplete."

"Yes, they are pretty spotty," he agreed. "Though the fragments are very rich."

Tess considered his problem for a moment. "I do know of a document in the collection that might help you. John Ames's wife kept a journal at their farm. We have some pieces of it. Maybe she mentions the quarantine."

"A journal? That's fantastic!"

Tess might have just told Jonathan he'd won the lottery. He looked so excited, she thought he was going to grab her and kiss her. *Not that I would mind that,* she realized.

"I don't know for sure if she mentions the quarantine," she reminded him. "But we do have most of the journal."

She glanced at her watch. "I'm on a break right now and need to grab some lunch. But I can come back later and find it for you."

"I could use a break," Jonathan said quickly. "I mean, if you don't mind company. Do you have time to run into town for a bite? Someplace other than the Clam Box," he added quickly.

Tess had to laugh at his expression when he mentioned the diner. "I don't have enough time left to go into town. There's an employee lunchroom here. The menu is limited, but the food isn't bad."

"Sounds fine to me," Jonathan said quickly. He grabbed his computer, and they walked down the long hallway side by side. The entire building was very quiet, one of the main reasons Tess loved working here. Through the open doors along the way, they could see other visitors studying documents intently and so quietly, you could hear the sound of turning pages as you walked by.

Downstairs, she led him to a door at the back of the first floor, where a sign read EMPLOYEES ONLY. They entered the narrow, light-filled space.

"Wow . . . this is nice," Jonathan said, looking around.

The employee café was actually very pretty, and Tess never minded taking her breaks here. The floor and one wall were stone, and the other wall had long windows. Wrought-iron tables and chairs were set in a row with a counter at the far end. The windows framed a view of a garden with a gravel path and arching white arbors.

"I think this space was a solarium and sort of an indoor greenhouse when the Warwicks lived here. The first owner's wife was an avid gardener and raised orchids indoors."

Tess found an empty table, and Jonathan put his belongings down on a chair. Then they walked up to the food counter. He turned to look out at the windows as they stood on line. "It feels like we're in a greenhouse— or actually sitting outside. What's in that garden?"

"Roses, all different kinds. Mrs. Warwick planned it so that there's always something blooming throughout the spring and summer. All the brides in town want to have wedding photos taken here, but the trustees are strict about it and very few are allowed in."

"I see. Serious business." Jonathan's tone was thoughtful, but she could tell from his eyes he was teasing her. "I guess when the time comes, you'll have good connections."

"I haven't given it a thought," she said quickly. Though the truth was, she really did want her wedding photos here . . . when the time came. "I suppose I'll have a fair shot if I can stay on good terms with Mrs. Fisk."

They both got coffee and sandwiches. When they came to the cashier, Jonathan quickly paid for both of them.

"Oh, you don't have to buy my lunch, that's okay," Tess said.

"I want to. You told me about that journal and you brought me to this interesting, hidden-away place."

That much was true. But he was almost acting as if it were a date. *Well, maybe it sort of is,* she realized. A "starter" date? They sat at their table and opened their sandwiches.

"So, how long have you worked here?" he asked curiously.

"Gee . . . let's see. Since high school, I guess. I was a summer intern my junior year. Now that I'm in college, I've been promoted. I actually get paid. Not much," she added with a laugh. "But I like the atmosphere."

"A little different than the diner?"

"A little. Though both have their charms."

"I can't see any in the diner, but if you say so."

"I like the people watching. There are all the regulars who live here . . . Reverend Ben, the Hegmans, Officer Tulley . . . He and Charlie go back to grade school. I already know what they'll order and can practically predict what they'll talk about, too." Jonathan smiled at her confession. "Then there are all the new people who come into town. Some are very interesting to talk to."

"Like me?" he asked. His dark eyes widened as he took a sip of coffee.

"Yes, I'd include you in that category." He looked pleased by her answer. Was he blushing a little? That was cute, she thought.

"So you work at this place and the diner and go to BU. How do you manage all that? Do you commute to school from here?"

"Oh no, I live on campus." *Not that far from your campus,* she nearly reminded him. "We're on intercession now, so I'm here until January. I work at both these places in the summer, so they take me back for a few weeks during school breaks. The extra money comes in handy for Christmas shopping. It would be too boring doing nothing all this time."

"I know what you mean. I'm on a break now, too. Most of the other people in my program are off skiing or under a palm tree somewhere, sipping a blended drink."

"Or home for the holidays?" She thought he would add that choice, but he didn't. *Interesting,* Tess thought.

"Yes, some went home," he said quickly. "But I'd rather be working, too."

Tess thought about asking what his plans were for Christmas, but some intuitive little voice warned her to stay on more neutral ground.

"So, it sounds like your research is going well today," she said.

"Even better than I expected. This place is a real treasure trove. I don't think I'm going to tell my friends about it." She could tell he was half-joking, but half-serious, too.

"Is your department very competitive?"

"Deadly. But probably no worse than anywhere else."

"Oh, that's encouraging."

He laughed at her reply. "Don't worry, Tess. I haven't known you very long, but I'm practically positive you'll hold your own in grad school . . . more than hold your own, I'd say."

She met his glance and didn't know how to answer him. His compliment was encouraging but had taken her by surprise. And so had the warm expression in his eyes.

He looked away, picking up his sandwich again. "What do you like best about studying history? I mean, what made you choose that subject instead of say, literature or biology?"

"I'm not sure exactly. I've always liked to read true accounts about events or biographies. I love novels, but true stories seem more compelling. I also like to understand why things happen. What are the influences— the social climate and small events that lead up to one momentous one? It is so amazing to me that if one simple little thing had not gone a certain way, an entire war could have been prevented—or a national leader would not have been assassinated. Or a revolution wouldn't have begun."

He nodded, his expression thoughtful. "I know what you mean. I think about that a lot, too."

"I love reading firsthand sources, like the letters and diaries kept here. It's like voices are talking to you from the past, telling you their very private, personal stories. I think places like this little building are so important, preserving the stories and legacy of so many people. Their struggles and victories. The mysteries in their communities, like the Marsh Fever epidemic. Maybe someone like you or me can figure it out someday. And all their suffering wouldn't have been in vain."

"It is like voices," Jonathan said. "And sometimes the voices seem to be calling out, across the centuries, asking you to help them. I feel the same . . . though you put it into words much better than I can. When I do intense research and sit reading documents for days, I end up hearing voices in my head," he confessed. He gave her a shy grin. "Sometimes I even start talking back to them."

Tess laughed, imagining him doing just that. "If you wear some earphones while you're working, people will just think you're singing along to your iPod."

"Good idea. I'll remember that." He smiled at her, and she realized he was looking at her a certain way again. An admiring way, she'd say if she had to put a name to it. She had to dress up a bit for this job and hoped it wasn't totally obvious that she had taken a little extra care with her appearance because she knew he would be here today. She had fixed her hair a little differently, gathered at her nape in a loose bun, and wore a black skirt and boots with a soft-looking blue-gray sweater that matched her eyes, and small pearl earrings.

She had also left her glasses downstairs, at the visitors' desk. She only needed them for reading—and to put off guys who didn't interest her. Jonathan definitely did not fall into that category.

"Can I get you some more coffee?" he asked. "I'm going up to get another cup."

"Thanks, but I've got to get back to work," she said, checking her watch. "Mrs. Fisk will be sending out the hounds in a minute."

Jonathan laughed. "We don't want that to happen. Not that I don't like dogs," he added quickly.

She had a feeling he was a dog person, as opposed to a cat person. She was a dog person, too. Not that it warranted discussion right now. Maybe at some point they would get to it. As she rose to go, she did hope so. "I'll come up to the reading room in about ten minutes and find that Sophia Ames journal," she said.

"Oh . . . the journal. Right. Yes, I'm excited to see it. I'll wait there for you."

She could tell by his expression, he had all but forgotten about the document while they were talking. Which gave Tess a good feeling. Had her company been so enthralling?

"Thanks for bringing me here," he added. "I enjoyed our break."

She smiled briefly. "Same here."

He seemed like he wanted to say something more. Maybe ask her out on a real date? But finally he didn't. He looked very serious and cupped his hand at his ear. "Uh-oh . . . did I just hear barking?"

Tess laughed. "I hope not. See you later."

"Right. See you."

She turned and quickly headed for the exit. At the doorway she noticed that he was still watching her. He smiled and she smiled back.

As she walked back to the office to sign in from her break, Tess felt a sudden rush of giddiness. Jonathan Butler was nothing like he had seemed at the diner. Nothing at all. And that was a good thing.

Just goes to show you, Tess. You can't judge a book by its cover . . . especially if it's all wet and soggy.

CHAPTER SIX

OE, IT'S SAM AGAIN. WON'T YOU ANSWER IT?" MARIE Morgan was in the kitchen with her husband, eating a quick breakfast before setting off for work. Joe stood right next to the phone as the machine answered the call and their son Sam's voice came on. But instead of picking up the phone, Joe just stood there listening.

"Hi, Mom. Hi, Dad. It's me again. Thursday morning. I'm just trying to reach you, Dad. Will you give me a call on my cell, please?"

"What if it's an emergency?" Marie said as the call ended.

"It's not an emergency, don't worry." Joe sat down with his coffee and a bowl of oatmeal and started to read the newspaper.

"He's left you messages all week. Maybe I should call him back if you don't want to."

Joe looked up at her. "You don't have to call him back. It's all right. I'll call him when I'm ready. I know what this is about."

Marie nodded and sipped her coffee. She eyed her husband over the rim of the mug. "I know. It's about your mother . . . When is she coming here for dinner? Didn't you invite her?"

"I did," he insisted. "But I'm working every night this week. I'm not even sure how long she'll be here."

"Maybe I should call her," Marie suggested, knowing that innocent sentence would get his attention.

Sure enough, Joe put down his paper. "Come on, honey. I told you what's she's up to. My mother has a way of twisting the evidence when she pleads her case. That's how she got Sam on her side. I'd bet even money on it. Are you thinking about jumping ship on me, too?"

"Oh, Joe." Marie shook her head. She could have predicted that last question. Sometimes her husband saw the whole world in terms of who was or wasn't loyal to him. "I'm not jumping ship. You know that. But I have to say that I understand that your mother wants to see peace between her sons before she dies. And that she wants to see her family come together again. I can't fault her for that, Joe."

He nodded without looking up at her, pretending that he wasn't really listening. But she knew he had heard every word.

At last he gave a heavy sigh. "It's more complicated, Marie. You know it is. Tell you what, I'll sleep on it." That was Joe's code for: *I'll forget we ever had this conversation.*

"And what's that going to do?" she began, but Joe's eyes narrowed as he noticed something in the paper. "Wait," he said, "let's listen to the weather. The paper here says it's going to snow this week."

Her husband reached up and turned on the radio. A fast-talking announcer practically shouted out the weather report, conveniently cutting off their conversation.

Marie finished her breakfast and brought her dishes to the sink. It was time for her to leave; she couldn't talk any longer anyway.

"Will you be late tonight?" she asked.

"Yeah, I will be. I'm not going to Spoon Harbor until three," he said.

Marie knew that meant he wouldn't head home before eleven tonight, at the earliest. But she did wonder now why he was already dressed in his kitchen whites. Then he said, "I'm going to Molly's shop this morning. Betty's still out and she needs a hand."

"That's nice of you. I hope she appreciates you working so hard on your time off." Marie put on her coat and grabbed her purse and keys.

"She just needs me to bake a few things. I don't mind. A few more years in the head office, and I'll forget how to cook altogether."

"That's what happens when you're the top chef, honey," Marie teased him. She kissed him good-bye and headed out the door.

Once outside, Marie took a few deep breaths of the cold, bracing air then got into her car. She started the engine, but didn't drive off right away. She needed a few minutes to clear her head and collect her thoughts.

Joe was a good man, but he had a stubborn side that was as impenetrable as granite. Especially when it came to talking about his angry parting from his brother.

I should have known it was useless to talk about it, she thought, *but I had to try. Maybe Sam will catch up with him and have better luck. Maybe I should say a little prayer for both of them on my way to work.*

By Thursday morning, Sam was sure of it—his father was avoiding him. Sam had invited Joe to have a beer and watch some football on his big, new flat-screen TV. The Patriots were battling for first place in their division, for goodness' sake. Joe brushed him off. Then Sam had asked his dad to come by the shop. He even tried to find him at home on one of his rare mornings off. No luck. Sure, the man worked like a dog, but Joe had always managed to fit in these visits before.

A wind swept off the harbor, and the fancy burgundy-and-gold-striped canopy over Molly's shop fluttered in the breeze. Sam saw the usual crowd of customers inside, though it wasn't yet lunchtime. He walked around the back to the employee entrance. His mother had told him that Joe was stopping by this morning to help Molly catch up with orders, since Betty Bowman, Molly's partner, was out again.

Sam was hoping that Molly was out. In fact, he was counting on it. He knew that on Thursdays she didn't come in until noon. He wanted some time to talk to his father without taking on both of them at once.

As much as he loved his dad, and agreed he had been wronged by the terms of his grandfather's will, Sam also knew that there was a time when wrongs had to be forgiven. Friendship, marriages, the relationships between parents and children . . . There always came a moment when it all hung on a thread, and forgiveness was the only way to mend it back together.

Sam's faith was central to his life, and his faith taught that the world could not survive a single day without forgiveness, for small slights and great ones. Still, he hesitated outside the shop. He didn't want to be in this position, going against both his father and his sister, but he couldn't avoid it. Sam knew he had to argue for love and forgiveness. Anything else was wrong. Anything else was turning away from the divine love that was every person's birthright. He sent up a silent prayer. *Dear Lord, I'm going to need some help here. Please give me patience. Help me get my dad to listen. Or maybe you could just open his mind to the idea of forgiveness? We all need to find a way back to Your love if we're ever going to find our way back to being a family again.*

Sam squared his shoulders and walked up to the back door. It was unlocked. Is that a sign, he wondered wryly. He opened it and walked in. The workroom was empty. He wondered if he had missed Joe after all. "Hello?" he called. "Anybody around?"

Joe came out of the walk-in fridge. He wore an apron and carried a big metal mixing bowl.

"Hey, Sam. Looking for your sister? She's out in Essex, visiting a client."

No, I'm looking for you. Didn't you get any of my phone messages this week? Sam wanted to say. But he checked himself from starting off on such a negative note.

"You just helping out today?" Sam asked, easing into the conversation.

"That I am. Betty is out with a bad back, poor thing. I had a little time before I have to get over to Spoon Harbor. It's funny, I hardly ever get to do any real cooking anymore over there, ever since the promotion. It's a lot of paperwork now, meetings with the managers, menu planning . . . managing all the nut jobs who work for me."

Sam had to laugh at his father's job description. "Come on, Dad. I know you love being the big boss. Besides, you had plenty of practice, bossing all of us kids around."

"Don't remind me. Your mother took the brunt of it. I was just the enforcer," he joked. "By the time I got home, you would be asleep in your beds, looking like angels, and she would be telling me what a rotten bunch you'd been all day and I could hardly believe it."

Sam remembered being a boy and feeling as if he never saw enough of his dad. His father would leave early in the morning and come home late at night, with only one day off a week to play with them. He often had cooking jobs at two or even three places, taking on different shifts and cobbling his income together. And he often took side jobs during the holidays to make a little extra money. Joe Morgan rarely had time to read them stories and tuck them in, or go to school events and baseball games.

But Sam always knew that his father loved them. That was the important thing. It was love that drove Joe, not ambition, love and a bone-deep sense of responsibility. That's the way his father was—hardworking, responsible, consistent. What you saw was what you got with Joe Morgan.

Sam began to understand this once he had his own children. It was hard to find any fault with a father who was so devoted to his family, that was for sure.

Now Joe began taking eggs from a large carton on the table that held over a hundred. He cracked them with one hand into the big metal bowl.

Sam tried to think of a way into the difficult conversation, but his father spoke first. "I saw your grandmother the other day, Tuesday morning. Up at the inn on the island. She must have told you."

Sam nodded and stuck his hands in his pockets. "She did say you stopped by."

"She told me why she came, so I can guess why you're here." Joe flipped off a cardboard divider and took out more eggs.

Sam felt the side of his mouth curl down in a self-conscious smile. "You got me, Dad. I told Grandma I would try to talk to you."

"No surprise there. Molly said you were on their side."

Sam bristled at the us-against-them terminology. "Is that why you've been avoiding me all week?"

His father just laughed. "I was hoping I'd tire you out and you would give up. I guess that tactic didn't work. Did you and your grandmother come up with a new strategy?"

"Why do we have to talk about it like that, like it's some battle campaign? And why do there have to be sides? Aren't we one family?"

His father was frowning now. He picked up a whisk and began to beat the eggs with a skillful, ferocious power. "I don't want to talk about it at all. You're the one who brought it up, you and your grandmother."

Sam found it hard to talk above the sound of the metal whisk hitting the side of the bowl. He waited a moment, but it didn't seem his father would be done any time soon.

You're not going to make this one bit easy for me, are you? Sam said silently. Resigned, he plunged ahead. "I know Uncle Kevin and even Grandma did you wrong. I know your folks, your father especially, went back on his promise. I know you had the rug pulled out from under you by your own brother. I know that hurt a lot . . . I saw it with my own eyes."

"You're darned straight. I'll tell you what hurt the most, Sam. That it was my own family. My own flesh and blood. I could have understood it all a lot better if these were strangers, people I knew in business, or people who pretended to be my friends. I could have understood that. But my family? You might say of an old friend, 'We were so close, we were like brothers.' But Kevin and me, we *were* brothers. You see why that makes it even worse?"

Sam nodded slowly. "Yeah, I do see. But you and Uncle Kevin are still brothers. And Grandma is still your mother. What would you think if I got mad at Mom for something and stayed angry for almost ten years? And you were gone and she had no one and I called once a week but didn't pay much attention to her otherwise . . ."

His father abruptly stopped stirring the batter and put down the spoon. Sam could see the little scenario had gotten under his skin. "I get the point. But 'what-ifs' don't matter. This really happened to me. You don't understand. It changed something deep inside, Sam. It's—" He spread one hand out, as if searching for words, then clenched his fist and said, "It changed something deep inside. It's like something twisted inside me, down in my heart. I don't think I can ever get it back the way it was again. I'm not just making an excuse."

Sam didn't know what to say. He had heard his father shout about the situation, but never talk like this, with so much emotion. He knew his dad was telling him that there was no solution, no way to bring everyone together. But Sam decided to press on. Maybe getting his father to express his grief was part of the process, like squeezing the poison out of a bite.

"I believe you, Dad. It was a huge loss for you. You had to let go of a dream, a new life that you'd imagined and anticipated for a long time."

Joe nodded, measuring brown sugar with a glass cup. "That's right. For years, I was hoping to move up to Vermont and get out of this cooking grind. It was the light at the end of a tunnel, that store. I was set up like a bowling pin . . . and knocked right down. Your uncle knew the store was mine. It was like he stole my entire future from me. I not only lost my father back then, I lost my brother, too. I didn't recognize him anymore, who he had become. To be a person who could do that to me . . . and your grandmother just stood by. She kept saying she thought it was the right thing. The right thing? For who? Not for me."

Sam was quiet a moment, watching his father work, adding spices and pouring in vanilla. The smell was sweet and soothing, in contrast to the difficult conversation. Joe added sugar from a big metal sifter that he squeezed over the bowl. He was either making cake batter or cookie dough, Sam couldn't tell which.

"You know Uncle Kevin was sick, Dad. He couldn't stop drinking. Grandma and Grandpa were worried he'd never earn a living for himself without the store. And they were wrong. He lost the store when it should have been yours. But that was years ago, and now Uncle Kevin pulled himself together and he's changed. He's a different person."

Joe glanced at him. "Because your grandmother says so? Take it from me, pal, that's a lot of wishful thinking. She always says that about Kevin—while he's lying in a gutter somewhere, not knowing which way is up."

"Maybe that was true in the past," Sam said carefully. "But Kevin's got his act together now. He hasn't had a drop for nearly five years, he has a really good job, and he got married again."

Joe shook his head. "Your grandmother should have been in public relations. If she can say all that about Kevin with a straight face, she ought to be able to tell people I won the lotto and was elected president."

Sam had to smile. "I know she tends to exaggerate to make a point. A family trait, I think," he added. "I spoke to Uncle Kevin yesterday. I called him at his office, and I checked him out on the Internet. Grandma wasn't lying. He does have a big job and is being transferred to New Zealand. The company even put out a press release . . . and I didn't see Grandma's name anywhere on that one."

"Ha-ha. Very funny." Joe yanked a sheet of plastic wrap off a big roll and covered the mixing bowl. "Just because he's holding down a job doesn't mean he stopped drinking."

"Well, he said he did. He said it a few times," Sam added. "He had no idea Grandma came down here. He said he was going to call her."

"Call her about what?" His father sounded edgy and angry again.

"He told me that he would be willing to talk things out with you. Or even just say hello after all this time. He said he was thinking of calling you before he left for New Zealand but . . . he was afraid to."

Joe set his mouth in a harsh line, his tone bitterly sarcastic. "Gee, my brother was always such a stand-up guy, that really surprises me."

Left myself wide open for that one, Sam thought. He felt like he'd been hit by a clean right hook. At least his father knew that Kevin was thinking about this whole mess now, too. Still, he didn't know what else to say.

Joe had pulled some large baking sheets out of a rack and was covering them with parchment paper. Sam stood by and watched him. His father was still so strong, skillful, and able. His moves were quick and sure, as if he could easily cook in his sleep . . . and had perhaps at times done just that when fatigue overwhelmed him.

"Dad . . . I'm sorry if talking about all this upsets you. I don't mean to do that. But it's like pulling a bandage off an old wound that never healed. It's going to hurt a little before it can get better again."

"Great. Thanks for the warning. But I never asked you—or your grandmother—to do that. We've been over this. Why can't you just leave it alone? Why do you have to stick your nose in where it doesn't belong? Because your grandmother asked you? Well, I'm your father and I'm telling you to just butt out, okay?" His father's voice had gone from a low growl to loud anger.

Sam had not heard his father yell at him this way since his teenage years, and at first he shrank back. But he felt his own temper quickly rising. Sam knew he shared the Morgan trait for emotional drama, as his wife often reminded him. With an effort of will, he managed not to answer his father's anger with anger of his own.

"Are you done now?" he asked Joe, barely suppressing his own annoyance.

Joe nodded, looking down at the empty baking sheets. "Yeah, I'm done. I said all I'm going to say about this. Now do me a favor and take off. I have work to do here."

Sam laughed and shook his head. "First you yell at me like I'm still a kid and then you give me that same old line you always used when you wanted to keep us from pestering you. It won't work, Dad. I'm a grown-up now. Things change. People change, too." He paused, wondering if his father was even listening. Joe wasn't looking at him now as he dropped spoonfuls of the cookie dough on the trays in neat rows.

"I'm doing this because I care about you. Don't you get it? It's not even about Uncle Kevin and Grandma. It's about you. Holding on to this bitterness and resentment only hurts you, eats at your soul. Makes you less of a person . . . It's practically a habit now, feeling angry and slighted by them. And it's a role that you cast yourself into. Your brother has changed. He's not playing the loser alcoholic anymore. He figured it out. You ought to just see him before he goes. He didn't stay stuck like you."

Joe picked up his head and stared at Sam. His face was red with anger, and his eyes were wide and shocked. Sam saw a vein throbbing in Joe's left temple.

I'm giving him a heart attack, Sam thought with alarm.

"Now you listen here, you have no right to say that to me. To take his side. How dare you." His father pointed his finger at Sam, jabbing the air.

Sam held up his hands in a gesture of surrender. He should have left a long time ago. Maybe his father was right. Maybe this wound was best left covered over and untouched. Maybe now was not the time.

But before he could answer, he heard the door open and turned. It was Molly, back early.

"I thought I heard your voice, Sam." She dropped her briefcase and bags, then took off her coat and hung it on a hook. Slowly, she looked from her father to her brother, reading the entire situation in that one glance. Then she turned on Sam. "What are you doing here, bothering Daddy? Getting him all upset? Look at him. He looks like he's going to burst a blood vessel or something."

Joe stood back from the table and was trying to calm himself. But his red face and angry expression told the whole story.

Molly walked over to his side of the table. "Are you all right, Dad? You want some water? I think you ought to sit down." Molly tried to lead Joe to a stool, but he shooed her back with his hand.

"I'm fine, Molly. Stop fussing." He finally did sit down and just glared at Sam.

"Okay, I'm leaving. You can all calm down. I'm sorry, Dad, but—"

"Just go, Sam. You've said enough." Molly's tone stung, like a sharp, cold slap. "Look how you upset him. Was it worth it? What has Uncle Kevin ever done for you . . . for any of us? I can't believe you would put Daddy through all this heartache for absolutely no good reason."

Sam sighed. His sister didn't get it, either. It was like talking to a wall. Talking to two walls. Sam knew when he was beat, but he couldn't resist one last reply.

"I know you think you're helping him, Molly, protecting him or something. But you're not."

"Just leave, Sam." Molly had been hovering over their father but now stood up and moved toward Sam, looking as angry as he had ever seen her.

Sam stared at her a moment, then turned and left the shop.

Just outside the door, he closed his eyes and took a long, deep breath and squeezed his eyes closed. Was he crying? He couldn't even tell. When had he fought like that with his father . . . and his sister? He couldn't remember.

Dear God, what's happening to our family? Did I do the wrong thing coming here? Please help us sort through this painful mess. I don't want my father and sister to be angry at me forever, too . . . the way they feel about Uncle Kevin. They don't seem to hear a word I'm saying. Help them understand, especially Dad. Please let him see he can put down this load he's been carrying. Carrying for much too long.

JONATHAN DIDN'T GET TO LILAC HALL UNTIL ELEVEN. PROFESSOR Pilsner had called just as he was leaving the inn, asking for an update on his research. Once his advisor got going, it was hard to gracefully exit a conversation. Jonathan usually relished these talks, feeling privileged to be on such close terms with the esteemed scholar. But as Professor Pilsner rambled on, all Jonathan could think of was Tess, waiting at Lilac Hall. He had told her that he would meet her there at half past ten, and he didn't even have her phone number.

He knew that he could have called the Historical Society and asked someone to find her, but that seemed a little complicated and maybe making too big a deal of his delay. Still, he hated the idea that she might be waiting and growing annoyed with him. Or worse yet, feeling hurt, thinking that he didn't care enough about her to show up when he said he would. He knew it had only been a few days since they met, but he did care. He cared a lot. He wasn't sure how and when that had happened, but he knew it was true.

After he drove through the gates and parked his car beside the mansion, he practically jogged to the building, trying to catch his breath as he walked into the big entry hall and looked around. Mrs. Fisk and a boy who looked like he was in high school stood at the visitors' desk. But there was no sign of Tess.

He wondered if she was already upstairs, in the reading room he had been using. He started up the steps and heard a voice, calling him back downstairs.

"Sir? You didn't sign in yet."

"Oh, right, sorry." Jonathan hopped down the steps and walked up to the desk. Mrs. Fisk slipped the sign-in book over to him, and Jonathan quickly filled in the information and showed his identification.

Mrs. Fisk looked it over very slowly, making Jonathan impatient. Finally she signed the approval slip and handed it to him. "Letters and diaries from the 1600s are on the second floor, North Room. Michael will go up and help you."

The high school student stood by smiling; he was eager to have something to do, Jonathan guessed.

"That's all right . . . Tess Wyler has been helping me. I think she might be upstairs already."

Mrs. Fisk looked at him curiously. "I'm sure she's not. Tess isn't here today." She smiled mildly at him. "Michael can help you. Don't worry."

Jonathan felt a jolt of disappointment. From the way the woman smiled at him, he was sure it showed.

"You'll need to put your belongings in a locker," she reminded him. "Michael will meet you back here."

"Right, I was just about to do that," Jonathan replied, though he had in fact forgotten. He walked back to the lockers and stowed his coat and bag, taking out his laptop and a pad and pencil. He met Michael again at the bottom of the staircase, and they climbed together without talking. All Jonathan could think of was Tess. He had left the inn in such a good mood, anticipating seeing her, and now felt his spirits sink, like a stone tossed in a well.

Where was she? Was she sick? Had she just called in sick, purposely avoiding him? No. That was silly. He had the feeling she really liked him. Besides, agreeing to meet at the Historical Society wasn't a real date. Maybe she had another reason. He hoped it wasn't a boyfriend.

He placed his computer on the table, next to the pad and pencils. Michael stood, looking at him. "What can I find for you?"

"I've been studying a journal written by Sophia Ames who lived in Cape Light during the time of the quarantine." Jonathan told him the exact date. "I think the microfilm is in the cabinet, up there."

Jonathan pointed to the cabinet where Tess had found the journal. Michael looked up at the shelf, seeming stumped. "I'm sorry, sir. I'm sort of new here . . . I'll go get Mrs. Fisk. She'll help you."

Jonathan sighed and sat down. "Good idea," he said.

He turned on his computer and pulled up the file with his notes on the epidemic. Mrs. Fisk soon arrived, announced by a rattling sound, produced by the big key ring that hung from a dark green cord she wore around her neck. He knew it as unfair, but she reminded him of a house-keeper in some gothic novel, like *Rebecca* or *Jane Eyre*. She even dressed the part. He wondered what Tess thought of the woman. Michael followed at her heels and was soon sent up a wooden ladder to fetch down the container Jonathan needed.

Jonathan set up the machine, then forced himself to focus and concentrate. Sophia's complete journal had not survived the years. About twenty pages, some of them just fragments, had been preserved on microfilm. It was a shame the pages weren't consecutive as large chunks of time were missing. But he did find entries about "the fever." Sophia wrote about plans to quarantine the sick, mentioning the names of a few of those "unfortunate souls" who were being sent to the island. Her own husband didn't survive the disease long enough to be among those quarantined, and Jonathan found a heartbreaking account of John Ames's rapid demise from Marsh Fever, along with Sophia's fears that it would take her as well. But there was no mention of strangers who arrived to tend to the sick on the island. There were no accounts of visitors, other than the villagers from Cape Light, who occasionally came to bring provisions and check on those who were quarantined. Jonathan doubted he would ever find documentation of the magical strangers who supposedly arrived to heal the sick ones and then disappeared, without a trace.

He had an idea about the truth behind the legend but, so far, no proof. He knew that if he was going to publish a paper in a scholarly journal and submit it to peer review, he had to be thorough. He couldn't propose a theory then risk some other scholar coming here and finding a single document that might discredit him. He had to examine as much of the firsthand material as he could find. He had a lot of reading to do, that was for sure. But it will be well worth it, he thought. No pain, no gain in the history game.

The only problem was, he felt too hungry and distracted to concentrate. Between his phone call from Professor Pilsner and rushing to meet Tess, he had skipped the inn's hearty breakfast that morning and run out with only a cup of coffee and a carrot bran muffin, which had been tasty but not nearly enough to keep his engine running.

He closed his computer, thinking he would go down to the lunchroom Tess had shown him. But he wasn't sure he would be allowed in without Tess, and it wouldn't be much fun without her.

Down in the entry hall, he took his coat from the locker and headed out to his car again. *The village isn't all that far,* he told himself. *I can grab a quick bite and go back to Lilac Hall for three or four hours before they close.*

He cruised down Main Street and without thinking parked in front of the Clam Box. Though he had promised himself he would never return, he couldn't resist taking a look to see if Tess was there. He walked to the door and pulled it open. There were a few tables filled, but he didn't see Charlie behind the long counter today. That was a good thing, he thought.

He did see Tess waiting on a table near the back. *And that is a very good thing,* he said to himself. He stood by the door, waiting for her to notice him. Finally she looked up and met his glance. She looked surprised but pleased to see him, he thought. He felt his heart beat a little faster than normal and told himself he was acting like an idiot. *Okay, she seems glad to see you. Even though you've practically stalked her today. But try not to be a total nerd?*

"Table for one, sir? Or are you meeting someone?" Tess asked in a very professional tone.

"I had hoped to meet someone today . . . but she stood me up," he teased back.

Tess looked shocked. "You're kidding. Well, maybe she had a good reason. I hope you'll hear her out. . . . Would you like a table by the window today, or a booth in back?" she added before he could reply.

"The window would be fine." He followed her to an empty table and she handed him a menu. "The specials are on the board. We're out of the firehouse chili. Can I get you something to drink while you're deciding?"

"Water will be fine." He looked up and smiled at her. He guessed she was remembering the mammoth spill that had happened the last time. He didn't want to tease her, though.

She soon returned with the water pitcher and efficiently filled his glass, then put a small travel umbrella next to his place setting, which she seemed to have produced from thin air.

"Just in case you happen to be reading the original Dead Sea Scrolls or the Gutenberg Bible while you're dining. Instead of a newspaper or magazine, like a normal person."

He picked up the umbrella and smiled. "Thanks. Very thoughtful. I do remember now that the service here is excellent."

"It is. Much better than the food. Why aren't you eating lunch at the inn?"

Because I wanted to see you, that's why. "Too far," he said. "I want to get back to Lilac Hall and do some more work today. How's the clam roll?" he added, glancing at the menu.

"As Nietzsche said, 'That which does not kill us makes us stronger.'" Her pencil was poised over the order pad.

He laughed. "In that case, I'll try the turkey club on whole wheat, no fries, and a cup of tea."

"Good choice. I'll be back." She walked away again, and Jonathan watched her head to the kitchen. Then he looked over at the little red umbrella on the table. She didn't mind poking fun at herself, did she? He felt happy again, and he knew it was only because he had caught up with her.

Tess soon brought his sandwich and tea, but had three more tables to wait on. Jonathan ate slowly, then ordered pie for dessert and had two more refills of tea. He was practically the only one left in the diner by the time Tess returned to his table for the fourth or fifth time.

"Would you like *anything* else today?" she asked again.

He looked up from the folder of papers he had been reading.

"I'd like you to sit with me a few minutes when you have a break. Is that possible?"

She looked surprised by the request, but pleased. "Charlie is out today, and you're my last table. So I think it will be okay. Just let me tell Trudy."

She walked off to talk to the other waitress, an older woman with dark red hair. Then she returned with a mug of coffee. She drank her coffee black, he noticed, no milk or sugar. He needed both.

"So, did you survive at the historical society today without me?"

Just barely, he nearly replied. "Mrs. Fisk and a volunteer named Michael were very helpful. Though she does remind me of the housekeeper in *Jane Eyre* or some other gothic masterpiece."

Tess laughed out loud. "Doesn't she? With that hairdo and those keys around her neck? I thought the same thing when I first met her. She looks like she must have been living in the mansion since it was first built. But she's actually very nice and knows every scrap of paper in the collection."

"Oh, she was very knowledgeable, no question." *But it's much more fun to work with you and sound out my ideas and hear what you have to say,* he wanted to tell her. But all he could do was sit back and smile.

"My hours were changed," she explained. "They need me there tomorrow instead of today. So I grabbed a few extra hours here. Sorry I wasn't able to get in touch. I guess I could have called the inn," she added. "But I didn't want to bother you."

It wouldn't have been a bother at all. But he knew what she really meant. She felt awkward hunting him down.

"No problem. I was just teasing you before."

"So, did Mrs. Fisk lead you to any other treasure troves of information?"

"I'm still working with the Sophia Ames journal, and I've found some good bits of information there. She does mention the fever and how her husband died. And she does mention the quarantine, which was proposed a week or two after his death. She wrote in her diary that his death was a cruel blow, but how much harder it would have been to have seen him taken away to the island, and to be separated from him in his final hours."

"How sad," Tess said.

"It is," Jonathan agreed. "Her writing is amazingly stoic and even poetic. Wait, I have a quote from the entry here somewhere. Listen to this . . ." He found the note on his pad, eager to share it. "She wrote, 'My dearest John breathed his last in his own bed, under our roof. He passed from my arms into the arms of the angels, the Lord bless and preserve his soul.'"

When he glanced over at Tess, her wide blue eyes were a little glassy. "That's beautiful," she said.

He had the urge to reach over and touch her hand. But the opportunity passed as Tess leaned back and said, "I'm glad you're finding the journal useful. I hope she's written more about the quarantine."

"Even if she didn't write a lot about it, I'm getting a good sense of the psychological state of the community. People were very frightened. I think it's fair to say they were panicked. They all knew that other colonies had been nearly wiped out by other epidemics, and everything they tried to cure the fever, or slow its spread, was failing.

"You know, the more I think about it, the more I realize that terrible as it must have been to be sick and quarantined on that tiny island in the middle of winter, it must have been even more dreadful to be one of the people in Cape Light who sent their loved ones away. I mean, to say good-bye like that to a sick husband or wife or child or parent, knowing full well that there is no cure for the disease, and you will never see them alive again. And that at least in part you are sending them away to save your own life . . . Wouldn't a situation like that, especially in that time, almost compel you to believe in God's mercy? They must have prayed day and night for their loved ones. They must have called on God and His angels and any other divine help they could think of. And it's really not a stretch from that point for them to believe that angels *answered* their prayers, because facing the reality of the situation without the belief in some kind of salvation was just too horrific."

Tess sipped her coffee. She seemed to be mulling over his words.

Jonathan waited for her to say something. "Well, what do you think?" he asked finally.

"You're saying the people who stayed in Cape Light came up with the idea of angels rescuing their loved ones because they couldn't face the truth of what they had done?"

"I'm not sure," he said carefully. "But I can't help wondering if maybe the legend isn't the sort of story that people tell themselves to make the unacceptable acceptable."

"I guess it's possible," Tess said at last. "But I don't know what kind of evidence you can find to support that idea. Besides, isn't it a little early to be drawing conclusions?" Her voice was calm and reasonable, not criticizing him. Just asking the question.

"Maybe I am jumping ahead a little," he agreed. "I need to finish going through the Ames journal and find more firsthand sources before I fix on any theories, no matter how tempting they sound." He smiled at her. "It's good to have someone around who won't let me cut any corners— or get carried away, thinking I have some brilliant solution."

"Don't worry. I'm sure you'll come up with a few more brilliant theories before you're done."

She could tell by his expression he thought she was being sarcastic.

"I actually meant that," she added. "I think you're smart and full of good ideas and seem to have a genuine empathy for this era. I think you may figure out something about the legend that no one else has."

Her compliment made him feel as if he had just won the Pulitzer Prize for this paper, and he hoped he wasn't grinning too widely. "Well . . . thanks. That's nice of you to say. I appreciate that, honestly."

"No problem. It's the least I can do . . . after blowing your first brilliant theory out of the water." She grinned and tucked a strand of hair behind her ear.

He had to laugh. That was true, but he hardly minded anymore.

"Listen," she said, "I know these older people in town who might be able to help you, Digger Hegman and his daughter Grace. They had ancestors who were founders, and I know they have a few letters from the first years of the settlement. Digger keeps saying he's going to bring them over to the historical society, but he never gets around to it. I could introduce you, if you want to see the letters and maybe interview them."

Jonathan stared at her. "That would be great, Tess. Thank you."

"I'll call them and ask if we can go over. Can you give me your e-mail or something?"

"Oh, right. Good idea . . . Here's my e-mail address and my cell number. Just in case."

Tess wrote down her e-mail and cell number, too, on the back of a table check. He took the slip of paper and carefully tucked it in his pocket. "Thanks," he said, glad to finally exchange e-mail addresses and phone numbers with her. Why had that taken so long? He suddenly imagined calling her while he was working at the inn, asking her opinion on some idea or sharing some special bit of information, like the note from Sophia Ames about her husband. Their connection added a whole new dimension to this work, he realized. A very unexpected but good dimension.

"I'll call the Hegmans later and let you know what they say," Tess told him. "They live just down the street, above the Bramble antiques shop. Grace runs the shop and Digger helps. Well, he tries to. He's getting pretty old and forgetful now. But he still tells some amazing stories about the old days in town when he was a boy. I've been thinking of doing a video interview with him and some other seniors in town, as an independent study project."

"That sounds interesting," Jonathan said, impressed.

"You'll have an interesting field trip if they let us visit," she promised. "It is good to get out and mingle with the natives."

"Yes, it is." He smiled at her, thinking of one native in particular.

A bell above the diner door jingled and a family came in. They looked hungry and haggard. The two small children, a boy and a girl, hung on their mother's coat as the father looked around for some help being seated.

Tess took one last sip of her drink and quickly stood up. "Looks like my break is over. Time for the crayons and color-in place mats."

"I'd better go, too. I'll call you later," he promised, "to hear what the Hegmans say." *And just to hear your voice,* he nearly added.

She smiled quickly at him then walked toward the fidgeting family, grabbing a stack of menus on the way.

Jonathan left a handful of bills on his check and a coffee mug on top of that. Once again, he had overtipped. She was going to think he was a millionaire in disguise or something. Which wasn't that far from the truth, he reflected as he slipped on his jacket and grabbed his bag. If he had been willing to follow his father's plan for his life—finish law school and join his dad's firm—he would be enjoying a very affluent lifestyle by now. One he would never enjoy on an academic's salary. But he was content with the choice he had made and the path he was following. These past few days, away from the campus and out on his own, immersed in this new research, he felt happier and more sure of that than ever.

As he walked to his car, he wondered how much meeting Tess had to do with that. Probably more than he wanted to admit. He was glad he would see her again soon and talk to her even sooner than that.

CHAPTER SEVEN

*M*OLLY . . . ARE YOU ALL RIGHT?" MOLLY'S HUSBAND, MATT Harding, stared down at her, a mug of coffee in one hand and box of high-fiber cereal in the other. He put both on the table and took a chair, facing her.

Molly shrugged. "I'm okay, just a little tired. Getting Betty on the bus was a day's work. She couldn't find her homework, didn't like her lunch, and her ponytail was too tight." Their youngest daughter, Betty, who was almost five now, was named for Molly's partner, Betty Bowman, and like her namesake, was definitely her own person. Molly only hoped that one day little Betty would acquire bigger Betty's gifts of tact and diplomacy, neither of which ran in the Morgan clan.

"She's getting distracted by Christmas. She's counting the days," Matt said. "And you're working too hard, as usual." He frowned at her as he shook some cereal into his bowl.

"It's the holidays, honey. It always gets crazy this time of year. And having my right-hand woman out so much the last few weeks hasn't helped." Matt knew Molly meant Betty Bowman, who in addition to being Molly's partner, was her best friend and mainstay.

"I just worry about you. I don't want you run-down and sick by the time the girls get home and we have our own Christmas. And your sister Laurie's coming with her twins," he reminded her.

"I know, don't worry. I'll perk right up once the house fills up. I had an e-mail from Lauren this morning. She's finishing up her classes this week. I can hardly wait to see them."

She and Matt had four children altogether, all girls: Lauren and Jill from her first marriage; Amanda from Matt's first marriage; and Betty, whom they had brought into the world together.

They had been married for over five years. Lauren and Amanda, best pals as well as stepsisters, were both in graduate school now. Lauren was at Columbia, studying art history, and Amanda was following her passion for music at Julliard. They shared an apartment in Brooklyn with two other students and traveled by subway in the city. Their lives were so very different from their quiet upbringing in Cape Light, but they loved their visits home and filled the house with energy and excitement.

"Besides, Dr. Harding, you always say the same thing this time of year," Molly pointed out. "And I can't even remember the last time I came down with anything for Christmas . . . except when I was pregnant with Betty and kept running upstairs to puke my guts out. That doesn't really count, does it?"

"No, it doesn't." Matt gave her one of his looks then checked the newspaper headlines.

He was trying not to smile but couldn't help it. He always laughed at her jokes. Her sense of humor and blunt, uninhibited way of expressing herself—just the opposite of his style—had drawn them together and kept their relationship lively all these years.

Her husband knew her very well and was an expert at reading her moods. Molly knew that she wasn't just tired today. It was more than usual work pressures causing this blue mood and low energy.

"There is something bothering me," she confessed.

"What is it? Can I help?" He put aside the newspaper and gave her his full attention.

"I had a fight with Sam yesterday, at the shop. I was out seeing clients and he had cornered Dad there, to talk about this thing with Grandma and Uncle Kevin again."

"Your grandmother is still in town? You haven't mentioned her. I thought she must have gone back to Vermont."

"She's still around, up at the Inn at Angel Island. I just didn't feel like I wanted to call her. I don't know what she's doing there, aside from hanging around, waiting for Sam to plead her case. From what I saw, it was more like my poor father was up on the witness stand, getting interrogated. Is that fair? He's the one who was slighted in all this. I felt so bad for my dad. It was a complete ambush. By the time I came in, he looked like he was going to have a heart attack or something. I had to get him a chair."

"Sam ambushed and interrogated your father? That doesn't sound like your brother at all," Matt said.

"I know, but that's what happened. The minute I walked in I could see they had been arguing. Dad looked so upset. So I just blew up and started yelling at Sam and sort of . . . threw him out of the shop."

Matt sat back and blinked. "You threw Sam out of the shop? You love Sam. He's your hero."

Molly winced. It was true . . . most of the time. Sam was her big brother and had always been there for her. Especially when her first marriage broke up and her ex-husband, Phil, disappeared and the girls were so young and totally dependent on her. Sam had always been there to fill in the gaps and was only a call away, twenty-four/seven. On nights when the girls were young and difficult, and the heat in their drafty little apartment was barely working, and Molly thought she had reached the end of her patience and strength, Sam would show up with a pizza and a movie, and suddenly everything was warm and cozy and fine again. She didn't know how many times she had given thanks that she had lucked into Sam for a brother.

"I know . . . I know . . . That's why I feel so bad. But why does he have to be such a turncoat? I feel bad for my father, too, and I can't hurt his feelings even more by siding with Grandma Addie. And I don't see how Sam can do it, either."

Matt reached across the table and covered her hands with his. His simple touch was a comfort, a balm to her troubled heart. Her husband had large, strong hands, but they were gentle, too. The perfect touch for a doctor, she always thought.

"I knew something was bothering you and it wasn't just being overworked."

"Well, I guess this mess is just the icing on the petit fours now."

"I hate to see you torn in two like this, honey. But I don't see how fighting with Sam is going to solve anything. It's only going to make things worse."

She sighed. "Duh . . . Yeah, I know that now. I just wish Grandma had never come down here and stirred all this up. It was like poking a stick in a hornets' nest. How is this ever going to get solved? Dad is just . . . Well, he doesn't want to see Uncle Kevin. He doesn't even want to talk to him on the phone. Sam did speak to Uncle Kevin. He told Dad that, too."

"That's a big step. So far there were only Cape Light hornets buzzing around. Does your Uncle Kevin want to make amends?"

Molly shrugged. "I don't know." She withdrew her hands from his. This wasn't why she had confided in him. She didn't want to talk about Uncle Kevin and what he wanted. She just wanted some sympathy, not the possibility of solutions. "I'm not sure it matters what Uncle Kevin wants. Or even Grandma. It's really up to my father. It's what he wants that counts, don't you think?"

Her husband looked stung by her sharp tone, and Molly felt instantly sorry. "I'm sorry. I didn't mean to sound like that. It's just that this whole subject makes me crazy."

"I can see that," Matt said quietly. "But that isn't helping any, either."

Good grief, now she was about to start arguing with Matt. Molly took a few deep breaths. She thought she had gotten a lot better at controlling her emotions, but this situation had pushed her backward, almost to square one.

"Are you really sure your father doesn't want to settle things?" he asked her.

"I'm positive. You should have heard him after Sam left."

"Well, the talk with Sam must have been difficult and your father was probably just venting. But maybe now he's had time to think about it more, and maybe his feelings are changing. He should have time to think on his own, without any pressure, Molly," Matt concluded in a firm tone.

Pressure from her, he meant. Pressure to dig in his heels, the way she always did. She did take after her father that way.

"I'm not pressuring him, honestly." She looked down at her coffee and thought about it. Was she? Just by being so stalwart and in his corner? "I'm . . . supporting him," she concluded.

Matt gave her a thoughtful look. "I understand. But try to just let him make up his own mind now. You and Sam need to stay out of it. And what are you doing fighting with your brother? You're just repeating the same problem between Joe and Kevin. Is this some strange virus spreading through the family?" Matt smiled weakly at his own slim joke. "It seems ironic to me. Do you really want to do that?"

"No, I don't," Molly said quickly. "I totally disagree with Sam on this, but I don't want to stop talking to him over it. That would be really stupid."

"Yes, it would be," Matt agreed. "Somebody is going to have to take the first step and make up. I mean, between you and Sam. We'll just have to see how it goes with Joe and Uncle Kevin."

Molly sighed. "Good advice," she said, though she wasn't sure at all if she could follow it. Every time she thought about this situation, she felt her emotions get out of control all over again.

Matt rose and touched her shoulder. "Feel any better now?"

"A little. Thanks for talking to me about it."

"Anytime, honey. I know it's hard but let's not let this spoil our Christmas, okay?"

Molly understood what he was saying. With the two older girls grown and out of the house, they were able to bring their whole family together so rarely now. The holidays were a precious time for them.

"I understand. Don't worry, Matt. It won't come to that."

Though deep in her heart Molly wondered if she could keep that promise . . . and was it even hers to give?

After Matt left for his office, Molly set to work cleaning up the kitchen and doing some laundry. The large, newly built home had seemed the perfect size for a growing family when they moved in. Coming out of some hard times, she had thought the house a dream come true, with its huge, gracious rooms, gleaming hardwood floors, a super-deluxe kitchen, three full baths, and every possible extra. But now that the older girls were gone and Jillian was about to leave the nest next September, it was starting to feel like the house was way too big and empty. It was a lot to take care of day to day, along with running her business. But once the girls came home and her sister Laurie arrived with her twins, all the rooms and then some would be filled.

They were going to decorate this weekend and set up the tree with just the lights. Amanda and Lauren insisted that they couldn't miss out on the family tradition of hanging the rest of the trimmings.

There was a lot to do before Christmas. She hadn't even started her shopping. Molly knew she should sit down this morning and make a big, long list. She didn't have to be in the shop until noon, though she would be working late tonight, setting up a holiday cocktail party. She tossed in a load of laundry, grabbed another cup of coffee, and sat in her planning place, on a high stool at the granite-topped island in her kitchen.

She sat with her pen poised over her pad and dutifully started her list. But her thoughts kept wandering back to Sam, back to the argument in her shop, back to her hard words to Grandma Addie. Back to the pain in her father's eyes whenever he tried to talk about his brother.

It was no good. She put her pen down. She couldn't concentrate on a Christmas to-do list this morning. She was too worked up. Her little boat was rocking from side to side, as if hit by a sudden squall.

She checked the time and decided to leave for the village a little earlier than she had planned. Maybe she could catch Sam at his shop. Maybe they could talk about this without arguing.

Molly reached the village a short time later. She saw Sam's truck in the driveway, next to the Bramble. Sam was working with one of his employees, loading the bed of the truck with long white columns that Molly knew would soon be bracing up the porch roof of someone's Victorian.

She parked her SUV across the street from the Bramble and started toward him, brushing aside a sudden attack of nerves. Why should she feel nervous approaching her own brother? Maybe because he had glanced at her car but hadn't looked her way once since then?

He still did not look at her as she stood near the truck. He was crouching on the truck bed, securing the columns with heavy nylon cord.

"Hi, Sam . . . Busy today?"

He glanced at her a moment. "I have to get back to a job right away. What's up?"

It took a lot to make her brother mad, but she definitely saw the signs of that rare occurrence.

She shrugged, feeling her courage drain through her toes.

"Nothing. I just thought we should talk. I guess it can wait."

He was at the far end of the truck bed now, facing away from her. "It will have to. For one thing, I don't have time right now. For another, I'm not sure there's anything to talk about." He stood up and turned to her. "Unless you've changed your mind about Dad and Uncle Kevin?"

Molly took a breath. She had to be honest, she had not. She shook her head. "Not really, no. I'm still on Dad's side, if that's what you mean."

Sam's bland expression suddenly darkened. "How can we even talk about this if you make it into some sort of war? Some sort of contest about which of us is more loyal to Dad? I love him just as much as you do, Molly. You don't have any copyright on that," he said angrily.

Molly was shocked and took a step back. "I never said that, Sam. Don't put words in my mouth now—"

"Maybe you never said it, but you act that way. Do you think staying mad at his brother till they both die is a good thing? Never mind poor Grandma. Is that the side you're on—being unforgiving and clinging to all this old baggage and these grievances?"

Molly suddenly felt as if a red-hot flare were shooting through her bloodstream. "How dare you talk to me like that? You've got all the answers, right, Sam? I never said you didn't love Dad, but I will say, you really don't get this at all. None of this—not one bit of this entire mess—is Dad's fault. And you're still blaming the victim."

Sam jumped down from the truck bed and faced her. For a moment, Molly was honestly afraid of what he might say next.

Then he shook his head. "If that's how you see it, there's nothing else I can say. When Dad decides—not you, but Dad," he said emphatically, "that he does have a choice here, that he can put this aside and move on, maybe we'll have something to talk about."

He brushed past her and got in the cab of the truck, then slammed the door shut and started the engine.

Molly felt sad they had fought again, and angry at him all at once. She tromped back along the icy ground to her car, trying to watch her step as her sight grew blurry and her eyes filled with tears. She got in her SUV and fastened the seat belt but couldn't drive away.

Sam, you big idiot, she shouted in her head. *Why can't you just get over it and be nice to me again? We always disagree, and you just laugh it off. Why do you have to stay so mad at me this time? Why does this even matter? Why can't things just stay the way they were, before Grandma came down here and turned everything into such a huge mess . . .*

Molly dried her eyes and headed for her shop. Two weeks and five days until Christmas Eve, when Sam and Jessica would have the big family party at their house. She thought about the promise she had made to Matt. How she wouldn't let this family feud ruin their holiday.

Sorry, honey, but I just made things even worse. Sam can't stay mad at me until Christmas . . . can he?

She didn't even want to imagine what would happen then.

JONATHAN DROVE INTO THE VILLAGE ON FRIDAY EVENING, JUST AS darkness was falling. The weather forecast had predicted snow today, but once again, the area had only been dusted by a few flurries. Jonathan thought the village looked like one of those miniatures set under a tree, with just the edges of rooftops and lampposts and cars frosted by a light coating of snow.

The Bramble fit into this picture perfectly. The building, once a Victorian house, was decorated for Christmas with lights and garlands strung around the porch and front door and a big pine wreath. He parked in front, got out of his car, and waited for Tess. She was meeting him here at six but he was a little early.

A path leading up from the street to the shop had not been shoveled yet, but he could still see the remains of flowerbed borders and flowerbeds all around the porch and picket fence. The porch was packed with collectibles: wooden benches and rocking chairs, painted signs, milk cans, old bottles, and lanterns. He wondered how much was actually valuable and how much was just junk that the shopkeeper hoped to pass on. If he ever had a house, he knew he wanted a lot of old, interesting things in it, treasures from the past. He wondered if Tess would like that, too, then caught himself, feeling silly for even wondering how she would decorate a house.

Small candles glowed in all the windows, and Jonathan could easily imagine a time when a family lived here, when a horse and carriage rolled up the gravel drive and parked in the back, near the barn. He could picture the mother, wearing an apron over a long dress, taking something out of the oven. The table was set for dinner, and a fire glowed in the hearth. The children were playing games and reading. There was no TV, computers, or video games, of course. They ran to greet their father when he came home in from the cold and jumped into his arms. Oh, and there was a dog, Jonathan decided, a big, friendly yellow dog, stretched out by the fire.

Would he ever fall in love with someone and have a home like that? Would he have children? Would he ever live such a simple, happy life? It seemed a dream, so different than the way he had grown up.

He smiled to himself, wondering what had sent his thoughts into such a sentimental tailspin. He did get nostalgic around antique stores. It was easy for him to imagine the lives of the people who once owned all these things. But he also knew it was something more. The holidays coming, maybe. Meeting a girl like Tess . . .

He suddenly felt someone watching him and noticed a woman looking out from behind the curtains on the bay window. She either realized he had come for the interview and wondered why he didn't come in—or she was about to call the police.

He checked his watch and when he looked up, Tess was walking toward him down the sidewalk with that long, graceful stride of hers. He waved and started toward her.

She waved back and smiled. She wore a dark blue peacoat, jeans, and boots, with a red-and-white-striped scarf slung around her neck. Her long, shiny hair hung loose, waving around her shoulders, and when she finally faced him he noticed two red circles on her cheeks from the cold. Like a china doll he might find inside.

"Waiting long?" she asked. "Sorry I'm late. My mother was going to give me the car, but she was held up at work. So I had to walk."

"No problem, I got here early. I could have picked you up. You should have called me."

Tess didn't answer, just smiled. She wasn't used to asking people for help. So far, all the guys she dated had disappointed her that way. Jonathan seemed different. He was older for one thing and did seem more mature.

He was definitely a cut above in the looks department, if that counted for anything. He looked very handsome tonight, she thought, in a dark brown leather jacket, worn jeans, and a burgundy scarf. The dark red color brought out his brown eyes and thick lashes. Some girls would kill for lashes like that, she wanted to tell him. But of course, she didn't.

He suddenly leaned closer and she wondered why. Was he going to kiss her hello or something? Instead, he whispered in her ear, "I think we'd better go in. A woman keeps peeking out from behind that curtain."

Tess followed his glance, and they both saw the lace panel on the bay window slip back in place again.

"That's just Grace," Tess explained. "She can be a little nervous. You'll get used to her."

They walked up to the porch and Tess rang the doorbell, an antique, brass pull-style that had a high, sharp ring.

Grace opened the door a few seconds later. "Hello there. Come right in. I've been waiting for you," she told Tess.

It was dim inside the shop, with only the light coming from the Christmas candles in the windows and a small milk glass lamp on a table near the door. Tess hoped that Jonathan could still get a good look around at the various rooms off the entrance and the interesting items that filled them.

She saw Jonathan's head turn as they passed the room to the right of the door, which displayed old sets of china on tables covered with hand-made lace and flowery chintz. There were also china dolls and lamps, elephants, and pugs. Many, many china pugs. They must be a popular item, Tess reasoned.

The room to the left held antique furniture, a graceful fainting couch, with carved wooden edges and vibrant fuchsia silk upholstery and fringed pillows. There were love seats and velvet-covered rockers and ballroom chairs that looked too fragile to be sat on by a modern-day body. In and among these furnishings, Tess spotted other smaller items—antique teddy bears and toys, clocks of all sizes, glass ginger jars, and punch bowls set randomly on end tables. A hat rack was covered with dusty hats, some trailing long feathers, and several bookcases held brown tattered volumes.

The walls of all the rooms were covered with framed watercolors, sketches, silhouettes of Victorian ladies and gentleman cut from paper, cross-stitched scenes, and homely mottos. There were two more rooms in the back, packed with more treasures, but out of view in the shadows. A glass counter just across from the entrance held jewelry. Tess loved to browse here but had so far never bought herself any of the antique earrings or necklaces she admired.

Grace took their coats and scarves and hung them on a coat tree with arms that looked like deer antlers. She was a small, thin woman with a narrow face and pointed chin. Her hair, silver and dark brown, was straight and thin, cut to her chin and held back on each side with a bobby pin. She wore a black cardigan sweater with a blouse underneath, buttoned to the top. The lace edge on the collar and pin-tuck pleats made it look antique.

"This is my friend Jonathan," Tess said. "The one I told you about. He's a graduate student at Tufts in the history department."

"Welcome. Nice to meet you," Grace said, tilting her head.

"Nice to meet you. Thank you so much for having me here." Jonathan smiled and held out his hand.

"Oh, it's no bother. My father loves to talk about the old days. He can hardly wait to show you his letters." Grace was shy with strangers, Tess knew, and didn't look Jonathan in the eye when she spoke, though she was trying to smile.

They followed Grace up a flight of steps. "How is Digger?" Tess asked. "Is he feeling well?"

"Oh, he's still fit," Grace reported. "Stronger than I am. But he's so forgetful now, I have to watch him every minute," she added in a hushed tone.

Tess had told Jonathan last night on the phone that Digger was a bit senile. Digger's concentration and state of mind seemed to come and go. Tess warned Jonathan that there was no telling how reasonable the old fisherman would be tonight, but Jonathan seemed willing to take his chances. Digger's condition might compromise the interview, he told her, but it wouldn't compromise the value of the letters. "Dad? Our guests are here," Grace announced as she led them to a living room off the landing.

"Remember, I told you that Tess was coming with a friend who wanted to see your letters?"

"Yes . . . yes, I remember. Hello, Tess. You look prettier every time I see ya."

Tess saw Jonathan smile as the old man enveloped her in a big hug. Digger always looked the same to her, but she knew that he was getting older and must look very eccentric to Jonathan.

His long white hair melded into a long beard that started at the top of his cheeks and hung down to his chest, though both hair and beard looked smoothly combed and freshly washed. And when he hugged her, she had smelled his old-fashioned, spicy cologne.

Sparkling blue eyes, which didn't seem the least bit confused, peeked out from under bushy silver brows and the edge of his woolen fisherman's cap, which was pulled down low on his brow. He wore a thick brown cardigan sweater that looked hand knit, perhaps by Grace, Tess thought. He wore a gray pinstriped vest under that and a plaid flannel shirt. His baggy corduroy pants looked brand-new, and his heavy black work boots were freshly polished.

Digger stepped back from the hug and pressed a hand to his head, making sure he hadn't lost his cap.

"This is my friend Jonathan. He's studying the epidemic that struck the early settlers in Cape Light and the quarantine on Angel Island." Tess tugged on Jonathan's sleeve to bring him closer to Digger.

"Oh, you're the one," Digger said, nodding at him.

"That's me." Jonathan nodded. "I hope we haven't kept you waiting."

"Oh, no problem, son. I wasn't doing anything special . . . Just thinking about my family. I've got some very special letters that have been passed down to me by my great-granddad and his great-granddad before that. The museum up on the Beach Road wants them. Says they'll give me money. I won't sell," he added quickly, shaking his head. "You can't sell away your family heritage."

"Of course you can't," Jonathan agreed with him.

"You're darn right." Digger's tone was vehement, as if Jonathan had been arguing with him.

"Dad, they came to see the letters. Do you remember? What did you do with them?"

"I have them right here, Grace. In my pocket, don't trouble yourself . . ." He reached into the pocket of his pants but came up empty. Then he tried the other side. Still nothing. Then he tried the pockets of his brown cardigan.

Jonathan glanced at Tess nervously. She knew what he was thinking. *If letters that old had survived all these years, the documents could not be roughly handled, stuffed into pockets, or stored without extra care.* Tess wondered if the letters would be legible at all, or torn to shreds.

"They can't be in your pockets, Dad. We keep them in a special box, remember?"

Tess shared another glance with Jonathan. She could practically hear him sigh with relief, and she felt the same herself.

"That's right, in a box. I was just holding the box on my lap, thinking about what was inside. The paper is old, see? It breaks off in your hand," he explained to Jonathan. "You can't touch it much or put it in sunlight. Once a year maybe, or less. I don't want them letters to crumble away to dust."

Jonathan nodded again. "Old documents are fragile. They shouldn't be handled at all."

"Or just thrown about and lost," Grace added, looking around the room for the storage box.

Digger seemed distressed. "Geez, I hope those people from the museum didn't come and take them when I wasn't looking. They've been after me, calling and calling . . . They know where we live, too," he said quietly to Jonathan. "But I keep the letters hidden. In a secret place. Nobody would think of it," he said proudly.

"Good, that's good, Digger." Jonathan wondered if the documents were in this secret place right now . . . and Digger couldn't think of it.

"Is this the box?" Tess had wandered over to the Hegmans' Christmas tree, which stood in a corner of the room. There was a crèche scene below the lowest branches and a few gift-wrapped packages. But one package, about the size of a shoe box and made of plain dark brown cardboard, seemed out of place. When she knelt down to get a better look, she knew in an instant it was an archival storage box, the kind used at the historical society to protect documents from humidity and light.

"Smart girl. You found it under the tree?" Digger seemed amazed at her discovery. "I never put it there. Maybe Grace did . . . and she forgot. She gets like that."

Grace gave him a look, her mouth twisted to one side. "Yes, maybe I did. In my sleep, I guess."

"All right, let's take a look at these now . . . once a year." Digger's thick, gnarled fingers trembled as he tried to open the box. "Here, Tess. You open it. My hands are tired and complaining today."

That was a good way of putting it, Tess thought. She imagined when a person got older their spirit still felt very lively—at least it seemed that way for someone like Digger—but their bodies were like worn-out machinery, frustrating to operate.

Tess sat on the love seat across from Digger's chair. She set the box on the coffee table, carefully opened it, and removed the letters, handling them with great care.

"I read somewhere that the antique documents need to be kept in a special box like that and covered by a plastic sleeve. So I've been keeping them like that for a long time now," Grace explained. "It took Dad a while to understand, but he knows now they won't last otherwise."

"Grace keeps them right. As good as in the museum," Digger insisted. Jonathan had been standing next to Tess and now sat beside her on the love seat. She counted five sheets of paper protected in plastic covers.

"How many letters are there, Grace?" Jonathan asked, looking at the pages over Tess's shoulder.

"Three altogether. But we don't have all the pages of one of them."

"May I see a page?" Jonathan asked her.

Tess handed him one of the sheets, and he examined it carefully. Digger and Grace watched him, waiting for his opinion, Tess suspected.

"Well . . . what do you think? Real treasures, right?" Digger said finally.

Jonathan looked up and nodded. "Yes, they are. Truly. You've taken very good care of them," he said, glancing at Grace. "From the paper and ink marks, I'd say these letters would be prized by any historical society."

Digger beamed with pride. "Hear that, Grace? This fella's in the business. He says our letters are treasures."

Grace seemed proud, too, but was shy about showing it. "I heard what he said, Dad. We have to take care of them. We can't be tossing that box around the house, like an old pair of shoes, can we?"

Digger made a face like a little boy who's been scolded but didn't say anything.

"When were the letters written?" Tess asked, scanning a page for a date.

"Oh, way back there. When the village founders first came over from England. Sixteen thirty-three, I think it was. The settlers all came up here from Cape Cod in the spring, built shelters, set up their crops. Come fall, that's when the sickness started. The Marsh Fever, they called it."

"That's exactly right. At the end of the first year." The old man could remember historical facts and even dates, Jonathan noticed. It was the present he had trouble with. "Who wrote these letters, someone in your family?"

Digger nodded. "That's right, my ancestor on my daddy's side, Mary Newell Hegman. Her husband was Ezekiel. They had eight children and they all caught the fever. Seven died in their beds, and Mary was sent over to the island with the baby in her arms. . . . Oh, those were dark days, son. Dark days."

"Very dark," Jonathan agreed.

"People made some hard choices and had to live with it, come what may." Digger sighed heavily.

"What happened to Mary and the baby? Did they survive?" Tess asked.

Digger nodded. "It was a part of the miracle. The good Lord had mercy. Mary came back after the winter cured and the child cured, too. He grew up to be a fisherman named Philip . . . same name as me. He kept the family line going. There would have been no more Hegmans in the New World if he hadn't hung on."

Tess felt a tingling excitement as she heard the story. She glanced at Jonathan, sensing he felt it, too. She could tell from the light in his eyes and his excited expression.

"Did Mary write these letters to her husband from the island? Does she mention anything about the quarantine and the . . . the visitors who came to take care of the sick ones?"

He almost said angels. But he couldn't quite manage it, Tess knew. She knew Jonathan even questioned whether human visitors had come to care for the sick.

"The angels, you mean? Is that what he's talking about?" Digger seemed confused and turned to Tess.

"That's right, Digger, that's what he means." She lifted her eyes and smiled at Jonathan.

Jonathan smiled back. He knew Digger believed in the legend, and he wasn't about to start a debate with the old man, just to prove a point.

Tess already knew Jonathan was kind and wasn't out to hurt anyone's feelings or insult their beliefs, though he was committed to finding out the truth, if he could.

"What do you think, Digger? Did angels come to nurse the quarantined villagers? Or was it some group of merciful folks from another settlement, or maybe even some Native Americans who helped them?" Jonathan proposed.

"Wasn't any other settlements nearby at that time. Lots of Native Americans, though. Wampanoag," he added, naming the tribe that had lived in the area.

"Yes, that's right. . . . What do you think?" Jonathan repeated the question.

"Oh, it was angels. No question, young man. Couldn't have been anything else. When you consider the time of the year, the harsh weather, the land bridge impassable for weeks at a time . . . You say Native Americans come over in their bark canoes? When even a big, seafaring vessel could hardly handle those rough seas."

If there was one thing Digger knew—and still knew—it was the sea and the weather. He had a good point, too, Tess thought.

Before Jonathan could answer, the old man said, "Here, you sit right there." He pointed to the couch. "You read them letters. Take your time. Then you tell me what you think," he added with a challenging note. "You decide for yourself. I don't have to tell you what to think. You're in a big university studying to be a professor, right?"

Jonathan nodded. "That's right."

"Well, you're a heck of a lot smarter than me. So you decide for yourself," he repeated.

Jonathan carefully picked up a page again. He held it out so that Tess could read it, too. They sat shoulder to shoulder on the small couch, and Tess focused on the dark purple letters. The ink was made from berries, boiled bark, and even ash from the fireplace, and the pen, a sharped quill at the tip of a feather. The old writing was very hard to make out, and Jonathan's nearness was a further distraction.

"Can you read it, Tess?" Jonathan turned to her, his face very near. "I can hardly make out a word," he confessed.

"I think I've got the first line." She pointed with her fingertip and read aloud. "*'My dearest heart, We arrived on the island safely. The baby is still feverish . . .'*" She looked up at him. "I can't make out much more after that. I think you would need a magnifying glass."

"Yes, that would help," Jonathan agreed, sliding the page back into its plastic sleeve. He looked up at Digger. "I'm sorry . . . I think I will need some time to read these. The ink is faded, and the handwriting is hard to make out. I don't want to rush and miss something important," he added.

Digger nodded. "Wouldn't be right to rush. There's a right way to do something and a wrong way. You don't want to miss a word. What would be the point of that?"

"Would it be all right if Jonathan borrowed the letters?" Tess glanced at Grace and then back at Digger.

"Oh, it's all right with me, as long as he handles them carefully and keeps that box in a cool, dry place, out of the sunlight. But I expect he knows about all that," Grace replied. "But it's not really my place to say. It's up to my dad," she added.

Tess looked over at Digger. "It will only be for a few days, and he'll copy them down and type it all out. Then he'll give them back to you with the type-written pages, so that if you want to read them, you don't have to take them out of storage."

Digger looked surprised at the idea. His bushy eyebrows rose into the edge of his hat. "You'd do that for me? That would be a good thing," he agreed.

"I'd be happy to," Jonathan replied. "Or, if you're not comfortable with me taking the letters off the premises, perhaps I could come back here a few times and try to transcribe them for you."

Tess could tell he really wanted to study the letters on his own, but didn't want Digger to feel pressured. It was thoughtful of him to offer to study them here. That might be a good compromise, she thought.

But Digger surprised her. "Oh, that's okay. I trust you, son. I have a sixth sense about folks and you're a good one. I can just smell it on a person."

"Well . . . thanks," Jonathan said. "Thanks for the compliment."

Digger nodded. "Sure thing. I can live without them letters in the house for a week or so. I do want to help you get the story right, so you can put it in a history book. Ain't that what you're aiming for?"

Jonathan had to smile at that. "Yes, that's exactly what I'm hoping."

Grace had left the room but now returned with a silver tray, holding a teapot and cups and a dish of cookies. They were plain butter and molasses cookies, brown on the edges, and looked homemade.

"I've made some tea. It will take the chill out."

While it was cold outside, the apartment felt quite warm to Tess. But she knew that older people often felt chilled, so it was probably just right for them. Grace offered her a cup of tea and she took it, saying thank you.

"Jonathan here is going to borrow the letters, Grace. He's going to study them and type up what they say, so we don't have to worry about tearing the pages if we want to read them over."

"Oh, very nice. Why didn't I think of that?" Grace asked no one in particular.

"He's got to read them slowly, so he doesn't miss the part about the angels. It's all in there . . . you'll see," Digger promised.

Tess could tell Jonathan didn't want to disagree but was probably thinking he wouldn't find any conclusive evidence to support that claim.

Still, she sensed they were both excited to see what they would find in these documents.

"You see, some folks who were healed on the island went on to become healers, too," Digger continued as he sipped his own cup of tea. "It was a gift passed down in families. Like blue eyes or singing."

"He understands, Dad. You don't have to go on about it."

"I'm just explaining, Grace. No harm in that."

"I understand," Jonathan said. Though Tess suspected he found this claim even more doubtful than the one about angelic healers. "Do you know anyone in town I can interview who is descended from this group? Someone who has the . . . the healing touch?" Jonathan asked.

Tess watched Digger consider the question. He stroked his long beard. "Hard to say. People don't like to flaunt that sort of thing."

Jonathan nodded. Tess was sure he thought that was because the claim was more fantasy, part of the legend.

"There is someone, though," Digger continued. "Claire North. People say her family line traces down from the healers, and she's got the gift."

Tess nearly laughed out loud at Jonathan's surprised expression.

"Claire North lives on the island. She works at the inn over there," Grace told Jonathan.

"Yes, I know . . . I'm staying at the inn. I'll ask her about that," he said. Tess watched him take a breath and then reach for the box of letters. "Well, thank you both very much for your time and for letting me examine these documents. I really can't tell you how much I appreciate your help, Mr. Hegman—"

Digger interrupted him with a sharp laugh. "Ha! Can't recall the last time anybody called me that. That's rich, that is." He looked over at his daughter. "Hear what he called me, Grace? *Mister* Hegman."

Digger practically melted into his beard, chuckling.

Tess glanced at Jonathan and smiled. He seemed a bit bewildered, not totally understanding what he had said to send Digger into this spasm of mirth, but he also seemed amused by the moment.

Grace sighed while they waited for Digger to stop chortling. "I think my father is getting tired. You probably ought to go."

"Yes, of course. I was just about to. Thanks again. It's been a real pleasure meeting both of you," Jonathan said sincerely as he shook the old man's hand and then shook Grace's. "I really appreciated our talk and your help. I'll take very good care of the documents. Please don't worry."

"I ain't worried, son, not one bit. You seem like a fine, responsible young man . . . and you got Tess peeking over your shoulder, keeping an eye out for me, too." His playful smile lit up his old blue eyes. "You're a lucky fella, you know that?"

Tess blushed, catching Digger's meaning. He thought something was going on between her and Jonathan. Something more than friendship and a mutual love of history. Well . . . maybe there was. Jonathan also looked taken by surprise, his smile suddenly frozen. She sensed he felt a bit embarrassed, too.

But before Digger could say more, Tess leaned down and gave him a quick hug. "See you soon, Digger. Take care of yourself."

"Same to you, dear. Grace has got me working hard these days. It's the Christmas rush, you know."

Grace made a face and shook her head. Jonathan could only imagine Digger dealing with her customers.

"Yes, it's the rush. We're all set, right, Dad?" Her father solemnly nodded. Grace turned to Tess and Jonathan. "I'll show you out. I have to go down anyway to lock the door."

At the bottom of the steps, Grace handed them both their coats. "Thank you again for your help and hospitality," Jonathan said.

"It was no trouble. We like to have visitors. Gets a little quiet around here." Grace smiled briefly at him, then opened the door. "You both be careful. Just take it step by step on that path. I haven't had a chance to shovel yet."

Grace shut the door, and Jonathan and Tess started down the steps. At the bottom, he took her hand. "Here, hold on to me. There isn't much snow, but I think it's iced over."

Tess wound her fingers with his, as if it was the most natural thing in the world. "Okay, thanks . . . whoa . . . you're right. It did get worse."

They walked along silently for a moment, concentrating on keeping their balance.

"So, what do you think? How did you like meeting one of the village's most famous and revered citizens?"

"He was everything you promised, and more. I can see why people love him so much. He's a genuine character."

"Totally genuine," Tess agreed. "They just don't make 'em like that anymore."

"No, they don't. I really enjoyed talking to him. And it was good of him to let me borrow the letters. Thank you for asking. I wanted to ask, but didn't want to pressure them," Jonathan admitted.

"I didn't see how you were going to get anything out of those letters without being able to study them for a while. It's amazing that the documents have held up so well. Luckily, Grace knows a lot about antiques. I guess she knew that they needed special handling and found out what to do."

"Yes, she did a good job with that. I can't wait to see what I'll find. If the letters really were written by a woman left on the island, they might provide some conclusive evidence—one way or the other."

"About angelic visitors, you mean?" Tess asked.

"About any visitors at all," Jonathan said. "Digger doesn't seem to think the Wampanoag boats could have made it out to the island in the winter. He thinks the water was too rough."

Tess nodded. "I did hear him say that. But he has his own ideas about what happened. So I guess you would have to consult with an expert on the Wampanoag in order to confirm that."

"That's just what I was thinking," Jonathan agreed. "I'm just entertaining possibilities, Tess. My mind isn't made up yet," he promised her. "Until I read the letters, I don't know what they'll say."

"And you don't know what Claire North will say either, speaking of possibilities," she added. "You didn't even know about that wrinkle in the story."

He didn't answer for a moment. She knew that this lead was the wildest and most unbelievable yet and wondered if Jonathan would even bother interviewing Claire. Or just write off the whole idea as an exaggeration of a partly senile, old man.

"Okay, it's another avenue to explore," he conceded. "But I've been living under the same roof as Claire North for almost a week now. I think I'd notice if she had . . . superpowers."

Tess wrinkled her nose. "He didn't say she was flying around in a cape and boots and catching bank robbers."

"She'd wear an apron and boots," Jonathan corrected her. "And go after folks who are bad cooks, or insisted on eating take-out food."

Tess laughed at his description as they reached the sidewalk. The treacherous path was behind them. But as they proceeded down the street toward his car, Jonathan didn't let go of her hand. Which was fine with her.

"I don't know, Tess. Maybe I'll read these letters and interview Claire and I'll believe in angelic visitors, too. You never know. Anything is possible," he said finally. He smiled at her, the corner of his mouth turned up. "Happy now?"

She thought about his question a moment. "Yes . . . I am happy."

They stood face-to-face, so close that the puffs of frosty air from their breath mingled. He stared into her eyes for a long moment and didn't speak. She thought he was going to kiss her and could hardly breathe. Instead he said, "Would you like to get a bite to eat? We could go somewhere nice. Somewhere very un–Clam Box?"

"Are you asking me on a date? I mean, a real date?"

Jonathan looked like he wanted to laugh, but didn't. "Well . . . yes, I guess I am. Is that okay? I mean, you don't have a boyfriend stashed away somewhere, do you?"

She opened her big leather bag and looked inside. "Nope, no boyfriend in there. I don't have one stashed anywhere, actually. And I'd love to have dinner with you—someplace very un–Clam Box. But I can't tonight. I have to get home. My folks are going out, and I have to watch my brother."

"Oh, okay." Jonathan looked disappointed. "Maybe some other time then? Soon," he added.

"Yes. Definitely. Anytime," she said.

"Can I give you a ride home at least?"

"No, thanks. I'm going to walk. I need the exercise . . . If you talk to Claire tonight, let me know. I'm curious to hear how that goes."

"Don't worry, you'll be the first to know what she tells me."

"Good. I can hardly wait." Then on sheer impulse, she put her hand on his shoulder, leaned up on tiptoe, and kissed him on the cheek. His skin was smooth and very cold. As she stepped back she saw his dark eyes light up with surprise.

"I've got to go," she said quietly. "See you."

"Bye, Tess." He waved and watched her walk up the street.

She felt so happy, she could have been walking on air. But it was more than just that giddiness you feel when you meet someone you're attracted to. She felt that she and Jonathan had shared an adventure tonight, like a team of investigators on a case. A case of historical investigation, she amended. She was starting to feel in sync with him in so many ways, the way they reasoned things out and laughed at each other's jokes, even the way they walked together, in rhythm with each other's steps.

They were not completely alike, she knew. But their differences seemed to complement each other.

At first she had thought it was just their common interest in history that made it easy to be with him. But now she felt it was more. Much more. She was as eager to know where this relationship would go as she was to find out what was in Digger's letters.

CHAPTER EIGHT

~⋆~

RIDAY NIGHT'S DINNER AT THE INN HAD BEEN DELICIOUS AS usual, Adele thought. Claire had outdone herself with a salad of mixed greens, chilled beets, and goat cheese, followed by a scrumptious entree of roast salmon with dill sauce, green beans, and wild rice mixed with mushrooms.

It had been a full table, too, with Claire, Liza, and Liza's boyfriend, Daniel Merritt, a carpenter and all-around handyman, who did all the repairs and renovations on the inn. Then there was Jonathan, the history student, of course. He seemed in particularly good spirits, telling them more about his research but also asking the others a lot of questions about living on the island. Especially Claire, who had lived there all her life and had ancestors who went back to Cape Light's founders.

Adele was grateful for the lively conversation. It distracted her from the worries that preyed upon her mind. She had seen little of her family since Tuesday, hoping that Sam would be able to work things out with Molly and Joe. So she had waited, mostly staying around the inn, often finding herself helping Claire with the cooking or some other task that went faster with two sets of hands and some diverting conversation.

After dinner, Jonathan offered to help Claire clean up, so that Liza and Daniel could make it up to Newburyport in time for a film they wanted to see. Claire and Jonathan shooed Liza out of the kitchen, and Adele went into the front sitting room and took out her knitting, as she had most other nights since coming here. She knew Claire would arrive a short time later, with her own knitting and a tray bearing a teapot and homemade cake or cookies.

Adele wasn't sure she would have remained on the island this long if she had not been at the inn, enjoying Claire and Liza's relaxing company so much. It was such a peaceful, gracious place, a safe haven from the turmoil in her family, a touchstone for her troubled heart.

She took out her knitting and began to stitch. She was making a little hat for her great-granddaughter, Lily. A pink cap with purple trim. It was a small, simple project, but she hoped she would be done in time to give it to Lily before she left town.

Now, as she knit, her troubled thoughts returned. She had to face it. She had come with good intentions, but she hadn't thought this peace-making mission through. Maybe she was just too old for the job of smoothing these troubled waters.

Sam had stopped by the inn late that afternoon. He tried to make light of the situation, but there was no progress with his father, and it sounded as if things between him and Molly had gone from bad to worse.

That's when Adele told him, "You've tried your best, dear, but it's time for me to go. I'm doing more harm here than good."

"Don't give up yet, Grandma. It's just that Molly's stubborn. She's always been that way. But this is like a chess game. If we can just move Queen Molly out of the way, I can get to Joe."

Adele smiled at his analogy. "When did you start playing chess, Sam?"

"My son Darrell taught me. I can't win a match off him, but luckily, I still hold my own on the basketball court."

"Good for you," Adele said with a laugh. "I wish I could see those boys and Lily before I go."

"What do you mean? Of course you can't go until you spend some time with us. The kids have been asking me all week when you were coming. How about Sunday? We can meet at church and you can spend the day with us. We're lighting the Advent candle this week at the service, and we're going to decorate our tree in the afternoon," he added.

Every Sunday of Advent, the four weeks just before Christmas, a special candle was lit on the altar to honor the days leading up to the birth of the Savior. Each week a different family was chosen from the congregation to light the candle and say the prayers. It was an honor, and Adele wanted to see her grandson and his family perform the little ceremony.

"Of course I'll come. I'll be there front and center," she promised. Her drive home could wait until Monday.

After Sam left, Adele felt a wave of melancholy. She was excited to visit with Sam's family but wished she could see Molly's girls, too, before she left. Visits to Vermont from Molly and her crew were far and few between. None of Joe's other children—Jim, Eric, Glen, and Laurie—lived in New England now, though Laurie and her twins were coming up from Florida for Christmas. *I will miss seeing them all,* Adele reflected.

She felt a sudden sharp pain clutch her heart. She had imagined their Christmas gathering so clearly—the sights, the sounds, the cheerful conversations and laughter. The simple but inexplicable warmth of her family gathered around, like a beautiful, warm blanket.

She felt as if the comforting feeling had been yanked away and she now stood stunned and sad, chilled and alone. That was the problem with expectations, with hoping and praying for something so hard. Prayers are not answered in our time, but in God's time. She knew that. But it was always a hard lesson to be reminded of. She had no choice but to accept it. Accept that she had tried and failed. It was simply not to be. Not this Christmas, anyway.

Adele heard someone coming down the entry hall, and Claire appeared in the doorway with her tray full of tea things and her knitting tote over one arm.

"You've already gotten started, I see." Claire set down the tray on the low table and took her favorite seat in the wing-backed chair near the fire.

"I didn't get too far. Just sitting here thinking, mostly," Adele admitted.

"That's going to be a sweet little hat. For one of your great-grandchildren?" Claire guessed.

"Yes, for Sam's little girl, Lily. I hope I can finish it by the weekend. I'm going to visit them on Sunday. They've invited me over for dinner and to help decorate their tree."

Adele had only hinted at the real reason for this visit and had yet to tell Claire the full story. Though Claire had probably overheard something of the conversation when Joe had visited on Tuesday morning and Sam has come to see her here today. Something about Claire's sympathetic expression and calm blue eyes suggested she had a good idea by now of what was going on with the Morgan clan.

Claire had never been one to pry or ask too many questions. A wonderful quality, Adele thought, and a great relief.

"That sounds like a perfect Sunday afternoon to me. Liza and I need to decorate the tree this weekend, too. She and Daniel picked out a tall one this year." She glanced over at the Christmas tree that stood in a stand in the corner of the sitting room.

It was tall, Adele saw, and beautifully shaped with long swooping boughs in perfect proportion. Decorating had started on the rest of the room, too, with a pine garland draped around the hearth and Christmas decorations, most of them antique, set about the room. Adele noticed an old snow globe made of heavy glass, a set of three tall nutcrackers, and a golden Glockenspiel.

"Perhaps we can enlist some helpful guests to add the finishing touches," Claire said.

"I'll help you if I can," Adele replied happily. "I won't be putting up a tree this year for myself. I might as well help everyone I can down here."

Claire checked the teapot then poured them both cups of steaming herbal tea. Adele had the feeling she was going to ask a question now.

But before any words were exchanged, Jonathan appeared in the doorway. "Everything's done in the kitchen, Claire. I turned on the dishwasher. I hope that was all right?"

"That's just fine, Jonathan. I appreciate your help. We never put our guests to work. I hope I haven't given you the wrong idea."

"Not at all. I wanted to help." He did want to help her, since Liza had to leave and Claire was left with the whole job of cleaning up. After she had cooked such a fabulous meal, too.

But he had also wanted more time alone with Claire to ask about her heritage. She had answered all his questions, but somehow, he still hadn't learned much about her. Claire North had a real talent for deflecting attention and preserving her privacy. He had finally given up on drawing her out, but he had learned more about the history of the settlers and had enjoyed talking to her.

"Come in and sit with us a minute, have a cup of tea," Claire urged him.

"The fire's just right and these are excellent cookies," Adele added, offering him the plate of large, freshly baked chocolate chip cookies. Golden around the edges and chewy looking, just the way he liked them. Jonathan could not resist.

"Thanks. Don't mind if I do." He took a seat in an armchair and helped himself to the tea and confections.

"Claire's looking for more volunteers this weekend to help decorate the tree," Adele told him. "But perhaps you're not staying that long?"

"I'll still be here."

"I'm glad of that, but you don't have to help if you're busy. Only if you want to," Claire said, taking out her own knitting.

Jonathan didn't answer. It had been a long time since he had decorated a Christmas tree. He could hardly remember the last time.

"How long do you think it will take to finish your research?" Adele asked. "I don't think you mentioned that at dinner."

"Hard to say. It's going well, but will probably take a few more weeks."

Claire paused in her work and examined the stitches. "Will you be with us for the holidays? Or take a break and come back?"

"I'm not sure. I might go back to Boston for a few days," he said. "I might go back just to do a little work in the school library . . . Can I stay over Christmas if I need to?"

"Of course you can. We'd love to have you. It will be a quiet day here. Just myself, Liza, and Daniel for dinner. Audrey and Rob Gilroy, who run the goat farm next door, might come, too."

"Sounds nice. But I don't want to intrude on your private dinner. I used to love Christmas when I was a kid. Now, though, it's just another day for me." That wasn't entirely true, he knew. It did matter to him. Or it would—if he had a close family, or even close friends, to celebrate with.

Claire looked genuinely distressed. "Christmas isn't just another day," she gently corrected him. "Does your family live far from here? Is that why you don't go see them?"

"Oh no, they're right in Boston." There wasn't that kind of distance between them. Just the emotional kind, which was the hardest to bridge. "I don't have a big family. I'm an only child and my mother passed away when I was seven. It's always been just me and my father . . . until he got married a few years ago to Gael," he added. "They met at his firm. She's very nice. Has two little girls, so I have these cute stepsisters. They're all going skiing in Utah for Christmas. My dad asked me to come but I'd rather just work. . . . I may not even be done here with my research on the island."

Claire nodded. He could tell she was hearing the story that was written between the lines.

"I never took to skiing much myself, either," Adele said. "Everyone in Vermont where I live is just crazy about it. I did enjoy the cross-country style . . . What does your father do for a living, Jonathan? If you don't mind me asking."

"He's an attorney. He runs a big firm that was founded by my grandfather. The plan was that I would follow him into the firm when he retired. The problem was, I didn't like law school. I tried it for a year, but it wasn't for me."

Claire nodded, efficiently finishing off another row of her knitting. "You love history, no question. It's a blessing in life to find something you love and have a talent for doing. A great blessing."

Jonathan smiled, feeling she really understood something very important, something essential to finding a real sense of purpose and satisfaction in life.

"That's exactly right. I could have pushed myself through four years and passed the bar, but I knew I would have been miserable for the rest of my life. I knew it wouldn't be good for me, and it probably wouldn't have been good for the firm, either."

"Sounds like you made the right choice," Adele said. "It must have been hard to tell your father."

"Yes, it was. He's still angry at me, though he tries to act as if he's not." The hardest part, Jonathan thought, was knowing that his father would never feel truly proud of him, no matter what academic heights he reached. Academia and scholarship were not on his father's yardstick of success.

After that the women fell silent. The only sounds in the room were the clicking of knitting needles and the yellow flames crackling in the hearth. The smell of the fire mixed with the fresh scent of pine was deeply relaxing. Jonathan suddenly realized that he had been talking so openly with Claire and Adele, though it was not at all his way. But he did feel comfortable and somehow very safe here. He took another cookie and more tea.

"Perhaps someday your father will come to see how happy and fulfilled you are in your work," Claire said finally. "That seems to me all a parent could want for a child."

"I hope so. I just wish that in the meantime, I didn't feel as if he was so disappointed. But there's not too much I can do about that."

"No, there isn't. Have you tried talking to him about how you feel?" Claire added.

"When I quit law school I tried to talk to my dad about it, but he was too mad at me to even listen. And now . . . Well, I sort of gave up."

"I'm sorry to hear that," Claire said. "You seem too young to give up on anyone."

Jonathan didn't know what to say. "I haven't given up on him exactly. But he doesn't understand what I do, or what's important to me. I'm not sure he ever will. Maybe when I finish my doctorate and find a position at a good university and get a few papers published . . . maybe he'll get it then."

"That's a lot of maybes," Adele observed.

Jonathan had to laugh. "Yes, it is."

"Do you mean you need to wait until you're a success in your field before you can work things out with him, is that it?" Claire asked.

"Yes, I guess so."

Adele looked over at him, seeming surprised. "But you're already a success, Jonathan."

"She's right," Claire said gently. "And I like to think that all of us are always good enough to make peace. It's one thing we don't need a degree for, thank the Lord. Maybe it's just a matter of it being the right time. All things in their time."

"I take your point," Jonathan said with a smile.

It was surprising to him that he didn't mind this discussion at all. He rarely talked about his father, and Claire was practically a stranger. But there was something about this cozy room and the fire and her calming presence that had drawn him out. And given him something to think about.

Now it was time to go upstairs and do some more work before he turned in for the night. He was eager to get a start on Digger Hegman's letters.

"Thanks for the tea," he said, coming to his feet. "This was a very nice break. But I have to go up and get back to work."

Claire smiled at him. "You do work very hard. I hope you'll get out and see more of the island before you go. It's an unusual place, and you might find the answers to some of your questions here."

Jonathan wasn't sure how studying the landscape would help him, but it might give him a deeper understanding of the experience of being quarantined here. And it was a beautiful place that he had not seen enough of.

"I'll try to do that, Claire," he promised. He said good night again and left the ladies.

As he walked up to his room, he felt calmer and even encouraged about his work here. Had his talk with Claire North done all that? She did have a peaceful, understanding presence. Was that a trait passed down from her ancestors, or just her personality?

Another question he might not ever answer. But he did want to talk to Tess and tell her he had at least tried.

He pulled out his phone and checked the time. It wasn't too late to send Tess a text. She had told him to report in right away if he talked to Claire.

Tess—Asked Claire about her heritage tonight. I didn't learn too much. But we had a good talk anyway.

He sat and thought a moment. Then typed some more:

Are you free tomorrow? Can you drive around the island with me? Claire thinks a tour will answer some of my questions.

Then he sat and waited. He got worried when ten minutes passed and she didn't answer, but twenty minutes later his phone buzzed, signaling a message:

Clam Box, all day :(How about Sunday?

His heart fell when he read the first line. Then he quickly recovered and answered her:

Come to the inn at 12. I'll bring some lunch and you can show me the sights. :)

Sunday suddenly seemed a long time to wait, even though he had plenty to focus on between now and then. He hoped the weather would be mild enough to walk a lot and eat a picnic lunch. He was sure that Claire wouldn't mind packing something delicious for them. But it would be good to go back to the cliffs and take a long walk along the shore. Especially with Tess.

ADELE LOVED THE IDEA OF GOING TO CHURCH WITH SAM AND HIS family but also felt a little nervous. She worried what might happen if they met up with Molly and Matt. Or Joe and Marie. She didn't want poor Sam to stick his neck out any further for her than he already had. She would be leaving town tomorrow. He had to stay and face the music.

But when she saw Sam's family pull up at the inn in their huge SUV, her heart skipped a beat. She was dressed and ready, with her coat and gloves on, standing by the inn's front door. Sam hopped out and helped her down the steps. Jessica was waiting outside the vehicle and gave her a big hug. "Hello, Grandma Addie. You look wonderful."

"So do you, dear, pretty as ever." Jessica dismissed the compliment with a self-effacing smile, but it was no lie. She had to be over forty but looked as fresh and pretty as the day Sam brought his bride-to-be up to Vermont to meet her.

"Here she is, kids. Here's your great-grandma," Jessica announced as she helped Adele into the front seat.

The three children greeted her, their manners perfect. "Hello, Grandma Addie," Darrell said politely. "It's nice to see you again."

He was a young man now, talking with a deep voice. Sam and Jessica had adopted Darrell when they were convinced they could never have children of their own. They could not have loved him more, and he had grown into a fine young man, making them very proud with his excellent grades and as the captain of his varsity lacrosse team.

"It's so good to see you, Darrell," Adele said. "My, how you've grown since the summer. I bet you're as tall as your father now."

"Almost," Sam said, getting back behind the wheel.

"Are you going to come home with us all day?" Lily asked, leaning over the front seat. "Do you want to see my room?"

"We're going to decorate our Christmas tree," Tyler said. He was seven now and tall for his age. He had Jessica's curly hair and Sam's big blue eyes.

"Yes, I know. I'm going to help you," Adele said happily. "Right after church. We'll all go back to your house and you can show me everything."

Lily seemed particularly pleased by the answer. "Okay," she said, sitting back in her seat, "but that will take a long time."

"We'll have plenty of time," Adele replied. "Don't worry."

How she wished she did have more time with these children. They were growing so fast. They had changed considerably from their last visit this past summer. Especially the boys, who had both grown taller.

A short time later, Sam held her arm as they all filed into church. A row near the front had been saved for their family because they were lighting the Advent candle.

Adele had just gotten settled in when Reverend Ben walked over. "Good morning, folks. Ready to light the candle?"

"We all know our parts, Reverend. We rehearsed at home," Jessica said.

"Very good. I'm sure it will go fine. Hello, Adele. Are you going up with the family this morning?"

Adele hadn't even thought of that. Before she could answer, Jessica said, "Why don't you, Grandma? It will be fun."

Adele was taken by surprise. "I don't know. I might not do so well on those steps. I didn't bring my cane."

"You'll be fine. Darrell and I will help you," Sam said.

Adele didn't know what to say. Part of her thought it would be nice, probably the last time she would ever light an Advent candle.

The other part warned her that Joe and Molly would be annoyed with Sam as soon as they saw her sitting here. She didn't need to add fuel to the fire.

"I don't think so. Thank you anyway. I'd prefer to watch all of you. I'll enjoy that much more," she said honestly.

They finally gave in, though Adele caught a certain look in Sam's eye. She guessed that he knew why she was avoiding the spotlight today.

As they waited for the service to begin, Adele spent the time catching up with the children, asking questions about school and their sports teams. The choir soon walked in and sang the opening hymn. Then Sam and his family lit the candle, each taking a turn with the parts of the prayers. Adele watched in delight, wishing she had a camera.

Sometimes it was better to just sit quietly and soak it all in. Take mind pictures, she called them. She was swept back in time to a Sunday long ago at this very church, when her own family stood there. Joe and Kevin had been a bit younger than Sam's boys. Joe was the oldest and always big and strong. He had lifted his brother up to light the candle when Kevin struggled. A tear came to her eye, remembering.

The ceremony concluded and they were soon seated beside her again as the service continued. Last week she had felt isolated and solitary, alone in the back row. But she felt very different here this morning as her voice melded with those of her family, reciting prayers aloud or joining in a hymn. She felt connected to her loved ones, like pearls on a string.

At the end of the service, Adele rose and gathered her things. She followed her family out of the row and into the flow of congregants leaving the sanctuary.

"Would you like to say hello to Reverend Ben?" Jessica asked her.

"Yes, I would," Adele replied. Her real reason, though, was that she wanted to say good-bye. She had not told anyone in her family about her private chat with the reverend last week.

The center aisle became a little crowded as most of the congregants lined up to greet Reverend Ben on their way out of the sanctuary. Adele was feeling a bit jostled when her great-grandson Darrell took her arm. "Let me help you, Grandma Addie."

Adele tilted her head to look up at him. Darrell didn't resemble either of his adoptive parents physically, but in his temperament he so reminded her of Sam, it was uncanny.

"Thank you, Darrell. What a young gentleman you are. Just like your father—" Adele was about to go further with her compliment when she stopped in her tracks. Her son Joe suddenly stood before her, filling her vision.

"Hello, Mom. I didn't know you were still in town."

How would you? You haven't come to see me or called the inn since Tuesday. But of course, she couldn't say that.

She didn't know what to say.

"Joe . . . Marie . . ." Adele glanced at her daughter-in-law standing beside Joe, just a step behind him.

Poor Marie, she looked nervous and confused about what to do: greet her mother-in-law as she normally would and have Joe think she was disloyal? Or stand there awkwardly, as if they were strangers?

A moment later, she came toward Adele and gave her a quick kiss on the cheek. "Hello, Adele. Did you like the service? Didn't the kids do a great job with the candle lighting?"

"It was lovely. I was so happy to be here," Adele said honestly. She looked at her son. "Remember when we lit the candles, when you and Kevin were—"

"Of course I remember," he cut her off quickly. "Do you think talking about the past is going to change my mind?"

Adele hadn't meant that, had she? Now he had her all confused.

Marie looked concerned and touched his shoulder. "Joe, calm down. You're still in church," she reminded him.

Sam had been talking with friends at the end of the line and following the family at a distance. Now he suddenly appeared beside his grandmother. "Grandma is spending the day at our house. She's leaving for Vermont tomorrow," he told his parents.

"Oh . . . how nice." Marie nodded, trying to make things seem normal again, though there was little hope of that.

Joe didn't say anything. He frowned, making a big crease between his eyebrows the way he had done since childhood. His father would always ask if he was confused about something when he did that.

"I'm not confused, I'm just thinking," he would practically shout back at him.

At least he was thinking about her departure, Adele realized.

"Good-bye, Joe. Good-bye, Marie. You have a good Christmas," Adele said sincerely.

If Joe had any doubts, she wanted him to know that she had given up her quest. She was waving a white flag of surrender.

"Oh, I'm sure we'll speak to you before then," Marie said quickly. She looked at her husband.

"I'll call you, Mom. Watch your driving," Joe said.

Adele nodded. She hadn't even expected that much.

Sam looked upset. "Is that all you have to say to Grandma? Watch your driving. I'll give you a call?"

"Sam . . ." Jessica touched his arm. "We'd better keep moving. We're holding up the line."

But everyone on the line had walked around them by now. There were few people left in the sanctuary, and Reverend Ben walked back inside and came toward them.

"Good morning. Nice to see everyone here today." He glanced around the circle. His eyes settled on Adele. "So you stayed through the week. Enjoying your visit?"

His question was mundane enough, though Adele caught his real meaning. She looked at Joe and could see his cheeks had flushed. At least he had the decency to be a little embarrassed about his uncharitable behavior in front of his minister.

"I enjoyed the service today and seeing Sam and his family light the candles," she said honestly. "I'm going to visit with them today and go back to Vermont tomorrow."

Reverend Ben looked concerned about that reply. Adele guessed he had picked up on the note of resignation in her tone.

"Well . . . I'm glad you could be here today. You have a great day with your family and a safe trip. Please stay in touch. I would love to hear from you."

He leaned over and gave her a quick, gentle hug.

"Thank you, Reverend. I will do that," she promised.

Reverend Ben turned his attention to Joe and Marie, speaking briefly with them and shaking Joe's hand. Joe seemed suddenly docile and deflated in the presence of his minister. He glanced over his shoulder and briefly waved as he and Marie left the sanctuary.

"I'm sorry about Dad," Sam said quietly. "I just don't know how to get through to him."

Adele patted her grandson's hand. "Please don't blame yourself, Sam. And please don't stay mad at him or Molly. That won't help. I don't think either of us can do any more right now." She glanced around the quiet sanctuary, the soft light filtering through the stained glass windows and the white candles in the pine wreath on the altar still flickering.

"Maybe I was overreaching to think I could come down here and create some sort of family miracle. We can only give this over to God now and pray. Only He can truly change your father's heart."

WHEN TESS ARRIVED AT THE INN SUNDAY AFTERNOON, JONATHAN WAS on the porch waiting for her. He was holding a map of the island, she noticed, and also had a backpack and a picnic basket.

"Right on time," he greeted her. "And we have a great day for our exploration."

Tess had to smile. The island was only a few miles long and a few miles wide. Jonathan was as excited as someone about to explore the Amazon Rainforest. It was sort of cute, she thought.

"Yes, the weather is cooperating. Where is all that snow they keep talking about?"

It seemed to Tess that almost every other day this week the weather forecasts had warned of a sizeable snowfall. But so far, all their area had seen were a few mild flurries, with soft, fluffy snow that quickly melted.

"I don't know. I'm just glad it's not here yet." Jonathan met her at his car, then opened the doors and put in their belongings. "Everyone around here is worried about having a white Christmas. Looks like they might be disappointed this year."

"I wouldn't go that far. You know what they say about weather in New England. If you don't like it, just wait twenty minutes."

"Right. Could be a new state motto," he agreed, making her smile. "Let's hope it doesn't apply today."

They fastened their seat belts, circled out the drive, and were off. "Which way should I go?" Jonathan asked as they reached the road.

Tess shrugged. "Which way do you want to go?"

He turned to her, looking surprised. "Didn't I tell you? You're the official guide today. I'm going to rely on you entirely to give me the full tour of Angel Island."

"Really? I'm honored. In that case, I think you should turn right. We'll be traveling through the island's charming village center," she added in her best tour guide voice, "where passengers can disembark for refreshments and souvenirs."

"I think Claire has packed enough refreshments for an entire busload of passengers." Jonathan glanced over his shoulder at the large picnic basket. "But she was short on water bottles. I guess we can stop up there."

"That's the Angel Island General Store, where Walter and Marion Doyle will be happy to help us." Tess turned to him and grinned. "Don't I need a clipboard and a microphone?"

"Don't worry, you're doing great." He was watching the road, but she could see he was smiling. A view of the ocean was visible on the left side of the road, with the countryside on the other. They were passing the Gilroy Farm, and Tess spotted the goats prancing around in the meadow, and a big shaggy dog chasing after them.

"Does this bus brake for goat cheese?" she asked.

"Normally, yes. But I think we have plenty of that, too. Liza Martin is best pals with Audrey Gilroy. I've been eating goat cheese three times a day, not that I'm complaining. I do love the stuff."

"Me, too," Tess said. "Maybe I'll pick some up on our way back. My mom makes great omelets with it on Sunday mornings. I love the lavender soaps and bouquets that Audrey sells, too. And the fudge." She turned to him. "I'm making myself hungry. When are we breaking into that picnic basket?"

She eyed the basket again. She had tasted Claire North's legendary cooking before. Now she could just imagine what was inside. It was a far cry from Clam Box takeout, she had no doubt.

"You're the boss. I'm just the driver. You decide."

Tess had to smile at his easygoing attitude. "Okay, I will. First stop, General Store. We'll take it from there."

They rounded the last bend in the road and found themselves in the island's village center. Jonathan slowed the car over the cobblestones that lined the square and quickly found a parking spot. "Don't we need a little narration here?" he asked as they got out of the car.

"Right, I'm forgetting my duties. Sorry." She turned and gestured with her hands. "Here we are in the island's scenic village center. A mecca of commerce." Jonathan winced, but she continued, trying not to laugh. "The General Store is the largest and most prominent, not to mention thriving, business here. But just across the way you can see Angel Island's medical clinic, open for twenty-four-hour care. And the much more cheerful sight of Daisy Winkler's tearoom and lending library," she added, pointing out the pale yellow cottage with the violet door.

"That is a cheerful sight. I noticed it when I was bike riding. Does someone really live there?"

"Daisy Winkler, who else?" Tess asked. "Come on, maybe she's there. We can say hello . . . Do you want to?"

"Sure, I'd love to meet the elf."

Tess arched one eyebrow. "Daisy is not an elf," she told him with mock-severity. "But I can see why her house would make you think that. And she is kind of amazing."

They walked across the square to the cottage, and Jonathan opened the rickety gate in the picket fence.

"It doesn't look like the shop is open," he said.

But before Tess could answer, she heard another voice. "Yoo-hoo! Young people . . . Don't rush off . . . I'm coming."

She turned to see Daisy Winkler, dressed in one of her long skirts and shawls, tramping through the frozen vegetation of her front yard garden.

"Hello, Daisy. I'm glad you're here. This is Jonathan Butler. I'm showing him around the island today."

Daisy greeted Tess with a wide smile. "What a beautiful day for a tour, Tess. How nice to meet you," Daisy added, extending her hand to Jonathan. Her hands were covered in dark blue velvet gloves that reached up to her elbows, Tess noticed. The gloves, hardly standard gardening wear, seemed to be Daisy's acknowledgment of the winter weather, along with a fluffy lavender scarf. "And where have you come from?"

Her tone and manner were very serious, as if she were expecting him to say he was from some other galaxy.

"Um . . . just Boston. I'm a student there," he added.

Daisy nodded with a knowing expression. "We are all students, Jonathan. When you understand that, your life will open up in a much richer way . . . like a flock of butterflies."

Jonathan nodded but did not reply.

"I can open the shop for you," Daisy offered with a hopeful expression.

"That's all right, Daisy," Tess said. "We haven't really gotten started yet. We have a lot of ground to cover."

"That's nice of you to offer," Jonathan added politely.

"I would love to visit your shop sometime. Maybe another day."

Daisy seemed satisfied and nodded. "Another day it will be then. In the meantime, I have a poem for you . . . yes, I do . . . It's in here, somewhere . . ." She reached into her skirt and a handful of miscellaneous treasures appeared in her velvet-covered palm. Tess and Jonathan waited as she sifted through them—a ceramic button painted with a flower, a piece of hard candy, a lace-edged hanky, two hairpins, a rubber band, a large old-fashioned skeleton key, and finally, a balled-up scrap of paper. She picked that out like a prize.

"Here it is. I knew I had it." She presented it very formally to Jonathan. "This is for you. I found it this morning and knew it was for someone . . . a friend whom I hadn't yet met," she added.

Jonathan looked down at the ball of paper, which was now in his outstretched hand. "Well . . . thanks very much. I'm sure I'll enjoy it."

"I am sure, too."

Daisy headed into her shop. Tess and Jonathan headed back across the square toward the General Store. "So that was Daisy Winkler," Jonathan said finally. "Does she get much business there?"

"More than you would think. Sooner or later, everyone who visits the island stops in there. And I've heard that her shop is listed in some real tours of the area. Honest," Tess said, glancing back over her shoulder.

"Oh, I believe you." Jonathan laughed. "And everyone who visits gets their own poem?"

"No, not at all. That means you're special," she told him, knowing it was true.

"Well, then I'm honored, I guess. Let's see what it says." He stopped in front of the store to unfold the scrap of paper and read it aloud.

"I started early—Took my Dog—
And visited the Sea—
The Mermaids in the Basement
Came out to look at me—"

Jonathan stopped reading and looked at Tess. "Emily Dickinson," he said, "one my favorites."

"Mine, too," Tess said, pleased that he knew the poem. "Is that all she gave you?"

He nodded, turning the scrap over. "That's it . . . Isn't it enough?" A smile broke out across his handsome face, and she had to smile back.

"I think so. There's plenty there to think about, the way there always is in a great poem."

They had not started off early, or brought a dog, but Tess still felt the poetic fragment perfectly fit their outing. The sea was all around them today, and perhaps Jonathan would meet up with something as unlikely and fanciful as a mermaid—or at least open his mind to the endless possibilities.

They walked into the General Store, and Tess's senses were immediately filled with the varied sights and scents of the place. The store carried everything from canned corn to car oil, fresh pickles to fishing line, baby wipes to wiper blades, and everything in between. The wooden floors gave off a slightly musty scent, mingled with the smell of fruits and vegetables, hot coffee, and the cooked foods at the deli counter.

Marion Doyle, who ran the store with her husband, Walter, stood in her usual spot at the register, sorting a bundle of mail into the rows of pigeonhole boxes behind her. The store was also the island's only post office and Marion, the official postmistress.

"Hello, Tess. What brings you around today?" Marion greeted her. "Working up at the inn?"

"Just being a tourist. I'm showing my friend Jonathan the sights," she added.

Jonathan had found the cold drink case and came to the counter with several bottles of water, where Tess introduced him to Marion.

"Nice to meet you," Jonathan said. "You have quite a store here. I could browse all day."

Marion seemed pleased with that compliment as she rang up the water. "We're here to supply the necessities . . . and then some."

"I can see that. You do very well on the 'then some,'" he added, making her smile.

"We try our best. Enjoy your day."

Tess and Jonathan thanked her, then headed outside again. "I didn't know you worked at the inn, too. How many jobs do you have in this town?"

Tess laughed. "I like variety. It's all good experience," she added. "I only work at the inn if Liza is putting on a wedding or a big party. Or if she has a lot of guests and is shorthanded. In the summertime, mostly."

"Do you work part-time when you're at school, too?"

Tess shook her head. "No, only at home. I need all my spare time at school to study."

Jonathan smiled at her. "*All* your spare time? There's never an hour or two left for having fun or . . . going out on a date with someone?"

"That depends on which someone asks me out," she answered playfully.

"Oh, I see." He nodded, taking in the information. "Any special qualifications needed?"

"Of course," she answered tartly. "Let's see . . . the someone has to love history . . . be kind, generous . . . and despise the sight and smell of clam rolls almost as much I do."

"Hmm . . . I'll make note of all that. Not sure if I qualify," he said, pretending to write in an imaginary notebook. "But I could give it a try once we get back to Boston."

"Yes, you should. I think you'll have a good chance."

"That's encouraging." He smiled warmly at her. They were standing in the little stone-covered square right next to the fountain. The village center was near the top of a hill, affording a breathtaking, panoramic view of the sea. "Wait, I'd like to get a photo here," Jonathan said, taking out his camera.

"For your research?" Tess asked.

"Yes, and . . . just because it's so beautiful." He snapped one or two frames, then said, "Stand by that wall, and I'll take one of you."

Tess felt a little self-conscious at the request. She didn't like being in pictures and her hair was all messy and she didn't have on a trace of makeup. But it also seemed a very nice compliment and encouraging to think that Jonathan wanted a picture of her.

"All right, but only if we're in it together," she said.

Jonathan laughed. "Okay, I'll try. I hope my arms are long enough."

He stood next to her by the stone wall and put his arm around her shoulder, holding her close. Then he extended his other arm out as far as he could reach, pointing the camera at them.

"Okay, smile now," he said. Tess didn't need the reminder. She felt very happy in his embrace and was already smiling widely.

"I hope I got it. That could look really nice," he said, checking the shot on the camera's screen. "Yes, perfect."

He showed it to her, and she was surprised by what a good picture it was. They looked happy and relaxed—like a couple who had known each other a long time.

"Not bad," she agreed. "Will you e-mail me a copy?"

"Absolutely. When we get back to school . . . I'll send it with my application," he said. "A nice photo like this should help, don't you think?"

For a moment, Tess didn't understand what he meant, but then she laughed. He was talking about her screening process for dating.

"Yes, it will," she promised, glad to hear that he seemed to want to continue their relationship once they both left Cape Light.

They got back in Jonathan's car and started off again. "Where to now?" he asked.

"There's a little fishing village on the south side of the island you should see. Right down here," she said, showing him the map.

"Sounds good. Maybe we can find a place down there to have our picnic."

Tess was all in favor of that. It was already her usual lunchtime, and she felt hungry.

The fishing village was a bit farther off from the island center than Tess recalled, but the scenery along the way was worth it. A small wooden sign for Thompson's Bend appeared, stuck to a post in the main road, and she pointed it out to Jonathan.

"We made it. You can turn right there, at the sign," she told him. Jonathan made the turn onto a much narrower road, and the car instantly began bouncing around. "Cobblestone streets," Tess said. "It's a very old spot."

Tess directed him around a few more turns, down winding streets with evocative names, like Fish Bone and Teapot and Hasty Lane. The rustic old cottages matched the street names well, each property quite unique.

"This is a pretty place," Jonathan said, driving slowly as he looked around.

"It was once just a summer colony, a group of shacks where fishermen lived in the warmer months so they could go out on their boats more easily. Then their wives and children started coming here, and some families winterized their houses and stayed year-round. And some cottages were sold and became summer homes for people who live in the city."

"It would be wonderful to live in one of these someday, away from everything. It's so quiet here, you could really get some good thinking and writing done."

Tess was surprised at the direction of his thoughts. She had just assumed, for some reason, that Jonathan liked the city better than an out-of-the-way place like Cape Light or the island. She realized that she was glad he saw the beauty and value of a place like this and didn't think it was boring or too rough and unsophisticated.

"I have no idea where I'll want to live once I finish school," she told him. "But I'll always come back to the village and this island. I know I'll always love this place."

"It's easy to see why."

They drove over to the dock and spread out their picnic on a long wooden bench. "Let's see what Claire gave us." Jonathan seemed excited as he unpacked the basket, as if unwrapping some wonderful surprise package.

There was lobster bisque, packed in a thermos and steaming hot when he poured it into two matching mugs. Then two lobster rolls, stuffed with sweet lobster chunks on toasted rolls. There were cups of coleslaw, tomato and avocado salad, and thick slabs of chocolate cake for dessert. They dove into the feast as if neither had eaten for days. As Jonathan poured Tess a second cup of coffee from another tall thermos, she carefully licked some icing from her fingertips.

"All that food, it was so good," she said with a sigh. "I can't move."

"Neither can I," Jonathan agreed. "I think I need a nap."

Tess laughed. "If it was summertime, we could spread out a blanket and sleep off this feast on the beach. But I don't think it's quite the right weather for that."

"Good point," he said, covering a yawn with his hand.

"I think we should take a walk instead. That will wake us up."

He looked doubtful but said, "It's worth a try."

The beach near the dock was too short and rocky for a good walk, so they got back in Jonathan's car again. Tess directed them through some winding streets and then back onto the main road, where the ocean soon came into view again.

"This is a good place," she said a few minutes later. "There are a lot of paths along the road. You can park anywhere on the shoulder. And we're not far from the cliffs. You wanted to see them again, didn't you?"

"I do. Now that you mention it, this does look familiar. I guess I recognize this area from my bike ride," he added.

Jonathan had told Tess that he had ridden a bike here on one of his first days on the island. She was glad that he wanted to come back. She hadn't realized it before, but she had been looking forward to visiting the cliffs with him. It meant something to her, though she wasn't quite sure what.

They found a path through the dunes and walked down toward the water. The sun had already reached its zenith for the day and was starting its slow descent into the horizon. "This is the best time at the beach, any time of year," Tess said.

"Great minds think alike," he agreed with a grin. "I like the late afternoon at the beach best, too." They had walked across the sand and reached the shoreline, washed smooth and hard by the tide.

The sun sparkled on the blue water, and Tess cupped her hand over her eyes to look out at the sea. "Looks like low tide. We can make it all the way to the cliffs. It's not very far."

"Yes, I remember. It's easier walking down here, but don't get your shoes wet," he warned her.

"I'll be careful." Just as she said the words a fast wave rushed in. It was just about to wash over her when Jonathan grabbed her around the waist and lifted her off her feet.

They were suddenly very close. He was much stronger than he looked, she realized, and then her mind was filled with a million other thoughts about him.

The foamy seawater retreated, and Jonathan set her down again, out of the tide's reach.

"Thanks . . . you saved me. My sneakers, at least," she added.

His answering smile warmed her, almost as much as the sun.

"My pleasure. I couldn't have you walking around with soggy feet today on my account. It's still December."

Tess was having such a wonderful time, it was hard to remember that it wasn't the middle of summer. He took her hand and they continued, walking on higher ground.

"So, you never told me . . . have you read through Digger's letters?"

"I started working on them, but it's slow going," Jonathan replied. "The ink is faded and the handwriting is hard to make out. So far, I've only transcribed the first few paragraphs of what I think is the first letter. I have to make sure I don't miss a word or mistake any words. One inaccuracy could change the entire meaning of a sentence—or the whole letter."

"Very true," Tess agreed. "You know what Mark Twain said, 'The difference between the almost right word and the right word is really a large matter—it's the difference between the lightning bug—' "

" '—and the lightning,' " Jonathan finished. He glanced at her and smiled. "I will say that so far, the first letter is just about heartbreaking. Digger's ancestor, Mary Hegman, had been taken to the island with her three-month-old baby. It sounds like her husband, Ezekiel, wanted to go with them, even though he wasn't infected. But—you probably know this—the village council issued a proclamation that all fit, able-bodied men had to stay on the mainland, I assume, because so many had already died off."

"Exactly," Tess said. "Men were needed to hunt and fish and protect the community."

"So far in the letter, she's just telling him that she arrived safely and understands why he couldn't come with them."

"She must have been very brave," Tess said.

"I think she was. You can almost tell that from the very first words she wrote."

Tess was a little disappointed that Jonathan had not read more of the letters yet. She was eager to hear what they said. But of course, it would

167

be difficult and time-consuming to interpret the pages. She had seen the scrawled, faded script for herself, and was barely able to make out a word.

Would the letters reveal some startling bit of evidence about what happened on the island? Some clue to the true identity of the visitors who had helped the villagers quarantined there? Or would Mary Hegman's letters show that there never were any visitors and, as Jonathan proposed, that the legend was just a story that evolved to give a sad event an acceptable ending?

But before Tess could ask him more, the cliffs came into view, their silhouette golden against the stark blue sky. She stopped in her tracks and so did Jonathan, still holding her hand. "There they are. I'm always amazed by the sight," she admitted.

"It is pretty amazing," he agreed, "the way that entire chunk of stone looks so light. As if it could break off at any moment and fly away. It's totally . . . counterintuitive."

Tess totally agreed. She couldn't have said it better herself and didn't need to reply. They started off again, walking faster now. Finally they reached the cliffs and stared straight up.

Tess was tired and took a seat on top of a big flat rock that was still warm from the sun. A good thing, since the sun was going down faster now and the shadows growing longer.

She watched Jonathan amble around the base, viewing the rock formation from different angles and taking photos.

"How long do you think it took for the wind and water to carve away the stone like that?" Jonathan asked.

"That's a good question. I guess you could ask a geologist."

"Want to go up to the top? There's an awesome view."

"Can we get up there?"

"There's a path, but you need an official tour guide." She hopped down from the rock and took his hand again. "Follow me."

She led him to the path on a hillside beside the cliffs. Jonathan stood at the bottom, looking up. "You want us to climb all the way up there? Have you done this before?"

"Sure, lots of times." She actually had only done it once before but was eager to try again. "It's not as hard as it looks—and it's definitely worth it," she promised. When he still looked doubtful, she added, "I dare you."

He stared at her a second then said, "Okay, I dare you back." She started off first, with a burst of energy, but soon slowed down to a reasonable pace. The path was winding and steep, though not impossible to ascend. Tess was glad now that she was wearing sneakers. Jonathan had fallen a few yards behind her, and she glanced back to check on his progress.

"Are you all right back there? Too much sitting in reading rooms, Jonathan. You have to get into better shape if you want to do this sort of field research."

"Sad but true. I'd better get in shape to keep up with you."

Tess turned around and smiled. He looked fit enough to her. She'd just been teasing him. But that was something they could work on together, she thought.

Finally, she reached the summit. The very top of the rock formation was a flat, smooth space. Not so small that she was afraid of falling off, but not all that large, either. When Jonathan joined her, it seemed even smaller.

"So, was it worth a few sore muscles?" she asked.

"Absolutely. What a spectacular view! I feel like I'm sitting on a cloud," he said, staring down at the water and beach below. "But I wouldn't come up here on a windy day."

"Not without a parachute," she agreed.

He laughed and placed his hands on her shoulders. "A parachute is a great idea. Do you have one handy? We could ride down together and skip that long hike back down the hillside."

She turned to face him and found herself in his arms. "No . . . I don't. I guess I'm not that great a guide, after all."

A few wisps of her hair blew across her face, and he brushed them aside with his hand. When she saw him clearly again, he was smiling down at her, and she felt as though they were the only two people in the world.

"Don't say that. I think you're the perfect guide. I think you're just plain . . . perfect," he said quietly.

He dipped his head toward her and kissed her, softly at first and then deeper, holding her very close and tight.

Tess felt herself melting against him, his kiss feeling so exciting and new and at the same time so familiar and right. She had never felt this close to anyone before, as if they shared the same thoughts and feelings. The same way of seeing the entire world.

She wasn't sure how long their kiss went on, but when he slowly pulled back, her head was spinning. "Are you all right?" he asked quietly.

"A little breathless . . . but in a good way."

"Me, too," he admitted. He leaned forward and hugged her tight a moment. "Thanks for daring me to come up here, Tess. Thanks for a spectacular day."

Tess didn't think he had anything to thank her for. But it was sweet of him to say that.

Jonathan put his arm around her shoulder, and they gazed at the view a few more moments. Finally it seemed the right time to return to his car and go back to the inn.

"Well, shall we start back down? Ladies first, I guess," he said, returning to the top of the path they had taken.

"Don't worry, there's another way we can go, and we'll end up on the road, near the car."

Tess brought him to another path that led away from the cliff and the shoreline, over a few sandy dunes and up to the road. They still had to walk to his car, but it was much easier going than hiking back along the beach, especially since the tide had started to come in again and would have blocked their way.

"Oh, this is good. I'm glad you knew of this way, too," he said. Then after a moment or two, he stopped. "Wait a minute . . . you mean, we could have just driven the car over and walked out on those dunes to the top of the cliff?"

She nodded. "Yep, but it sort of ruins the fun. Anyone can go that way. Don't you want to blaze new trails?"

He stared at her a moment and she thought he was angry, feeling annoyed that she had made him work so hard. Then he leaned his head back and laughed. "Yes, I do. Promise me that when we come back here, you won't let me take the easy way."

"Okay, I promise," Tess said, feeling happy inside again that he was seeing her in his future.

They drove back to the inn without saying much. Tess felt pleasantly tired and exhilarated from their hike and from their entire afternoon.

"Would you like to come in and visit awhile?" he said when they reached the inn. "I'm sure Claire would make us some tea. Or I could make some for you."

"Thanks, but I have to get back home. I had a wonderful time today, Jonathan."

"So did I . . ." His voice trailed off as he stared into her eyes. "When will I see you again? Will you be at Lilac Hall tomorrow?"

"Yes, my hours start at ten. Look for me when you get there."

"I will . . . good-bye, Tess. See you." He leaned over and kissed her, quickly this time.

Tess touched his cheek and then got into her car. She had to take a moment to clear her head so she could drive.

She knew that part of her was still on the summit of the angel wing cliffs, with Jonathan's arms around her. Feeling as if they were floating on a cloud.

CHAPTER NINE

S AM DIDN'T PICK UP HIS CELL OR THE PHONE IN HIS SHOP ON
Monday morning, so Adele left a message.

"I'm just about to go, Sam. You told me to give you a call. I want to
thank you and Jessica again for such a beautiful day yesterday. Please
give the kids a big kiss for me. You must all come to see me very soon in
Vermont. You can go skiing. The boys would love that," she added.
"Okay, good-bye now, dear. I'll let you know when I get home."

Claire had already carried Adele's bags down from her room after
breakfast and stowed them in the trunk of Adele's Subaru. She was just
coming inside again and met Adele in the entry hall, near the big antique
coat tree and mirror. Adele checked that she had all the cold-weather
clothes she came with—her hat, gloves, and scarf—which had all come
in handy during her walks on the beach.

"Are you sure you can't stay another day or two? The Christmas Fair
committee will definitely miss you," Claire said.

Last week Adele had filled in some of her idle hours helping Claire and a group of other church members prepare for the annual Christmas Fair. Adele had enjoyed making the crafts that would be sold, and even more, catching up with some of her old friends, like Sophie Potter and Vera Plante. She and George had joined a church in Vermont, but it was not nearly the spiritual home that Reverend Ben's congregation had always been.

"I would love to stay longer, Claire, but I just heard another forecast this morning that a storm is on the way. I don't want to get stuck down here. I'd better take advantage of the good weather and get on the road while I can."

"I understand. I was just hoping I could tempt you to change your mind," Claire confessed. "And I was going to make your favorite for dinner tonight, crab cakes," she added.

"That's not fair," Adele said with a laugh. "You and Liza have spoiled me rotten this past week. I don't know how I'll ever put up with my own cooking again . . . and I'm fattening up like the proverbial Christmas goose," she added, making Claire smile. "That's another reason I have to go."

"We'll miss you, Adele. You must come back very soon and stay longer next time." Claire leaned over and gave her a hug.

"I'll try." Adele heard someone on the steps and turned to see Liza.

"Adele, are you leaving already? I'm glad I didn't miss you. I hope you had a good stay."

"It was perfect, dear. You've done wonders with this place. You're a born innkeeper. Your aunt and uncle would have been so proud. In fact, I'm sure they're up in heaven somewhere, just beaming."

"Thank you, Adele. It means a lot to me to hear you say that." She hugged Adele good-bye.

When Adele stepped back, Claire held out a basket covered with a blue-and-white checked cloth. Now where had that come from? She seemed to be a magician at times.

"A little something to tide you over on the road. It's a long trip, and the food at those road stops generally isn't very healthy."

"Or very edible," Liza added, more to the point.

"That's so thoughtful. I will enjoy this." Adele was sure of it. Though it would make her feel a little wistful, missing this place even more as she traveled homeward.

But she missed her own bed and her own snug little house, too, she reminded herself. Back to her place she must go. "Well, time to get my show on the road. Good-bye now . . ."

Claire and Liza walked out with her, and Claire helped her down the porch steps to her car and saw that she was safely inside with her seat belt secured.

"Now remember, if you feel tired at all, just pull over and rest. Will you give us a call when you get home, just so we know you got there safe and sound?"

Adele promised that she would and finally started the engine and pulled down the drive. She saw Claire and Liza in the rearview mirror, waving good-bye to her.

Adele drove down the main road, headed for the land bridge. She suddenly felt a little teary, all of her dashed hopes and failed plans gathering like dark clouds in her heart, though the sky above was clear and crystal blue.

Oh, God . . . I'm bringing home failure after all. I didn't expect that . . . But maybe I deserve it, ignoring this problem for so long . . .

But her heartfelt prayer was abruptly interrupted by an awful sound. Her little car hopped and swerved on the road and she quickly pulled over. She parked on the sandy shoulder and pressed on her warning lights. Slowly, she got out of the car and walked around to the back to see what had happened.

A rear tire had blown out. It wasn't just a simple flat but a huge tear on the tire's wall. It looked as if it had exploded. She glanced back on the road to see if she had driven over something that caused the damage. But she didn't see a thing.

How odd. She'd had the car checked by her mechanic before this trip, to make sure everything was in order. She knew he checked the oil, antifreeze, and brakes. Didn't he look at the tires, too?

Well, there wasn't much she could do about it. She was able to change a tire at one time in her life but wouldn't even attempt to look for the jack now. Besides, this was more than a quick fix. She knew that she didn't have a full-size spare in her trunk, just the emergency donut tire that came with the car. That certainly wouldn't get her all the way back to Vermont. It would barely get the car into the village to a service station.

She got back in the car, pulled out her cell phone, and called the now-familiar number. Liza picked up on the second ring. "The Inn at Angel Island. May I help you?"

"Liza, it's Adele. I didn't get very far. I'm just a few miles down the road, actually. I've had some car trouble. One of my rear tires blew out. Could you please come and get me?"

"Oh, Adele, what a shame. Of course I'll be right there. We'll have to call a tow truck from the village. There's no mechanic on the island, but we'll figure all that out once we get you back here."

Adele was sure they would. So, she would have more time in Cape Light after all, despite her plan to go. She would have crab cakes for dinner and take part in the work of the Christmas Fair committee tonight.

Beyond that, who could say?

"We called you right away, Molly, but we didn't know how to stop it. We put a bucket under there, but all the sheet cakes got wet."

Molly had come running to the shop this morning after an urgent call from her assistant manager, Sonya. A leak had sprung sometime during the early morning, and now a steady stream of water poured down from the ceiling at the back of the shop.

"I called the plumber, but I just got the answering service. I guess he'll call back soon . . ."

"Don't worry, Sonya. You did what you could." Molly had pulled off her jacket, her gaze stuck on the leaky spot. "I doubt it's a pipe. There's no plumbing back there. It must be a rotten spot in the roof or something. I guess that little dusting of snow we got this week is up there melting."

"Oh, right. I didn't know who to call for that."

Molly smiled grimly. "I do."

She owned the building now, so there was no more complaining to a landlord about repairs. She did know someone who could fix this disaster in the blink of an eye . . . if he wanted to.

Her brother, Sam, of course.

In the past, he would drop everything and ride to her rescue, no matter what the situation. Especially when she had been a single mother, working two jobs, and Lauren and Jillian had been so young. Her parents had done their best to help, but Sam had been the one, the only one, who was always there for her.

She sighed. She had been hard on him, and it was time to apologize. A sincere apology this time, not the halfhearted one she had tried to pull off on Friday. Sam had seen through that easily.

No pain, no gain, she reminded herself. *No patched roof, either,* the dripping sound reminded her.

She picked up her phone and called his cell. He picked up on the second ring. "This is Sam."

"It's me, Molly . . . Can you hear me?" He sounded like he was on a construction site somewhere. The sound of banging hammers and male voices filled the background.

"I can hear you. What's up?" His tone was curt, but at least he hadn't hung up on her. That was a good sign, wasn't it?

"I . . . I need your help. There's a huge leak in the back of the shop. I'm pretty sure it's coming from the roof. There was a bad spot up there that was patched about two years ago, when we bought the place."

"Yeah, I remember."

He had looked the building over, along with the official inspector, and told her back then that she needed a new roof. She was glad that he didn't say "I told you so" now.

"Well . . . you were right," she said, hoping to get on his good side. "We did need that roof job and now I'm paying for it. It's making a gigantic mess, Sam. We already lost a day of baking and a lot of money in wasted supplies."

She heard her brother sigh. "I have to stop at the shop to get some roofing material. I'll be there as soon as I can."

"Thank you!" she said, nearly collapsing in relief. "You are the best brother ever!"

"Right," Sam said with what sounded like a weary laugh. Then he hung up.

SAM HAD BEEN SURPRISED BUT RELIEVED TO HEAR HIS SISTER'S VOICE on the phone. He'd been thinking about calling her. He knew he had to apologize for his behavior on Friday when Molly had come to his shop. Grandma Addie had encouraged him to take that step, and he knew it was the right thing to do. Because now he could also understand better how his father and brother had sat with their anger so long that it hardened into its present unyielding state.

He pulled up in front of Molly's shop and went around to the rear door. She was holding a rubber bucket and opened the door with her free hand.

"I'm so glad you came. Thanks a million," she said sincerely as she led the way inside. Sure enough, a steady stream of water was coming through the ceiling. "It's even worse than when I called you," Molly said with a groan. "If the Board of Health decides to stop by unannounced, they could close me right down."

"You could stall them with a few croissants," Sam suggested.

He reached up and poked the leak with a screwdriver, and even more water rushed down. "It's the roof," he said, confirming their guess. "I'll get the extension ladder and check it out. This shouldn't take too long."

She nodded bleakly. "Okay, do what you have to do."

A little over an hour later, Sam came back down. The leak had stopped and the bad spot was patched. "That will hold it for a few months, depending on the weather. But it's also a low spot, and you have to get a real roof guy over here."

"Will do. You recommend someone, and I'll call him right away."

"Aren't we Miss Agreeable today?" Sam teased.

"We are," she promised him. "How about I make you one of those chicken and cheese panini things you like? I'm sure you had to skip lunch to get over here so quickly."

"I did," he admitted. "All right, I guess I at least deserve a free meal out of this."

Molly set a place for him at the end of the metal worktable. She served him a toasty, plump sandwich stuffed with roast chicken, tomato, and arugula and oozing with melted cheese and some secret dressing he couldn't quite identify.

"How is it?" she asked after he took a bite.

"Real good, thanks."

"So . . . are we friends again? Or at least . . . siblings?"

"I'm willing to wipe the slate clean if you are. I know you don't agree about Dad and Uncle Kevin, and I don't see it the way you do. But if we stay mad at each other, we're sort of repeating that unhappy chapter of family history. That seems pretty dumb to me."

"I thought of that, too. It is dumb. Let's not do that, Sam. We're smarter than that, don't you think? You and I have butted heads since we were kids. But that's just our way. You know, like baby goats playing on a hillside."

"Baby goats?" He made a face at her. "How am I like a baby goat?" He was trying not to laugh while he ate, but it was a challenge.

"Oh, you know what I mean. What I'm trying to say is, even though we argue from time to time, it doesn't mean anything. We never really get mad. But this time . . . this time was different. It felt so scary . . . and final," she admitted. "You know, when I saw that leak I wanted to call you, but I knew you were probably still mad at me, and I just felt so awful," she managed in a faltering tone. A tone that was very un-Molly, he knew. "I was thinking about all the times I used to call you when I was first divorced. The slightest little problem would come up and I would be crying on the phone. And you would come, no matter what you were doing. You'd come and help me."

"They weren't little problems," Sam said gently. "The way I remember it, you were strong and independent, and you didn't call unless things got pretty rough. Besides, I never minded helping you and the girls. You know that. I enjoyed it. It gave me good practice before I got married and became a father."

"Sometimes I think you got married just so you had an excuse not to help me so much."

"Maybe," he agreed, smiling. "But don't tell Jess I said that." Sam had finished his sandwich and now set the plate aside.

"How about some dessert? I just finished icing the mini-carrot cakes—"

Sam held up his hands. "No, I'm good, thanks. You are a danger to my waistline. But I do want to talk."

Molly nodded, and he could see that his sister didn't really want to get into this topic again, but they had to try. This was as good a time as any.

"So, what do you think now about Dad and Uncle Kevin? Do you still feel the same?" Sam watched her expression as he asked the question. She looked wary, and he didn't want to put her on the defensive. "I just want to know how you feel. Grandma has given up. She drove back to Vermont this morning. She left me a message."

"She did? I didn't know that . . . I wanted to see her at least one time before she left." Molly sounded sad.

Sam almost snapped at her again. *How* could *you know if you didn't try to see her or even call her on the phone while she was here?* But he stopped himself.

"She missed seeing you again, too," he told her. "She was sad it didn't work out," he went on. "Yesterday after church she told me she was handing it over to God."

Molly sighed, suddenly somber. "I should have been nicer to her. I just felt so bad about Dad, it got my hackles up."

"Let's not even go there," Sam said quickly. "The question is, what do we do now? Anything? Do you think Dad will take any steps at all to solve this? Will you take any steps?" he asked pointedly. "Or do you still feel the same way? And I'm just asking," he reminded her, "just to get a show of hands. I'm not going to fight you anymore on this. So you can be honest with me."

Molly seemed about to answer, then bit her lower lip, as if stopping her mouth from reacting before her mind had caught up. Then she slapped the metal table with her hand. "All right, I'm in. I'm in," she repeated. "I feel bad for Dad, but you know what? Life goes on, Sam. Life goes on. We have all been hurt by people we love. You have, and I have, too," she reminded him. "When I was thinking about how you used to help me when I was first divorced, I started thinking about Phil, too, of course. How mad I was at him, and how it made me so short-tempered and mad at the world sometimes."

Sam rolled his eyes. "Really? We never noticed."

Phil Willoughby and Molly had gotten married right out of high school, but their marriage had broken up when Jillian was still tiny. Phil disappeared for a while, not even helping with child support, making Molly's load even heavier.

Molly made a face back. "Yeah, I'll bet. The point is, when he cleaned up his act and wanted to be a real father again, I had to forgive him. I was remembering that, too. That was hard, Sam. You know how hard it was for me. But if I hadn't taken that step and let go of the past, who knows where I would be now? I never would have worked things out with Matt . . . I never would have had this shop or this great life I have now," she added. "I was definitely stuck. So maybe Daddy is, too."

Sam felt so relieved that his sister finally understood, he nearly leaped over the table and hugged her.

"I think he is, Molly. That's why I want him to work it out. This anger and bitterness is only hurting him, secretly eating at his heart. . . . I'm glad you see that now."

Molly nodded. "I think I do. But what should we do—try to bring them together? Is that what Grandma wanted?"

"I think that was her plan. But now she'll have to come back down here again. Or someone will have to go get her. I guess I could do that," he offered, "if we could set a time and place for this to happen."

"We would have to surprise Dad," Molly said. She rose and poured herself a cup of coffee. "I'm thinking it should be a big family party, not just the two of them, one on one. You know Daddy; he wouldn't handle that too well."

"A family party sounds good. We could get to meet Kevin's new wife and their children. He's never even seen our little ones, Lily and Betty."

"You spoke to him. Do you think he would come?"

"Yes, I do. I think he wants to make amends with Dad. He just doesn't know how to start."

"Well, from my limited perspective, a big party is always a good idea. We can have it at my house. There's plenty of room, and I'll make all the food here. Consider it done. All you have to do is get Grandma Addie back down here."

"I can handle Grandma, no problem. But are you sure you really want to go ahead with this? I don't want to feel as if I backed you into a corner. I know you have a ton of holiday parties to cater right now. With Betty out and Christmas coming, I'm sure you don't need any more on your plate. I really just wanted us to talk this out without fighting again."

Molly reached over and patted his arm. "I know, Sam. But you know how I am. Up until now, I've just accepted Dad's stubbornness because that's who he is. And because I'm like that, too," she admitted ruefully. "But we both know that's not always a good thing. So do you think this could work?"

Sam nodded, feeling as if a huge load had been lifted from his shoulders. "I do, and you know what they say in that baseball movie, 'If you build it, they will come.'" He smiled at her. "If you make that pâté of yours and those spinach puffs, they will come and have a good time and maybe figure this out."

"I hope so, Sam. At least we can say we tried . . . together, right?" She offered him her hand across the table and he folded it in both of his own and shook it.

"Right. We're in this together, pal. We either rise or fall."

His phone rang and he checked the number. "Look at that, it's Grandma. I told her to call me when she got home, but she can't be in Vermont already," he reasoned. "Unless she's started speeding in her old age . . . Hi, Grandma, what's up? I hope you're not trying to talk on the phone while you're driving."

"I'm not driving, don't worry. I'm still at the inn. I had some car trouble this morning, and I didn't get too far. A rear tire just plain exploded. So I had to wait for a tow truck from the village, and now they have to order the right sort of tire for my car. I'm going to stay over at the inn at least one more night . . . could be longer."

"Really? That's . . . amazing. I'm really glad to hear that . . . I mean, not that you had car trouble. But I've just been talking to Molly and we had this idea. Wait, I'm going to put her on and let her tell you yourself."

He covered the phone before handing it to his sister. "Grandma had car trouble. She's still at the inn. What luck, huh? Why don't you tell her about the party? It was your idea. She's going to be so happy."

Molly took the phone, and Sam listened to her side of the conversation as she explained their new plan to Grandma Addie.

Sam could tell from the expression on Molly's face and the many pauses in the conversation that their grandmother was pretty overwhelmed but totally thrilled by the idea.

When Molly hung up she looked happy, too. "She can hardly believe we want to do this. She said her prayers were answered. Isn't that sweet? I'm going over there tomorrow to visit and figure things out. I'm thinking the sooner we have it, the better, like maybe the end of this week?"

"Sounds good to me. You pick a day and we are there."

"You'd better be," Molly warned him. She sighed. "Well, at least we made our grandma happy. And figured out how to bring peace to the family . . . and you fixed a hole in the roof. Pretty productive day, wouldn't you say?"

"And it ain't over yet," Sam reminded her. "I think I'll take that carrot cake to go with a cup of coffee. Skim milk and one sugar, you know the way I like it."

"Yeah, I know . . . and you know where the self-serve station is, right up front. Help yourself." She grinned at him like she always did when he tried to boss her around.

Sam didn't mind. Things were back to normal between them, and that was fine with him.

CHAPTER TEN

ONATHAN DIDN'T GET TO LILAC HALL ON MONDAY UNTIL nearly one in the afternoon. He walked into the entry hall and checked the reception desk. Mrs. Fisk was there, but there was no sign of Tess. He walked over to sign in, eager to see her.

"Is Tess Wyler around?" Mrs. Fisk glanced at him over the edge of her glasses. "She's been helping me a lot with my research," he added quickly.

"Tess is not in today. She's at home with a cold."

"A cold? That's too bad."

She didn't seem sick yesterday, he thought. Maybe she had hidden it from him—or ignored it. That would be like her. Had he kept her out on the beach in the cold too long? Maybe her feet did get wet in the waves.

He suddenly felt very inconsiderate. He had been so caught up exploring the island, he hadn't even noticed that she didn't feel well.

"Mr. Butler? I can take you upstairs now. You need to store your belongings in a locker," she reminded him.

Jonathan looked up and realized that Mrs. Fisk was waiting to take him to the reading room. She must have been talking to him, and he hadn't heard a word.

"You know, Mrs. Fisk . . . I just remembered. I forgot some important notes. I really can't work without them. Stupid of me," he said as he quickly signed himself out again. So far, he had only taken off his muffler. He slung it around his neck again, then tucked the canvas bag with his laptop under his arm. "See you tomorrow. Have a nice afternoon."

The curator stared at him quizzically, her mouth in a tight line. "Same to you."

Jonathan trotted quickly to his car and jumped in. He pulled out his phone and called Tess's cell. It rang and rang. Finally, he heard her voice on the other end. She sounded like she had a clothespin on her nose.

"Jonathan? Are you at Lilac Hall?"

"I just got here—and I'm just leaving. They said you're home sick."

"I have a cold. It's a doozy." He smothered a laugh. Only Tess would use a word like that. "I meant to text you, but I was sleeping most of the morning."

"That's all right. I feel awful. You must have felt it coming on yesterday, and I kept you out all day in the cold. Why didn't you say something?"

"I felt fine yesterday. It just came out of nowhere last night, honestly. Besides, being out in the cold doesn't give you a cold. It's caused by a virus or bacterial infection. Actually, it's been scientifically proven that walking outside in cold air can speed up recovery."

"I'm sure." He smiled to himself. Even completely congested, Tess was getting the facts straight. "Listen," he said, "can I come by and see you? I could bring you some things from the drugstore or supermarket. Do you have enough orange juice and tea and honey and all that? How about tissues? There are never enough of those."

Tess laughed. "My mom went out this morning and stocked up on supplies. But there is one thing I could really use."

"What is that? Your wish is my command."

He heard her laugh, a croaky sound that made him feel all concerned again. "I need to finish a paper that's due when I get back to school, and there's a book I reserved at the library in town. They just called and said it came in."

"I can get it for you, no problem. What about your library card? Should I stop by first and pick it up?"

"Don't worry. I know all the librarians there. I'll call and let them know you're coming for it. They'll know what to do."

"Great. Now . . . where do you live?"

Tess gave him her address and directions to her house and the library. Jonathan headed back to the village and soon found the library, which was on Main Street, not far from the village hall. He quickly retrieved the book Tess had on hold, a thick volume on colonial history. As he was about to check it out, he noticed a woman next to him at the counter returning a DVD of *Notorious*, a classic Hitchcock thriller that was suspenseful and romantic. He thought Tess might like it if she wanted to take a study break. The librarian was nice enough to let him have that, too.

He headed back to his car with the book and movie and started off toward Tess's house. Even though she told him she had all she needed, he still felt he ought to bring something to cheer her up. He was passing a big supermarket, the kind that sold everything from donuts to doorknobs, and he pulled into the lot. There had to be something in there that he could bring a person who had a bad cold—a very sweet, pretty person whom he cared about a lot.

After his stop at the market, Jonathan found Tess's house. She lived on a narrow street with tall trees, not far from Main Street.

It was a very pleasant-looking street, he thought, like something out of a painting of classic America. The houses were modest, mostly Capes in the saltbox style that was so popular in New England.

The Wylers' house was neat, well kept and dark blue with white trim. It was a cloudy day and a lamp shone in the front window. He could see a cozy living room inside with a couch and big armchairs and a Christmas tree in the corner. Colorful Christmas lights were strung around the bushes outside and around the front door, along with a strand of pine garland and a big wreath.

He thought of the house he had grown up in. His father never let the caretaker put lights up, though they did have a large wreath every year on the front door. Even the wreath was rather bare-looking, its only bit of decoration a big red ribbon from the florist's shop.

Few people saw it, so what was the difference? The huge brick colonial was set back on several acres in Weston, one of Boston's wealthiest areas.

Tess's house was about the size of his father's six-car garage, but there was something very warm and welcoming about it, Jonathan thought as he came up the walk. He realized he was eager to see the inside, to see where Tess lived and learn more about her.

At the front door, he rang the bell, balancing the packages in his arms. The door slowly opened, and a boy stood there and stared up at him. He looked a lot like Tess, with the same thick reddish-brown hair and blue eyes. He was about ten years old, Jonathan guessed. "Hi," he said. "I'm here to see Tess."

"I can't let any strangers in. Wait here."

The boy shut the door, and Jonathan shifted the packages in his arms. How long was this going to take?

Then he heard a loud, clear shout from just behind the door. "Tess-sss-ss! Some guy is here to see you. Did you order groceries?"

He heard footsteps and Tess's voice. "Groceries? What are you talking about? I didn't order anything."

The door opened again. Jonathan smiled at her. "It's just me. I got your book and some other stuff," he added, now feeling self-conscious that he had sort of overdone it.

Tess's blue eyes widened. "Is that all for me?"

He tried to shrug, acting like it was no big deal. "Just some flowers . . . and some soup and crackers . . . and some organic spearmint tea. Opens up those nasal passages," he explained. "Oh, and I saw these really nice-looking oranges and strawberries. It's important to get lots of vitamin C."

Tess took a bag from him and peered inside. "And a chocolate cake? Is that good for a cold, too?"

"Chocolate is very good for you. It's an antioxidant and lifts your mood. It will help you study, really."

He had heard all this stuff someplace, though he wasn't sure if any of it was actually true.

"Come in, come in." Tess was practically laughing at him. "That's very sweet, Jonathan. I would give you a hug, but I don't want you to catch anything," she said in a quieter voice. Her brother might be listening, he realized.

"I really just wanted the book and didn't even want you to see me like this. I'm a total, unmitigated . . . mess." She covered her face with her hand.

He gently pulled it away. "You look great. As always," he added quietly.

Her nose was a little red and her cheeks were pale. Her hair was tied up in a sloppy knot at the back of her head, coming loose in all directions. She wore jeans and fluffy slippers and a huge sweatshirt that said Cape Light Lacrosse, a leftover from high school, he suspected.

They carried the packages into the kitchen, and he helped her unpack everything and watched her put the flowers in water.

"These are beautiful. Thank you."

"I didn't know what color you liked, so I asked the lady to mix them up." He had gone for the deluxe bouquet, a dozen multicolored roses—pink, yellow, white, and a purple-hued red. Her wide, amazed smile made it entirely worth it.

"My brother, Billy, is home sick from school today, too. I must have caught this bug from him, the little stinker. Germs, that's about all he ever gives me."

"I heard that. I'm telling Mom!"

They both heard Tess's brother shout from the other room, over the sound of the TV. Jonathan looked at her and they started laughing. She waved her hands, urging him to be quiet. "Shhh . . . he has extremely good hearing, like a vampire bat," she whispered.

"Okay, I'll be quiet, don't worry." It was just so good to see her again. He loved being around her. Even with her stuffed nose and watery eyes.

She started to sneeze, and he quickly handed her the box of tissues he'd brought. "They're the kind with lotion," he explained, then immediately felt ridiculous. Who actually discussed lotion on tissues?

"Thanks," she managed after a sneeze or two.

"Maybe the flowers weren't such a good idea," he realized, looking at the big bouquet. "I can put them outside, on the porch or something."

"Oh no, don't do that. They're so pretty. No one ever bought me roses before."

He felt good about that. He would buy her a roomful if she liked them that much.

Tess put two oranges on a plate and led him into an L-shaped living room and dining room. Her schoolwork and laptop were spread out on the table.

He took the library book from his pack and gave it to her. "I almost forgot. Here's your book. I also got this movie from the library. It's an old Hitchcock film. You've probably seen it."

"Yes, I have. About ten times," she teased him. "But it's one of my favorites. I really should study but I'm starting to get a headache." She frowned, rubbing her forehead with her fingertips.

He touched her cheek and looked into her eyes. "I'm sorry you feel sick, Tess. I know you said it wasn't, but I can't help thinking this is my fault."

She shook her head. "I told you, it was my brother. He's a little germ bucket, honestly."

She was making him laugh again. "All right, if you say so . . . I just want you to feel better."

She looked into his eyes and smiled. "I do already. Honest."

He did, too. He could have pulled her close and kissed her, germs and all. But they both heard footsteps and turned to see Billy walk into the room. "I can't find the chocolate syrup, Tess. Did you use it all up?"

"No, but you can't have milk anyway, remember? It will make you even more congested."

"You're kidding, right?"

Jonathan could see Tess was tired, and Billy was tired and didn't feel well, either. "How about some of that Super-C Tropical Splash? It has pineapple, orange, mango, and strawberry juice, and it's organic. I brought it for Tess, but you can have it. It will help your cold," he promised. Jonathan knew he sounded like a car salesman, but the pitchman voice worked with his little stepsisters.

Billy squinted at him and then looked at his sister. "Who is this guy again?"

"He's a friend of mine, Bill. Don't be fresh," she warned him.

"All right. I'll try it." Billy shrugged, and Jonathan followed him into the kitchen and poured him a glass of juice.

"Hey, here's an idea. How about some club soda in it? That's what my favorite—" He was about to say, "That's what my favorite housekeeper always gave me," but caught himself. "That's what I liked to drink when I was sick."

Billy took a tentative sip, then decided he liked it and took the rest of the glass into the TV room. "If you get bored with Tess, you can play a video game with me," he told Jonathan.

Jonathan felt honored by that invitation, though he doubted he would get bored with Tess anytime soon. "Thanks. I'll see how it goes."

He found Tess in the dining room at the table, reading something on her laptop. "Thanks for dealing with him for me. He's a good kid, but we've been stuck together all day."

"I get it. I have two little stepsisters. They're cute but tough negotiators."

He sat down at the table and leafed through her books and papers. "What's your paper about? You never told me."

Jonathan felt a little guilty when he realized that. They talked so much about his work, and he had never even asked her about hers.

"Indentured servitude in the North American colonies," she replied. "There's plenty of material about it. Too much," she added. "My problem is just putting the information in order and writing something that makes sense."

That was his strong point. He enjoyed the research, but he loved making an outline and the actual writing of the paper. "Want me to take a look? I'm a pretty good writer," he added. "Maybe I can help you."

"Be my guest." Tess moved the document back to the first page and turned the laptop screen toward him. "I'm going to make some of that mint tea you brought. Would you like some?"

"That would be great."

Jonathan started reading Tess's paper and made some notes on a pad he found on the table. By the time she returned with their tea, he was more than halfway through what she had written so far.

She sat quietly across the table, looking at the book he had brought from the library. She suddenly snapped the book closed. "It makes me nervous to watch someone read my writing. I should go in the living room."

"I'm almost done—and this is good. You don't have to go," he assured her. It was true, too. And he didn't want her to sit in the other room, so far away from him.

"So, what do you think?" she asked when he finished. "It rambles all over and makes no sense, right?"

"It could use a little tightening, but it makes perfect sense to me. I think your premise is very original, too. It's hard to come up with any new ideas about indentured servants and their impact on colonial communities."

"Are you sure you're not just trying to be nice to me? If it's lame, I'd really rather know the truth. I can take criticism—if it's constructive. I won't get all nutty."

"I'll keep that in mind. But this paper is fine," he replied. "I only have a few comments and questions. I really do think it's good."

"Okay. Show me what you think needs fixing." She came to the other side of the table and sat next to him, so that they could look at the computer screen together. Her nearness was distracting as he scrolled through the paper, page by page, talking over his suggestions with her.

Tess was so smart. She had a different style of thinking, a different way of attacking a problem or question than he did, and her ideas always surprised him. She was never predictable, that was for sure.

They had reached the end of the paper, immersed in their conversation about the main idea of her thesis. Suddenly, they both became aware of someone else in the room. He turned to see a woman standing in the dining room doorway. She wore a coat and had grocery bags in both hands. Jonathan realized instantly that she was Tess's mother.

"I'm home, Tess. Didn't you hear me calling you?"

Jonathan felt suddenly self-conscious, sitting so close to Tess with his arm slung around the back of her chair. Tess jumped up and walked over to her mother.

"No, I guess I didn't . . . This is my friend Jonathan. I told you about him, remember? He brought me a book I needed from the library."

"Nice to meet you, Jonathan." Her mother's tone was polite.

When she smiled, Jonathan saw a striking resemblance to her daughter.

He quickly rose and would have offered to shake her hand, but she was still loaded down with grocery bags. "Nice to meet you, Mrs. Wyler. Can I help you with those bags?"

"If you don't mind. There are a few more in the car," she said.

"No problem. I think Tess should stay inside. She's still sneezing."

Her mother seemed surprised by his concern. "Yes, she shouldn't catch a chill. That's very thoughtful of you, Jonathan."

Jonathan went out to the car that was parked in the driveway and collected the rest of the bags. When he came inside again, Tess's mother had taken off her coat. He noticed she wore a uniform and had an ID around her neck from a hospital. He wondered what she did there. He would ask Tess when he had a chance.

Billy was sitting at the kitchen table, eager for his mother's attention. "I think I'm too sick to go to school tomorrow," he announced.

His mother turned from the sink and smiled at him. "We'll see. Why don't you do your homework anyway, just in case? I made a special trip to school to pick it up for you."

Jonathan left the groceries on the table and found Tess in the dining room. "I'd better get going," he said. "I don't want to be in the way."

"Don't go yet. You can stay for dinner if you like. My mom always seems a little frazzled when she gets home," she added in a quieter voice.

Jonathan smiled. "That's all right. She's not expecting a guest for dinner. And you still have to take care of yourself. Do you think you'll feel better by Thursday?"

She frowned at him. "I guess so. What's so special about Thursday?"

"I noticed that there's some chamber music in Newburyport, a Bach quartet. I thought we could go to the concert and then have dinner up there. Are you free?"

"That sounds great. I love baroque music. I listen to it sometimes when I study. They say it helps your memory, but I just enjoy it. It's the only classical music I have on my iPod."

"I'll pick you up around six o'clock," he added. "That should give us plenty of time to get there."

Tess agreed and walked him to the door, where he put on his coat and slung his long scarf around his neck.

"Well, thanks again for stopping over. And for the beautiful roses and the pineapple, mango, strawberry juice and the book and the movie—and for helping me with my paper."

"Don't forget the tissues with lotion," he added with a grin, feeling happy he had pleased her.

"Best gift of all, I'd say. You may have saved me from looking like Rudolph the Red-Nosed Reindeer this week at work."

He sighed and placed his hands on her shoulders. "Thank you, Tess. Now I know my life has true meaning."

Tess laughed, and he quickly kissed her forehead. "Feel better. I'll call you."

"Please do," she said as he headed out the door.

Tess stood by the door as he walked down to his car. "Go inside," he called out. "You're going to get cold."

He could see a sneeze coming on as she nodded and waved again, and quickly shut the door.

If she wasn't well by Thursday, that would be all right, too. He could come visit and they would watch a movie or just talk. He didn't care. He just liked spending time with her. More and more, every time they were together.

* * *

TESS CLOSED THE FRONT DOOR AND WALKED INTO THE KITCHEN. HER mother had put an apron on over her uniform and was starting to cook dinner.

"How's your cold, honey? Feeling any better?"

"I'm all right. I think I can go back to work tomorrow. I think the worst is over."

"As long you don't have a temperature." Her mother unwrapped a package of string beans and began snapping the ends off. "I guess your friend Jonathan helped speed up your recovery. He seems very nice. Did he bring those roses?"

"Yes, he did."

"They're very pretty." Her mother glanced at her and smiled.

Tess knew what she was thinking: Friends don't buy roses. Boyfriends do, though. She felt her cheeks get warm. "Well . . . we're sort of dating, a little. I guess. He asked me out for Thursday night, to a classical music concert and dinner in Newburyport. But that's our first real date," she clarified.

"That sounds very nice. So, you met him at the historical society, right?"

She had told her mother last week about meeting Jonathan and how she had been helping him with his research.

"At the diner, first. I waited on his table and spilled water on him," she admitted. "Then he showed up at Lilac Hall the next day. It was such a weird coincidence."

"That is a coincidence," her mother agreed. "He's doing some research about the village?"

"About the quarantine on Angel Island the first year the settlers arrived from England. It seems to be taking longer than he expected. He's working on his doctorate at Tufts," Tess offered.

Her mother nodded, looking impressed. She stuck the colander of beans under running water. "He seems very nice, Tess, very thoughtful. But just be careful, okay? You may see him when you get back to school . . . and you may not. Don't set yourself up for getting hurt."

Tess wanted to argue with her. Jonathan was so sweet. Didn't she see that? He had run over here today with an armload of presents just because she had a little cold. No guy had ever done that for her before.

But she didn't bother arguing about it. Her mother didn't know him yet. She didn't understand. She was just doing her Mom-thing, being all protective. Tess had a feeling that she would be seeing Jonathan a long time after he finished his research and left town. He had made that very clear.

Tess took out the dinner plates and silverware and started to set the table. "Don't worry, Mom. Jonathan's not like that."

"I hope so," her mother said.

Tess didn't reply. She didn't have to. He would never date her only to dump her once he left Cape Light. He was just not that kind of guy.

"THIS IS DELICIOUS, CLAIRE. MAYBE YOU'LL GIVE ME THE RECIPE." Molly smiled across the table at her grandmother as she finished the last bite of her seafood crepes.

Adele knew that Claire didn't normally cook such an elaborate dish for lunch in the middle of the week, but she had gone all out when she heard Molly was coming.

"I'd be happy to send the recipe to you. Glad you could join us today," Claire said.

"Are you kidding? How could I pass up that offer? It's great to eat someone else's cooking, especially when it's better than my own."

Claire just smiled at the compliment. Adele thought her granddaughter and Claire were pretty equally matched in the kitchen, with each having their specialties. Molly had come to the inn to talk about the family party she was planning. But Adele also wanted to enjoy her granddaughter's company a little, too.

Claire soon cleared the dishes and brought in coffee and dessert, a fresh fruit salad, and slices of flan she had served the night before. Then she left to clean up the kitchen, leaving Adele alone with Molly, who carefully tasted a bite of the flan. "Wow . . . this is awesome, so light. I have to get this recipe, too. Do you think Claire would ever come cook for me?"

"I doubt it," Adele said honestly. "She seems very settled here. Besides, the inn wouldn't be the same without Claire."

"You're right. It would disturb the entire ecosystem here. I couldn't do that to Liza, either." Molly sighed and sat back in her chair. "So, Grandma, thanks for inviting me here. I do need to say that I'm sorry for the way I acted when you first got here. I didn't understand what you were trying to do . . . but I didn't have to get so mad at you. The things is, I always feel good for a few moments after speaking my mind. But it never solves anything."

Adele was touched by Molly's apology. "I appreciate that, dear. Now I must apologize for the way I came down here, expecting everyone would just see things my way and fall right into line. I'm sorry for that. It obviously wasn't the right thing to do."

Molly nodded as she took another bite of flan. "A little warning might have been a good thing, now that you mention it." She paused and patted her mouth with a napkin. "I say we're all square and on the same page now—you, me, and Sam. I hope this family reunion idea works out. It was all we could think of to get Dad and Uncle Kevin together. Sam and I think Dad will come if we say that you're still in town and we wanted to get together before you went back to Vermont. But we don't think we should tell him that Uncle Kevin is coming. You know Dad. He probably wouldn't come."

A Season of Angels

"I was thinking the same thing myself," Adele said. "I do hate to trick him, but it's for a good cause."

"Frankly, Grandma, it's not like he's given us any big choice here," Molly pointed out. "Is Uncle Kevin as stubborn as Daddy? We'd better rethink this if he is."

Adele laughed. "No, not at all. He's just the opposite. Your father got all the Morgan genes for that trait."

"Good news." Molly practically sighed with relief. "Well, the only thing left is to invite everyone. Sam says he's going to call Uncle Kevin. But you should call him, too, and explain everything. Is that all right with you?"

"I think that's a good idea. I've been speaking to your uncle this past week, so he has some idea of what's going on. But when will the party be? Did you already tell me and I forgot?"

Molly smiled. "You didn't forget. I didn't say yet. We've set the date for this coming Saturday night, at my house. I'll take care of the rest."

By the rest, Adele knew she meant food, drinks, flowers, and every-thing else needed for a party of—what would it be? Thirty people or so, with Kevin's family and Joe's other children and their families, who lived outside of Massachusetts now.

"That will be quite a crowd," Adele noted warily.

"The more the merrier," Molly replied. "Piece of cake for me, Grandma." Molly's phone buzzed and then she checked the screen and jumped up. "So sorry, I have to get back to the shop. Mini emergency with some mini cream puffs."

"I understand. You go now if you have to. But this is so generous of you. It must be making a big crimp in your work schedule and your pock-etbook," Adele added as she stood up to walk her granddaughter to the front door. "You must let me help you out in some way."

"No worries, I've got it all covered. I could do this in my sleep. Besides, I've thought about it and talked it over with Matt. We know how much this means to you. We're happy to help you if we can."

"I do appreciate it. From the bottom of my heart." Adele put her arms around Molly and gave her a big hug, the way she did when Molly was a little girl.

Molly hugged her back. Then she stood back and looked down at Adele. "I know this has been a difficult visit, Grandma, but I'm not sorry that you came. Maybe we did need our grandma Addie to come down here and kick some . . . Well, you know what I mean."

Adele laughed. "Yes, I do, dear. I think you all needed some of that."

After Molly left, Adele felt happier than she had in weeks. She felt as if a terrible burden had been lifted from her shoulders. She couldn't wait until Saturday night to see both sides of her family together again.

Her light, hopeful mood persisted into the evening when she went into the village with Claire for the Christmas Fair committee meeting at the church.

They were a few minutes late. The other committee members were already gathered in Fellowship Hall, sitting at long tables and working on the craft items that would be offered at the church's biggest fund-raiser of the year. Each table was focused on a different project—wooden pull toys, Christmas tree ornaments, painted boxes, and holiday table center-pieces.

Adele had no preference and was content to follow Claire, who liked working on the painted boxes. She had a real talent for painting delicate flowers and other designs from nature once the wood was covered by a bright glossy paint.

They had worked out a system where Adele painted the base coat on the box and Claire did the special design. It worked out well, and they were quite productive.

"Oh, hello, Adele. I didn't know you were coming back to help us tonight." Sophie Potter joined them at the table. "I thought you left for Vermont."

Adele was not surprised that Sophie knew of her plans. It was a small congregation, and any sort of news traveled fast.

"I had some car trouble, so here I am," she explained. "I should be here until Sunday, actually," she added, though she didn't say why.

"Good idea to stay put. There's snow coming. Lots of it."

Vera Plante sat across the table, carefully coating a small round box with bright blue paint. "And that gives me a good idea. I'm going to paint white snowflakes on this one."

Adele hoped the snow wouldn't affect the party plans. But weather forecasters were known to get all excited about nothing. Besides, folks in New England did not panic over a few inches—or even a few feet—of the white stuff.

Grace Hegman sat at the far end of the table. She had already painted several boxes in pale but interesting lavenders and greens and was now using a very fine brush to add the details. "Everyone loves a white Christmas . . . unless they have to go out shopping in it," she observed.

"Has the shop been busy, Grace?" Claire asked.

"We have a lot of browsers, not so many buyers yet. They all rush in at the last minute, wondering where the pin or the ring or the teacup they've been eyeing for weeks disappeared to. Well, someone else thought it was a good bargain, too." She poked her brush into a small jar of craft paint and pursed her lips. "I try to stay pleasant and patient, hold on to the holiday spirit and all that at this time of year, but it's not easy."

Adele bit back a smile. Grace had never been known for an easygoing personality. Then again, she did have a great burden to bear, caring for her elderly father, which she did with great grace and forbearance. She could easily be excused for not being the most relaxed shopkeeper in town, couldn't she?

The women chatted and worked as the time flew by. At one point, Adele looked up and saw Reverend Ben walk in, a stack of folders under one arm. Adele guessed he had just come out of a meeting, perhaps the trustees or church council. He sat on so many committees, she didn't know how he kept them all straight. But after so many years, running the church must come automatically to him cause he did it so very well.

He stopped to talk to Sophie, who was the head of the Christmas Fair committee, but when he noticed Adele, he smiled and walked over to talk to her.

"I thought you left for Vermont yesterday. Are you back so soon?" he teased her.

"I started on my way, but didn't even make it over the bridge. A tire blew out. Luckily, I hadn't gone very far and wasn't going very fast."

"That is fortunate. A blowout can be very dangerous on the highway. So, you're just waiting for the car to be repaired then? Will it take very long?"

"It didn't take long," Adele told him. "I picked it up this morning. But the situation has changed a bit around here. It looks like we're going to have a family reunion on Saturday. At Molly's house," she added, trying hard to tamp down her excitement. "So I don't want to miss that."

Reverend Ben's eyes widened. "Of course not. Will the whole family be there—your son Kevin and his wife and children, too?"

Adele nodded. "He'll be invited. He knows that I came here and why. But we aren't telling Joe that Kevin is coming," she added. "I know it seems underhanded, but we didn't want to risk him skipping the party."

She hoped the reverend wouldn't think she was being dishonest and manipulative, tricking Joe this way.

Reverend Ben did look concerned. "I understand your reasoning," he said finally. "I hope that you're not disappointed. I hope it works out well for everyone."

"Thank you, Reverend. We have to take our chances, I guess. Please say a prayer for us?"

"I already have you on my list," he promised.

They talked for a few moments more, and then Reverend Ben was called away to another table.

Adele's high spirits were dampened a bit by his realistic reminder. You can bring a horse to water, but you can't make him drink. She and her grandchildren could set the perfect table for reconciliation, but that didn't mean that Joe and Kevin would partake.

But just as she'd told Reverend Ben, that was a chance they had to take.

CHAPTER ELEVEN

~~~

*W*HEN MOLLY WOKE UP ON FRIDAY MORNING SHE WANTED TO cry. But she knew it wouldn't help. After all her fine promises to her grandmother and Sam, she wasn't really sure how she could pull off such a big party in such a short time—and keep up with her own business, which was hitting the annual holiday peak of insanity. Her partner, Betty, was still out, which didn't help matters. Molly felt as if she had been pulling double shifts for the last two weeks.

She was sipping her coffee, trying to make a list but staring into space, when her husband's voice finally caught her attention. "Molly . . . did you hear anything I just said?"

"I'm sorry, hon. I was just thinking."

Matt sat down across from her. He had on his overcoat and was already holding his car keys. "When I put Betty on the bus she said, 'Tell Mommy, please don't forget the cupcakes.' I assume you know what that means?"

"Oh, right . . ." Molly had promised cupcakes for Betty's class party today. Thank goodness the child had remembered. "Got it covered." She quickly made another note on her pad.

"Are you okay? I know you didn't sleep well last night. You were tossing around like a fish. You know, you don't have to do this big party for your family if you don't want to. We can all just go out to a restaurant. I'm sure that would be all right with everyone."

"Not at this time of year, honey. Every decent place with a room big enough for this clan is booked solid. Hey, why don't we all go over to the Spoon Harbor Inn and surprise my dad at work? There's a solution."

He gave her a look. "I'm serious, Molly."

"Sorry, I'm just getting punchy or something." She sighed. "I know I was totally against this idea at first, but I changed my mind. I think it's the right thing to do. I have to step up and help Grandma Addie . . . and help Dad, too. Besides, I can't back out of it now. It's tomorrow night. Everything is set. Everyone is coming."

"I guess you can't," he agreed. "Your uncle is coming, too?"

Molly nodded. "Uncle Kevin is totally onboard and ready to work things out with Dad. I just want it to be really nice. A real holiday feeling, warm and welcoming. Candles, garlands, everything really pretty. I want to set the right tone, know what I mean?"

"Honey, you couldn't throw a bad party if you tried. It's going to be just great. At least the girls are home to help. That should make you feel better."

"Thank heaven. I have to admit, I think it's a sign. Someone up there is trying to help me." Was it luck, or had some of the desperate prayers she had mumbled this week been answered?

Matt was still watching her carefully. "So what's on the menu?"

"The menu?" Molly shrugged. "I just added on to whatever the crew was preparing for parties already being catered this weekend. As for the chairs, tables, plates, silverware, flowers, and so on, I just wrote up an order for us. Sonya will have it all carted over here sometime before tomorrow morning."

Matt nodded, looking satisfied that she had it all in hand.

But there was still the house to deal with—cleaning, decorating, rearranging the furniture. How would all that get done? Molly had imagined doing it all herself, staying up until two in the morning.

Then yesterday her older girls, Amanda and Lauren, had come home together from New York a few days earlier than they had planned. Their homecoming cheered Molly's heart and made her feel she was on the right track. The family had spent the evening trimming the Christmas tree and eating pizza, which was just the break she needed. Before the night was over, she had recruited their help with the party and had already left a long to-do list for them on the kitchen counter, right next to the coffeemaker, where they wouldn't miss it. She was sure they would sleep in, but they were pretty fast workers once they got going.

"The girls will be a huge help, no question," Molly told her husband as he finally got ready to go to work.

"Don't worry, honey. It will all work out," he promised her. Molly just nodded. She was starting to feel cautiously encouraged.

But the biggest surprise and boost came when Molly arrived at the shop later that morning. Betty Bowman—her business partner and best friend in the entire world—stood at the metal worktable, dressed in her burgundy Willoughby Fine Foods apron, as she checked a row of covered aluminum trays against a work order.

Betty looked up and smiled when Molly walked in. She didn't say a word. She knew she didn't have to. Molly would do the shouting for both of them.

"Betty! What are you doing here? You said next week or maybe even after Christmas."

"I didn't say that, my doctor did. I had an appointment yesterday and told him I just couldn't stand being in the house anymore. He was going to have to change my back support for a straitjacket—or give me one for my poor husband."

Molly knew that wasn't true. Betty and Nick had the perfect relationship. They had found each other late in life and had only been married two years. They were still in the honeymoon stage, and seemed like one of those couples who might never leave that phase.

"Don't give me that. I think Nick probably hated the idea that you were going back to work today," Molly said. She laughed and gave Betty a hug. "You might end up needing a straitjacket anyway if you hang around here long enough."

"Yeah, I know." Betty nodded, and her smooth blond hair fell across her eyes. "If I see any angry Morgans, I'll just hide out in the pantry."

Molly and Betty were in constant contact on the phone and by e-mail, so Betty knew everything going on in Molly's family.

"Good plan. I'll come with you." Molly took off her coat and left it on a chair. "I hope you didn't come back here before you were totally recovered, just because I'm having that party tomorrow night. That better not be the reason. Or I'll send you right home," Molly warned.

"Oh, I know you can pull that together blindfolded and still manage this place. Honestly, my doctor gave me a total all clear. I just can't lift anything heavier than a stuffed mushroom. Maybe I'm a medical miracle . . . or maybe you're trying to do the right thing for your family and someone up there is trying to help you along?"

Molly wasn't sure about the answer to that question and didn't have time to figure it out. "Honestly, Betty, when I got up this morning I wanted to cry. But I knew it wouldn't help."

"And now?" Betty asked.

"I think it might be all right. I think it might just all work out."

Molly tried to hold that good thought as she worked hard the rest of the day. The hours went by much faster with Betty around, and she was able to leave the shop in time for dinner.

Lauren and Amanda had finished their list and made a big dent in the housework and decorating. They had also fixed dinner for everyone. Betty would be in the shop tomorrow managing their business, which left Molly with an entire day to put the final, professional touches on the party.

It was all falling into place, Molly realized as she went up to bed that night. And she had even remembered to get the cupcakes over to the school for the class party.

"So, are you pleased? Everything seems to be going fine so far." Matt had come up beside her and put his arm around her shoulders.

Molly turned to her husband with a small, cautious smile. "So far, so good. But we're hardly done with the first act."

Her husband laughed quietly. "You're always your toughest critic, Molly."

That was true. But it was hard for her to let go and go with the flow tonight. She was sure she wouldn't relax until the night was over, though the stage for this family gathering had been perfectly set. Even she had to admit it. Her large, gracious home never looked better than it did during the holidays and rarely as welcoming as it looked tonight.

Their grand Christmas tree—even taller than usual this year—was the focus of the living room. The star on top practically brushed the twelve-foot ceiling. Sam was still admiring it, a beer in hand, as he kidded Matt about driving a cherry picker into the living room to put the lights on. Matt was notoriously un-handy, and Sam never tired of teasing him about it.

A fire crackled in the big stone hearth, and the mantel was covered with a green garland, a row of white ceramic angels, and glowing tapers.

Candles of all shapes and sizes were placed throughout the house, casting the rooms in a warm, friendly light. A pleasing scent of cinnamon and ginger mingled with the fresh pine.

The tables were set with matching golden tablecloths and dark green runners. The centerpieces, which she had made herself, were a combination of pine, holly, and long-stemmed white roses accented with golden bows. White china plates and thick linen napkins were stacked at the end of the long buffet, and large silver platters offered only the very best from her shop's kitchen—giant shrimp and snow crab on cracked ice, baked clams and Oysters Rockefeller, miniature crab cakes, and spinach feta puffs. There were trays of gourmet cheeses; smoked salmon dotted with crème fraîche and bits of caviar; cool, tart vegetable dip; and even Grandma Addie's hot artichoke and cheese spread. For the kids, pigs in a blanket, mini pizza bites, and carrot sticks, though some adults liked those choices, too. Molly would politely look away when she found grown-ups cruising that table.

As Molly checked the trays, making sure nothing needed to be replenished, her grandmother suddenly appeared beside her.

"Can I help you with the something, Grandma?"

Her grandmother shook her head. "Maybe later. Everything looks so good, almost too good to eat. I'm honestly overwhelmed. You didn't have to go to all this trouble."

"Well, I'm not going to say it was a total snap," Molly admitted. "But it was definitely worth it."

Worth all the trouble and more, just to see the look on her grandmother's face when she had come in the door. No one could say whether their plan would work, but Molly felt she had done the right thing to help in the way that she could.

"I think it's wonderful, dear. Truly magnificent. If I knew this side of the family was partying in such a fashion, I would have come for a surprise visit much sooner."

Molly laughed and slipped her arm around her grandmother's shoulders. If Adele was nervous about what the evening would bring, she didn't seem to show it. Molly was definitely nervous but doing her best to hide it. That was a certain form of courage—to feel the fear and keep going anyway. Maybe it was a family talent.

"I'm not saying we don't have nice parties, but this one is special. It reminds me of how we always loved coming to your house after Christmas. Now, that was special." Molly felt wistful, thinking about those annual visits that had ended right after her grandfather died.

"Yes, it was. I hope you'll all come back very soon. You come any time. Don't wait until it's too late."

Molly knew what she meant. They had all waited a long time to come together again. Too long, perhaps. Her grandmother would not live in that sweet old house forever. "We will, Grandma," Molly promised. She meant it, too.

Sam and his family had arrived first, bringing Grandma Addie with them. Then her brother Eric and her brother Glen and their families showed up. Their oldest brother, Jim, and his wife had just walked in a few minutes ago. Laurie, the youngest sister, was still in Florida and not due to arrive until next week. That was a shame. Molly had a feeling that Christmas Eve was going to seem like a footnote after this get-together. But Sam and her sister-in-law Jessica always made a wonderful night for the family. Maybe they would do things a little differently this year, but it would be no less fun. The point was being together, as family, whether the menu was caviar or pizza.

Jessica was in the living room, too, talking with Eric's wife, Cindy, and their youngest son, Aaron. The house was full and lively, just the way Molly liked it. She had been brooding about her empty nest and looking forward to seeing the rooms full for the holidays. Well, be careful of what you wish for, she thought. This was a bounty she had never expected.

Lauren, Amanda, and Jillian were hanging out in the family room with their cousins, Darrell and Tyler. Molly knew these events could be boring for kids, but she also knew they liked them anyway.

Lily and Betty, who were great pals, were heading upstairs to play in Betty's room. Then they turned and walked toward Molly. Betty tugged on Molly's satin skirt. "When are the new cousins coming, Mommy?" she asked for the umpteenth time.

"Soon, honey. They should be here any minute." Molly checked her watch. Uncle Kevin was almost a half hour late. Not enough to worry about, yet. *But he did have a history of being unreliable,* a little voice reminded her. Then she stopped herself. As Sam had told her all week, they all had to wipe the slate clean in this relationship. Uncle Kevin had changed a great deal and if this evening was going to work and the family was going to come back together, they had to *all* stop judging their uncle and stop seeing him through their father's eyes—and see him through their own.

Easy to say, hard to do, Molly realized as Sam walked up to her. Just from the look on his face, she could tell he was thinking the same thing. "Did you hear from Uncle Kevin?" she asked. "Maybe they hit traffic or something?"

"He hasn't called, but I'm sure they're on their way." Sam didn't sound all that sure, though, Molly noticed, and he obviously hadn't called their uncle, either. Maybe he'd been afraid to. "What about Mom and Dad? How come they're not here yet?" Sam asked.

"I told them to come about half an hour later than everyone else. I just thought it would be better if they didn't meet Uncle Kevin out in the driveway . . . though now it looks like that might happen anyway."

"Let's hope not. And I hope Dad didn't figure out what we're up to and decide not to show."

Molly had thought of that, too. Though they warned all their siblings that the reunion was top secret, confidences had a way of leaking out in the Morgan family. There wasn't one person who was really good at keeping secrets.

The doorbell rang. Sam and Molly stared at each other. Matt walked to the large entry hall to greet the new guests.

"That's either Dad or Uncle Kevin," Sam observed.

"And I think the curtain's rising on act two," Molly replied. She stood stone still, listening for voices echoing in the foyer. She didn't hear her father and mother, so she took a breath. It was Uncle Kevin and his family . . . finally.

She put her glass aside and went to greet them. Sam had already started off ahead of her. Then she saw Matt lead her uncle into the living room. She hardly recognized him. He looked so different now. For one thing she expected him to look much older. Nearly ten years had passed since she had last seen him, but he actually looked younger than she recalled. He was fit and trim, with short silver hair, a square jaw, clear blue eyes, and a warm, relaxed smile.

Molly felt herself smiling, too, as their eyes met. A rush of memories filled her heart and mind—all the fun times she'd had with her uncle when she and her siblings were kids and he was a footloose bachelor who never tired of amusing them.

But before she could greet him, Grandma Addie stepped between them and embraced her son. "I'm so happy to see you here. Thank you for coming," Molly heard her grandmother say in a shaky voice. When she stepped back from Kevin, Molly could see that Grandma Addie was crying. But they were tears of joy, and maybe of relief, too.

"Now, Mom, no tears. No need to thank me, either. I'm happy to be here." He looked over at Molly and took a step closer. "Thank you, Molly, for making this beautiful party. I'm very grateful."

"We're glad you could come, Uncle Kevin." Molly hugged her uncle and stepped back. "Really glad."

Kevin gently held the arm of his wife, Janine, as he introduced her. She was a slim, pretty redhead, probably a few years younger than he was, Molly guessed.

"What a lovely home. Thank you for inviting us," Janine said. She introduced her children, Jackson who was a high school senior and the same age as Jillian, and Nora who was in her first year of college.

"Hi, kids. Thanks for coming. The younger generation is hanging in the family room." Molly pointed them in the right direction. "You'll pass the food on the way. Please help yourself to anything you like."

The teenagers drifted off, and more guests came to greet Uncle Kevin and Janine, though Adele remained close by his side.

Molly took a break from her hostess duties to sit with her uncle and new aunt in the living room. Practically all the adults at the party were gathered around him. Sam was keeping the conversation going, with questions about Kevin's new career, how he had made the jump from engineering to telecommunications, and about their plans to move to New Zealand.

Molly mostly sat and listened. Uncle Kevin not only looked different, he was different inside, she realized. Calm and open, he seemed willing to answer all their questions and appeared to be genuinely interested in their lives, too.

When the others drifted away to refresh their drinks or move on to other conversations, Kevin came to sit next to her on the sofa. "I'm so pleased to see how things worked out for you, Molly," he said. "When I last saw you, things were tough. You were struggling. But your girls have grown into lovely, accomplished young women, and your grandmother tells me you have a successful business. Your husband, Matt, seems like a great guy. You two look very happy together."

"Thank you, we are. I've been very lucky," Molly said. "And very blessed."

"I'm sure that's true. But there's an old saying: 'The harder I work, the luckier I get.' Anyone can see you've worked hard, Molly. You should be very proud."

"You've worked hard, too, Uncle Kevin. I don't think we've been fair to you and I'm sorry for that."

She knew her apology was fumbling and impulsive. She wasn't even entirely sure what she was apologizing for.

Her uncle seemed to understand. He took her hand. "I appreciate that, but the responsibility to reach out and make amends was mine," he told her. "I wrote to your father a few times, but he never answered. I had to accept that he wasn't ready to hear me out. And I should have tried harder or not accepted his rejection so easily. The past is over and done. There's no way to change it. I made a lot of mistakes back then, but I've forgiven myself. I've forgiven him, too. All we can do is come together tonight to talk things out and go forward, to start a new page in our family story, right?"

Molly nodded. That's what they all wanted. Except for Joe. But she sent up a quick prayer that her father would finally be convinced that this was best for all. Could he really reject his brother again when everyone had gone to so much trouble to make this a night of peace and goodwill? Everyone here was ready to put aside the past and build a bridge to the future.

Molly heard the doorbell and felt a nervous clenching in her stomach. She took a deep breath. Act two, scene two. Joe and Marie had arrived. She heard them in the foyer. Since it was a party, they hadn't waited for someone to answer the door.

She suddenly felt self-conscious sitting next to her uncle, but she forced herself to stay where she was. She wasn't going to insult Kevin by jumping up, acting as if she felt guilty for being nice to him in front of her father. Though in truth, that had been her instinctive response.

You've got to update the program, Molly, she told herself. *Delete those old files. Remember what Sam said, we're not going to get anyplace tonight if we all start taking sides again.*

Her uncle glanced at her. "Sounds like Joe is here. Let's go say hello," he said lightly.

Molly forced a smile, and they both got to their feet. Molly walked toward the entranceway between the foyer and living room. Matt came to stand beside her, resting his hand on her back.

Joe's eyes were wide and curious as he looked around. "What is this . . . Christmas Eve already? Did I make a mistake on my calendar?"

His gaze fell on Molly first. "You said this was just a little get-together, to welcome the girls home."

"It's a little more than that, Dad," Molly admitted. "There's someone here to see you," she added. She looked around for Uncle Kevin. He was standing with his wife by the Christmas tree, but now walked toward his brother.

"Hello, Joe. I'm happy to see you."

Molly watched her father's face turn white. Her mother touched his arm, but he shook her off.

"You? This is all about you, isn't it? I get it now. You all tricked me."

"We did," Sam admitted. "But we didn't know how else to get you over here, Dad."

Joe turned to Sam. "I should have seen this coming. You just don't give up, do you? You and your grandmother."

"Oh, Joe, can't you just stop being angry for one minute and listen?" Adele implored him.

"Don't be mad at Sam, Dad. We planned it together," Molly said. "It's not about Uncle Kevin . . . or you. Look around. It's all your children and grandchildren . . . and your mother. It's a real family reunion, and long overdue," she tried to explain. "But we all need you and Uncle Kevin to make up and forgive each other. We just want to all be one family again, don't you get it?"

Joe shook his head, and Molly could see that he didn't get it at all. She had an awful feeling that whatever her father was about to say was not going to be good.

"That's right, blame me for everything," he said finally. He lifted his glance and stared at her. "Molly, you cut me to my heart. I thought you were on my side . . . How could you, of all people, do this to me?"

Molly felt a pain in her heart. Had she really betrayed her father? He looked so wounded and sad. She was about to go to him and apologize. But something stopped her. "Dad, we're all on the same side. Honestly. Won't you just talk to Uncle Kevin for five minutes? Just hear him out?"

Joe gave her a cold look, then turned to Molly's mother. "Get the coats, Marie. Let's get out of here."

Uncle Kevin stepped forward. "Come on, Joe. I'm sorry for the surprise. That wasn't right. But you and I can still talk a little, can't we?" When Joe didn't answer, he said, "Did you ever read the letters I sent?"

Joe shook his head. "I threw them out unopened. I knew what you were going to say. I didn't want to waste my time."

Uncle Kevin didn't look surprised or angry, Molly noticed.

"I made mistakes, Joe. I know that. I know taking the store wasn't right. I was desperate back then. Desperate people don't care who they hurt. I was going down and grabbed on to the lifeline Dad tossed to me. I told myself that you would understand."

Molly saw a flicker of sympathy cross her father's face. Then his expression became hard and closed again. "Spare me the psychology class. I don't need this," he said to himself as much as anybody.

"Yes, you do. You need to hear your brother out, once and for all," said Grandma Addie, who had been standing quietly beside Sam and Jessica. Now she suddenly stepped forward and got between her two sons. "I remember when you used to play too rough together and one of you would come to me crying. I would make you both say you were sorry and hug each other. Dear God, how I wish I could do that again," she said.

"Mom, it's all right. Don't get so upset." Kevin rested a hand on Adele's shoulder.

"Of course I'm upset. He doesn't understand. He doesn't want to. He doesn't know the whole story, either," she added, staring at Joe. "Your father and I had our reasons, good reasons—"

"I know. I know," Joe said in a tired voice. "Kevin was drowning himself in a bottle. He was always the weak one."

Kevin didn't respond. He didn't even look fazed by the horrible insults. Perhaps he had expected all of this, and worse.

"It wasn't that," Adele quickly countered. "He has to tell you," she said, looking over at her younger son. "Maybe he already did, in all those letters you didn't read."

Kevin stepped forward. "There was something else, Joe. Something you didn't know about. I made Mom promise not to tell you. Though I'm not sure if it will make any difference to you now."

Joe looked ready to listen, then suddenly changed his mind. "Give me a break, both of you." He turned to go.

But Marie blocked his path. They stared at each other for a long moment, and Molly could see what she had often observed as a child: Though her mother was smaller and quieter than her dad, she was every bit as strong and determined.

"Joe, you just wait one minute now," Marie said, her voice gentle but firm. "You just hear your brother out."

"What, you too now?" Joe looked at her with surprise. But when he saw she wouldn't budge, he finally turned back to his brother. "What is it, Kevin? What is it that I don't know?" Joe crossed his arms over his chest, almost daring his brother to say anything that might change his mind. Molly saw her mother rest a hand on her husband's arm, but he didn't seem to notice.

"It's hard to tell you this. I never wanted you to know. But it's important to be honest and get things out in the open, out where they can't hurt you anymore. That's what I've learned," Kevin began. "When Dad was failing, he kept telling me that he wanted to leave me the store, but I said I didn't want it. It was yours. Then, a week or two before he died . . . I tried to kill myself. I got drunk, cut my wrists, and got in the bathtub. I just could not stand my life anymore. I was a disappointment to everyone I ever loved, including you. I had failed at everything I ever touched. I gave up. I wanted to end my life. I would have succeeded, too, but a drinking buddy of mine who had the keys to my place came by to crash and found me. He somehow sobered up enough to wrap my wrists and call an ambulance. He died a few weeks later in a car accident," Kevin added.

Molly gasped out loud. She felt Matt's arm tighten around her shoulder.

"Your father was desperate to help your brother after that," Adele continued. "To give him something to hang on to. Wouldn't you have done the same for your own child, Joe?"

Joe took a long breath. The story had finally gotten his attention, Molly could see. Though she couldn't predict how he was going to react.

Joe's brow was furrowed in concentration. He looked at his mother and brother and waved his hands at them. "I don't know . . . I don't know what to think of any of this," he practically shouted at them. "How do I even know it's true?"

Molly realized he was confused now, and maybe that was a good thing. But it wasn't enough to make him want to stay.

He suddenly turned to his wife. "Marie, you stay here if you want. I'm going home. You all have a nice visit," he added in a bitter tone. "Toast the guest of honor for me," he added, looking first at his brother, then straight at Molly.

Molly saw frustration flash over her mother's face, then a resigned expression. She came over to give her daughter a quick hug.

"Good night, Molly . . . I'll call you tomorrow," she said in her usual way. "I know you tried, honey," she added quietly.

"We all did, Mom," Molly said. But as she watched her parents make their way to the door, she knew that somehow, it hadn't been enough.

CHAPTER TWELVE

*L*ESLIE HAMMOND WAS PROBABLY THE LAST PERSON ON Earth that Jonathan wanted to meet for lunch on Monday. But she had called him in the morning and said she was driving to Maine to visit her family and remembered that he was just off the highway, in Cape Light.

"I thought it would be nice if we had lunch together. I bet you're dying to see a friendly face and have some intelligent conversation."

Jonathan had almost replied that there had been no lack of intelligent conversation the past two weeks. Not since he had met Tess.

But the less said to Leslie, the better. He already knew that. She was not exactly a friend, but not really an enemy. More of a . . . frenemy, he would have to say. As doctoral candidates in the same program, they acted like comrades, but they both knew that under the thin veneer of social niceties, they were actually serious rivals.

Leslie's visit was not so much a social call as a snooping mission. She wanted to find out what he was up to with all this field research—and

THOMAS KINKADE AND KATHERINE SPENCER

whether she needed to worry that he was getting ahead of her in the department pecking order.

He knew he had to see her and convince her there was nothing for her to worry about. Or her efforts would get even more creative once he returned to the department. Like, "borrowing" a flash drive from his computer or "accidentally" taking a file from his desk. She had already done both of those things.

It was unfortunate, but he couldn't trust her—or trust that if she knew what he was working on, she wouldn't try to steal his idea.

Jonathan wasn't even sure right now what that idea was. The shape and direction of it seemed to keep shifting, like a cloud floating in the wind. At first he was sure that he had come to find the real reason that those quarantined on Angel Island had survived the epidemic. But now, he wasn't so sure at all.

Leslie didn't have to know that, either. He had told her to meet him at the Clam Box at twelve sharp. He knew that Tess wasn't working there today because he was due to meet her at the historical society at two.

Imagine that, a guy like me having to keep two women apart. It's like a scene in some silly date movie. He had to smile at the idea, even though Leslie was far from a romantic interest.

Tess . . . now she was another story. A wonderful story. When Thursday night had rolled around, she was still too sick to go out on their big date. But they hung out together at her house, watching the Hitchcock movie he had found at the library and eating popcorn. Which was even better than the night he had planned. Jonathan had been invited for dinner with her family, too, and when Tess's mother heard he had no plans for Christmas, she asked him to come to their Christmas Eve party. He had even let Billy beat him at a video game. He couldn't remember when he'd had a better time with a girl . . . unless it was their tour around the island last Sunday.

When he left on Thursday night, he had made it very clear to Tess that he wanted to see her once they got back to Boston, and she seemed more than fine with that plan.

Jonathan felt so happy every time he thought about her he could barely keep his mind on his work these past few days. This sneak attack from Leslie was just a blip on the screen. His radar was set for Tess, and he could hardly wait to see her.

He would have plenty of time to get Leslie out of his hair and back on the road by two, he was sure. He knew that Leslie had a little crush on him. They had gone out on one or two dates last year, but nothing had come of it. She was smart and attractive, but definitely not his type. They were fine being colleagues . . . at least he was.

He arrived at the Clam Box a few minutes before twelve. There were plenty of empty tables, and the older waitress, Trudy, met him at the door. She even knew his name by now.

"Just yourself today, Jonathan?" she said.

"A friend is joining me. She should be here soon."

She led him to a table by the window. "I'll leave two menus. Be back in a minute to take your order."

Jonathan nodded and looked out the window to see if Leslie was coming down the street to the diner. He checked his watch. She was usually very punctual. He hoped she hadn't gotten lost. Timing was important here today.

"Hey, what are you doing here? Did you track me down again?" He heard a cheerful voice and looked up. It was Tess, in her waitress uniform. She looked so cute, his first impulse was to jump up and kiss her.

But he knew Charlie wouldn't like that, and he didn't want to get her in trouble. Instead, he just smiled. "No, I didn't stalk you. I thought you weren't working here today."

"Charlie called me in for some extra hours, breakfast and lunch. I'll be off soon. I can still meet you later."

"Oh . . . well, good. That's very good," he repeated awkwardly. Jonathan forced a smile but didn't know what to say.

"Give me your order. I'll tell Charlie to rush it."

"That's okay. I don't want to jump the line. I don't know what I want yet . . . and Trudy is my waitress, I think," he added. Tess gave him a puzzled look. "Besides, I'm meeting someone . . . a friend of mine from school."

Jonathan was about to explain more—that Leslie was more of a snooping rival than a friend—when Leslie entered the diner. She saw him, and a big smile stretched across her face. She waved wildly, as if she were on a cruise ship and he was down on a dock, awaiting her arrival.

Jonathan managed a weak smile and a wave in return. Tess followed his gaze. "Is that your friend?"

He nodded. "We're in the same program. She was driving by on her way to Maine."

Leslie came to the table and Jonathan stood up politely. She greeted him with a big hug. "It's so good to see you, Jonathan. I feel like you've been gone for months. There's no one left to talk to. No one funny or smart," she added.

She sat down and put her handbag on the seat beside her. Then she glanced at Tess. "Just a glass of water please, miss, with plenty of ice. What a quaint place. I guess there aren't too many choices here." She leaned toward Jonathan. "Anything decent to eat? I have a sensitive stomach."

Tess looked a little put out by Leslie's imperious treatment, but she took it on the chin, Jonathan thought. She was about to walk away, but Jonathan stopped her.

"Leslie, this is Tess," Jonathan said quickly. He was going to describe Tess as a friend, but she seemed so much more now. Still, he felt wary of calling her his girlfriend. It didn't seem the time or the place to announce that to the world. Was it? he wondered.

Leslie was still reading the menu and glanced up. She looked at Tess, as if seeing her for the first time. "Oh, how do you do? Leslie Hammond." She stretched out her hand and Tess shook it.

"Nice to meet you," Tess said evenly. She looked at Jonathan. "I'll go find Trudy for you. Have a good lunch."

Jonathan followed her with his gaze. He couldn't tell if she was mad or not. Leslie had treated Tess like she was furniture, but he had introduced her, trying to make up for that.

I'll explain everything to her later. She'll understand, Jonathan told himself.

Trudy came and they ordered. "A salad's usually safe," Leslie said as Trudy left. She picked up her fork and rubbed it with a paper napkin. "How's the research going, Jonathan? People keep asking where you are. There must be something pretty important for you to camp out here in the wilderness."

"Oh, it's not such a big deal. But it is time-consuming," he replied.

"Everything worthwhile is. Waldham says you've got some Native American thing cooking out here. I bet him twenty bucks he was wrong."

"Really? You two must be pretty bored." Jonathan smiled, acting amused. Did she expect him to chomp on that bait? He even doubted that Leslie had made a wager with Mitch Waldham, another doctoral candidate, though he didn't doubt that they gossiped about him.

She shrugged and tilted her head to one side, her smooth brown hair falling across her shoulder. "We're all stuck in the trenches together, Jon. We have to have some amusements."

Jonathan took a sip of his water and sighed inwardly. He hated when people shortened his name like that, but he didn't bother to tell her. He snuck a peek at his watch. Had they only been sitting here ten minutes? It felt like hours.

"So what are you up to these days, Leslie? How did it go with that article you did on the mining strike? Have you sent it to any journals yet?"

"A few. These editorial review boards take so long. It's ancient history by the time they get back to you. I almost had a hit on the last one, *American Scholarly Review*. But one reader sent it back with about a million queries. I think she even complained about the typeface I used."

Trudy brought their lunch, and Leslie stabbed a slice of tomato with vigor. Jonathan shook his head in sympathy. "That's too bad. Sometimes I think these journals are more interested in rejecting material than publishing anything. Just to keep their standards up." While his observation was true, and Leslie was smart and ambitious, Jonathan knew she was also a pretty sloppy, slapdash scholar. He wasn't surprised her paper had not met their editorial standards. She churned out papers but got few published. He, on the other hand, was slow and careful, the tortoise who didn't turn out much but crept to the finish line.

The conversation lapsed for a moment as Trudy returned and filled their water glasses.

"Okay, not Native Americans," Leslie suddenly. "Now I'm guessing the seeds of the Revolution?" It took Jonathan a moment to catch up with her. Then he realized she was still trying to guess the topic he was researching. "I hear there was some interesting activity among the local population, spies in the British army who sympathized with the colonists. Could have been a real lynchpin of the entire war. No one has ever been able to document it, though. Do you think that's true?"

"Really? That would be a good study . . . Wait, let me get this down." Jonathan took a pen from his pocket and pretended to jot notes on a napkin. He already knew about that footnote of Revolutionary War history, but it wasn't his beat.

"Jonathan!" Leslie laughed and reached out to cover his hand with her own. "Just stop. I know when you're putting me on."

"And I know when you're trying to inveigle information out of me," he replied with good humor that he really didn't feel.

"Inveigle?" Leslie's eyebrows rose. "Isn't that a harsh thing to say about a friend?"

Jonathan felt someone standing by the table and looked up to see Tess again. Leslie's hand was still covering his, and he slowly pulled it away.

"Tess, do you have a minute?" he said impulsively. "Come and talk to my friend Leslie. She's giving me all the dirt about the department."

Inside he felt like a melting dish of ice cream. His false cheer was annoying even to his own ears, and Tess was looking at him with a totally puzzled—and repulsed—expression.

Still, he persisted. He couldn't help himself. "Tess is studying history, too. At Boston University," he told Leslie. "She's also specializing in the colonial era."

Leslie glanced at her. "I didn't know they let you specialize as an undergrad. Is that a special program?"

"I'm in my senior year, and I've been allowed to take some grad courses."

"Oh, good for you. You must be very bright," Leslie said, as if she were talking to a five-year-old.

"Tess works at the historical society in town," Jonathan added quickly before Leslie could somehow manage to insult her again. "She's a docent there. She's been a great help with my research."

As soon as the words came out, Jonathan realized he had made a big mistake.

Leslie turned and focused her full attention on Tess. "Really? I could always use a good researcher. What sort of material did you unearth for him?"

Tess looked taken aback by her tone. "Some letters. About the Marsh Fever quarantine on Angel Island. It wasn't called Angel Island back then though, of course—"

"And when was that, exactly?" Leslie acted as if she was just curious, but Jonathan knew she was digging for information.

"Oh, it was just a few letters. Nothing important," Jonathan cut in before Tess could go any further.

He tried to send Tess a message with his eyes, but she wouldn't look at him. He knew he was being rude, but he couldn't let Tess give away the entire subject of his study. She had already given Leslie a huge clue. He knew he might seem paranoid to Tess, but he didn't want anyone to know what he was working on.

Good research ideas and theories were stolen every day in academia. And some people, like Leslie, were such gossips. Even if she was only interested to find out if his paper was any better than her research, she would tell the whole world about his ideas and someone out there would find them worthy of stealing.

"Tess . . . Charlie wants you. Looks like he's got an order up," he said suddenly.

Charlie stood behind the counter making sandwiches. He had looked their way a few times with his usual scowl, but he wasn't trying to get Tess's attention. Not now, anyway.

Tess looked over her shoulder. When she looked back, Jonathan could tell she knew he had just made an excuse to get rid of her. To his astonishment, she played along.

"Thanks. I think you're right. I don't want to lose my great job here." She smiled at Leslie and snapped her gum. "Enjoy your lunch." Then she flounced off with an exaggerated walk. Jonathan watched her with a sinking feeling.

"Do you eat here much? You seem to know her pretty well." Leslie had only finished half her salad but pushed the dish away.

"I do know her. She's . . . a very interesting person."

Leslie gave him a skeptical look.

She's more intelligent and interesting than you, he nearly said.

But it wasn't Leslie's fault. He was the one who had made a mess of things. Tess felt hurt now, and he didn't blame her. He only hoped he could get rid of Leslie quickly.

He would catch up with Tess at Lilac Hall later. *In a little while, we'll be laughing about this,* he told himself.

When Trudy came to the table a few minutes later, Jonathan asked for the check. Leslie looked a little surprised. She hadn't finished her coffee. "Don't let me rush you," he said politely as he picked up the check. "Take your time, finish your coffee. I have an appointment. I didn't realize how late it was."

He did have an appointment, an important one . . . meeting Tess. She no longer seemed to be in the diner, and he wondered if her shift was over and she had left through the kitchen.

"Oh, that's too bad. I thought we could walk around the town a little, and you could show me the sights. Maybe I should wait for you somewhere. How long do you think you'll be?"

Leslie was nothing if not persistent, wasn't she? Jonathan almost had to marvel at her.

"I'm sorry, I don't think that will work out. We'll catch up after the holidays. Maybe you'll win that twenty dollars from Waldham after all and you can take me out to lunch."

Leslie laughed. "I would, but I can't win it if you don't tell me what you're working on."

"Good point." Jonathan was already standing. He gathered his jacket and bag. "Have a safe trip. Merry Christmas."

"Same to you, Jonathan. Thanks for lunch. It was great to see you." Leslie stood up and gave him another big hug and a big kiss on his cheek. Then she just stood with her arms around his shoulders. "Will you be back for New Year's Eve? My roommates and I are having a party. I hope you can come."

"Sounds fun. I'll let you know," he said, quickly slipping from her embrace. "See you soon."

Jonathan was finally out of her reach and quickly walked to the door. Out on Main Street, he practically jogged to his car and drove straight to Lilac Hall.

"HOW ABOUT THAT SANDWICH YOU MADE ME LAST WEEK—WITH THE chicken and cheese and arugula? Got any of those around today, Moll?"

Molly had asked Sam to stop by the shop on Monday. Of course, he had come at lunchtime, though she never minded feeding him.

They hadn't spoken after the party Saturday night. They both felt stunned by what Kevin and Adele revealed and shocked that, even in the light of that revelation, their father had remained so angry and unforgiving. But after Joe and Marie left, the gathering had continued. On a more subdued note, to be sure. Still, everyone had enjoyed spending time with Uncle Kevin and his family. Reconnecting with them was the one good thing that had emerged from this heartbreaking situation, Molly thought.

She set the sandwich and a cup of coffee in front of her brother and sat down across from him.

"So, what do you think now?" he asked her.

"I think we've lost a father . . . but gained an uncle?" She tried to smile but couldn't quite manage it.

"Don't joke. Did you call Dad yet? I tried yesterday. He wouldn't talk to me."

"I figured. I didn't even try. He needs some time to cool down, Sam. You know how he gets."

Molly was honestly afraid to call her father. The way he had looked at her, it hurt all over just to think of it.

"So . . ." Sam's tone was cautious. "Are you going to say I told you so? I mean, if you are, let's just get it over with."

She sat back and looked at her brother. Maybe, at some other point in this saga, she would have said that. But Molly knew, somewhere along the line, something inside her had shifted. She saw this whole story differently. The view from her head . . . and her heart.

"No, I'm not going to say that. For once," she added, making him smile. "I think we did the right thing. What I told Dad was true. It's about more than him and Uncle Kevin. We're all connected. Or should be. At least we tried, right?"

Sam nodded. "Yeah, we did. But I can't help feeling things are even worse now than when Grandma Addie got here. Though I'd never tell her that."

"I wouldn't, either," Molly agreed. "She'll only feel guilty. I spoke to her yesterday on the phone. She's still up at the inn. She felt too tired for the drive on Sunday, poor thing."

The entire evening had been emotionally wrenching for their grandmother. Molly wasn't sure how she had gotten through it. She was stronger than they all gave her credit for, that was for sure.

"Is she staying until Christmas?" Sam asked.

"No, she said she was leaving this week. As soon as she feels up to it."

"Christmas is only a week away, Moll. What's going to happen if Dad's still angry? It will ruin the entire holiday for the kids, for all of us."

Molly had thought of that, too. "Do you and Jessica want to skip the Christmas Eve party this year? We'll understand," she added quickly. "We can all just hang out at home and get together on Christmas Day for desserts or something, so the kids can open their presents together."

"I've been wondering the same thing," Sam confessed. "Should we really cancel Christmas over this? The whole idea seems crazy, but if Dad stays this angry, there wouldn't be much joy in a party. It would almost be as if we were getting together just to spite him. But what about the kids?" he added. "They don't understand what's happening."

Molly thought the same. The teenagers, along with Tyler, had been in their own world, at the back of the house with their loud music and

TV-screen dance game. The little ones, Betty and Lily, had been playing with dolls up in Betty's room. Luckily for everyone.

"I know. But it's up to you and Jess. We'll do whatever you want."

"We talked about it. Jess wants to have the party whether or not Dad and Mom want to come. Her family is counting on it. We have to think of them, too."

Jessica's sister, Emily, was the town mayor. She and her husband, Dan, and their youngest daughter, Jane, were always at Sam's house for Christmas Eve. Emily's older daughter, Sara, and her husband, Luke, usually came in for a few days from Boston, and sometimes Dan's daughter Lindsay, who ran the *Cape Light Messenger*, came with her family, too. It was a full house, no question, and it was the biggest party of the year. Everyone looked forward to it.

"You know how Jessica's mother gets," Sam said, talking about his mother-in-law, Lillian. "She hates any change of traditions or plans. If we wanted to cancel this party, we would have needed to send her a registered letter back in July."

Molly had to laugh. But it was true. Lillian Warwick and her husband, Dr. Ezra Elliot, would not understand such a disruption in their schedule. Molly knew that the Morgan family—with all their boisterous displays of emotion—was still a mind-boggling experience for Lillian. She could never understand why her younger daughter had chosen Sam Morgan . . . and never would.

"It's settled then. Game on for Christmas Eve. No matter what kind of mood Dad's in." Molly tried to sound positive but knew she didn't quite pull it off.

No question about it. This year Christmas was going to be a forced march, one she sort of dreaded now. She hated to blame Grandma Addie, but Sam had a point. Things were worse—much worse—than they had been before their grandmother got here, and Molly wondered now if it had all been worth it, despite what she had just told Sam. Even though it had been good to reconnect with Uncle Kevin, he was off to New Zealand in a week or two.

But her father . . . oh, dear . . . her father lived just a few blocks away and was a major part of her life. Or had been. The way things were going, she thought bleakly, Joe Morgan might as well be moving halfway around the world, too.

"I MADE A BIG MISTAKE COMING HERE. I CAN SEE THAT NOW. A LOT OF good it did me." Adele sighed and brushed her hands with flour. She had been sitting in the kitchen, watching Claire knead bread dough, and now took a large flour-dusted pillow herself and began punching it down.

"Addie, don't be so hard on yourself. Your grandchildren wanted to help. I'm sure they don't blame you." Claire looked up a minute from her work and met Adele's gaze.

"I'm not sure about that. I apologized to Molly when she called yesterday. She was good about it, but I know she's upset. Now her father isn't speaking to her, or to Sam. What kind of Christmas will they have? All thanks to me. What good has it accomplished?" Claire didn't answer. Adele didn't expect her to. "I should go tomorrow. I feel fit enough for the drive," she said before Claire could ask. She had felt so worn out after Saturday night, she had slept until nearly one on Sunday, and this morning she got up late again.

That was the way she had always dealt with emotional turmoil and stressful confrontations. Some people stayed up worrying all night. But emotional scenes drained her, like a battery that runs out of juice, more so now that she was older.

"Why don't you stay here through Christmas, Addie? It's only another week. We'd love to have you with us. You can see your family . . . or spend Christmas Eve here," Claire said evenly. "It will just be me and Liza and Daniel Merritt. Our neighbors, Rob and Audrey, may come . . . and

Jonathan might stay. I haven't asked him yet, but I don't think he's done with his research."

It was an intriguing invitation. If she stayed, would she see her grandchildren and their families again? She hoped they weren't too angry with her now for the big mess she caused. Jessica and Sam had invited her for Christmas Eve. But it might be too hard to stay here if they didn't really want to see her now.

Still, Adele didn't look forward to going home and being alone with her thoughts in her empty house. She had left Vermont in such a rush. There were no decorations up, no Christmas tree, no presents or baking done. She didn't really want to face that overwhelming emptiness, either.

"I'm not sure what to do, Claire. I'm really not sure," she said honestly. "It's all Joe, you know? Nothing we say or do can change his heart. But I see now I should have realized that. I should have known, after everything that Kevin went through. George and I pulled our hair out, trying to make him give up alcohol. We cried, we bullied, we bribed him. Right to the very end," she admitted. "But we didn't change him. Not one bit. He was the only one who could do that." She sighed, punching down the pile of dough again, turning it around and around, then flipping it over. "It's the same with Joe. I see that now. Everything Molly did with that beautiful party. Everything Kevin said and I said . . . You can't convince someone to feel something they don't feel. It just doesn't work that way."

"That is true," Claire agreed. "You can't talk someone into a feeling. It has to come from inside of them."

She stopped her work and looked down at the dough, which she had coated with a light touch of oil and returned to a large yellow bowl.

"Bread is so much work. It takes so long to rise. Sometimes I don't think it's ever going to amount to much. It sits and sits. Then I turn around and . . . there it is, doubled up and ready for the oven. The yeast is so slow. But it always does its job."

She covered the bowl with a clean cloth and placed it back on the counter in a warm spot, so it could sit some more.

Adele glanced at her. She had finished punching down her dough, too, and was preparing for its second rise. "You mean, I have to be patient and let Joe sit with this and see what happens?"

Claire glanced at her but didn't answer. "There are two more meetings of the Christmas Fair committee, one tomorrow night and one on Thursday. Then the fair is on Saturday. Do you really want to leave after you put so much work in? We could definitely use your help at the table." Before Adele could answer, her friend said, "I'm going to make some soup while the bread sits. Would you like to help?"

Adele didn't have any place she would rather be at that moment. "I'd be happy to," she said.

JONATHAN HAD TRIED TO CATCH UP WITH TESS AT LILAC HALL ALL afternoon, but she kept avoiding him. He could tell she was mad. It was so frustrating. He was sure that if she would just give him a chance to explain, she would understand and forgive him.

It wasn't like her to be this way. She was usually so calm and logical. He hated knowing she was upset with him. He tried to work in the reading room, but he couldn't concentrate. He kept glancing at the doorway every time he heard footsteps, hoping she was coming to see him. But she never did, even though he texted her several times.

At four o'clock he had to go down to sign out with the rest of the visitors. He finally saw her at the front desk. "Can I walk out with you, Tess?"

She shrugged and didn't look at him. "I'll be a while. I have to check all the rooms upstairs."

"That's all right. I'll wait," he promised.

Mrs. Fisk soon shooed him outside. It was chilly and getting dark, but Jonathan waited near the entrance, afraid that if he got into his car, he might miss Tess.

Finally, she came out, the collar on her dark blue peacoat flipped up and that candy-cane-striped scarf wrapped around her neck.

She faced him at the bottom of the steps, her hands stuck in her pockets. "I have to get home, Jonathan. What is it? Something important?" she asked pointedly.

He knew she was mimicking what he had said to Leslie. That the letters Tess had found were "nothing important."

"I'm sorry about what happened in the diner today, with Leslie Hammond. She's such a snoop. She was just trying to find out what my research is about. She so competitive, I can't trust her. That's why I interrupted you and said the letters you found weren't important. I didn't mean that," he insisted. "They're very important. You helped me immensely—"

"Good. I'm glad. That's what I've been trained to do here. Now, if you will let me pass—"

He took hold of her arm. "Tess, please don't act like that. I'm trying to explain. I'm really sorry . . . I never know how to handle that woman."

Tess shrugged and stepped away from him. "Oh, you seemed to be handling her fine. Or she was handling you. It was hard to tell."

He knew what she was talking about. He knew how it had looked to her, too. If he had been in her place, he would not have liked seeing some other guy acting so familiar with her.

"Okay, she took my hand while we were talking . . . and she gets very . . . huggy when we say hello. We dated once or twice," he admitted. "But she's not my type at all. We're just friends. Just barely."

"Oh? Well, perhaps you ought to tell *her* that. I think she's confused." Tess started to walk toward her car, then turned back to him. "Listen, I get it. It's all right. I believe she's just your friend. Honestly. And you don't have to explain yourself to me. We hardly even know each other."

He was pleased to hear that she believed him, but that last line stumped him. "We don't?"

She shook her head slowly. "Not really . . . I think this has just been a . . . a fun thing between us while you were in town and I was home from school. I didn't really think anything would come of it. I mean, after you left here. I don't think that's what I want now, anyway," she added.

Jonathan felt stunned by her words. Was she just saying that to get back at him—to protect herself?

"You don't? But we talked about this, just . . . Thursday night." *The best night of his life*, he wanted to add. "I thought we both felt the same, I thought we had all this figured out—"

"I know what we said, Jonathan, but it wasn't very realistic. It was a very special night and I think we just got a little carried away. But you have your life and I have mine. I don't think the timing is very good at all. Once you get back to Tufts, you'll be teaching classes and writing your dissertation. And I'm totally overloaded next semester with my course work. I don't see how we'll ever get to see each other—"

"But we could. If we really want to. We could make this work easily . . ."

Then he caught himself. She was dumping him. He hadn't understood at first. Something had changed her feelings about him. Something that had happened today.

"So you don't want to be in touch when we get back to the city," he said just to make perfectly sure he understood her.

"I don't think it's a good idea," she said quietly. "I'm sorry."

He nodded. "I see. I see . . ." He didn't know what to say after that. He felt his eyes sting and get suddenly watery. Was he actually crying? That couldn't be. He had just been standing here in the cold too long. "Well . . . good-bye, Tess. I'll see you around town, I guess. I'll be here a few more days."

Tess looked suddenly sad, like she, too, might cry. Didn't she want this? She was the one who had started it.

"Okay then . . . so long. Good luck with your paper. Oh, and don't forget to get those letters back to Digger before you go. I have a feeling he's forgotten that you borrowed them."

He nodded curtly. "I won't forget. I'll return them. Don't worry." He raised his hand and waved stiffly. "Good-bye, Tess."

She waved back, then turned and walked off to her car.

He walked to his, but sat in the driver's seat a long time before he could gather his concentration to head back to the inn.

What had just happened? What had he done? Everything had seemed so good between them. So easy and right.

It was over. In the blink of an eye. Jonathan couldn't believe it.

She'd swept into his life and lit up every room in his lonely heart. Now, just like that, she was gone.

Lights out.

CHAPTER THIRTEEN

⟋⟍

O N SATURDAY MORNING, JUST TWO DAYS BEFORE CHRISTMAS, Adele found herself still at the inn. She probably would not have stayed through the week—that had never been her plan—but Claire had persuaded her, one day at a time, to put off her plans to go.

First because she was too tired for the long drive on her own, then to help at the fair committee meetings, and then to help at the actual fair, which Claire claimed was very shorthanded this year.

Adele had spoken to Kevin a few times since the unsuccessful reunion. He had been concerned to hear she was so tired and decided that since she had stayed in Cape Light this long, there was no point in her trying to rush home to Vermont for Christmas. He and his family would come down to the inn on Christmas Day to visit her. The day after Christmas, he would drive her home to Vermont in her Subaru. Janine and the kids would follow in their car. That way, they could spend the holiday together, and they would know she got home safely.

"You don't have to do that, Kevin," she insisted. "I'm perfectly capable of getting myself back home. I've just enjoyed the company down here, and they need my help for an event at the church—"

"I'm leaving here soon, Mom. There's not too much more I can do for you. Let me help you this once, okay?"

She was glad that he hadn't listened to her excuses. And relieved that she didn't need to make a big dinner and entertain guests. Or drive all over New England.

"All right, if you insist. I've been invited to spend Christmas Day at the inn with Claire and Liza, so it all works out." Adele nearly asked if she should tell the rest of the family he was returning, but she decided not to even go there, as the young people say.

She had been worried about his sobriety, at the party and afterward. The emotional confrontation with Joe had certainly put that at risk, and if Kevin had lapsed in his recovery because of her . . . well, she never would have forgiven herself.

It was a difficult question to ask, but ever since he stopped drinking, he had encouraged her honesty. She did ask him, and she was assured that while he had been deeply disappointed by Joe's reaction, he had never thought to soothe his pain with drink.

"That path is closed to me now, Mom. It's closed for good," he promised her. "Though I will say this was the hardest test I've faced so far."

Had this all been just a test of Kevin's recovery? Had that been God's purpose after all?

Adele was so confused. She had no idea of what to think of all of it and decided it was best if she didn't even try. She only hoped that she lived long enough for the true meaning to be revealed to her.

"It's good fair weather. Good weather for a fair, I mean. It will bring out the customers," Claire said, making a little joke as she parked in back of the church.

It was a fair day, with clear blue skies, not nearly as cold as it might have been two days before Christmas. The snow that had fallen after Adele's arrival had all but melted away. It didn't look as if it was going to be a white Christmas after all. Better for travelers and all that, but Adele did love to see a fresh white blanket of snow on Christmas Day. It didn't really feel like Christmas without it.

Adele and Claire made their way into the church, which was already bustling with activity, though the fair had not yet opened. Adele had forgotten how completely the church was transformed by the event. Every available space was filled with tables and activities. With a huge wreath on the big wooden doors, pine garlands in the hallways, and a beautiful tree in the sanctuary, the church was decked out for the holidays, and she could not help but feel the spirit that abounded there.

She and Claire made their way into Fellowship Hall, which had been set up the night before as the main marketplace.

"Here's our table, number nine," Claire said, reading from a sheet of instructions sent to the committee members. "We have the White Elephant, china, odds and ends, and collectibles. You can find a lot of gifts here if your list is short," she suggested.

Adele's list was very short. It was practically nonexistent, though she had picked up a few things around town during her afternoon walks. She hoped to find a few more small gifts today and at least leave them at the inn for her family, if she didn't get to visit with them. It saddened her to think that she could be in town for the holiday, and no one would invite her to join them. But she could understand it, too. She had come down here and stirred everything up, upset the entire applecart . . .

Oh, no use dwelling on it. Or feeling sorry for yourself. You did what you thought was necessary, she told herself briskly.

Sophie Potter came over and gave them instructions for running the table, showing them how every item had been priced and ticketed with a little sticker. "Some people will try to bargain with you. That's all right if things aren't moving very well or it's the end of the day. I'll trust your judgment," she told Claire and Adele. "If there are any outrageous offers—say on this big alabaster lamp—just come find me. This is a fund-raiser. We don't want to give the store away," she warned them.

Adele nodded, knowing she was most likely to do that. Even though she and her husband had run a store for many years, she had never been very good at business.

It was just past nine a.m., and the fair was not due to open until ten. There was plenty of time to visit with the rest of the volunteers, and as Adele was greeted by all of her old friends she wasn't one bit sorry that she stayed. A vision of herself home alone in Vermont in an empty, bare little house was definitely not more appealing.

Reverend Ben and his wife, Carolyn, were there, too. Carolyn was working at a table across the room that sold wooden toys, puzzles, and small drums and woodwind instruments for children, and Reverend Ben was helping everyone get settled in their places.

Adele wondered if he would notice her. She had not attended the service on Sunday because she was too exhausted. The reverend probably thought she was already back in Vermont.

Finally, he did notice her and quickly walked over to say hello. "Adele . . . still here? I thought you were headed home."

"I couldn't abandon the Christmas Fair committee, Reverend. They persuaded me to stay." *One committee member in particular,* she wanted to add. But Claire was not at the table with her just then. She had forgotten something in her car and gone back to get it.

"How about your family? Did they persuade you, too?"

Adele looked at him a moment, then shook her head. "The get-together we had last Saturday at Molly's house . . . my son Kevin came," she added. "But it didn't go well . . . not as I had hoped."

He seemed to understand without her needing to say more. "I'm sorry to hear that. I know how you were counting on it. But please don't lose heart. No sincere attempt at forgiveness is entirely lost, Adele. Think of it like drops of water, wearing down stone."

She did think of her son Joe's heart as stone sometimes, though she knew it was unfair of her. All she could do was nod in agreement.

"So will you be spending Christmas Day here?"

"Yes, I will. Liza and Claire have invited me, and Kevin is coming on Christmas Day with his family. Then he's going to drive me back home. I guess my children are starting to worry about me," she added with a laugh. "I've been acting a bit . . . erratically."

"All for a good cause," he reminded her. He smiled and briefly touched her shoulder. "I won't say good-bye now. I'll look for you in church on Christmas, okay?"

"I'll be there," she promised. "See you then, Reverend."

There were no volunteers at the table next to theirs that sold pine wreaths, centerpieces, and roping. But soon after Reverend Ben had gone, Adele noticed Sam's wife, Jessica, and her sister, Emily Warwick, along with their two young daughters, Lily and Jane. Emily was just as Adele remembered her, tall and slim with smooth brown hair and bright blue eyes. She was about ten years older than Jessica, but didn't look her age; she never had. Adele guessed that her daughter Jane was about seven now, a lively little girl with blue-gray eyes and reddish-gold hair.

The women rushed into the room, each holding their little girls firmly by the hand, as they searched out and consulted with Sophie. Sophie directed them to the table full of pine. Lily was the first to notice her great-grandmother. Though she didn't seem to think it was unusual to see her there, which Adele found amusing.

"Grandma Addie! What are you selling? Can we help you?" Lily asked.

"Of course you can. I definitely need some good helpers today." She bent to receive her sweet kisses and hugs. How that made her day. *Thank you, God, for this*, she said silently.

When she stood up, Jessica was there, too. She also gave Adele a kiss and hugged her warmly.

"Grandma, are you really working here today? Does Sam know? He didn't tell me."

"I kept planning to go home all week. But somehow, here I am," Adele explained.

She had spoken to both Molly and Sam a few times since Saturday. They had both been concerned about her, but a little distant, too, she thought. "I told Sam I would let him know when I left, but so far that hasn't happened, as you can see."

"We're still having our family party on Christmas Eve. If you're here, you must join us."

Adele wanted to go to the party, but if Joe was going to be there, she didn't want to spoil everything again with another scene.

Jessica seemed to sense this dilemma and quickly said, "I don't know if you've heard from Sam's father. But he still isn't speaking to Sam or Molly . . . or any of us, actually. So we don't expect him. Molly is coming with her crew, and my sister and her family will be there." Jessica glanced at Emily, who stood arranging their merchandise into neat rows.

"Oh, that sounds wonderful," Adele said honestly. "But I don't have gifts. I haven't done any real shopping—"

"Please don't worry about that. The kids already get too many gifts, and the adults don't need a thing. We just want you with us. That will be our gift," Jessica insisted. She was a very sweet woman. Her grandson had chosen well, Adele thought.

Despite all the strife and drama, at her age could she really pass up a chance to spend such a lovely night with her family? Adele didn't think she could.

"If you don't want to drive at night, Sam will come and get you," Jessica added, leaving Adele no way to refuse.

"All right. I'll be happy to come. Thank you, Jessica."

"Please don't thank me, Grandma. That's what Christmas is about. That's what families are about. It's time we all started remembering that."

Before Adele could reply, Emily waved hello and then beckoned her sister back to the table. There seemed some question to decide with their girls, and Jessica's input was needed.

Claire bustled back and came to stand beside her. "Sorry I abandoned you, Addie. I made some cinnamon bread for the bake sale and forgot all about it in the car. Is everything all right?"

"Everything is just fine. And I wanted to thank you," Adele added, "for persuading me to stay. I think staying out the week here was the right thing to do."

"Well, that's good then." Claire didn't seem at all surprised as she checked the price on a sticker under an old pocket watch. "Look at this old watch. I wonder if it still runs." She wound the stem, held it to her ear, and then put it down. "I often wonder what sort of watch God carries in His pocket . . . I know His sense of timing is rarely in sync with ours."

That was very true, Adele thought, and worth remembering.

Sophie opened the doors to the Fellowship Hall, and the first customers walked in. Adele and Claire were happily occupied the rest of the afternoon. There wasn't much time for conversation. Or more worrying about family troubles. Which, Adele had decided, could not solve anything.

JONATHAN WAS ALONE AT THE INN ON SATURDAY AFTERNOON, though the stillness all around him did not help his concentration. All he could think about was Tess and how stupid he had been to hurt her feelings just for the sake of protecting his research. He had been so excited about this study and the original eyewitness evidence he had found here, but none of that seemed very important now. So much of the excitement, he now realized, had been working with her, their unexpected but synergistic partnership. He had avoided Lilac Hall ever since their argument. Her rejection had been a blow, and he wasn't ready to face her again. He wasn't sure if he ever would be.

He had enough materials at the inn to keep him busy for a few days more. Particularly, the Hegman letters, which were slow going. He had transcribed four of the five pages so far. Though few women of her time were taught to read and write, Mary Hegman clearly had a talent for it. Her descriptions of her surroundings and the people she had been confined with were rich with detail—the rough huts and sparse provisions and the deep faith that sustained them. She thanked God continually that her child had survived and that she was strong enough to nurse him.

He was finding it surprisingly hard to read these reports of hardship and sacrifice, even though it had all happened hundreds of years ago and these people were long gone from this world. He was no stranger to the scrutiny of hard times and even violent events. But for some reason this time Jonathan felt the personal accounts of this epidemic and quarantine penetrate his heart. He had lost some protective force field, some emotional armor he had never even realized had been there. Perhaps it was his scholarly objectivity.

It was all about Tess and his feelings for her. *She's robbed me of my super-scholar powers,* he tried to joke to himself.

Jonathan picked up his magnifying glass and forced himself to focus on the last letter. All he had was a single page, though it appeared that the missive had been longer. It began with Mary's usual greetings to her husband, with hopes that he was still healthy and getting by without her. But toward the bottom of the page she began to talk about *"an odd happening here and surely, there was God's hand in it."*

That line caught his eye and he eagerly read on, though the faded ink and scrawling writing was doubly frustrating to him now.

She wrote that Joshua Swift, a farmer they both knew from the settlement who was also quarantined, had been so near death, *"a shallow grave had been prepared for him in a patch of sandy earth, just beyond the encampment, where the departed have been laid to rest while the ground remains frozen.*

"But next morning, Joshua Swift walked about freely, fully healed. Even the violent boils that erupted on his face and arms had vanished while my own persist these long weeks. People speak of two visitors who came in the night. How they rowed ashore, we cannot fathom. The sea was high and a storm swept over the island through the night, likely to dash a small boat to pieces. Indeed, this man and woman did not appear to have come by sea, though they delivered several barrels of grain and dried cod and even one of apples. Blankets, much needed, as well.

"They walked about in thick dark cloaks and fine boots, no better to be found at the King's boot maker. Some say even the sandy earth did not soil them and that they moved in a heavenly light. They walked from hut to hut, searching for the sick ones and . . ."

Jonathan came to the end of the page. He sat back, stunned. Then he quickly looked through the other pages he had transcribed, hoping that by some miracle, this letter continued and he had somehow not noticed the missing page. But he was right the first time. Though Mary continued her account to her husband, Ezekiel, the rest of the letter had not survived.

Jonathan felt a lump in his throat. Visitors? In fine clothes? What could this mean?

It still doesn't mean that the visitors were angels, he reminded himself. *There must be some logical explanation for all this. Or perhaps in her grief and sickness, Mary Hegman was delusional.*

Though throughout the other four pages of her letters, Jonathan had to admit that she seemed very sane and rational in all she thought and reported.

He felt a pang of longing deep inside. He wanted to call Tess, so he could share this discovery. He could just imagine her reaction. Yes, she would say it proved him wrong. But they would discuss the importance of these spare, faded lines of writing, the possible significance. If only he could talk this all over with Tess, Jonathan knew he would enjoy this discovery so much more.

As it was, he felt a bit overwhelmed now . . . and confused. As if the rug had been pulled out from under him in more ways than one.

He gazed out the window over his desk at a sweeping view of the shoreline and sea. He couldn't help but remember their walk to the angel cliffs, how they had stood on that very peak and kissed, with just blue sky all around them.

He had lost his heart to her that day and left it up there in the clouds somewhere. Nothing in his life would ever be the same again. Jonathan knew he had a lot more work to do here. He had to go over the letter many more times and transcribe every word and punctuation mark, even the spelling errors and crossed-out words.

But he was too worn out to start that tedious process. He took off his glasses and got up from the desk. Then he headed downstairs, thinking a cup of tea and one of Claire's home-baked treats might lift his spirits and give him a little more energy.

He had just put the kettle on when Liza came into the kitchen through the back door. She was carrying a basket of packages that all bore the colorful label of the Gilroy Goat Farm.

She took off her jacket and scarf and hung them on a chair. "Have you been inside all day working, Jonathan? You ought to get out for a while. It's beautiful weather again today."

"Yes, I think I will. A walk on the beach will clear my head. I've been going over some very . . . intense material today," he told her. The kettle whistled, saving him from having to explain more. "Would you like some tea, Liza?" he asked, fixing himself a mug.

"In a minute. I'm going to put this food away." She started unpacking the basket, setting the items on the table. There were round packages of goat cheese and big bars of freshly made soap. The farm's trademark lavender scent filled the room. Jonathan suddenly remembered that he had stopped at the farm on Monday morning before he and Tess had broken up. He bought her a small gift there—a heart-shaped wreath made of lavender and wildflowers that he thought she would like. He didn't know what he would do with it now.

"I guess Claire and Adele are at the fair." Liza glanced at him as he sat at the table with his mug. "I didn't get a chance to go this year. They should be back soon."

The fair. Claire and Adele had been talking about it all week. Jonathan had meant to visit them there, but he had totally forgotten. "Is that today? I meant to go, too, but it slipped my mind entirely."

Liza laughed. "Sometimes you're like an absentminded professor, Jonathan. I think we have to take care of you."

Jonathan smiled. At least somebody was.

"You do remember that Christmas is coming two days from now, right?" She teased him in a good-natured tone as she put the packages of cheese in the refrigerator. Before he could answer, she added, "We would love to have you join us if you're free."

Christmas . . . now there was another painful topic. He had been looking forward to spending Christmas Eve with Tess and her family. But he was sure that they weren't expecting him now. How could he stay here, knowing that he could have been with Tess? He didn't think he could do it. It was best to just leave town, even if he wasn't completely finished with his research.

"Thank you . . . I'm sure you'll have a wonderful holiday here. But I'm definitely going back to Boston by Christmas. I just . . . really need to get back. I hear there's snow coming," he added, reaching for any excuse.

"Oh, that won't be much. Just a flurry or two. It might even pass us altogether," Liza added.

Jonathan had heard the same report. She must know he was making an excuse. He could see that Liza sensed there was more to the story, but she didn't pry.

"If you change your mind, even at the last minute, we would love to have you. It's no trouble to set another place for you, Jonathan," she assured him.

Jonathan forced a smile. They were so kind here. Sometimes he thought he could stay at this place forever. But he knew that the sooner he left, the better.

"WILL YOU CHECK THE ROOM UPSTAIRS, TESS? I THINK THERE'S STILL someone working up there." Mrs. Fisk checked the sign-in book at the visitors' desk. "Yes, one more to go. Dan Forbes," she said, naming one of their regular visitors.

And one of the only people who would spend the entire Saturday before Christmas at Lilac Hall. Ten years ago, Dan had given the reins of the village newspaper, the *Cape Light Messenger*, to his daughter Lindsay. He now spent his time writing books on local history. He was married to Emily Warwick, the town's long-running mayor. Tess was acquainted with him from his many visits here. She wondered why he had never focused on the Marsh Fever epidemic and the quarantine on Angel Island. He probably would be a good person for Jonathan to interview, she thought as she climbed the stairs. Dan knew so much about the history around here, especially during the colonial period.

But Jonathan would just have to do without one more connection from her. She didn't want to speak to him or even send an e-mail. The way he had acted with his friend Leslie—or whatever she was to him—had hurt her so much, even though he tried to apologize and kept asking her to meet him in order to talk things out. What was there to talk about? He had been like another person sitting there, practically making fun of her along with that woman. It still made her furious every time she thought about it.

Jonathan had e-mailed and texted her a few times since Monday, but she hadn't answered any of them. None had come today. Maybe he had given up on her or gone back to Boston. That made her feel worse, even though it was what she wanted him to do. It was the only way she could even start to get over him.

Tess had really believed they were growing close by working together. She had felt sure that their relationship had a future. But clearly, he had just been using her because she lived here and helped him find so much material for his work.

Maybe he hadn't even realized what he was doing. He didn't seem conniving, but it added up to the same thing. Jonathan obviously didn't respect her or consider her his intellectual equal. His entire attitude changed when he was in his own circle again. That was how it would be once they both got back to school and their studies. It had just been a little fling for both of them, something to offset the doldrums of winter break.

No matter how many times she considered answering his calls or agreeing to talk things out, she knew it was better to end it here. It would only hurt worse later.

Tess walked down the long, dim hallway and glanced in the reading room. Dan Forbes sat at the same table Jonathan liked and with his head bent over his laptop. The sight made her blink. It could have been Jonathan sitting there. She drew in a quick breath, feeling a pang in her heart.

It was going to take a long time to forget Jonathan Butler.

Like it or not, she had to.

CHAPTER FOURTEEN

WHEN MOLLY WOKE UP SUNDAY MORNING IT WAS STILL DARK outside. She had left her cell phone next to her bed and set the little alarm, so that Matt would not be disturbed. She had come in around two in the morning, after catering a late party. Matt had been asleep then, and now she crept out of bed without even speaking to him.

She wished she could have just rolled over and pulled the covers over her head. She didn't know how she had any energy left, but somehow she stumbled into the shower, pulled on her work clothes, and grabbed a quick cup of coffee from the superfast single-brew gadget in the kitchen.

The roads were empty as she drove into the village. Though she knew there would soon be traffic everywhere. It was the last day of shopping. That night was Christmas Eve, when only loonies and workaholics— like her—went out to grab a few more gifts.

She wasn't even sure if she would be able to sneak that mall crawl in tonight or tomorrow. There were still more parties to manage on her list and she was still on her own. Despite Betty's high hopes, she had only lasted a few days at work before her back gave out again. Poor Betty, Molly felt so bad for her friend. But she felt even worse for herself, left to manage the glut of party jobs as the countdown to Christmas Day neared its end. When pressure like this hit, Molly would always call her dad. No matter how hard his schedule was, he always found an hour or two to run to her rescue.

But not this time. Joe was still incommunicado. The best she and Sam could do was get her mother on the phone. Marie would report the same thing over and again, "Your father doesn't want to talk yet. I'm sorry."

Molly felt sad about that, too. But she pushed herself to keep going. Molly was glad now that Sam and Jessica had stuck to their plan and were still having their Christmas Eve party. She was glad Grandma Addie would be there, too. She'd had some mixed feelings about another family event after last Saturday's fiasco. But now she could see that there had been some pluses, along with the minuses, and family was important on Christmas. That's what the holidays were all about. Last but hardly least, she was glad to attend one party that she hadn't had to put together herself.

MOLLY WASN'T SURE WHEN THE SNOW STARTED FALLING. MAYBE SOME tiny flakes were coming down when she and her crew started setting up a holiday brunch in the private section of Lilac Hall for the board members and big donors of the historical society. Most of the guests were seniors, like Lillian Warwick. They took the bad weather as a personal affront—or some sort of lapse in responsibility of the forecasters.

"I don't know where this snow is coming from," Lillian snapped as she entered the party. "There was no call for snow on any of the channels. Ezra and I have been watching closely. My granddaughter Sara is coming from Boston for the holidays. She's a reporter for the *Boston Globe*. She's doing very well there and they've given her a column."

This was a detail about Lillian's family that everyone in the room already knew. It was also one that Lillian could not resist repeating.

Edna Fisk, the director and curator at the society, helped Lillian off with her fur coat, which was now a little frosty. "I think it will just be a dusting. It may not even stick."

Molly hoped so. She had heard there was a chance of a brief flurry or two and had not given it much thought at all. It was nice to have a white Christmas, but she certainly didn't want to be driving around in the snow all day and into the evening in her van.

As the day wore on, and she checked on three other parties going on simultaneously in the village, the snow came down heavier and heavier. The flakes were falling so fast, the windshield wipers were having trouble keeping up. Molly hated driving in those brief moments when she couldn't see a thing, but on she plowed, not even considering a change in her schedule.

The van rolled along slowly, the tires making a muffled sound. The snow seemed to seal the van in a pillow of silence. Her assistant manager, Sonya, sat beside her in the passenger seat. Molly could tell she felt nervous being on the road. Molly was driving slowly, but the heavily loaded vehicle did swerve a bit. She hadn't seen a snowplow yet, probably because the town wasn't prepared and hadn't lined up extra drivers.

"What's with all this snow?" Molly grumbled. "Why can't they figure this stuff out? They keep saying we're getting snow for weeks—and no snow. Now they don't say a thing—and *boom*! We get dumped on."

Sonya nodded. "Exactly. Nobody said it was going to snow like this."

"All those satellites and computers and radar, and nobody can see a snowflake is coming?" Molly continued to rail. She was losing her temper, but she couldn't help it. She was overworked, overtired, and she had miles to go—and five more parties—before she could sleep. She did not need ten tons of snow right now.

"I think we'd better put the weather on again, Molly. Maybe we have to cancel the Elks Lodge. That's way out of town. It's going to be bad driving . . ."

Molly turned on the radio and tried to find the all-news station.

"I can't cancel a party, Sonya. That will ruin our reputation. I don't care if we're the only ones there. It may just be you and me and the food trays, balloons, and the DJ, but—" She paused, hitting the brakes during another temporary whiteout on the windshield. "Come to think of it, that DJ might not show, either."

Sonya didn't answer. She glanced at Molly, then stared straight ahead. The weather report was coming on, and Molly raised the volume.

"Well, folks, what's all the white stuff out there, you say? It's the surprise storm of the season. A slow-moving system of moist air has hit a cold front to the north, just sitting there on the Canadian border. That warm, moist air keeps pumping up from the south. In other words, it's a meteorological gridlock up there. And it looks like the snow will come down through tonight and tomorrow, tapering off sometime Christmas morning, and—"

"Christmas morning?" Molly echoed. "Did he really say—"

"Quiet, quiet!" Sonya practically put her hand over Molly's mouth so they could hear the rest of the forecast.

". . . We'll be hit with at least two to three feet and even higher drifts in some areas before it's all over. Back to you, Al . . ."

"Three feet of snow?" Molly's voice rose in a panicked yelp. "We can't get three feet of snow. We have five more parties. . . ."

Molly's cell phone rang. She saw the number on her dashboard. It was a client, and she answered the call with her hands-free device.

"Hello, Mrs. Gaines. It's Molly."

Mrs. Gaines had obviously heard the weather report, too, and was postponing the party at the Elks Lodge. "I think we'll try to arrange a new date. Nobody wants to go out on a night like this. It could be dangerous. Can we arrange a new date, maybe one night next week?"

"No problem," Molly replied in her most professional tone, which was no small feat, considering that the driving now demanded her complete and full attention.

She had barely hung up when another call came in. This time it was a client with a party just two hours away, also postponing. Molly hung up with him and turned to Sonya. "I think I'd better drop you off at your house and get home myself. While the van can still make it." The catering van was not exactly an off-road vehicle; it didn't even have four-wheel drive.

Sonya happily agreed. There was some party food in the van that couldn't be frozen or stored, and Molly gave most of it to her employee. She and her staff had worked so many long hours this week, she now wondered if Sonya had shopped or prepared at all for her own family's holiday.

Too late for that now, but at least they would have a nice dinner catered by Willoughby Fine Foods, Molly thought as she slowly made her way home in the catering van. If this snow really kept up, her family would be dining on the same.

JUST AS THE FORECASTERS PREDICTED—TOO LATE TO HELP ANYONE— the snow fell steadily through Sunday. Reverend Ben even cancelled the Sunday service, which was one of the only times that had happened in the entire history of the church. Sam was a deacon and had to make many of the phone calls to the congregation.

"There was another time when a nor'easter hit," he told Jessica later that afternoon. "The minister was stuck in the church for a week, and all he had to eat was a bushel of clams."

"At least he had something. But I would have gotten sick of clams by then."

"Me, too," Sam agreed. "So what do you think about our party? I think we have to call it off."

He was standing by the glass doors in the family room that led outside to their property. The snow was piled so high against the doors, he would have been waist-deep if he had been outside.

Jessica sighed. She had baked more cookies with Lily during the day, having little else to do, and was now decorating them with swirls of colored icing and sprinkles.

"I guess we have to. Even if it stops before they say, the roads will be a mess. I would hate it if anyone got stuck or had an accident on their way. Maybe it will be better tomorrow? We can have everyone over for Christmas Day."

"Maybe. I don't think they have any other plans. I'll call everyone and find out."

Jessica glanced at him. "How about your parents?"

"I'll call them, too, and leave a message. Maybe my mom will come without Joe. It's Christmas for her, too."

Jessica knew it was hard on Marie to miss out on the holidays because her husband was so stubborn. But she was so loyal to him, Jessica doubted she would come alone.

"The bridge is still out, and we're still officially stuck on the island until the snowfall ends," Liza reported.

It was Sunday, the morning of Christmas Eve, and Jonathan was sitting in the kitchen with Claire and Adele, having breakfast. They were listening to more weather reports on the radio when Liza came in from outside. She was barely recognizable under her cold-weather gear: down jacket, heavy boots with thick laces, big mittens, and a hat and scarf that covered everything but her eyes.

He had been conflicted about staying or going all weekend. Now Mother Nature had decided for him. He honestly didn't mind. If he had to choose the ten best places to be stuck during a snowstorm, the inn would have to be at the top of the list. It was elegant and comfortable and beautifully decorated for the holidays. There was plenty of good food and pleasant company. What more could you ask for? He was surely more comfortable here than he would have been at even the most luxurious resort in Utah.

The roads might be passable tomorrow, but he would stay until the day after, he decided. There was nothing and no one waiting for him back in the city. He thought about Tess, picturing her with her family, in their cozy house surrounded by the tall trees. He wondered if she was thinking of him at all.

Probably not. She hadn't answered any of his phone calls or texts. That was a clear enough message for him. She wouldn't even give him a chance to explain. No hope there of getting back together again.

Maybe she was right. Maybe it wouldn't have worked out, and breaking it off now was the right thing. The easiest thing. But it really didn't feel that way to him right now.

"Marie, why do you keep looking out that window? What do you expect to see, Santa Claus flying down from the sky?"

"I was just looking at the snow, but you never know."

Marie put the curtain back in place and turned to her husband. They were sitting by their Christmas tree, which was surrounded by piles of wrapped presents. Most of them were for their grandchildren. Marie was not a shopper the rest of the year, but for Christmas she tended to go overboard.

Joe sat in his armchair, reading a book about Winston Churchill. Marie couldn't help but recall one of the most famous quotes from the great British leader: "We will never surrender." Which seemed to have become her husband's motto lately.

Marie had worried all week about whether or not to go to Sam's house tonight without her husband. It was a difficult choice to make for so many reasons. The snow had lifted that burdensome decision from her shoulders. The snow or God had, she thought. She wondered if they had been isolated here tonight for a reason, an important reason.

She walked to the tree and picked up some packages that had slipped out of place. She carefully smoothed out the paper and puffed up the bows.

"What's the matter, Marie? Are you still brooding about Sam's party? Look at it outside. We couldn't go anyway. I bet he's not even having it."

"He isn't. They moved it to tomorrow, if the weather is all right."

Joe shifted in his seat. "When did you hear that? You didn't tell me."

"Sam left a message this afternoon. I guess I didn't think it mattered to you one way or the other." Marie sat down on the sofa across from him.

"It's just the idea. You should have told me."

"Really? Well, it's just the idea that if they were having the party and there wasn't a blizzard out there, we would still be sitting here. That's the idea that bothers me, Joe."

Her husband put his book down and stared at her. She rarely raised her voice to him.

"Go on, what's on your mind? You've been sitting on this all week, I can tell."

"All week? More than that, Joe. You've always been so sensitive about the subject, I could never tell you how I really feel. Because you refused to discuss it. But now I have to tell you. You're carrying this on too long. What have you gained by holding on to this anger? Nothing. What have you lost? A lot, Joe. And you may lose even more if you don't watch out."

Her husband didn't answer; he just scowled at her. She wondered if he was even listening or just brushing aside her words, still too stubborn to see the truth.

"Look at your life, Joe. This is a good night for it. Like that story by Charles Dickens, wasn't it?"

"Oh, so now I'm Scrooge?" He almost laughed at her, but she could see he was getting angry.

"You tell me," she challenged him. "I know how unfair it was when Kevin got the store. I know how hurt you were. But that's in the past, and what we have here now is good. Do you think our lives would have been any better up in Vermont? Staying here, in Cape Light, has let us be part of the lives of our children and grandchildren all these years. *That's* been the best part of our lives. I know you always wanted your own business, but you did much better than you ever expected down here. Maybe even better than if you had taken over that store. Maybe it wasn't even Kevin's fault when the store failed. It could have happened anyway, no matter who was running the place, once the big-box stores came in on the turnpike up there. You told me that yourself." Marie took a breath and tried to finish what she wanted to say. "Look at your life, Joe. You are blessed and everything—every single thing—turned out for the best, as far as I can see."

Joe rubbed his chin. He didn't seem as angry as she had expected, though his expression was tight and cold. "Well, that's your opinion, I guess. I never knew you felt that way. Maybe you should have told me sooner."

"Really? What good would that have done? Were you ready to hear it? Are you even ready now? Your brother put his hand out to you. He said he was sorry, and I think he really meant it. What did you do, Joe? You pushed him away. That's not like you. It wasn't what we taught our kids to do, either. Right or wrong, it's time to forgive. Do you really want to keep this anger, this ugliness, in your life?"

Her husband shrugged. "I'm sorry, Marie. I can't help the way I feel. Would you rather I lied to him? Would you rather I said, 'Okay, I forgive and forget.' And not really mean it?"

"Of course not. But you have a choice to make, Joe. And I have to tell you, I'm ashamed of the way you're acting."

His expression changed. Now he looked genuinely stung.

"Yes, it's true," she said quietly. "I never thought I'd say that to you, and we've been married over forty years."

Joe leaned toward her. She could see a wave of anger wash over his features, but suddenly he looked very sad and even confused. "Marie . . . please . . . what do you expect me to do?"

Marie shook her head. "I don't know. It's not for me to say. But I do know you can't just push this aside anymore, like you've been doing all these years. We're in our sixties now—you, me, Kevin. Your mother is nearly ninety. Who knows how many years any of us have left? Kevin is moving to New Zealand. We may never see him again. You have to face it now and figure it out."

THE SNOWSTORM HAD ENDED JUST AFTER DAWN. ADELE WOKE EARLY and looked out the windows of the inn. She heard the sound of shoveling outside, but couldn't quite see who was working or if they had made any progress yet.

The entire world was covered with white, even the beach front, which she knew was unusual. It had to be one of the biggest storms that had ever hit this village on Christmas. Certainly the biggest she recalled.

Would the Christmas Day service be cancelled, like yesterday's service had been? That would be a shame, she thought, but it might be necessary.

A quiet knock sounded on her door. "Adele, are you awake?" Claire called softly.

"Yes, I am. Come in." Claire opened the door and smiled at her. Adele had thought she was up early but Claire, as usual, had beat her. She was dressed in a down jacket, heavy wool pants, and high boots. Adele guessed she must have been outside already, helping to clear the snow.

"Merry Christmas," Claire said.

"Merry Christmas to you." Adele smiled at her dear friend. "What do you think of all this snow? Are we stuck on the island till spring? Not that I'm complaining," she added quickly.

Claire laughed. "It looks bad, doesn't it? But the plows have been out, even on the island. Liza said she heard the bridge and the main road are almost clear."

"Oh, that's good to hear." Adele was thinking of Kevin. They had talked on the phone last night and had left their plans up in the air. The storm had missed Vermont, he reported. But they would still have to wait to hear how the roads in Massachusetts were for traveling. The thruway into Cape Light was another question.

"And one of the deacons called from church," Claire added. "The service has been moved up to noon. I think we'll be dug out by then and will still have time for a nice breakfast. Liza has a big SUV, and Daniel will follow in his truck. In case we get stuck," she added.

It would take a caravan to ensure their safe passage from the island today, Adele thought. But it was Christmas. "Count me in," she told Claire. "I can't miss church on Christmas."

"I thought you'd say that."

After Claire left, Adele looked around the room for her heaviest clothing. She had a few things that would do and knew that Claire could loan her a pair of snow boots, which she would certainly need. She had a nicer outfit planned for the day, but would change into that once they got home from church. For now, warm and dry were her fashion priorities.

She began to get dressed and was hungry for breakfast. She certainly couldn't help clear the snow, but she could help in the kitchen. It was all hands on deck today. She wondered if the rest of her family would make it to church. Sam and his family would be there, she felt sure of that. Sam was a deacon and was probably there already, digging out the parking lot. Molly was also a determined soul and would wrangle her daughters and husband, even if they balked at going out.

Joe and Marie were a question mark, though. Joe might be working today at the Spoon Harbor Inn, she realized. But he would probably come to church if he had the day off. She had not heard from him since Molly's ruined reunion, but if she saw her son today, she would hold love and charity in her heart and greet him with the spirit of Christmas, no matter how he acted toward her. Adele promised herself—and promised God—that she would do that.

And she still didn't know where she would be spending Christmas Day, here at the inn or in the village, with her family. Sam and Jessica had put off their Christmas Eve party, and everyone was gathering at their house today. Everyone except Joe and Marie.

Of course they wanted Adele to join them, but she was expecting Kevin, and if Joe decided to go to Sam's at the last minute . . . Well, no one wanted a repeat of the meeting at Molly's house. Adele had decided that if Kevin and his family were willing to come down today, they would just spend a quiet day on their own at the inn.

The various complications made her head spin. She squinted down at the buttons on her wool cardigan, closing it up to her chin. She already knew that Christmas this year was not going to be the usual. But she had hardly expected it to be this mixed up—or challenging. She made up her mind to be thankful. Thankful for what she had, instead of feeling sad and disappointed about how she had hoped things would be.

The ride of a few miles, from the inn to the bridge, had been a challenge. Adele rode in Liza's SUV along with Claire, while Daniel followed slowly behind in his truck. Jonathan, who had helped with all the shoveling, jumped into the truck at the last minute and had come along to church, too. Adele knew he wasn't a churchgoer but felt glad he had come with them. The idea of leaving him alone at the inn didn't seem right somehow.

Snowplows had been out all night, and village crews were dispatched in the morning. The village streets were narrowed by piles of snow but were mainly clear. The church parking lot had been plowed and shoveled, too, but high piles of snow made parking spaces rare, and it was the day that everyone turned out for the service. Adele wondered if they would even find seats inside. Liza dropped Adele and Claire off at the door, so that Adele didn't have to walk too far.

The sanctuary was just as crowded as she had expected, though it did look lovely, decorated with candles and pine and a big display of red and white poinsettias around the altar table.

The choir was singing the opening hymn, "O Come, All Ye Faithful." Adele looked around for a seat and Sam suddenly appeared, looking very handsome in a navy blue suit and red silk tie. "Merry Christmas, Grandma," he said, kissing her cheek. "I have a seat for you." He quickly showed Claire and Adele to two seats in the side section, in the row behind his family, and handed them programs for the service.

Adele settled into her seat and found her hymnal. Claire was already singing in a rich, full voice and showed her the page. Adele sang, too. She couldn't help looking around the church for the rest of her family. She spotted Molly on the other side of the church with her husband, Matt, and all four of their girls. She saw Liza slip up the side row with Daniel and Jonathan. They found seats, too, before the hymn was over.

Finally, she saw Joe and Marie sitting up toward the front in the middle section. She sighed, thinking of how the scattered pattern of her family in church mirrored real life so well. They were all present and accounted for . . . but all very distant.

"Merry Christmas, everyone," Reverend Ben greeted the congregation. "I'm so pleased you could all make it here today, despite the weather. Let us come together now to worship, to share in the joy of Christmas and the gift of our blessed Savior, born this day."

The reverend led the congregation in the opening prayers and then

Sophie Potter stepped forward from the choir to read the first scripture from the Old Testament. Then Reverend Ben stood at the pulpit and read the second passage, from the second chapter of Luke in the New Testament, which described how the angel visited the shepherds guarding their flocks and told them of the birth of Jesus.

"—And this *will* be the sign to you: You will find a Babe wrapped in swaddling cloths, lying in a manger. And suddenly there was with the angel a multitude of the heavenly host praising God and saying: Glory to God in the highest, and on earth peace, good will toward men!"

If only that angel would appear to my family and give that same decree, Adele thought. *But at least I tried my best to bring them all together. I did try to make peace.*

She glanced at Joe, wondering if the passage had touched him at all. It was impossible to tell. He sat facing forward, eyes straight ahead. She wondered if he had even noticed her sitting here. It was impossible to tell that, too.

She brought her wandering thoughts back to the service. Reverend Ben had begun his sermon and was talking about the storm.

"Well, we finally got that snow they've been talking about," he said, eliciting some laughs. "I had my sermon all planned for today. But when I woke up this morning and looked outside, a new idea came to me. Perhaps I should say, a new realization."

He paused and everyone waited. The sanctuary was so quiet you could hear a pin drop.

"God's love is like a snowstorm. A blinding blizzard, in fact. We are up to our necks in His love and mercy . . . but we don't even realize it. And what better sign of His love than the birth of Jesus? The precious gift God gave us, forgiving all our past missteps, wiping the slate clean. Making us brand-new, too. Pure as the driven snow, as they say. Pure as a newborn child. So that we may live in His eternal peace and love forever."

Reverend Ben paused again and gazed around the sanctuary.

"What a magnificent and beautiful sign of God's love the snow is. What a miracle when you think of it . . . billions of minuscule bits of ice, each uniquely patterned, literally falling down from heaven to cover us. An amazing white blanket tucked all around us, the way a loving mother covers her infant while they sleep. How blessed we are this day, to see the snow and understand it this way, as the gift of God's love and the gift of His forgiveness.

"Isn't that what Christmas is about? Aside from all the gifts and parties and general hoopla. It's about the way God has forgiven us and wiped the slate clean, by sending His Son, our Savior. And how we must extend this kind of love ourselves in our own lives, every day. Forgiving each other for our angry outbursts or our hurt feelings. Forgiving each other for our mistakes. We are, after all, only human. But we are also created in God's image. This is how each one of us can directly experience the message of our Savior, Jesus Christ, the very meaning of His birth on this day. By practicing love and forgiveness, as God has forgiven us. By sharing it and showing it to each other.

"That is what this magnificent snow—what a white Christmas— means to me. A blanket of love. Faith. And forgiveness.

"So while we're shoveling and plowing . . . and complaining about traveling to our Christmas parties, let's pause and be silent a moment and give God His due for creating such a masterpiece. Such a miracle. No less amazing or divine than a baby's new life, or the peace and promise that a child brings into our world . . . if we open our hearts to Him."

He paused, smiling gently. "Let us go forward this Christmas Day, thankful for this storm that can remind us that we are forgiven and made pure today, too. A new page has been turned in our lives. We have all been born brand-new today, in God's love and the birth of His son. And this magnificent love and mercy and forgiveness are all around us, truly a divine miracle.

"May God bless us all. Merry Christmas."

The choir began to sing, "Hark! The Herald Angels Sing."

Adele sat back and let the joyful notes wash over her. She had always thought Reverend Ben gave sermons that helped his congregation see their experience in this world in a more divine light. His words today had done just that, giving her much to ponder and bringing some peace to her heart.

When the service ended, the aisles were so crowded that Claire and Adele decided to wait a few minutes. Adele was soon greeted by Jessica and Sam, who had been seated in the row in front of them.

"Are you coming to our Christmas party today, Grandma?" Jessica asked after they exchanged greetings. "You can come home with us right now," she added. "Sam will drive you back to the inn tonight."

"I'd love to, Jessica, but Kevin is coming down from Vermont with his family to visit me today."

"Oh . . . well, they can all come to our place," Jessica replied. She glanced at Sam, who answered with a tight smile.

Adele could see he didn't know what to say. Especially since Joe and Marie were now walking toward them.

"Merry Christmas, everyone," Marie said in a cheerful but firm tone. Then she leaned over and singled out Adele for a hug. "Merry Christmas, Mom. It's good to see you. I'm glad you were able to get to church today."

"Thank you, dear. I am, too. It wouldn't seem like Christmas without going to a service."

"Merry Christmas, Dad," Sam said loudly.

His father met his eye and nodded. "Merry Christmas. Merry Christmas, everyone," he added, taking in Jessica and even Adele with a sweeping glance.

"Merry Christmas, Joe," Adele answered. She paused, considering the question that popped into her mind. Then she couldn't resist. "How did you like Reverend Ben's sermon?"

She was prodding him, no question. But sometimes mothers couldn't resist.

"A little off the cuff, I thought. I wonder what the sermon was like that he first planned to say."

"Oh, Joe . . ." Marie shook her head. "I thought it was wonderful. Very thoughtful, original, too." She seemed about to say more, when Joe interrupted her.

"Marie, we'd better go. I think our car is in a bad space. We might be blocking people."

Marie glanced at her husband, looking surprised. Then she looked resigned. "Just a minute, Joe. I'll be right there." She took Adele's hand. "Are you coming to Sam's house today, Mom? I hope so."

"Oh, I'd love to, but Kevin is coming down from Vermont with his family. He called before I left for church. He says the roads are clear enough and he's on his way."

"Oh . . . well, I'll be at Sam's. Maybe you should all come there. I'm not sure about Joe . . ." She turned her head, looking for her husband, but he had already walked away. "I guess I'll ask him at home." Marie shrugged and hugged Adele again. "I'll be there. Maybe I'll see you."

"Maybe," Adele said, though she doubted it. Joe or no Joe, she just didn't want to risk upsetting everyone's Christmas.

After Joe and Marie left, Adele turned to Sam. "It's good of you and Jessica to offer, but I don't think I'll bring Uncle Kevin to your house today. I don't think it's a good idea. Your mother might persuade your father to come, after all. And frankly, I couldn't take another scene like the last time."

Sam looked sad but slowly nodded. *Neither could anyone else*, she could almost hear him say.

"I understand, Grandma. I'll come by tomorrow morning, before you all leave, and say good-bye."

"Oh, Sam, you don't need to go out of your way like that."

"It's no trouble. I'd like to see Uncle Kevin, too," he insisted. "You have a good Christmas, okay?"

"You, too, dear. Wish everyone a Merry Christmas for me."

Adele walked to the front of the church with Sam and Jessica. She had hoped to see Molly, but the church was so crowded and Molly and her family were so far away, all she could do was wave from a distance. She stopped on the front steps of the church and looked around, but didn't see them come out. Then Liza's SUV swooped by, and Claire appeared and helped her into the vehicle.

Adele was soon on her way back to the island. She tried to turn her thoughts to the day she would have there, with Kevin and his family and all her good friends. She was looking forward to that, truly she was, though a piece of her heart felt torn away, yearning to spend Christmas Day in the village with the rest of her family.

WHEN THEY RETURNED HOME FROM CHURCH, MARIE FOLLOWED JOE into the kitchen. He always made himself a big sandwich or an omelet after church, and today was no different, even though it was Christmas. Confronting the family after church had made him nervous and when Joe was nervous, he ate.

"Gee, I'm hungry. What time is it?" He stared into the refrigerator, then took out an array of leftovers from the dinner he prepared for them the night before. He took out dishes of olives and bits of gourmet cheese, a seafood salad, and a plastic bag of pepperoni slices.

"You want a snack, Marie?" he asked, adding a box of crackers to his bounty.

"No thanks. I'm going to Sam's house. I'm sure they'll have plenty of food there."

He looked up and frowned at her, but didn't say anything. Then he took out a plate and set one place at the table. "You're really going over there without me?"

"Yes, Joe. I'm going. You can come if you want. I'm sure they would love to see you there, too."

He sat down but didn't take any wrapping off the dishes. "Are you really going to leave me here alone? It's Christmas."

"That's right. It's Christmas. I want to see my family . . . my children and my grandchildren. I want to watch them unwrap all the presents I bought for them. Now, if you don't want to go, that's your choice. Suit yourself."

She saw his shoulders sag. He let out a long, slow sigh, then pushed his empty plate away. "Okay . . . I'll go. But what about my mother?"

"She's staying at the inn. You don't have to worry about seeing her."

Joe didn't answer for a moment. Then he looked up at her. She could see he was upset, his eyes wide and glassy. "I didn't mean it that way . . . I meant, I should see her, too. It's Christmas and . . . I was thinking about what you said to me last night . . . and what Reverend Ben said in his sermon." He turned to the window and gestured with his hand. "Look at all the snow out there, Marie. I feel like it's mocking me or something. Like it's a big, fat white sign. With invisible writing."

Marie had to smile at her husband's description. Though she could tell he was perfectly serious, even upset by his revelation.

"What does the sign say?" she asked quietly.

Her husband shook his head. "It says a lot of things. Mostly, 'Joe Morgan, clean up your act.' I have to be a bigger man. I have to be a better son to my mother . . . and a better brother. Like you said last night, I've got to make up my mind to forgive and bring peace to the family. Peace on earth, goodwill toward men. Including brothers." He stood up and gazed at her. "I have to wipe the slate clean, Marie. Today is a good day for it."

Marie was so surprised that for a moment she felt breathless. She answered him carefully, wondering if she had misunderstood. "So . . . now you want to be with the family today and your mother, too?"

He nodded, looking about as contrite as Joe Morgan ever did. "That's right."

"That's good, Joe. That's very good but Kevin is coming down from Vermont today to spend Christmas at the inn. Didn't you hear your mother say that? Oh . . . I guess you had left us by then," she recalled.

"Is he really?" Joe looked surprised. It was a setback, she thought sadly.

"Maybe you could see her tomorrow. Before she goes back."

Joe didn't answer. He spread a cracker with cheese and chewed noisily. He thought for a moment, then took out his cell phone and began punching in a number.

"Who are you calling?" Marie asked.

"Sam and Jessica . . . then I'm going to call Molly." He glanced at her. "I think it's my turn to plan a party. I think we should all go over to the inn and—"

Before he finished the sentence, Sam came on the line.

"Sam? It's your father," Joe announced, as if Sam could possibly not recognize him. "I know you've done a lot of preparing for the family coming over today. But I was thinking of Grandma, alone at the inn, and I had an idea. What if we all went up there and surprised her?"

Joe paused and Marie wondered what Sam would say.

"Yeah . . . I know Kevin is coming. It's . . . it's okay with me. I want to see him, too," Joe finally managed to say. "I'm thinking this could be like a do-over of Molly's house. The party I screwed up for everybody," he added, avoiding Marie's surprised look.

Marie could tell from Joe's expression that Sam was in favor of the plan.

"All right, you call the inn and I'll call Molly. We'll meet you over there in say . . . an hour or so? Your mother bought out the mall this year. We have a lot of presents to pack up. I might need two cars."

He glanced at Marie and rolled his eyes. She just smiled back in answer.

When he hung up, she walked over and put her arms around his big shoulders. "I'm proud of you, Joe. I know how hard this is for you. But you're doing the right thing."

He rested his hand on hers. "I hope my brother isn't mad at me now. I was pretty rough on him," he admitted.

"Well . . . if he is, you'll just have to apologize for that, too. The main thing is that you're making the effort. He's got to give you credit for that. And your mother will, too. I think Adele will be thrilled."

Joe nodded, looking glassy-eyed again. "I think she will be happy. But it makes me ashamed now to think how stubborn I've been and so willing to make her unhappy." He sighed. "Why do we hurt people that we love, Marie? You would think God would make it so that we just couldn't do that."

Marie was surprised by the question and her husband's philosophical turn of mind. "I don't know, Joe. They say it's human to err, but divine to forgive. Maybe God is giving us a chance to be more like Him?"

Joe shrugged. "Guess I'm getting my chance today. I hope I don't blow it."

She patted him on the back. "I think you're going to do fine."

She believed that, too. For some reason—through the grace of God— her husband's heart had finally come around. And after that, everything else would follow.

CHAPTER FIFTEEN

*A*DELE THOUGHT SHE MIGHT FAINT. SHE HAD TO SIT DOWN and practically collapsed into a chair. "So, what do you think, Grandma? Would that be all right with you?"

"All right with me? You know this was my dearest hope. What I've been praying for," she said honestly. "Of course I want you all to come here today. I just can't believe your father agreed to it."

"It was his idea," Sam explained. "He doesn't mind Uncle Kevin coming. He said he wants to see him."

Joe wanted to see Kevin? Did that mean he wanted to finally make peace with him? Adele wasn't taking anything for granted. It was enough for her that Joe was willing to be under the same roof as his brother on Christmas Day.

"Oh, Sam . . . words fail me," she said honestly. "But we need to ask Liza and Claire. They might not be up for an unexpected invasion of Morgans, today of all days. Let me talk to them a minute, and I'll call you right back."

Claire was working in the kitchen, starting to prepare a roast duck for the Christmas dinner she had planned. Liza was there, too, working on the vegetables.

Liza glanced over at Adele. "Do you need something, Adele?"

Adele pressed her hands together, hoping they weren't trembling. "I just got a phone call from Sam, and well, it's a long story, but my family all want to come here today to be with me . . . and to be together. I think you know that I was trying to patch things up between my two sons. Now it seems Joe is willing to try again. They'll bring all their own food and drink," she quickly added. "And paper plates." She glanced between the two women. "But it's too much to ask. I'm sorry."

"Adele, it's fine with me. We would be happy to have them. That's what we do best around here. Right, Claire?"

Claire nodded, slipping the duck into the hot oven. "Absolutely. I was thinking it was going to be too quiet around here. I would love to see your family."

"Really?"

"Yes, really. I think it's a great idea," Liza insisted. She glanced at Claire.

"We know how much this means to you, Adele. We're happy to help you. You know, I knit you a little hat. It's under the tree. But consider this a special gift to you, from me and Liza."

"Thank you both. Thank you so much!" Adele could hardly believe her good luck. She felt tears well up in her eyes. These women were so special and dear to her. How could she ever repay them? Someday, she would try.

"Now call your grandson back and let me talk to him. We need to coordinate the menu." Claire waited while Adele dialed Sam back.

"Sam . . . it's all set. Liza and Claire are willing to have us."

"Happy to have you," Liza corrected her.

"Happy to have us," Adele said. "Now Claire wants to talk to you about the food and such. Here she is . . ."

Adele handed over the phone and sat back, taking in deep breaths to calm herself. A family reunion. Just what she had prayed for.

Even better than she had hoped, she realized. Because this time, Joe was not coming, kicking and screaming. It was—miraculously—all his doing.

Forgive me, God, for ever doubting Your goodness. You truly know what is best for us. Thank You for working in Joe's heart and bringing us all together today. I am so grateful . . . and blessed.

Adele felt as if she were twenty years younger as she ambled about the inn, trying to help prepare wherever she could. Liza and Claire worked as a team, as if they were suddenly one body and mind. They talked in short-hand about the setup of the dining room and sitting areas. Daniel and Jonathan were called on for some heavy lifting—retrieving extra chairs from storage in the basement and moving the long dining table and other pieces of furniture to create an L-shaped buffet area.

A little over an hour later, the inn was transformed and could have easily hosted a wedding.

"You are amazing, ladies," Adele said as Liza smoothed long linen cloths over the tables and added candlesticks and a pine centerpiece.

"It isn't perfect enough for a magazine layout. But not bad for crisis mode."

"We work well under pressure," Claire added, seeming energized but content. She never seemed to hurry or feel stressed but always got so much done, Adele thought.

"And having your family bring all the food certainly helps," Liza said with a laugh. "We're lucky that so many of them are such terrific cooks."

"That does help," Adele agreed. Still the transformation of the inn seemed like another miracle.

A short time later, the inn was teeming with guests. *My family . . . they're filling every room*, Adele thought, smiling softly to herself. There was eating, drinking, talking, and laughing. The children were outside playing in the snow. Lillian Warwick and Dr. Elliot had taken seats by the fire, close enough to watch the action but out of harm's way. There was one more chair there, and Adele considered joining them.

It wasn't hard to tell that Lillian had been upset by the change in plans today. But she did seem distracted by the inn's architecture and was avidly discussing the moldings and ceiling medallions with her husband. "Do you suppose those are original to the building? I must ask Liza Martin. Perhaps this place should be listed on the registry."

Adele looked around and could not help but smile. *George, George. Look what we created! If only you were here to see this . . .*

"Having a good time, Mom?" Joe walked up beside her and put his arm around her shoulder.

"This has to be one of the happiest days of my life. Almost as wonderful as the days you and Kevin were born. Certainly the best Christmas I can remember." She clutched his hand, feeling she was about to cry again. "Thank you, Joe. Thank you for giving me this."

Joe squeezed her hand, then gave her a hug. "I'm sorry, Mom. I'm so sorry it took me so long . . ." His voice trailed off, and he stared down at her. "Do you forgive me?"

Adele sighed and stared up at him. "Of course I forgive you. Do you forgive me for my part in this whole mess?"

"I do, Mom. We all made mistakes. We all played a part . . . But we don't need to go over that sad story again. What's done is done. We can't change the past. But we can turn the page. We can start again. It's a good day for it, don't you think?" he asked her, his voice thick with emotion.

"I do, son. I truly do." Adele got up on tiptoe and took his big face in her hands and kissed him on the cheek. "I love you, Joe."

"I love you, too, Mom."

Joe helped her over to the armchair she had been eyeing and then went to get her some food from the buffet. She heard voices in the foyer and realized that Kevin had arrived. Sam and Molly were both there to greet him and his family. Adele levered herself up on the arms of the chair so she could hurry to join them. Lillian and Ezra stared at her.

"My son, Kevin, from Vermont," she explained. "It sounds like he's here."

"I'm sure he'll be staying awhile if he's come all that way. You shouldn't rush like that," Lillian warned her. "You'll break something. Believe me, it's no picnic."

She had a point, Adele knew as she headed for the foyer. But it was hard to take it slow today. She was so happy and excited . . . and eager to see how Joe and Kevin would greet each other now.

Adele saw Joe coming out of the dining room. Kevin was handing his coat to Claire when he turned, and the two men faced each other.

Marie stood at Joe's side and Kevin stood with his family—his wife and her kids, Nora and Jackson. Molly and Sam stood watching from the doorway of the sitting room.

Everyone was suddenly so quiet Adele could practically hear her own heartbeat.

Joe walked toward Kevin with his head bowed a bit. He stood before him a moment without saying anything. Kevin waited. When Joe didn't speak he said, "Hello, Joe. Merry Christmas."

Joe nodded, still unable to look Kevin in the eye. Adele wondered if he was having second thoughts or if his anger was welling up inside again, taking over his good intentions.

He slowly lifted his head and looked at his brother. "Hello, Kevin. Glad you could make it." He stuck out his hand. "Merry Christmas," he added quietly.

For a moment Kevin looked shocked at the simple gesture, and then a huge, warm smile broke out across his face. *How he looked like George when he smiled,* Adele thought. *Especially now that he was older . . . and Joe did, too,* she realized.

The two men shook hands long and hard, Joe reaching out to clasp his brother's hand in both of his own. *Was Joe crying? His eyes were shining. But with tears of love and even gratitude,* she thought. He was grateful to Kevin for accepting this simple, tentative gesture of reconciliation.

Marie stepped forward and greeted her brother-in-law. Kevin hugged her and presented his wife and her children. Adele realized that Marie and Joe had left Molly's house so abruptly they hadn't met yet.

Suddenly it seemed the party was in motion again. Adele walked up to her two sons and smiled at both of them. "So, you made it," she said to Kevin. "I hope the traveling wasn't too difficult?"

"Mom, I wouldn't have missed this party for the world." Kevin smiled at her, and she knew that he meant every word.

She glanced at each of them. Her sons, together again. That's all she wanted to see. She was so grateful and happy. She felt . . . at peace.

"YOU DID VERY WELL, JOE. I'M PROUD OF YOU," MARIE WHISPERED AS Joe followed her on the buffet line.

"Thanks, Marie . . . but it's not over yet. I still want to talk to him. Privately. We still need to hash things out."

Marie nodded. "All right. One thing at a time. So far, so good," she encouraged him. "Gee, this food looks good. Did Jessica and Sam make all this?"

"Most of it. I recognize Molly's stuffed mushrooms. And I think Claire North made the roast duck. . . . It looks first rate," he noted. "Nice presentation, too."

"It does. I'm going to try some." She glanced at his plate, which was still empty. "Aren't you hungry?"

"I am but my stomach's all jumpy." He looked at the food and then put his dish down. "I'm going to look for Kevin and see if he'll talk things out with me. Better to get this over with, right?"

Marie nodded. "I think you'll both feel better once you clear the air. He probably wants to talk, too, but he's as nervous as you are. Don't worry . . . you're doing fine."

Joe nodded at his wife, then turned and left the room. He looked around for Kevin but didn't see him at first. Then he spotted him out on the porch, where he was talking with Molly's daughters who had congregated there with his two stepkids.

Joe took hold of his courage and walked outside. It was chilly, but the bracing air felt good. The inn was warming up with all the company and two fireplaces going.

When Kevin saw him, he left the others and walked over.

"So . . . I surprised you today, huh?" Joe tried to smile, but the gesture felt forced.

"You did. I won't lie. Sam called me while I was driving down here and said you wanted to see me. I didn't quite believe him at first," Kevin admitted.

"You gave up on me. I don't blame you."

"I said I was surprised. I never gave up on you. I never did and never would."

His sincerity and loyalty, after all these years and all Joe had done to reject his attempts at reconciliation, made Joe feel sad and guilty.

"I'm sorry I made you wait so long. I know that doesn't sound like much after all this time, but it took me a long time to see how stubborn I've been. How . . . wrongheaded. I'm sorry, Kevin. I really am."

"I'm sorry, too. For all the time we lost and how I acted when Dad died. I shouldn't have accepted the store. I know that now and I knew it then. I knew it was wrong and I knew that it hurt you," he admitted. "You had every right to be angry me. Every right," he repeated.

Joe nodded. It was hard to even talk about this, to be reminded of that dark time, the stunning blow he had been dealt by his own family. "I was hurt," he said, "real bad. But now I understand. Dad was desperate to save you, to give you something to keep you safe once he was gone. I would have done the same to save one of my kids. Maybe I just didn't get that back then."

"That's true. Dad was trying to help me. To save me even, I guess. But he didn't realize that I had to save myself. That was the only way to climb out of the dark pit I'd thrown myself into. But I could have been more honest with you, Joe. I was ashamed of myself, I was so weak and my life was such a mess. You had it all together, a wife and a family and you always had a good job. I didn't have anything. I'd lost my job, my home, my wife . . . I was a failure. I hated myself. And I was drowning in self-pity," he added. "I was so jealous of you. That little store didn't even seem like much compared to the life you had."

Had Kevin really seen him that way? Marie's words from Christmas Eve night came back to him. "I am blessed. But I've taken it for granted, pining after something I didn't get." Before Kevin could reply he said, "Did you really try to . . . to end your own life?"

"I did," Kevin admitted quietly. "I was in a lot of pain, and it just seemed easier. I wasn't the strong person you were. That wasn't even the bottom, either. I had to lose the store and at least a year or more of my life to finally face myself. That was the cost. I'm sorry for that. Sorry for taking what should have been yours. I have no excuse for it. But I am sorry."

Joe nodded, taking in Kevin's words. "I've been thinking about all this, Kevin, thinking about it a lot. I sort of decided that the store wasn't mine if I didn't get it. It wasn't really Dad's to give. Everything comes from God and He wanted you to have it, for whatever reason. Who knows how my life would have turned out if I did get the store? Maybe my marriage wouldn't have been so happy. Or I would have regretted leaving my kids behind here. Marie never wanted to leave Cape Light. Maybe the big stores on the turnpike would have put me out of business, same as they did you. There are no guarantees in this life."

"I appreciate it, Joe, but you don't have to say that to make me feel better."

Joe shook his head. "I'm not. Honest. It's just that we don't know what would have happened if I took the store away from you. I do know that I've had a good life and I don't have anything to complain about. Even though you would never know it from the way I've been acting lately."

Kevin laughed. "I have a lot to be grateful for, too. I'm five years sober and I've got my life back. I'm strong inside. The way I always thought of you . . . my big brother, Joe."

Joe felt embarrassed by his words, but touched. "I'm not so great. A big man doesn't act the way I did. But I'm trying to do better . . . Why did we waste all those years? We can never get them back again."

"That was foolish. But at least we have a second chance."

Joe nodded thoughtfully. "Just in time for you to move to New Zealand."

"Planes fly both ways, Joe. We should have our next family reunion there. Or maybe at some halfway point."

Joe laughed. "I'll have to check a map and get back to you. I have no idea what's halfway between New Zealand and New England."

He slapped Kevin on the back, then hugged him. "Merry Christmas, Kevin. I know I told you that before, but it's been too long since I said those words."

Kevin hugged him back. "Let's promise each other, this is the first of many more Christmases we'll celebrate together."

Joe smiled and nodded, but he felt as if he was holding back tears, too. "You're a good man, brother . . . I can't argue with that."

*   *   *

THE MORGAN FAMILY PARTY ON CHRISTMAS DAY WAS NOT AT ALL
what Jonathan had expected. Then again, his entire stay in this place had
been one long surprise. He had actually enjoyed himself with the Morgans, along with Liza, Claire, and their friends. He could not remember
ever being at such a big, raucous holiday party.

When he thought about it the next day, it was probably just the distraction he needed from his sad thoughts about Tess and his qualms
about leaving here with everything so unsettled—with her, and with his
work.

But it was time to head back to the city. Past time, perhaps. Yesterday in church the minister had talked about forgiveness and wiping the
slate clean. He had made it sound so easy. But it wasn't so easy. Not for
Tess. Jonathan had looked for her at the service. He remembered she said
her family attended church there. But the sanctuary was so crowded, he
hadn't caught sight of her. Still, that didn't mean she wasn't there.

What did it matter? He would leave today. Their relationship was
over and done.

He packed quickly and went down to the kitchen. Claire was there
with Liza. The buttery, rich scent of French toast filled the air, mingling
with the smells of coffee and bacon.

"First one down," Claire greeted him. "Everything's set up in the
dining room this morning, Jonathan. You can help yourself to coffee. I'll
bring the food in shortly."

Jonathan headed to the coffeemaker and filled a mug. Adele's son
Kevin and his family had stayed over, so there would be a full table this
morning. Jonathan didn't feel much like talking to strangers and wasn't
even that hungry.

"Are you leaving today?" Claire asked, turning from the stove a
moment to look over at him.

"Yes, I'm all packed. I wonder if you could do me a favor, Claire. I've been trying to return something to the Hegmans, a packet of letters they loaned me to study. I went by the Bramble on Sunday morning, before the snowstorm, and there wasn't anyone there. A note said they won't be back until the New Year."

"Grace and her father sometimes spend the holidays in Vermont, with her sisters. I guess they headed out early this year, trying to beat the bad weather. Even though the forecasters weren't calling for a storm, Digger has a knack for predicting on his own," Claire added. "I think he must have convinced Grace heavy weather was coming."

Jonathan just nodded. Digger would have such a talent. Everyone around here seemed strangely charmed—in a subtle, almost inexplicable way. His logical mind was boggled by so many things around here. He just had to accept it . . . and go on.

"Well, I guess that's what happened then," he said finally. "I wondered if you could give the letters to the Hegmans when you get a chance. There's also a little package for Tess Wyler," he added. "I'm going to send her a note and tell her to pick it up here. If she wants it."

Claire glanced at him. "I can bring the letters to the Bramble, don't worry. And I think Tess is coming here this afternoon, to help us clean up after the Morgans leave. She can get your package then."

His heart jumped up to his throat. He could see her again if he waited around. But he guessed she would treat him in that cold, distant way she had the last time they'd seen each other. He didn't think he could bear it.

"Great. If you could pass all that on, I'd appreciate it."

"No trouble at all . . . This French toast is ready. Can I fix you a dish?"

"It looks great, but I think I'll hold off for now. I want to take a last walk on the beach before I go. Maybe when I get back."

"It will be here. You go out and have a good walk. It's a nice clear day, though a little windy. You ought to wear a scarf," she added.

"I will," he promised, not minding the way she mothered him.

Jonathan found his jacket, scarf, and boots and headed out the front door of the inn. It was a clear day. The sunshine was nearly blinding, reflecting off the piles of snow. Though coastal areas like Cape Light and the island typically did not get as much accumulation as inland areas, the snow on the island was still plenty high, and Jonathan walked carefully down the road across from the inn.

The wooden steps were covered with snow and were not a viable route down to the shore. He walked on farther, but the snow between the road and beach still seemed too high to traverse. Not without snowshoes, he thought wryly, though Liza probably had a pair or two of those in her big barn, along with everything else.

It was windy, too. Sudden gusts blew off the water and drove high, puffy white clouds across the sky. Jonathan stuck his hands in his pockets and plodded on, feeling himself battered by the chilly breezes.

The sea looked different every day, he reflected, and he never tired of looking at it. He had only been here a few weeks, but he would miss this place. He would have to return sometime. In the summer. He could only imagine how amazing it must be here then, though even the thought of that visit made him sad, his heart heavy with regret about Tess.

He had never gotten to tell her about Mary Hegman's letter, what she had written about the strange visitors. He had never gotten to tell Tess so many things.

After considerable thought about Mary Hegman's letter and what it might mean, he had decided to put this project aside. While he still didn't accept that supernatural beings had tended to the sick during the quarantine, he had to admit something mysterious had happened here. Something . . . elusive, uncanny . . . something that was probably impossible to verify or ever completely explain.

In other words, he had to admit he was stumped. Certainly stalled in an attempt to write a scholarly study that would stand up to peer review.

He would leave it to some other historian to figure out. Or perhaps he would return to this puzzle someday when he was older and wiser and had more time. He couldn't help but picture himself alongside Tess, working together, investigating the past, and making amazing discoveries . . .

But that was not to be.

The landscape along the shoreline had changed, and he found himself on a cliff overlooking the sea. It was a high, sheer drop, much like the cliff on the other side of the island, which was shaped like an angel's wings. Only this one had no special contour that he could see.

He walked to the edge and looked out at the ocean and sky. He couldn't help but recall his moments with Tess at the very peak of the angel cliffs, how they had held each other and kissed. And it seemed like just the beginning of something . . . amazing.

He closed his eyes a moment, remembering.

"Jonathan!"

He heard someone call out his name, the voice carried on the wind. It sounded like Tess . . . but it couldn't be. He had to be imagining it. He spun around, looking for her—and saw her a short distance down the road. Standing by her car. Waving to him.

Dumbfounded, he waved back and quickly turned on the icy snowpack. In that instant he was hit full force with a hard gust of wind. His boots slipped out from under him and he landed on his back, stunned. Like a turtle on his shell, he was immobilized . . . then he suddenly slid down to the edge of the cliff as if he were on a water ride in a theme park.

He screamed and grasped for anything to hang on to, anything to stop his fall. In the distance, he heard Tess screaming. But all he could grab was more snow, then . . . nothing.

The ground disappeared from under him, and he felt himself falling through the air. The blue sky and blinding sunlight filled his vision and he said a prayer. "Dear God in heaven, help me. I really don't want to die . . ."

CHAPTER SIXTEEN

⌒

*J*ONATHAN! CAN YOU HEAR ME?" TESS RAN TOWARD THE cliff and down to the edge, not caring if she fell off, too. She was crying and gasping for air, afraid of what she would see when she looked over. She paused at the very edge, bracing herself.

Please, God, just let him be alive . . . I'd give anything . . .

"Tess? Are you up there?"

She heard his raspy voice and her heart skipped a beat. "Yes! I'm right here." She took a few steps more and peered over the edge.

Jonathan stared up at her. He had landed in a clump of pine branches jutting out from the rocks. The tree boughs had cushioned his fall and now cupped him like a hammock. Or a large, soft green hand, she thought.

"I can't believe it. I didn't fall to the bottom!" he shouted up to her.

"Are you hurt? Maybe we should wait to get you up. I can call the fire department or something."

"I think I'm all right, honest. There's a small ledge under the branches that I can stand on. And some rocks to hold on to climb up. If I go very slowly, I think I can get back up there."

Tess wished that he would wait for her to call for help, but she could hardly argue or blame him for wanting to get onto solid ground again.

"Okay. I'll help you." She watched from the top of the cliff as he slowly maneuvered off the branches and stood, balancing himself on the slim ledge. It was just wide enough for his boots and miraculously clear of snow. He took off his gloves to get a better hold, and she imagined that his fingers would soon be freezing.

She barely took a breath as she watched him slowly climb the cliff face, a yard or so at a time, until his head appeared at the top.

"Get back, Tess. Please. The ledge is so slippery and it slopes down. That's how I fell off."

"But I want to help you," she insisted. She braced one boot behind a big rock, then leaned over and reached out to him.

Jonathan met her glance and then grasped her hand. She pulled hard, and he managed to lift himself up on the cliff. Then he landed in a heap at her feet, practically facedown in the snow.

Tess dropped down beside him. "Jonathan . . . Thank God, you're all right." She touched his face with her hand. "It was so awful to stand there and see you fall . . . I thought you were gone. Forever."

"So did I. I was standing there thinking about you. About us. I felt so bad, Tess—"

"I'm so sorry. I really am. I should have answered your calls. I acted like a brat . . . can you please forgive me?"

He let out a long sigh, then put his arms around her and answered with a kiss. A deep, long kiss that filled him with the sheer gratitude and joy of being alive.

"Why were you even down here?" he asked as they parted. "Claire said that you weren't coming until this afternoon."

"Liza called me this morning and asked if I could come earlier. I guess she didn't tell Claire. When I got there, Claire said you went out for a walk so . . . I followed you. I wanted to see you one more time before you left. To say I was sorry."

"Thank goodness you did." He dropped a small kiss on her forehead. They sat close, holding each other for a few moments more.

"We'd better get up. The snow is starting to feel cold." She rose and stretched out her hand. Jonathan still felt a bit shaky after his fall and rose unsteadily.

"I can't believe the way I was—I was saved," he said as they walked to her car. "It was just amazing. A one in ten billion chance that I didn't just fall straight down to the bottom."

He turned and glanced back at the cliff. They could both see the branches that had caught him, a soft pine cushion.

"Those branches almost look like a hand," Tess said quietly.

She turned to him. "Or do you think I'm getting too . . . illogical now?"

Jonathan shook his head. "I don't know what to believe anymore, Tess. I found something in Mary Hegman's letters that I wanted to show you. She talks about visitors in fine clothes who came and cured some of the quarantined patients." He paused, looking very serious. "I guess that was a game changer for me. I can't go on researching this event. I'm going to put it aside for now."

"Why? You've come so far."

"I know but . . . I've changed my mind. I approached this study expecting to discover and explain what happened on the island during the quarantine. But now . . . I don't think I can ever discover what really happened. And even if I did, I don't think I could explain it. So I'm just going to put it aside for now and start on something new." He sighed and took her hand, then held it to his lips. "Besides, I've discovered something more wonderful and amazing than I ever expected coming here. I found you. And that's worth everything to me. I'm sorry for anything I did that ever hurt your feelings. Can we try again to make this work? I know that we could," he added sincerely.

Tess nodded and pressed her head to his shoulder. "I'm sorry, too. I acted like an idiot. I was just . . . scared that I wasn't in your league or something. So I ended it before you could find me out."

"Don't ever say that. We're a perfect team. Don't you think it would be fun to work together?"

"It would be wonderful . . . and so are you." She smiled and hugged him close, so relieved he had not been hurt and was right here with her. And everything between them was good again.

Finally, she leaned back and looked into his eyes. "Are you really sure you want to put this study aside? You're not afraid some other scholar will come along and scoop you on it?"

Jonathan hesitated, then shook his head. "No, I'm not worried about that. But if anyone publishes a study that debunks the legend . . . well, let's just say I'm prepared to write a very strong letter to the editor, recounting my own research and experiences here."

Tess grinned. "Maybe that's why the angels saved you."

"Maybe so. I'm not discounting anything right now. Not after what I read in Digger's letters and after falling off a cliff and living to tell about it."

Tess just laughed at him. "Okay, if you say so. But I'm going to hold you to that."

"I'm sure you will."

And it would be a long, happy, productive life, Jonathan thought. With Tess by his side, how could it be otherwise?

ADELE WAS UPSTAIRS, FINISHING HER PACKING, WHEN CLAIRE knocked on her door. "There's someone here to see you. Reverend Ben. He wants to say good-bye."

Adele was surprised and pleased. She left her open suitcase and followed Claire downstairs. Reverend Ben rose from his seat in the sitting room and took her hand.

"You didn't have to come out all this way to see me, Reverend. I was going to call you."

"That's all right, Adele. I came out to visit a church member who's ill and had to miss the Christmas service. How was your Christmas Day? Did you enjoy the visit with your son Kevin and his family?"

"Oh, Reverend . . . it was much better than that. They all came. My children and grandchildren. Everybody. And it was all Joe's idea," she told him, pleased at the surprised look on Reverend Ben's face. "Somehow, some way, he had a change of heart. He and Kevin talked everything out, and they've forgiven each other. And me," she added with a smile.

"That's amazing. It's just what you came here for—what you hoped to bring about."

"Yes, it is. My prayers were answered. I did get discouraged for a while and even believed I'd failed horribly and had made everything worse. But the good Lord worked in His own time, and His will for us prevailed. It all came about even better than I could have ever imagined." She reached out and took the reverend's hand. "Thank you for your prayers. I'm sure they helped."

"No thanks necessary. I'm not surprised," he said with a kind smile. "It wasn't just my prayers, but your faith and love. And perseverance. There are few things stronger than a mother on a mission to help her children."

Adele had to smile. "Maybe angels on a mission?" she asked.

"Possibly," Reverend Ben agreed. "Mothers and angels are certainly in the same category. In my book, anyway."